"The superlative Barry creates a vividly eerie, time-bending landscape that stretches back and forth between the Salem witch trials, the Goddess Murders, and the present-day mystery. . . . This spooky, multilayered medley of mysteries is sure to be a bestseller."

—*Booklist* (starred review)

"*The Fifth Petal* is a literary thriller that beautifully straddles the line between sensational and sublime, illuminating history and hysteria in a fictional context that never fails to resonate as being very much of this world. Barry melds mysticism, myth, and religion in this ambitious, multigenerational saga in near-epic proportions, resulting in a veritable witches' brew. In a publishing environment that values expediency, the author—who spent five years writing this book—proves that good storytelling, like perspective, often benefits from the passage of time. Prepare to fall under her spell."

—*The Strand*, John B. Valeri

"Murder is always a dark and strangely titillating subject, but when combined with madness and magic, it weaves an even more seductive spell. This is especially so when in the hands of bestselling author Brunonia Barry. Barry's tale isn't just an intriguing and evocative story but also a strong social commentary. Magic is not a malicious force of evil but a natural, earthy feminine power. . . . Women who wield any kind of power, supernatural or otherwise, are misunderstood or feared. Women who don't possess it are resigned to lives beyond their control. *The Fifth Petal* is an imaginative and haunting book that appeals to the emotions, the senses, and the intellect."

—The Book Beat, Jeanette Bouchie

"The power of modern magic, mythology, and history . . . Dark and suspenseful, Barry's well-constructed tale is filled with traps and red herrings as the truth is slowly revealed and Salem is forced to confront its sordid past."

—*Publishers Weekly*

"Banshees, lost memories, and secret pasts each play a significant role in this novel; enthusiasts of the author's earlier work and readers interested in the history of witchcraft and the occult will enjoy this return visit to Salem."

—*Library Journal*

"Brunonia Barry has done it again. If you liked *The Lace Reader*, you're going to love her new novel, *The Fifth Petal*. A real page-turner about murder and prejudice and love and what's possible and what isn't. Enjoy."

—B. A. Shapiro, *New York Times* bestselling author of *The Art Forger* and *The Muralist*

"A seductive combination of suspense, history, myth—with a sprinkling of the supernatural—*The Fifth Petal* is an enormously satisfying mystery novel. Brunonia Barry has created a world that is at once inviting and menacing, populated by characters both warmly familiar and surprising."

—Andrew Pyper, author of *The Damned* and *The Demonologist*

"There are many writers who write wonderful books. . . . Then there are those rare writers who make magic. Brunonia Barry proves once again she is a sorcerer. Transported to Salem, I was lost in a Gothic tale that only the author of *The Lace Reader* could have conjured."

—M. J. Rose, *New York Times* bestselling author of *The Secret Language of Stones*

"Written with pens dipped in magic and chills, *The Fifth Petal* uncovers hidden corners where myth, malevolence, and fervor converge in Salem, Massachusetts. Tendrils from the past and present wrap the complicated characters—and the reader's attention—until the stunning final sentence. Brunonia Barry weaves miracles."

—Randy Susan Meyers, bestselling author of *The Murderer's Daughters*

"*The Fifth Petal* is a brilliant and suspenseful tale that prods at embers still alive in a buried past. By weaving together the lost evidence of two Salem tragedies, Brunonia Barry's novel prompts profound consideration of the respect for history, the importance of resolution, and the power of voice. Highly recommended."

—Therese Walsh, author of *The Moon Sisters*

"Spellbinding! Clear your schedule—this beautifully written and seamlessly researched tale is a thriller, a romance, and a deeply felt investigation of the witch frenzy that haunts us to this day—and it's the book everyone will be buzzing about. Surprising, compelling, and profound—even revelatory—it will stay with you long after the last page."

—Hank Phillippi Ryan, Agatha, Anthony, and Mary Higgins Clark Award–winning author

ALSO BY BRUNONIA BARRY

The Lace Reader
The Map of True Places

The
Fifth
Petal

A Novel of Salem

BRUNONIA BARRY

B\D\W\Y

BROADWAY BOOKS

NEW YORK

Copyright © 2017 by BruBar LLC

All rights reserved.
Published in the United States by Broadway Books,
an imprint of the Crown Publishing Group, a division of
Penguin Random House LLC, New York.
crownpublishing.com

Broadway Books and its logo, B \ D \ W \ Y,
are registered trademarks of Penguin Random House LLC.

Extra Libris and the accompanying colophon are trademarks of
Penguin Random House LLC.

Originally published in hardcover in the United States by Crown,
an imprint of the Crown Publishing Group, a division of
Penguin Random House LLC, New York, in 2017.

Extra Libris material originally appeared on
Read It Forward (readitforward.com) in 2017.

Library of Congress Cataloging-in-Publication Data is available upon request.

ISBN 978-1-101-90562-3
Ebook ISBN 978-1-101-90561-6
International ISBN 978-0-451-49729-1

Printed in the United States of America

Book design by Andrea Lau
Illustrations by Meredith Hamilton
Photographs by Textures.com
Cover design by Tal Goretsky
Cover images: (diagram by Sir Isaac Newton) Granger, NYC—All rights reserved;
(women holding hands) Cover based on a photograph by © Gloria Mancini; (petals)
Dan Goldberg/Photographer's Choice RF/Getty Images

10 9 8 7 6 5 4 3 2 1

First Paperback Edition

For Gary

It will have blood, they say: blood will have blood.
Stones have been known to move, and trees to speak . . .

WILLIAM SHAKESPEARE, *MACBETH*

PROLOGUE

November 1, 1989
SALEM, MASSACHUSETTS

ISN'T IT A LITTLE LATE *FOR PRAYING?* TOM DAYLE THOUGHT but did not say. The child sat on a gurney just behind the privacy curtain in one of Salem Hospital's ER stalls, clutching what, to his lapsed Catholic eyes, appeared to be rosary beads.

It was an odd picture: a young girl, not more than five or six, prayer beads dangling from clenched and whitened fingers that were holding on to the crucifix part of the rosary so hard it drew blood, trails of dried reddish brown branching down her forearms and into the cracks between her fingers. Mean-looking scratches covered the child's arms and legs. If you could ignore the blood, she looked like one of Botticelli's angels: dark curls cascading down her back, alabaster skin not yet marred by tanning beds or summer sun.

The two nuns who accompanied her completed the angelic picture: the younger one sitting next to the child, holding her own rosary as she silently mouthed the prayers, the older one, whom he recognized as the mother superior from St. James's School, standing just behind, keeping watch.

It was the nuns who'd found her. He'd heard the story on his way over here. While the murders were being committed, the child had hidden in a patch of bushes, clutching the rosary and praying. The nuns, who'd admitted to hearing screams during the night, hadn't found her until the following morning, when the screaming faded to a mournful moan. They'd followed the sound along the North River and discovered the little girl standing by the pit where the bodies of her mother and two as yet unidentified young women had been dumped.

"Maybe she should have prayed you'd called 911 sooner," Dayle said to the older nun. He didn't say it so much to be cruel as to keep his own heart from breaking at the sight of the little girl. She looked the same age as his granddaughter.

One of the officers at the scene *had* asked the older nun why she'd waited to make the 911 call when the screaming continued into the night. "It was Halloween in Salem," she said, sadly. "It would have been strange if we didn't hear screaming." Another responding officer thought he recognized one of the young women as her body was hauled from the crevasse. Upon closer examination, he changed his mind.

This morning, they had picked up a person of interest, a local woman who lived over on Daniels Street, but he wasn't about to share that information with the nuns. "At the moment, we're still trying to identify the victims."

"One of the victims was the child's mother."

"How do you know that?" he asked, as if hearing it for the first time.

"She told us. She was talking to us when we first got here," the older nun said. "She only stopped when you came in."

In all his years as a detective, Tom Dayle had never seen anything as grisly as what had happened last night on Proctor's Ledge. Three young women, throats slashed, had been dumped into a narrow crevasse, the same mass grave where Salem had unceremoniously disposed of the bodies of those accused and executed for witchcraft during the hysteria of 1692.

A nurse hurried in and began to minister to the scratches on the girl's arms and legs. The child recoiled.

"I'm sorry, honey, but I have to clean these up."

"How'd you get those scratches?" Dayle asked the child. She didn't answer but stared as if seeing right through him.

"She was hiding in the brambles most of the night," Mother Superior said to Dayle. "That's how she got those scratches."

The nurse walked over to get bandages. "She's going to need a tetanus shot," she said.

"No," the child said, snapping out of her trancelike state and acting, for the first time since he'd arrived, like a scared little girl. She started to cry.

"It's okay, honey," the nurse said. "Tetanus shots don't hurt."

The child began to cry harder, recognizing a lie when she heard it.

"Let's see what the doctor says first," the nurse said, trying to comfort her. "Maybe you won't need any shots."

"I want Rose," the child said. Rose. That was the name of the woman they'd just picked up over in Broad Street Cemetery. When they'd found her, Rose Whelan had been covered with blood and babbling incoherently. The patrolman who'd picked her up was a rental cop. Salem used a lot of them on Halloween. He'd assumed Rose was just a leftover, someone who'd partied too hard last night and needed to dry out. It was a safe assumption. When he'd realized that the blood that covered her skin and clothing wasn't the fake stuff they sold in the costume shops but real—he'd seen enough bar fights and car accidents over the years to know—he'd taken her to the station, where the woman was recognized almost immediately, which made the story even more bizarre.

Rose Whelan was a noted historian who'd written several books on the subject of Salem's history and founded the city's Center for Salem Witch Trials Research, a resource library that drew scholars from all over the world. She was a well-respected woman, who, sometime between last night and this morning, appeared to have lost her marbles.

"She keeps asking for Rose," Mother Superior said. "Rose is the woman who pushed her into the brambles and told her to pray. She gave her those rosary beads."

"The rosary beads saved her," the young nun said, holding her own set out to him, its crucified body of Christ swinging like a pendulum. "It's a miracle."

The nurse finished washing the scratches but did not tackle the larger wound on the child's hand. "The doctor is on his way. . . . Don't open your hand, honey. We don't want you to start bleeding again. Hold it just like you're doing until he gets here." She left the stall.

With the nurse out of the way, Dayle focused on the child, pulling up a chair and sitting in an effort to be less threatening.

"What's your name?" he asked in his most gentle voice.

She didn't answer. She was clearly afraid of him.

"It's okay, he's a policeman. You can tell him," the younger nun said.

Dayle pulled his chair closer to the gurney. "How old are you?"

Again, she didn't answer but squeezed her hands tighter, fingers folded and ghostly pale, a single drop of fresh blood trailing down the inside of her forearm. Seeing the blood once again, the young nun picked up the pace of her own praying, mouthing her silent Hail Marys in rapid succession, as if a speedy invocation could erase all that was happening here.

"I have a granddaughter about your age," Dayle said, forcing a smile. "What are you, four maybe?"

"I'm five!"

"Five, huh? Five is a very grown-up age."

The child stared at him. "I want Rose," she said, starting to panic.

"Maybe I can help," he said. "Can you tell me Rose's last name?"

She nodded. "Rose Whelan."

"And do you know where I could find this Rose Whelan?" he asked, smiling at her. "If I wanted to get her for you. Do you know where she lives?"

Once again she nodded.

"Will you tell me the name of the street where she lives?" He hated to play her this way, but he had to double-check.

"I live there, too," she said, defensive.

"Can you tell me your address then?" Almost every child knew her address these days. It was one of the first things he'd made them teach his granddaughter.

As if reciting a rehearsed speech, she answered. "Sixty-two Daniels Street, Salem, Massachusetts, 01970."

The doctor came in, ending any further chance at dialogue. Annoyed, Dayle stood and moved his chair out of the way.

"Let's see this cut," the doctor said.

The little girl looked unsure.

"It's okay, you can let go now." He touched her hands gently.

One by one, she released her fingers from their prayer clutch, and then they all saw what she'd been desperately holding on to.

Upside down, embedded in her palm, was a wooden symbol Dayle didn't recognize: rounded and carved, with sharp ridges that dug deep into her hand. He didn't know what it was, but it certainly wasn't a crucifix.

Gently, using a scalpel to free the crusted edges, the doctor pried the wooden rosary free. It fell to the floor. Dayle reached down and picked it up.

It took a moment for the blood to find its way back into the girl's palm. Slowly, it pooled, turning the wound from white to red as it filled each layered level, creating a scarlet image of the medallion Dayle now held in his hand: a perfect five-petaled rose.

PART ONE

CHAPTER ONE

October 31, 2014
SALEM

There were no witches in Salem in 1692,
but they thrive here in great numbers now.
—ROSE WHELAN, *The Witches of Salem*

RAFFERTY HAD NEVER SEEN SO MANY TRICK-OR-TREATERS
on Chestnut Street. Nor had he ever been charged with escorting such
a large Witches' March up to Gallows Hill. There were at least 150 of
them this year—Wiccans, Druids, Celts, nature mama hippies with
psychic tendencies, pantheists and polytheists all—walking slowly behind his 1980 Crown Vic cruiser, the one he'd rescued from the junk
pile. For safety reasons, several streets had been blocked off. Traffic
was already backed up onto Highland Avenue as visitors streamed
into town for the festivities.

He'd been living in Salem for almost twenty years now. Back in
the nineties only summer and early fall were filled with tourists; by
midsummer you couldn't find a parking space anywhere downtown,
which was a pain in the ass. But come November 1, you could park
anywhere you wanted. Not so anymore. This was no longer a forgotten seaport. No longer an aging industrial city. Salem had been
discovered, and not just as a tourist destination but as the new hot
place to live. These days, you were lucky to get a parking space in
town at any time of year, which is why Rafferty always drove the
cruiser, even on his day off. As chief of police, he could double-park

anywhere. More often than not, a tourist would ask him to pose next to the cruiser so they could capture its Witch City logo: a police badge emblazoned with a flying witch on a broomstick wearing a pointed hat.

But all that was nothing compared to what happened here in October. The city had been dubbed the Halloween Capital of the World. That was no big surprise. But no one had expected it could turn into a monthlong celebration. Lately, it was even more than a month, which was great for the merchants: The population grew by at least 300,000 each October. Every year Salem imported extra police from Boston and Lynn and as far away as Connecticut, and each year they were still shorthanded.

The crowds tonight were something. Even here, in this residential neighborhood, the trick-or-treaters were waiting in long lines for their candy at the Federal mansions that were decorated for the occasion.

Rafferty drove the wrong way up Chestnut Street to the corner of Flint.

"Hey, Rafferty," yelled a man dressed as a pirate and known locally as Worms, "write yourself a ticket. This is a one-way street!"

Each year the pirate reenactors gathered at the Phillips House museum, the only historic home open to the public on Chestnut Street, to sing to the children, and maybe scare them a little, too.

"Scallywag!" his companion, Mickey Doherty, growled.

"Argh!" Rafferty shouted back at them.

"Them's fighting words, John," Mickey said, taking it as an invitation to approach the cruiser.

"*Argh* is only one word, Mickey," Rafferty said. Mickey Doherty was more entrepreneurial than almost anyone in town. He owned two haunted houses on Derby Street and the pirate shop on the wharf, where he sold a bit of weed on the side. Since possession was a misdemeanor these days, and Mickey didn't sell to kids, Rafferty looked the other way. "And if you don't know that, you should lay off the Dark 'n Stormies. Isn't this a kids' party?"

Mickey laughed and pounded the cruiser with his fist. "This kind of fortification's the only way I can stand the little demons!"

Rafferty shook his head.

"Hey, what're the streets like?" Mickey wanted to know. "I spoke to Ann earlier, and she warned me. There's a weird energy tonight."

Ann Chase. Salem's most famous present-day witch. "Well, if anyone should know . . ." Rafferty said, and Mickey laughed. "Actually, it seems pretty tame to me," Rafferty said. It was true.

Fall had come late this year, but now the air was chilling, and the darkness felt pervasive. He nodded to Mickey, turned on his siren, and pulled out, blocking incoming cars on Essex Street, so the parade could cross the road. As the candlelight vigil moved on, a driver blasted his horn, and others joined in chorus to protest the delay. The witches walked in formation, as slowly as brides.

Once the last witch had crossed the road on the way up to Gallows Hill Park, Rafferty's escort duties were over. He circled the city, checking on the rental cops and mounted police. *A weird energy.* He noticed that the Choate memorial statue at the corner of Essex and Boston Streets sported toilet paper streamers—nothing new or particularly weird there. Costumed children roamed more freely here, mostly without their parents: the little ones sugared up and bouncing, the older kids just looking for trouble. He spotted a few teens hanging out in the parking lot of an auto body shop on Boston Street. They scattered when they saw him coming—probably a drug deal. There'd been a lot of that lately in this area. He hoped the new senior center they were going to build here would turn the neighborhood around. That lot had been vacant too long.

He U-turned into the parking lot of the Dairy Witch and came back around when he got the call that there was some kind of disturbance in the Walgreens parking lot a few doors down. "I've got it," he said, thinking it was probably the same kids. But as he pulled into the lot, the kids were nowhere to be seen. He drove around back and spotted the hearse parked at the side of Proctor's Ledge. Hearse tours were big business in Salem; featured venues included everything from haunted houses to the apartment building over on Lafayette Street where the Boston Strangler had killed his only North Shore victim back in the early sixties. Salem entrepreneurs would go to any length to frighten the tourists, especially on Halloween, though the ghostly

Fright Tours logo hand-painted on the side of the hearse looked far more like Casper than Jacob Marley.

Unless the neighbors had a legitimate complaint, the police did little to discourage the fright tours or anything that made a dollar for the people who relied on Halloween to make a living. But this wasn't public property, it was private, and the manager of Walgreens as well as the neighbors up the hill resented the invasion of tourists. Especially lately, as the site of 1989's still-unsolved murders had become Salem's most popular tour.

He could see the candles from here. He recognized the voice of a local talent, someone they'd nicknamed Actor Bob, who'd made enough money with a voice-over commercial selling burials at sea to buy himself the old hearse and outfit it with cushy cutaway coffin seats lined with satin. Tonight, Actor Bob's baritone was far less comforting than his oceanic funeral voice. Tonight his voice was raspy, haunted.

"And now we come to Proctor's Ledge. Though some will tell you otherwise, many believe this place, not Gallows Hill, is where Salem executed nineteen accused witches back in 1692. This is also the place where, back on Halloween in 1989, three beautiful young women were brutally murdered: Olivia Cahill, Cheryl Cassella, and Susan Symms, whose ghostly white hair and skin were cut from her body to be used for some kind of Satanic ritual."

The crowd murmured, shocked.

Rafferty had heard Actor Bob lead the tour on several occasions. He always played to the crowd, changing and embellishing the story for effect, but this last part had been added recently—and embellished beyond belief.

"Remember their names. And remember the nickname the townspeople gave them. These young women were so beautiful and so bewitching, everyone called them the Goddesses."

More murmurs from the crowd.

"Neighbors on Boston Street and along the North River could hear their screams that night, but no one called for help until the next morning. It was as if a spell had been cast across the entire city of

Salem, and no one could break it. For what the girls were doing that Halloween had been forbidden, way back in 1692. They were trying to consecrate the mass grave of their ancestors, five of the women who had been executed during that dark time—for signing the devil's book."

Bob paused again.

"The ritual the Goddesses were performing that Halloween night in 1989 had been against Puritan law in 1692. To consecrate the ground where one of the Salem witches was buried was once an offense punishable by death. Which, ironically, is exactly what happened to those beautiful young women in 1989. Someone, or something, decided to punish them.

"Strangely, the bodies of all those executed in 1692 had disappeared shortly after the hangings, never to be found again. This is one of Salem's greatest mysteries. But the bodies of the Goddesses were left for all to see. Their throats were slashed, their corpses pushed into the same mass grave where their ancestors had once been buried."

Another lie, Rafferty thought. The bodies of the Goddesses had never been put on display. Where did Bob come up with this nonsense?

"There were only two survivors that night in 1989, a middle-aged woman and a young girl. The woman was found in Broad Street Cemetery, covered with the blood of the victims, ranting about the unearthly creature who, she claimed, had killed the girls. Most think the woman was the guilty one. A once-respected historian and scholar, she lost her mind that night and has never recovered. To this day, you can see her wandering the streets of Salem, predicting the death of everyone she meets. She has never been charged. No one could ever prove who the guilty party really was. Some think it was the crazy woman. Others believe the killer is a far more sinister creature, a screaming spirit of ancient powers who returns every Halloween to claim new victims."

On cue, a high-pitched scream pierced the air just behind Rafferty. The group gasped.

Rafferty spun around in time to see Actor Bob's accomplice run from the woods. "You'd better run," Rafferty said under his breath. He pushed through the brambles, swearing as a branch snapped back, slapping him on the side of his face.

"What about the little girl?" one of the tourists asked. "What happened to her?"

"No one knows," Bob replied, pausing once more for effect. "The little girl disappeared shortly after the murders. No one has seen or heard from her since."

At the sound of Rafferty's uncontrolled groan, the now terrified tourists reeled around. Even Actor Bob held his breath until he spotted Rafferty coming through the brambles.

"Are we just about done?" Rafferty asked. "Or is there more to this ridiculous story you're trying to sell these poor people? Bob, you know you're not allowed to do this here."

Rafferty hated that the still-unsolved case had become fodder for fright tours and tourist dollars, taking on mythical and paranormal proportions and embellished with exaggerated details that simply weren't true. The murders had taken place years before he arrived in Salem, but, to Rafferty's mind, the lack of closure was a stain on the police department that he now ran.

Rafferty escorted the tourists back to the hearse, then led the car out of the parking lot and onto Boston Street, turning left at the intersection and continuing downtown to the far end of Essex Street, which was party central.

As always, the pedestrian-only walkway was full of revelers: pirates, sexy witches, monsters, and zombies. *Lots* of zombies. The undead outnumbered the pirates and witches about ten to one. From the middle of the crowd, he could hear the amplified voices of the evangelists preaching fire and brimstone to the revelers, damning their souls to Hell unless they repented and stopped partying. They had added drums this year and cymbals that clanged each time a preacher mentioned Hell. The partiers were laughing and applauding. It didn't seem like there would be any confrontations between the groups tonight.

At a gathering on the corner, Rafferty saw a family wearing homemade costumes that featured bloody stumps where their limbs should have been. They were pulling a little red wagon full of body parts. He watched another man who stood on the sidelines dressed as an oven, complete with burners that turned off and on. A very convincing set of duct-taped Siamese twin dogs ran in front of his cruiser, nipping at each other's faces, frustrated by their unnatural confinement. The usuals were present and accounted for, too, the Frankensteins and the mummies posing for photos at their regular posts by the Peabody Essex Museum, out-of-touch vampires still sporting sparkling glitter in homage to *Twilight*. *They'll be zombies next year,* Rafferty thought. Vampires had been passé in Salem for quite a while now.

He felt sorry for some of the store owners, the ones who paid rent for shops no one could get to through these crowds. It happened every year. Dozens of fortune-tellers set up their booths on Essex Street right in front of the year-round shops that were vying for the same customers. The competition between the resident and visiting psychics had been a big problem a few years back. As a result, Salem now licensed its psychics before allowing them to set up their temporary booths in October.

"How the hell do you license a psychic?" Rafferty had asked when he'd heard about the plan. "I mean, do you have them do a reading and then just wait a few months to see if any of their predictions come true?"

"We'll follow San Francisco's lead," the town clerk had told him. "We're going to use their psychic licensing standards."

"Of course we are." Rafferty had laughed, relieved he didn't have to figure out how to do something so ridiculous. It turned out that all they had to do was check criminal backgrounds before granting licenses. Anyone without a past could now read the future.

From Essex Street, Rafferty drove over to Pickering Wharf. Traffic was bumper to bumper. Some partiers were heading out of the city before the fireworks at the end of the evening, but many were still trying to get in. He was happy to see that the group down by the harbor was fairly docile. He rolled down his window to speak to a patrolman who'd come up from Jamaica Plain.

"Just stick around long enough for the traffic to die down, then either head home or over to the party at the Hawthorne. Best Halloween party in town."

"Will do, thanks."

The Hawthorne Hotel hosted the famous Witches Ball annually, a few nights before Halloween. Tonight would be their more traditional costume party, with prizes given for the best creations; a few years back, Rafferty and his wife, Towner, had been judges.

He parked his car by Bunghole Liquors and walked over to the wharf.

Ann Chase was locking up her Shop of Shadows early tonight.

Six feet tall with thick red hair free-falling halfway down her back, and a "grey witch" by her own admission, Ann practiced neither white nor black magic but something in between. Tonight, she was wearing her traditional black witch's robe. It moved with her stride like a flock of blackbirds, making her look even more magical than usual, if that was possible.

People claimed Ann had a magnetic charge that defied normal boundaries. Depending on your own polarity, you generally found yourself standing either too close to or too far away from Ann Chase. Rafferty intentionally placed himself into the latter category—as much as he wished it weren't true, their history meant he kept her at arm's length whenever possible.

Ann had once explained to him why it was her choice to practice grey magic instead of the more common "white magic" that most Salem witches were into. A black magic witch—the bad, menacing kind you saw on television or in *The Wizard of Oz*—was an unnuanced caricature no self-respecting Salem witch would embrace. Besides, any witch worth her salt knew that every "black" spell you performed came back to you threefold.

"So why don't you stick with the love potions and lottery ticket enhancers that most witches sell around here?" he'd asked.

"The world is too messed up to be a bliss ninny, Rafferty. Sometimes you need to fight back. You of all people should know that."

Ann normally played the good witch, selling everything from

herbal remedies to lace. But sometimes, when she got bored with the tourists, she liked to scare them. Especially on Halloween.

"Had enough of the tourists, have you?" Rafferty laughed.

"That's an understatement."

"Mickey tells me you started a rumor that there's some weird energy out there tonight." His tone was dismissive. He looked at the wharf again. Nothing seemed amiss. People were now watching the fireworks exploding over the harbor, illuminating the docked replica of the *Friendship*. Looking at the great sailing ship, he imagined himself—for an instant—back in the early 1800s, when hundreds of the huge vessels still sailed from Salem, once the richest port in the New World.

"You doubt me, do you?" Ann's expression was one of amusement.

"Wouldn't dare." He laughed again, in spite of himself.

"It's the blood moon," she insisted, "and the eclipses." She gestured to the sky. The clouds had lifted, and now the waxing quartermoon shone with no remaining trace of red. The lunar eclipse a few weeks ago had occurred during the day and wasn't visible from the East Coast, but that night, the full "blood moon" had been the color of rust.

Rafferty knew the lore. His Irish American grandmother had called it a hunter's moon, but the Pagans had coined this more ominous phrase. It was simply October's full moon. "The blood moon rose a couple of weeks ago," Rafferty said. "So I doubt that's the culprit."

"It's the tetrad, Rafferty." Ann sighed as if explaining to a child. "Four lunar eclipses. This weird energy you don't believe in isn't going to end until September of next year."

As if to prove Ann right, a wind suddenly gusted around them, creating a screeching sound that would fit right in at the haunted houses on Derby Street. It stopped as quickly as it had started.

"You doing parlor tricks again?" Rafferty asked.

"Hey, I didn't do that. That one came from the other side."

More Pagan lore. Halloween and its Pagan predecessor, Samhain, were the time of year when the veil between the worlds of the living and the dead was supposed to be at its thinnest. The things Rafferty had learned since moving here! He didn't buy any of it, of course. "You think it's some kind of warning?"

"I think it's more like a preamble." She stared at him as she spoke. She was serious.

Despite his skepticism, Rafferty shivered.

The fireworks had ended, and the witches were gone. Rose Whelan settled her cart under the only oak left standing at the top of Gallows Hill, not far from the pavilion, with its caving roof and urine stench. The banshee music was in her ears tonight, and death was everywhere. Each fall, the leaves looked exhausted before they began to reveal the true colors that lay beneath their green masks. Every year, as they felt fall's inescapable death pull, they turned the reds and oranges and yellows that drew tourists to New England. The maples, whose leaves were always the first to turn, were naked now, their webbed branches sweeping the dark sky like witches' brooms. Only the oaks still held their scarlet flames.

Rose was exhausted, too. She greeted the tree as she sat down under it. Then she spoke to the pigeons; she was simply going to join them for the one night, she explained. Soon, she was drifting off, moving in and out of consciousness, dreaming a recurring nightmare from her stay at the state hospital. In it, the witches' hanging tree was chopped down, and then its massive trunk was floated along the North River toward open ocean, like a Viking ship carrying the souls of the dead to Valhalla. The dream woke her up, as it did every time she had it. Though she'd been dozing for only a short while, it took her a moment to get her bearings. It was the cooing of the pigeons that reminded her: Gallows Hill, a misleadingly named park that had nothing to do with what really happened here.

"If it weren't for me," Rose told the birds, "historians would still claim Salem built a gallows to execute them. On this very spot." She shook her head. "You wouldn't be living here if they had. You wouldn't build your nests where any such thing had happened, would you? Of course not."

The hanging spot, on Proctor's Ledge, sat unmarked, abandoned, and overgrown next to the Walgreens parking lot just below. The hanging tree, on which the condemned had been executed, had vanished long ago, and even the crevasse that had served as their mass grave was barely visible now, but Rose could still feel it there, unsanctified and cursing the whole area with bad luck. The Great Salem Fire had started right across the street in 1914, destroying hundreds of houses and leaving half the population homeless. To this day, there was crime, violence, and a darkness the neighborhood couldn't shake. The only way to stop it was to finish the blessing they had started that night on Proctor's Ledge, the night her girls were murdered.

Rose had been wrong that night, taking the girls up there. Not because the place didn't need to be consecrated, but because the remains of the executed from 1692 were no longer there. Shortly after the hysteria ended, the bodies had begun to disappear from the crevasse into which they had been thrown. Two of the bodies had been taken by their families and buried properly, but the remains of the others executed that dark year had simply vanished. What in the world had happened to them?

"Find the hanging tree, and you will solve the mystery," the oak trees had told Rose over and over, and she had come to believe them. "Find the tree and finish the blessing. For it is not just the wrongly executed who need God's mercy, but the tree itself for the part it was forced to play."

Rose had listened carefully when the trees began to speak. The oaks had saved her that horrible night in 1989, and she owed them a debt of gratitude. Finding the hanging tree had become Rose's sole purpose in life.

The birds appeared unimpressed, and Rose closed her eyes again, sighing. "There was a hanging tree," she mumbled, her speech slowing as she grew sleepier. "That is true. Down there." She pointed toward Proctor's Ledge. Rose hadn't been back to the spot since that night. This was as close as she dared get.

"The hanging tree disappeared . . . everything disappeared. The tree, the remains of the nineteen people they executed as witches, and even the young women I used to know." Rose began to doze. "You'll disappear one day, too," she murmured to the birds, her voice slowing even more. "You don't know that, but it's true. Everything disappears. The banshee takes them all . . ." Her head dropped to her chest, and she became silent.

"Hey, grandma, the witches all went home."

Rose's eyes snapped open. There were three boys standing too close in front of her. The one who'd spoken couldn't be more than fifteen. Low-riding baggy jeans and heavy boots made him look younger than the OG tattoo on his arm.

"I'm not a witch."

He moved even closer, smirking, his blue eyes in stark contrast to the dark look he focused on Rose. "I know exactly who you are. And I know what you did."

"Keep your distance from me," Rose warned.

"Good idea," he said, fanning his face. "You got a real stink there, grandma. When's the last time you took a shower?"

"Go home," the second kid said, shoving her.

"She doesn't have a home, do you, grandma?" OG laughed.

"Keep your hands off me," Rose said, pressing her back against the tree, hearing her pulse in her ears. "I'm not afraid of you."

"You should be," the second kid said, laughing.

"You're the one who should be afraid," Rose countered.

"Yeah? Why's that?" the second kid taunted. "You planning to kill me the same way you killed the rest of them? By screaming?"

"Screaming?" OG started to laugh. "She didn't kill them by screaming. That's just what she told the cops. She slashed their throats."

"I know," the second kid said.

"I don't want to kill anyone." Rose hoped she wouldn't have to. She thought of Olivia, Susan, and Cheryl.

"She's crazy," the third kid said. "Let's go."

Rose liked this one. His eyes were still soft. She spoke directly to him. "It's her you have to be afraid of. Not me."

"Who?" Soft Eyes asked, looking around.

She turned back to OG. "She could kill you right now and no one could stop her."

"Did you hear that? She said she could kill me." OG pulled a knife out of his pocket. "Seems like I'm the one holding the blade tonight. Be afraid, grandma. Be very afraid." With a quick slash, he drew the dull side of the blade across her neck.

Rose scrambled to her feet.

"I didn't say you could leave," OG said.

"He did." Soft Eyes turned to the second kid. "He told her to go."

"Well, I didn't," OG said. "Sit back down." He pushed hard, slamming her back against the tree, knocking the wind out of her.

"You're the one who needs to sit down," Rose choked. "If you don't, you're going to die."

OG laughed. "How's that?"

"You're in mortal danger. From the banshee."

"The What-she? Bee-she?" Soft Eyes said.

"You know the story," the second kid said. "She's the one who killed all those girls. Said a banshee did it. By screaming."

"That's right," Rose said. "She could kill you, too."

"I told you she was crazy," Soft Eyes said. "Come on, let's get out of here."

"No way," OG said, grinning at Rose. "I want to hear this. Tell my friend here about the banshee. It's Halloween, grandma. I want to hear a scary story." He held the point of the blade against her cheek.

She could see his life. There had already been violence in it, a lot of it. A string of brutality stretched out before him. She didn't see his death the way she could with most people. What she saw when she looked into his empty eyes was the death of everyone around him.

"Tell him, or I'll kill you right here. And no one can stop *me*. Tell him the same story you told the cops. About the banshee," OG insisted.

She turned back to the one with the soft eyes. This was the one who would need to understand one day. She swallowed hard.

"Tell him!" OG ordered. "Once upon a time . . ." he prompted, pressing the knife harder against her skin.

"All right," Rose said, taking a breath.

"When I was growing up, my Irish grandmother told me there was a sacred oak back in the old country called the Banshee Tree. It was a wild wreck of a thing struck by lightning years earlier."

Soft Eyes just stared at her.

"Some believed the Gaelic goddess of life and death was imprisoned inside that same tree for many centuries before the storm, tricked by the Christian priests who had come to Ireland to convert the Celtic tribes and would tolerate no gods but their own, and certainly no goddesses. Theirs was the one and only God, they said to justify her capture. Some say it was the Cailleach they imprisoned, but some called her by other names. You see, there were many goddesses who dealt with life and death. The imprisonment changed the nature of the goddess, diminishing her to the size of the fairies who dwelt in the mounds. It was a tragedy of great magnitude.

"But the tree loved the imprisoned goddess and took pity on her. Not yet loyal to the priests who had newly arrived, the tree hatched a plan: to free the captive goddess, the oak tree courted the strike."

The second kid snorted. "What the fuck are you talking about?"

"Shut up and she'll tell you," OG said.

"The storm that killed that oak was the worst in memory; the scream of the wailing wind circled the town once, twice, and then a third time, terrifying everyone. The lightning bolt vaporized the water in the wood, exploding its limbs and—some say—freeing the captive goddess. But freeing the goddess was the worst thing the tree could have done, for her imprisonment had changed her very nature, turning her from a goddess to a banshee, not the ones you've heard about, who only predict death, but one who actually kills."

"A killer banshee." The second kid laughed. "Right."

"I thought a banshee was some kind of ATV," Soft Eyes said.

"The tree should have left the goddess imprisoned, for freeing it would have consequences far beyond anything the oak could have imagined. The turning had made the goddess hate. Her size was still diminished, and her powers were no longer strong enough to determine life and death. She needed a host. Life no longer interested her; it was only death she craved now. Her sustenance became hate and fear, and where these baser emotions dwelled, the banshee goddess would always find a willing host.

"It was the tree that, perhaps, suffered the most, for it was forced to bear witness to the carnage it had unleashed. After the lightning strike that freed the turned goddess and forevermore, the tree's sap has run red, as if it were bleeding."

"Bleeding trees?" the second kid sneered. "Goddesses turning . . ."

Rose shuddered to remember just how that goddess had turned. That night in 1989, Rose had lost them all to the creature the goddess had become: the banshee. Those young women the banshee killed had been like her own daughters. On that horrible night, after it happened, after the shrieking stopped, the world had quieted and then disappeared. Rose had found herself staring into an eternal emptiness that stretched in every direction and went on forever. When the keening began, Rose had believed that the sound was coming from her own lips. Then she'd seen the tree limbs and branches start to move with the breath of the sound itself, their last leaves burning in the black sky like crackling paper. Then the trees had begun to speak. *Come away now,* the trees had said. *Come away.* Their mournful keen had jumped from one tree to another, and Rose had followed. But something had been unleashed by their ritual. What had been meant to consecrate had instead released something else, something that had jumped into Rose.

"You're out of your mind, old lady," OG said, enjoying the flash of his knife in the moonlight as he played the blade across her cheek, this time drawing blood.

It was the last thing he saw before the unearthly screeching began.

CHAPTER TWO

October 31, 2014
SALEM

A still wind is a dangerous wind,
for it calls down the banshee.
—ROSE'S *Book of Trees*

AT THE STATION, RAFFERTY PARKED IN THE SPOT RESERVED
for him. Just a few minutes earlier, as he'd been leaving the wharf, a
kid had lobbed an egg at his cruiser. It was a direct hit. The witch on
the broomstick was now wearing a frothy yellow-brown beard. A few
pieces of shell were stuck to her robe.

"Don't say a word," Rafferty said to an officer who was coming
down the station stairs looking amused.

"Wouldn't dream of it."

"Who've we got?"

"A few drunks."

"That's it?"

"And a couple of bar fights. Nothing much."

Rafferty went inside and stopped at the front desk, looking at the
arrest sheet.

Jay-Jay LaLibertie, the officer manning the desk, was in his midthirties but still had the look of a skinny high school kid. His hair was
uncombed, his uniform shirt untucked.

"Messages?" asked Rafferty.

Jay-Jay knocked over his soda as he reached for them, dropping the messages, soaking them. "Sorry, Chief."

Rafferty grabbed the fallen can, taking a whiff of it before handing it back.

"I'm sober this time, I swear," Jay-Jay said.

Rafferty sighed as Jay-Jay passed him the soggy pile. The top two were from his wife, Towner. He walked into his office and closed the door. He grabbed a Hershey's bar out of his desk and unwrapped it, taking a bite. Then he picked up the phone and dialed home. "What's up?"

"Nothing. Just missing you. When are you coming home?"

"Maybe an hour or so."

He picked up the cup of cold coffee he'd left on his desk, smelled it, then put it down again. He pushed the speaker button on the phone.

"So, how many strays have you taken in so far?" he asked.

Every Halloween, Towner kept an eye out for girls who were too drunk to get home after the fireworks. She knew only too well the kind of trouble young girls can get into, and she made it her business to help. "Strays" were always welcome in their home. Rafferty liked this about his wife. Truth be told, he liked just about everything about her. He'd almost lost her once, and it was something he couldn't bear to think about. "How many?" he asked again, aware that she was avoiding his question.

She just laughed.

"Be careful," he said. "I don't want to find one of them in bed with us."

"Oh God, I'd forgotten that! Remember her—"

Jay-Jay rushed in without knocking. "We've got a murder! Over on Gallows Hill!"

"You sure you haven't been drinking?" Rafferty said before he could stop himself.

"What's going on?" Towner's voice over the phone sounded worried. "Is that Jay-Jay?"

Rafferty took her off speaker.

"I swear! It's true. A kid is dead. Porter was over on Pope Street, and he took the suspect into custody," Jay-Jay insisted. "The kid's friends are saying the old lady killed him—"

"I'll call you back." Rafferty hung up, turning to Jay-Jay. "Slow down. Tell me what happened. Who's dead?"

"Billy Barnes! And his two friends are saying she killed him."

"Who is *she*?"

"That old homeless woman—the one who calls herself a banshee."

"Rose Whelan?" What the hell? He'd just been thinking about Rose. Now Rafferty could hear the chaos erupting out in the hallway.

"Porter arrested her?"

"Yup. Mirandized her and everything. They're putting the old lady in the holding cell right now. She's flailing around, looks like she's fighting with something none of us can see. You have to go look. It's spooky."

Rafferty was out the door and down the corridor before Jay-Jay had a chance to catch up.

"What the hell's going on?" Rafferty demanded of Porter, a heavy-set man in his midforties. *This is all happening too fast.* "You know you don't just go ahead and arrest someone."

"She wrote a confession," Porter said. "Signed it and everything." He handed Rafferty a piece of paper. It said: *Tell Rafferty I killed the kid. I had to do it. He was turning.*

Rafferty recognized the writing. And he was pretty sure the confession was written on a page ripped from Rose's journal. He'd seen the journal a few times, leather-bound with unusual handmade paper. The only things he'd seen in the book before were random drawings of trees.

"What the hell does that mean? Did she say anything?"

Porter shrugged. "She kept mumbling something in the car," he said. "It was kind of hard to make out what she was saying."

"Tell me," Rafferty said.

"Something about *the lesser of two evils.*"

Rafferty stared at Porter. "She said that?"

"That's what it sounded like."

"She has a nasty cut," Jay-Jay said to Rafferty. "We need to get someone in there to clean it up."

Two of the other officers who'd been watching the scene in the holding cell stepped back.

Rafferty looked inside: Rose was seated on the cot, and she seemed calm. She had a bloody gash on her cheek. Jay-Jay, who'd made the suggestion, took a step back. "I'm not going near her."

"Oh, for Christ's sake." Rafferty took the first aid kit down from where it hung on the wall by the exit door and let himself into the cell. "Rose," he said, kneeling next to her. "You're okay. We've got you now." He reached out to touch her arm, and Rose pulled back as if stung. "It's okay," he said. "It's just me, Rose. It's Rafferty. You know me."

The sound started as a low growl. It was so soft that Rafferty wasn't certain he was really hearing it until the pitch raised and grew in volume. All at once it was a shrieking that bounced off the cinder-block walls and caused the officers on the other side of the bars to cover their ears.

"Jesus Christ," said Jay-Jay. "Get out of there!"

Rafferty backed out of the cell quickly, unnerved. "Okay, Rose," he said, once he was outside. "I'll leave you alone for now."

"Stay outside," Rafferty instructed one of the officers. He assigned a guard to the cell. "Don't get too close," he warned, but he needn't have bothered. The officer stood as far from the cell as he could while still remaining in the corridor.

"Where are the witnesses?" Rafferty asked.

Porter spoke up. "They're down the hall. They had plenty to say on Gallows Hill, but now they insist they won't talk without a lawyer."

"Of course they won't." Rafferty sighed and ran his hand through his hair. "Back to the desk, Jay-Jay." Rafferty headed quickly to his office and closed the door. He picked up the phone and dialed Zee Finch, the psychiatrist who had been treating Rose on and off for years. He hated to call her at home.

"This is Zee," she answered, sounding groggy.

"Sorry to bother you this late," Rafferty said. "We've got a problem."

Zee listened as Rafferty explained what he knew so far.

"Oh God, here we go again," she said, when he was finished. "Let me get dressed. I'll be right down."

"Thank you." Rafferty hung up, then dialed again, this time calling Barry Marcus, a defense attorney who he knew did pro-bono work.

"Rose Whelan, huh?" Barry said. He hadn't been asleep. "What's she accused of this time?"

"Killing Billy Barnes."

"Billy Barnes?" repeated Barry. "Well, that's unfortunate . . ."

"Depends on how you look at it," Rafferty said. He knew Barry well enough to be honest. No one in Salem thought Billy Barnes was anything but trouble. But he was connected. His great-aunt, Helen, was one of Salem's most influential citizens.

"Are you the arresting officer?" Barry asked.

"What do you think?"

"I'm guessing no. So who was it?"

"Porter."

"Why doesn't that surprise me?"

Porter had a habit of arresting first and asking questions later, something that had gotten him into trouble more than once.

"What did the witnesses say?"

"I haven't questioned them yet. They've asked for a lawyer. Which means they think they're going to be charged with something."

"Are they?"

"I don't know yet."

"Fax me the police report." Barry sighed. "I'll be over in the morning. Meanwhile, don't let Rose talk to anyone. Let's not have a repeat of what happened last time."

"Agreed." Rafferty hung up, thinking about the '89 murders, Salem's most famous cold case. Rose Whelan had always been unofficially blamed for the killings, despite what he'd heard was an overwhelming lack of hard evidence. What they did have was "no truth, only speculation," which, as he'd seen with Actor Bob tonight, was dramatized and exaggerated by the locals for the tourist dollars. The facts were different and even more inconclusive: Three young women had been killed. It had been a bloodbath; the women's throats were slit, and they quickly bled out. One of the women, an albino, had hair and some skin taken from her body. A child and Rose herself had been the only survivors. It had all happened almost five years before Rafferty came to Salem. He'd wanted to reopen the case, but there had always been something more pressing to take care of in this city: drugs, street crime, domestic violence, all real and current. And then there was Halloween, which lasted longer and longer each year.

"Strange things happen here on Halloween," his predecessor, Tom Dayle, had told him as he handed him a few of the cold-case folders. The one they called the "Goddess Murders" had been at the bottom of the pile.

Rafferty had already heard the rumors about Dayle. Four years away from a full pension, the detective had suffered a mental breakdown, which had put him on medical leave for more than four years. The cops were whispering that it was the unsolved case that had sent him over the edge.

"The rest of the evidence is in storage," Dayle told him. "I wouldn't bother. There's nothing there." After reviewing current cases with Rafferty for one afternoon, he took disability retirement. Not for the breakdown, officially, but for "severe arthritis in his knees." Same money, better story.

Rafferty had heard a lot of stories around town about the case, random details that piqued his interest. Even now, twenty-five years after it happened, people were still talking about it, especially when it came to Rose Whelan. Now, twenty years into his own tenure, Rafferty would have to take a closer look. He threw out the rest of the Hershey's bar, got himself a fresh cup of coffee, and tried to recall what he knew about the case.

He'd never understood why the town believed Rose Whelan was the perpetrator and not another victim. He'd gotten to know her over the years, thinking, at first, that she was one of Towner's "strays." But Rose Whelan was far more than that. She had been a scholar, with specialties in both mythology and colonial history, particularly the Salem witch trials. When he'd questioned her once about the juxtaposition of two such seeming opposites, she'd dismissed him as if the connection was obvious. "To understand what happened with the Puritans in Salem, you must first understand the Pagan religions they so feared. To the Puritans, the Catholic acceptance of established Pagan feasts and holidays was just like summoning the devil."

But everything had changed for Rose with the murders of the three young women in 1989. She had been severely traumatized by the event, and because of her mental state and her presence on the hill that night, suspicions had begun to point in her direction. After all, the young women lived at her home. According to what Rafferty had heard, Rose had disapproved of their behavior and given them several chances to change it, then finally asked them to leave. He'd heard the ritual they had been performing the night they were killed was a last gathering, fulfilling some kind of promise the women had made to Rose, some condition of their living arrangements with her.

When they had died so mysteriously and brutally, accusations had begun to fly in Rose's direction. A grand jury had been convened, but—not surprisingly, in his opinion—it hadn't found sufficient evidence to indict Rose. All anyone could agree on was that Rose Whelan, once a respected local historian and authority on the witch trials, had not been in her right mind since that awful night on Proctor's Ledge. Rafferty believed in Rose's innocence. Besides Rose, there had been one witness to the crime; well, a witness of a sort, the other survivor, the five-year-old daughter of one of the victims. This child steadfastly insisted that Rose Whelan had helped her hide "from the bad thing" and then had gone back to try to save the others.

At the end of the day, instead of going to jail, Rose had been sent to a series of state mental hospitals. And after a full year of remaining mute, she'd regained her voice and begun to tell a wild story about what had happened to the three slain women, who by then had been dubbed "Goddesses" by the media and everyone in town. This was the reason Barry Marcus didn't want Rose to talk to Rafferty without an attorney present: Years ago, after prolonged questioning, Rose had alleged that the young women had been killed by a banshee. Rafferty knew of the banshee from his own grandmother's stories of Ireland: a banshee was a mythological female spirit whose mournful cries were considered omens of death. His grandmother had always claimed that Rafferty's family had a banshee that had predicted every death for generations.

But he'd never heard of a banshee actually doing the killing. Rose had claimed that, after the murders were committed, this banshee had jumped into her and that she was keeping the creature trapped inside herself to stop her from killing again. If she'd had a lawyer, she would have been advised against telling this tale to anyone, least of all the police.

Rafferty knew Rose well enough to know that she had fallen on hard times—she'd lost her home, for God's sake—but she was no killer. His cop's instincts had always been good; he'd stake them against the best out there.

"You want to tell me what happened?" Rafferty sat across from the two boys in the interrogation room. He drank the last of his coffee and stared at them. He'd seen them before, had a few run-ins with them during the last year. There was no lawyer present, but the two had had an extended phone consultation with someone before agreeing to proceed. No parent or guardian had yet come to the station.

He was far more familiar with the dead boy, Billy Barnes. Billy had been a bad kid. There was no way around it. Last year on Halloween, he had started a knife fight with a kid from Lynn, someone rumored to be a member of the Latin Kings. Though he was not a gang member himself, his OG tattoo was there to tell everyone he liked violence, that he wouldn't back down. *"Original Gangster" like hell*, Rafferty thought. Couldn't have been further from the truth. Billy Barnes was about as far from gangster as you could get. He was a poseur, a wannabe, as entitled as they come. Even so, he was dangerous.

No one had pressed any charges then, nor had they done so any of the numerous times Barnes had been picked up before or since. Some fancy lawyer had always bailed him out, and no charge Rafferty had filed against him ever stuck. Rafferty didn't think that did the kid any favors. If he'd been Rafferty's son, he would have left him in jail overnight or even longer, to give him a taste of what the correctional facility in Middleton would feel like. Probably do the kid some good—hopefully straighten him out. If his own daughter ever acted like Billy Barnes had . . .

"We told you. Rose Whelan is the killer."

"Right," Rafferty said. They were getting nowhere fast. The boys had clearly been advised to say nothing beyond the simple statement "Rose Whelan is the killer." He leaned across the table. "What about the cut on her cheek? Which one of you did that?"

The two boys looked at each other. Neither said a word.

"You two want to go home tonight, or do you want to share the cell across the hall from Rose Whelan?"

"You can't hold us," said the older one—whose last name was Monk.

Rafferty laughed. "Who told you that?"

When they didn't offer any answer, Rafferty sent them to a holding cell, not across from Rose but near enough to shake them up a bit. He waited for a new pot of coffee to brew before he called them back in, this time separately. Monk came first, avoiding eye contact. "I know what I saw," he said. Then he amended the statement. "What I heard."

The younger boy, the one called James, was different. Once Rafferty got him alone he was less reticent. "She warned him she'd have to do it," he said. "She thought *he* was going to kill *her*."

"Was he?"

"I don't know," James said. He shrugged. "Maybe." He looked like he was going to cry.

"What happened to the knife?" Rafferty asked. The knife that Billy Barnes had threatened Rose with had conveniently disappeared.

"Monk threw it into the woods."

"If I send someone out to retrieve it, is it going to be there?" Rafferty said.

"I don't know."

Rafferty kept eye contact but didn't speak.

"I don't think so," James said. "Not anymore."

"Was that your phone call, one of your gangster friends? Someone who would get rid of the knife?"

James quieted. His whole body was shaking.

Rafferty looked at the kid for a long time. "Tell me again. Exactly what happened. Between Billy and Rose."

"Monk told her to leave, but she wouldn't."

Rafferty wasn't surprised. People often harassed Rose. She'd learned to hold her own. Over the years, the skills she needed to survive on the streets had developed into a defiance that others perceived as either craziness or arrogance, or both.

"She should have gone," James said, starting to cry.

"What happened after that?"

"Billy threatened her. And then she threatened him."

Rafferty raised an eyebrow. "How exactly did she threaten him? Wasn't Billy the one with the knife?"

"Yes," James said.

"So how could Rose threaten him if he had the weapon?"

"She—she told him to sit down. Said she'd have to kill him if he didn't." Now the kid was hyperventilating. "It's the truth!" he said. "She said crazy things. About banshees and goddesses and bleeding trees that got hit by lightning."

Rafferty was familiar with some of Rose's musings. She was quite the storyteller, actually, though most of her yarns made little sense.

"Take a deep breath and hold it," Rafferty suggested.

The kid obeyed. Then, at Rafferty's direction, he exhaled slowly. Rafferty got up and got him a drink of water from the cooler. He sat back down and watched while the kid sipped.

"Okay?"

James nodded, wiping his eyes.

"Okay, then, tell me what happened next."

"A huge wind. Like a howling sound and then screeching. Horrible screeching. I've never heard anything like it. It hurt, man! I couldn't see, and everything went black—and then Billy was on the ground." James started to cry again. "His eyes were all bugging, like he was still seeing the thing that killed him."

"I thought you said Rose killed him?"

"It *was* her!"

"You said 'the thing that killed him.' "

The kid stopped crying. "She said she would do it, and she did."

"Dr. Finch is here," Jay-Jay announced when Rafferty came out of the interrogation room. "I put her in the cell with Rose."

Rafferty doubted Jay-Jay's judgment, and not for the first time. He hurried toward Rose's cell. Before he started interviewing the witnesses, he had checked in on Rose again. She seemed calmer, thank God.

Zee Finch was sitting on the cot next to Rose when he arrived, dressing her wound. She looked up when she saw Rafferty and tucked an errant strand of auburn hair behind her ear. "She's going to need stitches."

Rafferty nodded.

Rose appeared to stare at something no one else in the room could see.

"How long has she been like this?" Zee asked, as she finished bandaging the cut. "Has she said what happened?"

"She hasn't said anything to me," Rafferty said. He was standing at the opposite wall, keeping an eye on the hallway to make sure no one interrupted them.

"Are you charging her?"

"With what?" Rafferty asked. "Killing a kid by screaming at him?"

"Jay-Jay said there is a written confession."

"Yup," Rafferty said.

"You're not going to show it to me?"

"Not until I've shown it to her attorney," he answered.

"That's acceptable. But she needs to be in a hospital tonight. I'll call Salem and secure a bed in the psych unit."

Rafferty sighed. He hated the thought of Rose in a psych ward, but he couldn't release her, nor could he charge her, confession or no confession. According to the paramedics, the boy's body had been clean. No signs of violence or marks anywhere. "I think that's the best option. I can't do much of anything until I know what we're dealing with. At this point, I don't even know if a crime has been committed. We won't know that until we get the kid's autopsy results and tox screen. This isn't *CSI*; this is Salem."

They both knew that getting those results was going to take a while.

"Rose," Zee said. "I'm calling the hospital, and I'm going to get you a bed. You can rest there until we figure this whole thing out."

Rose made no response.

Zee took Rose's hand. Rose hadn't reacted at all when Zee cleaned her wound, but now, curling her fingers like a cat's claws, she went for the eyes, scratching Zee's face from temple to chin. Rafferty grabbed Zee by the arm, pulling her away from Rose.

"What the hell happened to her on that hill?" Zee asked, as she regained her composure.

"Tonight or twenty-five years ago?" Rafferty replied.

The first time he'd met Rose was soon after he and Towner had started living together. He'd come home late one night to find her sleeping under an oak tree in Towner's courtyard. "Well, you've certainly had a harrowing day, haven't you?" Rose had said without preamble.

"Who the hell are you?" he'd asked. "And what are you doing in my yard?"

"It's not your yard. It's Eva Whitney's yard, and she gave me this tree."

He'd realized the woman before him was Rose, whom he'd only heard about until that moment. She was right. Eva Whitney, Towner's grandmother, had been clear about that oak in her will. She'd left the huge brick house, the tearoom, and all her worldly possessions to Towner, but she had, in fact, left the oak tree to Rose. *I hereby bequeath life rights to the oak tree to Rose Whelan*, the will had specified. *If I could, I would leave her every oak in Salem. May it help her learn their secrets.*

After that initial meeting, they began to hit it off. She was always there, a fixture of the place, and she always said hello and asked about his day. Rafferty took to sharing bits of small talk and sometimes even philosophy with Rose when he'd come home from the late shift.

He thought of her as his sage, his oracle. Not that she was always prescient. A lot of what she said and the fanciful stories she liked to tell were nonsensical ramblings. But every so often, something she said resonated with him in a profound way. He'd come to like their interchanges.

It was Towner who'd told him about the woman's history. Rose hadn't always been strange. Before the Goddess Murders, she'd been a well-respected scholar. Rose had been credited with establishing the true location of the 1692 witch trial hangings, for centuries erroneously believed to be part of Gallows Hill Park. She'd also come up with the recently accepted theory that there were no gallows used in the executions back in 1692, but rather a hardwood tree, one that had long since disappeared, along with the bodies of the executed.

But Rose had changed since the murders. Her fixation on death gave folks the creeps. She would tell people how and when they were going to die. It made everyone uncomfortable, to say the least. To make matters worse, some of her predictions had come true. As a result, most people avoided her, crossing the street when they saw her coming.

The one case people always talked about was a death Rafferty could have predicted himself: a drunk with yellow skin and rheumy eyes he'd known from the Program who'd been off the wagon more than he'd ever been on it. Anyone could have predicted what would happen to him, but in front of a sidewalk full of witnesses, Rose had pronounced his death imminent. The next morning, his body had been sprawled on Lafayette Street in front of Red Lulu Cocina. It had simply been the law of averages, but people had wanted to believe it was sinister. And they'd wanted to believe Rose was to blame.

Some nights, when Rafferty came home late, Rose might make a comment that kept him thinking for days. "No one comes out of the womb and sees death on everyone. It happens over time and by degree, until, one day, you've seen so much horror that it turns you. That's when the banshee can jump in."

There were a lot of strange things in Salem that Rafferty didn't put any stock in, but he did believe in banshees, though he didn't go around advertising that fact. He'd told Towner the story once. He'd heard a banshee wail and moan the night his mother died; he was certain of it. He'd seen her, too: an old crone behind his childhood home, keening. When he'd approached, she'd disappeared, just evaporated like a water spirit. Of course, it had been back in his drinking days. He and his brothers *had* shared a few pints that evening. They'd kidded him about "seeing that old woman" for years. But Rafferty had seen her, a boggy spirit sitting on an aluminum lawn chair in Queens, mourning the death throes of his mother.

But Rose's flesh-and-blood banshee was something he didn't believe in. He and Rose had debated the subject on several occasions. Eccentric as she was, or even crazy as most Salemites believed, Rose was a well-educated woman; her arguments were often backed by her extensive reading on almost any subject Rafferty could imagine, mythology being one of her favorites. You almost always learned something talking to Rose Whelan.

Yet sometimes Rose was too strange and creepy even for Rafferty. Sometimes she looked at him as if she could see straight into his soul, and what she saw there was lacking.

One night he'd come home after a particularly gruesome day dealing with a victim of domestic violence who'd landed at the shelter on Yellow Dog Island, and he'd hoped Rose might be asleep under her tree, as she often was when he worked late.

Tilting her head, she'd looked at him curiously. "Do you think, inside, every one of us is a killer?"

"What?"

"If you thought killing was the lesser of two evils, would you be capable of taking a life?"

"I don't think about that kind of thing," Rafferty had said.

"You should. In your job."

Rafferty had hurried toward the steps.

"Have *you* ever killed?"

"No," Rafferty had said and hurried inside.

He'd heard her whispered reply as he closed the door.

"Liar."

If that wasn't a straight shot at his soul, nothing was.

CHAPTER THREE

You know who you are. You have always been other.

—Rose's *Book of Trees*

THE WOMEN SAT IN A CIRCLE, THEIR EYES CLOSED. THE note echoed as it orbited the room, the sound softening everything it touched, removing rough edges, rounding corners, relaxing those who were seated.

Callie stood at the front of the room, drawing the wand around the singing bowl. From a distance, she appeared to be stirring some great stew or tending a witch's cauldron, but the wand was actually being drawn along the outside rim of the bowl, not the inside. The tone it created was clear and true, circling and building in volume until it was so loud that Callie could feel the vibration in her bones. Placing the wand on the table, she listened to the sound waves the bowl continued to generate.

She had tried treating them separately, but the group energy was so strong when they meditated together that it had become obvious that this was their best healing modality. Today it was working for all but one of them, poor Margie, who was suffering from late-stage Parkinson's. Callie walked over, placing a hand on Margie's shoulder.

"Are you having trouble?"

"I can't concentrate with all that racket," Margie said.

"The bowl? You've never objected before," Callie replied, confused.

Then, as the sound of the singing bowl faded, Callie heard the news at noon blaring from the next room. Many of the elderly women at All Saints' Home, where Callie worked as a music therapist, had some degree of hearing loss, so the television in the rec room was always cranked high.

"The TV," Margie said. "It's bothering me."

"Hang on." Callie held up a finger and headed next door. "I'll be right back."

She closed the door behind her and walked into the hall. The smell of boiled cauliflower hung in the air. She poked her head into the rec room. The set was tuned to WCVB. "We were there for the entire week," a newscaster intoned. "We saw witches, pirates, and even an ugliest dog contest, as we do every year when we cover Halloween in Salem. And though it has been hokey and even otherworldly at times, it has always been safe and family friendly."

"Not always," the second newscaster commented.

"Too loud?" asked Edith as Callie walked in. Edith was one of the ladies who refused to come to Callie's music therapy sessions, even though Callie knew her arthritis was truly painful. She'd have to talk with Sister Ernestine—she'd be the one to convince Edith to join.

"Just a tad, Edith. May I have the remote?"

Callie turned to the screen as the broadcaster said, "A killer banshee."

The image shifted to a photo of an old woman pushing a cart. Her hair was long and white and wild, and it seemed to trail in her wake. She had a hateful look on her face. Underneath, the caption read: THE BANSHEE OF SALEM.

Callie stared at the screen. The woman looked so familiar, yet she couldn't quite place her.

"If looks could kill," the first newscaster said.

"Seems like they just might have," the other rejoined. "The alleged, and I stress that word, the alleged homeless killer banshee's name is Rose Whelan."

The remote clattered to the ground.

"If that name rings a bell for some of our longtime viewers, it should," the second newscaster said. "Rose Whelan was once the prime suspect in Salem's still unsolved Goddess Murders."

Callie couldn't speak. She did not reach for the remote but stood staring at the television and rubbing her left hand.

"Are you okay, dear?" asked Edith.

"The young victim's name has not yet been released, pending notification of his family."

Callie leaned down to retrieve the dropped remote, and Edith saw something on the young woman's left hand she had never noticed before. "Did you hurt yourself?" she asked. Was it a tattoo of some kind? No, not a tattoo. A burn maybe? Or a scar. Whatever it was cast a shadow across the young woman's palm. The older woman took a closer look. It was a scar. Why had she never noticed it before? Symmetrical and centered on Callie's palm was the image of Edith's favorite flower, a rose.

CHAPTER FOUR

November 1, 2014

SALEM

*No Christian burial was allowed for those hanged for
witchcraft in 1692. However, the account of Rebecca
Nurse's son rowing six miles down the North River to
recover his mother's body and give her a proper burial
is well documented. Later, though no one knows exactly
when, the remains of the others accused and executed
that dark year simply disappeared from the crevasse
into which their bodies were unceremoniously dumped.
Logically, the question follows: Where did they go?*

—ROSE WHELAN, *The Witches of Salem*

RAFFERTY WALKED BARRY MARCUS OUT OF THE POLICE
station. Except for the diamond stud in one ear, the lawyer looked the
way you hoped a successful defense attorney would look on his way
to court: dark blue suit, white shirt, red-and-blue-striped tie. Rafferty
fastened his coat, covering yesterday's rumpled button-down shirt,
now sporting a coffee stain on its breast pocket.

Shortly after sunrise, Rose had been transported to Salem Hospital via ambulance. Rafferty had her taken out the back door of the
station and instructed the ambulance crew to drive down Jefferson
Avenue to Salem Hospital's rear entrance and take her in through the
emergency room for admission. "You know you can't hold her," Barry
was saying to him now. "You can't even charge her without the kid's

autopsy results. Last time I checked, yelling at a juvenile delinquent who's threatening you with a knife wasn't a crime."

"There are no plans to formally charge her. Not yet, anyway. She's in the hospital on the orders of her doctor, Zee Finch."

They stepped outside into the morning glare as a reporter shoved a microphone in Rafferty's face.

"Is it true you've found a link between last night's killing and the Goddess Murders?"

"Who told you that?" Rafferty asked, not bothering to hide his annoyance.

"Several people," the reporter replied in a goading tone.

"Well, they don't know what they're talking about." As soon as he said it, he saw Barry raise an eyebrow, and Rafferty regretted the remark. He was exhausted. He'd had at least six cups of coffee, not counting the one he'd spilled on himself, and he hadn't been home at all, hadn't even called Towner to give her an update.

As they walked away, Barry leaned in. "Next time, just say 'No comment.' "

When they pulled up to the hospital, it was swarming with news teams.

"Is it true she killed a kid with her voice?"

"She's a descendant of a witch, is that right?"

"Did Satan make her do it?"

"What's wrong with you people? You can't kill someone with your voice!" Rafferty wanted to shout right back. But all he did was glance at Barry Marcus and say, "No comment."

The two men made their way to the locked psych ward on the seventh floor, passing through the security doors to find Zee waiting for them. She and Barry greeted each other.

"What happened to your face?" Barry asked, noticing Zee's bandage.

"Rose happened," Rafferty said.

"I'd like to see the confession," Zee said, her hand on Rose's door.

"I told her that was your call," Rafferty explained.

Barry reached into his briefcase and handed Zee a copy of the torn page from Rose's journal. She read it over a few times before she looked up. "This can't be admissible, can it?" She handed the paper back to Barry.

"If and when the time comes, that would certainly be my argument. Let's go in. It goes without saying," Barry added, "but I'll say it for the record: She will have no visitors while she is here—family and attending physicians only."

"I've already left that order," Zee said. "And I'll rebrief the staff about HIPAA compliance. We're going to have to hold a commitment hearing to keep her here."

"Not for any legal reason," Barry said.

"She's a murder suspect," Rafferty said. "That's legal reason enough."

"Not to hospitalize her, it isn't."

"On my orders. For her own protection," Zee said. "I've been treating Rose for some time. But she clearly needs hospitalization now. Still, we have to follow procedures, since she's unresponsive."

Barry nodded. "Who's the judge?"

"Usually Tremblay."

"He's not bad, but I need to be there. Just let me know when."

They pushed the door open and found themselves in a dimly lit room. Rose was staring at the ceiling and tied to the bed in four-point restraints. "Is that really necessary?" Barry asked.

"She was violent at the station," Rafferty said, gesturing to Zee's face.

"She was agitated," Zee corrected.

"What's her diagnosis?" Barry asked Zee.

"It's a little early for diagnosis—"

"Okay, then. What was the diagnosis twenty-five years ago? After the Goddess Murders."

"A conversion disorder as the result of complex trauma."

"And how long was she catatonic then?"

"I'm not sure *catatonic* is the right term."

"I'll rephrase. How long was she uncommunicative?"

"Almost a year."

"Okay," he said again. The three looked at Rose for an awkward moment. Barry shook his head. "Doesn't look like I'll accomplish much by talking with her. Let me know when the commitment hearing is. I'll be in touch with you both." He looked at the restraints again. "And get those things off of her ASAP." He headed for the door, and Rafferty opened it for him, just as a uniformed officer arrived to stand guard.

The lawyer left the room, and Zee and Rafferty stood together silently, watching Barry's back disappear down the hall. "I don't envy you this case," Zee said.

"Right back at you," Rafferty said.

"I mean, this can't be easy *personally*," Zee clarified. "You and Rose are friends."

She was giving him the opportunity to talk about his feelings, the way any good therapist might. But she wasn't his therapist, though she had once been Towner's. He pressed his lips together and shrugged. Truth be told, he felt a little uneasy around Zee Finch. It was she and Towner who were really friends—they worked together at the shelter for abused women and children that Towner's family ran on Yellow Dog Island and also at the tearoom Towner owned and managed in town, which employed the abuse victims who were ready to make their way back into the world. And even before that . . . Towner's terrible childhood and her breakdown were legendary in Salem. She had needed counseling, and Zee had a personal understanding of complex trauma that made her the right choice. She'd been instrumental in helping Towner recover. Still, Rafferty felt Zee knew too much, both about Towner's history and about their rocky path back together after their separation. Being around Dr. Finch for too long made him uncomfortable.

"I know you care about Rose," Zee offered.

"We all care about her," he said.

She waited for him to continue.

"I hate to cut this cleverly disguised attempt at a therapy session short, but I have to get back to work."

Zee laughed and shrugged. "I'll get you on the couch one of these days, my friend."

"Don't hold your breath."

CHAPTER FIVE

November 1, 2014
SALEM

*It may be most widely known as the site of the Salem
witchcraft trials of 1692, but this colorful, coastal
city has much to offer both residents and visitors:
a culturally diverse population, a rich maritime heritage,
an impressive display of historic architecture and
amazing stories that span almost four centuries.*
—The Comprehensive Salem Guide

CALLIE DROVE FROM NORTHAMPTON, PULLING OFF THE
Mass Pike onto 128, then following Route 114 to Salem, missing a
turn along the way and ending up down by the waterfront. She turned
left and drove up by the common, circling the statue of Roger Conant
to change direction and head back toward the station.

Rose is alive? How is that possible? They told me she was dead.

After the newscast had ended, Callie simply left the nursing home.
She didn't check in with her supervisor, the longtime prioress of both
the nursing home and the children's home where she'd spent most
of her early years. Sister Mary Agatha was her name, but the girls at
the home had nicknamed her Sister Mary Agony, and the name had
stuck. Though a big part of her wanted to storm into Agony's office
and demand to know why they had lied to her, Callie couldn't do it.
Not right now. Not without losing it altogether. She just had to get
out of there. She didn't tell anyone she was leaving. Instead, she went

home, packed an overnight bag, and started driving to a place she had once promised herself she would never set foot in again. She drove as if in a trance.

Rose was alive!

Salem didn't look at all the way Callie remembered it from her childhood: a struggling city, a historic seaport that had seen better days, its harbor district dotted with hippie houses and a few witch shops. What she saw now was a collection of upscale shops, restaurants, and restored homes whose grandeur rivaled the antebellum mansions of the south. Witch kitsch was liberally scattered through the downtown landscape, along with haunted houses and psychic reading studios.

Though Callie had only a handful of memories from her life in Salem, the moments she remembered were vivid and crystal clear, more like snapshots or videos capturing precise moments in time, with no trace of what came between. Her therapists—she'd had a few; the nuns had seen to that—had tried to get her to fill in the blanks, to paint a more comprehensive picture for them, but Callie hadn't seen the point. The few times she'd tried their exercise, it felt contrived or, worse, as if she were picking up their cues, giving them what they wanted in a effort to satisfy their morbid curiosity about what happened that night. Eventually she'd stopped therapy and stopped thinking about it altogether. Callie was a practical girl. Recreating the worst time in her life had done little to heal her; all it did was keep reminding her. If there were times she couldn't remember, it was just as well.

She did remember Rose, though. Not as much from the night of the murders as from before them. Rose had been a respected scholar of the Salem witch trials who had written several books on the subject and opened a research library in Salem, a place Callie's mother and her friends referred to simply as the center. People came from all over the world to research the witch trials, both for scholarly purposes and to look up the history of their ancestors. Each of the girls on the hill that night had initially come to the center looking for information about her ancestors, leapfrogging over present-day branches of family in favor of finding roots that traced back to 1692. In that way, Rose had always supposed that the girls were all a family of a sort, and she'd treated them as if she were their mother.

To the rest of the city, Rose had been professional, coldly academic, and dedicated to her research. She'd kept Salem's elite at a distance. But she'd been different with the girls and even more different with Callie.

Callie remembered how Rose would pick her up from school and the two of them would go walking all over the city together before they made their way back to their house on Daniels Street. It had always been Rose who came for her, or almost always. It certainly hadn't been her mother, Olivia. She could see Rose's long braid swinging as they strolled and felt her own shorter, curly ponytail keeping the same rhythm. Auntie Rose had liked to tie Callie's hair with a satin ribbon, a different color for every day of the week.

Callie took a right onto Derby Street, careful not to miss it this time, and turned right again on Central, following it to the police station. But the station had moved; the building was condos now. She pulled into a space and leaned out the window, asking the first man who passed by for directions, smiling flirtatiously to get his attention and nodding encouragingly as he gave her directions to the new station. She felt his disappointment as she pulled the car away.

She had to circle Riley Plaza twice before she spotted the broadcast vans blocking the stairs. She found a space, locked the Volvo, then elbowed her way through the news crews and up the stairs to the front desk.

"I'm here to see Rose Whelan," she announced.

"We told you all to wait outside," the desk officer said. "We're not dealing with any more reporters today."

"I'm not a reporter," Callie explained. "I'm her niece."

It was a small lie but an effective one. The officer looked surprised. Then he picked up a phone and punched in some numbers.

"I've got a girl out here says she's the banshee's niece."

A moment later the door opened and a tall man who seemed to duck more from habit than from necessity stepped through the doorway. He was muscular with bristly dark hair and brown eyes, good-looking in a rough way. He looked as if he were born with the jaded expression that defined his face.

"Rose has no family that I'm aware of," he said.

"My name is Callie Cahill," she said, working to keep her demeanor smooth; her therapists had always told her she was very good at hiding her anxiety. She could tell he recognized the name. "I'm not technically her niece—"

"John Rafferty," he said, holding the door for her as he showed her into his office, then closing it quickly against the officers who had started to gather.

Though he knew the name, he was still suspicious. "You sure you're not just some reporter pretending to be Callie Cahill?"

"Far from it," she said. Instead of explaining further, she shoved her hand across the desk, opening her clenched fist to expose her palm.

The stigmata. This was the part of the story that everyone had heard about and what everyone wanted to see. The nuns at St. James's had claimed it was a miracle when they found Callie the morning after the homicides, calling her a "sacred child" who had been saved from death by the mark of Christ. They'd worked closely with DCF to have Callie entrusted to their group home in western Massachusetts, promising to find her suitable foster care. They had probably thought they'd discovered a church miracle right here in Salem. But later, as the murder investigation had gotten under way and the grim details of the Goddess Murders had come out, rumors had begun to circulate about the "occult ceremony" the young women and Rose had performed on that Halloween night, and she remembered how quickly the narrative had turned.

Rafferty averted his eyes as if the looking itself was a violation. "Is it painful?"

His question took Callie by surprise. She considered it for a long moment before answering. "Sometimes." She felt awkward and quickly changed the subject, bringing it back to Rose. "How did the boy on the hill die?"

"I can't tell you that yet."

"The news called Rose a killer banshee."

"Yes, they did."

"What does that mean?"

"Rose says she had to kill the boy because he was turning."

"Turning? What does that mean?"

"At this point we don't know what she meant by that. She also claims to have killed him by screaming at him. Which we all know is impossible."

For a moment, it occurred to Callie that Rafferty might be wrong. The human voice could shatter glass, couldn't it? Hadn't she heard something about governments testing sonic weapons with the capacity to both maim and kill? Sound certainly had the ability to heal; she'd used it herself many times at the nursing home. If sound could heal, couldn't it also kill? But even if it were a possibility, the Rose Whelan that Callie remembered was not capable of intentionally killing anyone.

"Who is the boy?"

"He's—was—the grandnephew of a local Brahmin."

"What do you mean?"

"A bad kid from a good family."

"Does Rose say why she thinks she's responsible?"

"Rose isn't saying anything at the moment. I think she believes a banshee that lives inside of her killed him."

Callie stared at him.

"How much do you know about Rose?" Rafferty asked.

"Up until today, I thought Rose was dead."

Rafferty looked surprised.

"That's what the nuns at the children's home told me. My mother and Cheryl and Susan were all dead. And so was Auntie Rose. Or so they said."

"They lied to you?"

"Evidently."

"Rose isn't well," Rafferty explained. "She hasn't been the same since that night in 1989."

"I'll bet," Callie said. *How could Rose be the same? How could anyone?*

"You were there that night. What happened? What kind of ritual were you performing up there?"

She stared at him. His tone sounded vaguely accusatory. It reminded her of the nuns. "We went there to bless the unconsecrated grave of our ancestors," Callie replied. "Five accused witches who were executed on July nineteenth, 1692." She'd recited the story so many times after the murders that it seemed almost like one of the poems she'd memorized as a child.

"Rose had a breakdown," Rafferty said. "She was in a state hospital for a long time. When she came out, she wasn't the same woman. She also believed it was a banshee that killed your mother and the others."

"I just heard that," Callie admitted. "I'm not quite sure what that means. Especially in relation to Rose."

"According to Irish folklore, a banshee is a kind of specter who appears to those left behind when a loved one dies. But Rose's mythology takes things a step further. She believes banshees can kill, if they inhabit a human host who is 'turning.'"

"What does that mean?"

"Rose thinks it was a banshee that killed your mother and the others that night, and, after that happened, the banshee jumped into Rose, who has been holding her captive for all these years in an effort to keep her from killing again."

"That's crazy."

"This is what she believes. I've known Rose for a while, but it's difficult to understand her sometimes."

The Rose that Callie remembered had never been difficult to understand. Rose was direct, precise. If anything, it had been the other women, Callie's mother and her friends, who were sometimes confusing.

Callie struggled to recall Rose's tales about fairies and mythology. A lot of those stories were Irish, probably passed down through Rose's family, though Rose had grown up here. But all those stories were fairy tales or old myths Rose told her at bedtime. Auntie Rose had been quite the storyteller, but not in a way that was confusing or hard to understand. "She used to talk about fairies sometimes," Callie offered. "But I don't remember anything about banshees."

"I know a little about them," Rafferty said. "But I've never heard anyone but Rose suggest that banshees are killers in any traditional sense. Or human, for that matter."

Once again, Callie fell silent. Finally she pulled herself back from the dark place her imagination was leading her to. "Can I see her?"

"Of course. I'll drive you over to the hospital."

Rafferty parked in a spot marked MEDICAL STAFF ONLY, pulling in too fast and slamming on the brakes, jolting them forward in the seat, then back.

"Sorry," he said.

Callie looked out her window at Salem Hospital. The place she remembered had been much smaller. She'd stayed in the children's wing for a few weeks. Long enough for the nuns who had discovered her standing by the edge of the crevasse, with her hand cut and bleeding, to change their opinion of her: She'd gone from sainted to tainted in their eyes. People had kept coming and going: police, newspaper reporters, even clergy, unwrapping her bandage and making her show her wound over and over. She'd answered all their questions and told the truth repeatedly. But now she knew the nuns had lied to her. Those first days had been a bad dream: walking the entire length of the small hospital with the nurse who'd treated her, just trying to understand what had happened, telling the story again and again until it began to sink in that the whole thing was true, that they were all dead: Susan, Cheryl, and her mother, Olivia. They hadn't told her about Rose right away, hadn't said she was dead until they had taken her away from Salem, to their group home in Northampton, where nuns of the same order could protect her from the wild speculation and accusations that were to follow.

Today she could see that the hospital was huge, with many new wings and a big sign advertising its association with Mass General.

"Are those more news vans?" Callie asked, pointing.

"They are. Let's get inside."

The hospital was built into the side of a hill, with its main entrance at the top on the sixth floor. They took an unmarked stairway up one flight to the psych unit, pausing to be buzzed in at two different locked doors before they finally reached the nurses' station.

"This is Rose Whelan's niece," Rafferty said to the nurse at the desk. "Her closest relation." He didn't look at Callie as he repeated the lie.

"You can go in," the nurse said, "but only for a few minutes. Ten tops. I'm afraid there's been no change."

The officer they'd posted outside of Rose's door jolted awake as they approached and threw them a guilty glance. Rafferty nodded without acknowledging the slip. He hesitated, turning to Callie. "We are required by law to have a guard outside a murder suspect's room," he said. Then, as if to redeem himself, he added, "I called a lawyer for her this time. Before we even tried to talk to her. A good one who's defending her pro bono." He opened the door.

Callie had seen Rose's photo on the news, but she wasn't prepared for the scene before her: Rose was in four-point restraints. Her empty eyes stared at the ceiling, unblinking.

"She's been this way since last night," Rafferty explained.

If she was aware they had entered the room, Rose showed no sign. Rafferty saw the look of devastation on Callie's face and realized she needed a moment. "I have to make a phone call," he said. "I'll leave you two alone."

Callie didn't know what she'd been expecting; still, this was worse than anything she could have anticipated. *Rose isn't here* was the thought that came to mind. She felt her throat closing with the effort it took to hold back tears. In the last few hours, all she'd wanted was to have Rose back in her life. She chastised herself for such a stupid hope. She approached the bed. "It's me, Auntie Rose. It's Callie. I'm here."

She leaned down, trying to penetrate the empty stare, to see past the blankness of Rose's eyes to something behind them. Rose's eyes had always been so clear, so focused. Her mother and the other Goddesses had nicknamed her Old Eagle Eyes, because nothing got by her. Not ever, much to their chagrin.

"What happened to you?" Callie whispered. And then she sobbed in a way that erased all of the years she had put between herself and the worst moment of her life.

The lesser of two evils. Rafferty couldn't get the phrase out of his head.

In all the commotion, he'd never called Towner back. He dialed her number on his cell.

"Sorry," he said.

"It's okay," she said. "I saw the news." Then she continued. "So the little girl who witnessed the murders is back in town?"

"Was that on the news?" Rafferty sounded horrified.

"No."

"Then how do you know she's here?"

"I just know," she said.

He shook his head. He'd seen Towner do this many times—know about things before being told—but it still surprised him every time it happened.

Most of what Rafferty knew about the 1989 case, he'd learned from his wife. Towner hadn't lived in Salem at the time of the murders, but her grandmother Eva, who had been a friend of Rose's, had told her the story.

On the way back down the stairs, Callie stopped and turned to Rafferty. "Why would they lie to me? Why would they tell me Rose was dead? She was like my mother. I've missed her for so long, and she's been right here? Why would they do that?"

Rafferty had no idea what to say. It was clear from what he'd heard about the case that Callie had been traumatized. But that anyone would lie like that to a child seemed cruel. Especially since Rose would have been the only person Callie had left. He reached into his coat pocket, pulled out a half-empty packet of tissues, and handed them to her. "It's good for Rose that you're here now."

Neither of them spoke as they rode back to the station; Callie kept her face turned toward her side window, and Rafferty noticed her taking in everything as they passed.

"Where are you parked?" he asked as they pulled into the lot at the station. Callie pointed. Her face and neck were blotchy, her eyes bloodshot.

"Is that hotel down on the common still open?"

"You're staying?"

"If I can find a room." She pointed to the back lot. "My car's over there."

He nodded. Then, changing his mind, he U-turned and pulled out of the lot. "We'll get your car later. There's someone I want you to meet first."

Rafferty drove them away from the police station and across town to Salem Common, passing the elegant old Hawthorne Hotel and pulling instead into the long driveway of a massive brick house.

Callie read a sign posted on the side door: EVA'S LACE READER TEAROOM.

"That's the place," said Rafferty.

At the end of the driveway, they stopped in front of a smaller coach house. A lean woman with strawberry blond hair stood on a stepladder next to a huge oak tree at the entrance to the courtyard, scrubbing at graffiti that had been spray-painted on its bark.

"Damn it," Rafferty muttered.

It took Callie a minute to realize that the defaced area looked like a rose. Not like the stylized, five-petaled rose on her palm, but a more realistic one, complete with thorns and an inscription: *Kill the banshee!*

"Don't worry. I'll try painting over it if I can find a color that matches the bark," the woman said to Rafferty as he got out of the car.

She climbed down from the ladder, handing Rafferty the bucket. She kissed him hello, then turned to look at Callie.

"Callie, this is my wife, Towner Whitney. Towner, this is Callie." Seeing some girls from the tearoom, he stopped short of saying her last name. Towner saw his look and picked up the cue.

Towner extended her hand. "How nice to meet you, Callie. I only wish the circumstances were better."

"Me, too," said Callie.

"I thought I'd help Callie book a hotel room," Rafferty said.

"Oh, that's not necessary," Towner said. "You don't have to pay for a hotel. You can use Rose's room."

"I thought you might say that." Rafferty smiled.

"Rose lives here?" Callie asked, pressing her palms together as she spoke. "On the news they said she was homeless."

"Well . . . usually, she sleeps in our courtyard under her tree." Towner pointed to the huge oak. "That oak actually belongs to Rose. But that's a story for another day." She smiled, gesturing to the door. "We set aside a room for her in the house. She sleeps there sometimes. When I can convince her to. Please, come on inside."

Rafferty and Callie followed Towner up the front steps and into the foyer, where a spiral staircase wound three flights upward, seemingly suspended in the air surrounding it. On either side of the foyer were two matching parlors the size of ballrooms with a black marble fireplace at each end.

"I've been here before," Callie murmured.

"You have, actually." Towner nodded. "My grandmother once told me that you and your mother stayed in this house for a little while, before you moved in with Rose."

"I don't remember that," Callie said. "But I know I've seen that staircase."

"Rose's room is two flights up."

"I'll leave you two ladies to it," said Rafferty, excusing himself.

The women took the stairs to a large room with a comfortable-looking bed and a sink in the corner. Lining the walls were framed black-and-white photos of oak trees.

"Did Rose take these?"

Towner shook her head. "I took them. I was trying to lure Rose indoors. It didn't do much good, I'm afraid. She only comes up here when it's raining so hard it floods the parks."

"Strange," Callie said, unaware she had said the word aloud until she heard her voice echo in the huge room.

"Rose has a mission."

"What kind of mission?"

"She believes she can find the remains of the hanging tree that was used to execute the victims of the witch trials in 1692. The one that either died or was chopped down—back in, well, no one knows when. She had a vision that the tree was intentionally moved, and she's set her heart on finding it. She thinks it will lead her to the missing remains of those executed in 1692."

Callie looked surprised. "How would that work?"

"Your guess is as good as mine. Rose believes the oak trees of Salem hold some clue." Towner looked at Callie before continuing. "She says the trees speak to her."

"Oh," Callie said.

"She's had a tough time of it in the last few years."

"So I've heard." Callie's trembling voice belied her calm words. "Still, talking trees . . ."

"I know," Towner said. "Sometimes I almost believe her. I think my grandmother Eva did."

"Really?" Callie said.

"Eva and Rose had a special connection."

Callie waited for Towner to explain, but she didn't.

"Rose considers finding the hanging tree her life's work. The way she once felt about proving the real site of the executions, something she actually managed to do. I can't figure out how finding the remains of missing victims of the Salem witch trials relates to modern-day oak trees. Or to banshees, for that matter, but I know it must. Or at least it does in Rose's mind. Maybe you'll have better luck finding a connection. If you can get her to start talking again."

There was a long silence as Callie remembered how different Rose had been the last time they'd seen each other, before today. She had taught Callie and her mother so much, telling them stories, and Rose had instructed them all in the history of their ancestors, a history that, even now, Callie could recite the same way she could recite the Pledge of Allegiance. Or the Lord's Prayer. Rose, not the nuns who ended up raising her, had taught her that prayer. To think of Rose as she'd seen her today made Callie almost unbearably sad.

"I recognize that," Callie said, fighting tears and gesturing to the opposite side of the room. Framed on the wall was a map depicting Salem as it was in the 1600s, before landfill wiped out most of the North River. "I was raised on that map. Rose used it when she taught us lessons about our ancestors."

"Sidney Perley's map? Rose gave it to me," Towner said. "She said she knew every inch of it by heart."

"I wouldn't doubt that at all," Callie said, looking at the spot Rose had circled in red and labeled "Proctor's Ledge," the same location they had gone to the night of the murders, near where the map depicted Town Bridge. A snippet of poetry came back to her. Something written by Sidney Perley. *Poetry! the gem that gilds / The world of letters, and gives / Expression to soul beauty.* It was one of the first poems Rose had ever made her memorize. She could see the book in her memory, its fraying leather cover and broken spine: *The Poets of Essex County.*

She touched the circle on the map and remembered Rose sitting her down for her lessons. Teaching her to read before she attended school by memorizing poems and then reciting them, something her mother and her friends had found very amusing. When Rose wasn't home, her mother's friends had asked her to recite for them—sometimes in front of guests, sometimes for their own amusement. Rose had also taught her history, the real history of what happened in Salem.

"As I'm sure you remember, Rose was once an important scholar of the witch trials," Towner said, as if reading her young guest. "She uncovered so many discrepancies between the historical records and their accepted interpretations. When she was a professor at BU, she was awarded research grants from the Massachusetts Historical Society and honors from the Smithsonian, for God's sake. People forget just how important she was."

Callie remembered a few of the things Rose had told her about her research. How Puritan Salem had kept detailed expense records. And that none of those records mentioned any gallows being built, which had led her to conclude that it was far more likely the Puritans used a sturdy hardwood, possibly an oak, to hang the accused. How written accounts claimed one could see the bodies *hanging all the way over from North Street.* This public spectacle had been required by law, a warning to others of the consequences that befell those who *signed the Devil's book.* "Those bodies would not have been visible from Gallows Hill," Rose had always said. Since the accused would have been transported by cart, and since such transportation had been difficult, Rose had believed the condemned would have been taken to the first place beyond city limits with a hill visible from town, not Gallows Hill, but the actual hanging spot, one far more accessible by horse and cart back in 1692.

"Sorry. Let me climb down from my soapbox and show you where the bathroom is," Towner said, reading Callie's agitation at recalling this much information. She walked Callie down the hall. A woman was coming out as they approached. She nodded to Towner but looked at Callie with suspicion before moving on. "It's a shared space," Towner said. "I hope that's okay."

"It's okay with me if it's okay with her," Callie said. Towner opened the linen closet. "Clean towels and sheets are in here, though your bed was changed this morning." She paused, considering before she spoke again. "Most of the women who live here are from Yellow Dog Island."

"What's that?"

"It's a shelter for abused women that my family runs. The ones who are ready to come back to the world sometimes live here and work in the tearoom. It's a reentry program of sorts. So don't take it personally if they seem skittish. It's not you. I'll introduce you tomorrow—but only by first names. Most of them are part of the Domestic Violence Victims Protection Program. Their identities are kept secret in case their abusers are trying to locate them. So it won't be odd that I don't use your last name."

Callie was familiar with the program and with this type of abuse victim; she'd once volunteered as a music therapist at a shelter in Northampton.

Towner looked at her, then, keeping her voice lowered, she added, "You might not want to tell people your last name anyway. There are a lot of people in town who still remember what happened."

Callie was quiet as Towner walked her back to her room. At the doorway, she paused, as if to ask a question, then changed her mind. "Thank you for this. I'll get a hotel room if I'm still here tomorrow."

"Let's see what happens with Rose. Her room is yours for as long as you want to stay."

"Thank you," Callie said.

"John and I live in the coach house. I don't know if you're hungry, but we're cooking tonight if you want to join us."

"I'm really tired," Callie said. It was true. She hadn't realized how true until she'd heard herself say it.

"Okay, then, just rest. You can raid the fridge downstairs if you wake up starving. I open the tearoom from seven to eight thirty for the hungry and destitute. And then again at ten for our regular customers. If you're in the first group, you eat free and help serve or clean up. In the second, you pay for your breakfast. The menu's pretty much the same, so you can decide which category you belong in tomorrow morning. Personally, on any given day, I can fit into either one."

Callie tried to smile.

"Nice to finally meet you, Callie," Towner said again. "I'm glad John brought you home." She was gone then, disappearing down the long staircase.

Callie sat on the bed, looking out the window at the common, with its huge trees and decorative cast-iron fence. In the center of the park was a bandstand. Callie didn't remember staying in this house with Eva, but she did recall a night when she and her mother had slept on the cold floor of that bandstand, before Auntie Rose had given them a place to live.

Exhausted but far from sleep, she realized her bag was still in her car. She was too tired to walk back and get it, and she didn't want to bother Rafferty again. She looked through Rose's closet for something to wear, and, finding nothing, she undressed and hung up her clothes, crawling between the sheets in her underwear. She tried to focus her thoughts on Rose, tried to remember all she could about the woman who was once like a second mother to her. She knew they had some common ancestors. Hanging from each of their family trees was the name Rebecca Nurse. That genealogical connection was how she and Olivia had come to call Rose "Auntie."

All of the young women who had died that night had ancestors who had been executed on the same day in 1692. That was how they had found one another, why Rose had gotten to know the girls who became regulars at the center. Most had little education and lacked any background in research, so she had coached them, taking them first under her wing, and later, when she'd come to know their circumstances, into her home. In that way, Callie felt Rose and Towner were a bit alike. That was probably one reason Callie liked Towner immediately. It seemed as if both Towner and Rose were dedicated to helping the less fortunate citizens of Salem. Callie hoped Towner's luck would be better than Rose's had turned out to be.

Callie started to doze, then jolted awake when she heard a snapping sound. She turned on a light but saw nothing. It was the dream again. That sound was always part of the dream, branches and twigs snapping. Followed by a squirrel scrambling up a nearby tree.

She remembered hearing a snapping sound that Halloween night just before everything happened. Was it only a squirrel? Her memory was reaching too far back, getting too specific. She would not allow herself to remember that part of her past, not tonight. She had to keep from going there. She would fight to stay in the here and now. . . .

Every time she started to sleep, another memory jolted her awake, some detail she'd forgotten, some lesson Rose had taught her. More snippets of poetry: Longfellow, Emerson, Yeats. Rose teaching her to sound out words. Her mother and the others laughing until they cried as she tried to pronounce the new words they'd ask her to recite.

Her hand started to burn, the same way it had when feeling finally started coming back to it after the murders. It had been numb for a long time, more than a year. The doctors had told her that the scarred palm would probably remain numb forever, but, one day, it started to tingle, and then to ache, and finally to burn. The burning went on for weeks before feeling came back completely.

She rubbed at her hand, then buried it palm up under the cool of the feather pillow, the way she'd learned to at the home. If she could get it in the right position, the burning would stop.

Just before she fell asleep and began to dream, she remembered something Sister Agony had said when she'd cried about her burning hand. "They didn't hang witches back in Europe the way they did your ancestors," she told Callie. "In Europe, they burned witches at the stake."

He rowed down the North River, his palms blistered and burning from the six-mile voyage. Heaving the boat ashore, he quickly began to climb the hill, his dread building as he neared the pit. He dared not look up at the hanging tree: Its very existence filled him with rage. Instead, he kept his eyes low, searching for the crevasse where they had thrown his mother, hesitating before he lowered himself among the bodies. There were far too many dead, and the pit was deep. He felt his way among the corpses, touching first a cold leg, then an arm. He followed the skin, and his fingers touched her face. It was Susannah Martin. He gasped as he saw her blackened tongue, her bulging eyes . . . He began to choke, huge wrenching sobs. He had to leave her here. He only had strength enough to carry one body, and it was his mother, Rebecca, for whom he had come. Even as he told himself he would return for the others, he knew he would not. It would be too dangerous to come back to Salem Town. He had to find his mother, take her home, and give her a proper Christian burial. Standing deep in the crevasse, surrounded by bodies, he searched until he found the hand he knew so well, a hand that had so often held his own. He couldn't see her face: In its mercy, the sky had darkened against the vision he had no fortitude to bear. With the last of his strength, he hoisted his mother's stiffening body onto his back and made his way down the hill to the rowboat.

CHAPTER SIX

November 2, 2014
SALEM

*In a series of events that bears a striking similarity to those
of 1989, Rose Whelan remains in psychiatric custody at
Salem Hospital but has yet to be arraigned on any charge.*
                                        —*The Salem Journal*

CALLIE DIDN'T WAKE UP UNTIL THE SMELL OF CINNAMON
rolls climbed the staircase and slid under her door. She was starving.

Her nightmares had kept her from the deepest sleep. It had been
this way since childhood, and no amount of therapy had changed it.
Sometimes she dreamed in fragments from the night of her mother's
murder, mixed with pieces of her own life. Sometimes, like last night,
she saw other things that couldn't possibly be her own memories.
She looked at her phone. Almost 10:00 A.M. That made her one of
the regular people today, though she felt anything but. Her head was
pounding, and she couldn't quite rid herself of the traces of her dream
energy, so she showered and dressed, putting yesterday's clothes back
on, smoothing some wrinkles before descending the stairs to the
tearoom.

The walls were frescoed, vaguely Italianate. Small tables crowded
the room, and lace was everywhere, from the tablecloths to the curtains. Each table held a different teapot, with varying patterned cups
and saucers set on individual lace doilies. A long glass counter in the

far corner held canisters of tea, all hand labeled. There seemed to be hundreds of them. All of it made her yearn for coffee.

There were only a few customers: two distinguished-looking older women deep in conversation at the table by the window and another, younger woman sitting by the door. Callie took a seat at the smallest table, one near the fireplace and out of earshot.

"You can't get coffee here," the waitress said after Callie ordered a cup. She handed her a menu. "Only the tea."

Great. There were hundreds of varieties, from herbal and flower to hand-blended concoctions with names like Serendipitea and Chakra Chai. It made her head throb. Callie ordered a simple black tea with orange and mint.

"Let it steep until the sand runs out," the waitress said when she delivered it, turning over a small hourglass. She hurried back to the kitchen before Callie had a chance to order food. A minute later she was back with a plateful of pastries: scones, croissants, brioches.

"I didn't order these," Callie said.

"Towner always sends out the plate of pastries. You only pay for what you take."

"Oh. Thank you," Callie said, helping herself to an almond croissant. She ordered a soft-boiled egg and fruit. The egg came in a little silver eggcup, set on a china plate that matched her teacup. Next came a single pear—cut and perfectly fanned out on the plate, a tiny stripe of honey across the slices.

Callie ate slowly, paid for her breakfast, left a generous tip, then made her way to the kitchen.

"How did you sleep?" Towner asked, introducing her to Sally and Gail, two of the women who were cleaning up.

"Pretty well," Callie lied. "The bed is comfortable." Gail was the woman she had seen coming out of the bathroom the previous night. Callie saw her exchange a glance with Sally.

"Glad to hear that."

"I want to help out," Callie said, watching them clean. "What can I do?"

"You don't have to do anything," Towner said. "You're a paying customer."

Callie ignored her, gathering some dirty silverware and putting it in the dishwasher as Gail and Sally were doing.

"Okay, then, thanks," Towner said. "I've got to start making a salad for lunch." She went into the pantry.

Callie could feel the women's eyes on her. No one spoke. She saw them glance at each other again. She turned to face them. "May I help you with something?"

Sally said nothing.

Gail was braver. "You know Rose?"

"I do, yes." Somehow she couldn't imagine that it was Towner who'd spread the word, but it certainly had traveled fast. "Why?"

Gail said nothing. Sally blurted, "That woman's weird."

"What is that supposed to mean, exactly?" Callie held her eye.

Intimidated, Sally took a step behind her friend.

"She *is* a little scary," Gail said.

Callie started to defend Rose as Towner returned with a very large bowl. She looked back and forth among the women. "What's going on?"

"Nothing," Gail said, too quickly.

She and Sally hurried back to the tearoom to collect another round of dirty dishes.

"Making friends already, I see," Towner said.

"They wanted to know about Rose." Callie frowned. "They think she's *weird*."

"She is weird," Towner said. "But in a good way . . . I'm afraid you'll find that people have a lot to say about Rose in this town, not much of it good." Towner put the bowl on the counter and started to place salad greens inside.

"Wait!" Callie said.

Towner turned and looked at her.

"You're using that as a salad bowl?" Callie was horrified.

"I usually do. Why?"

"That's a singing bowl!"

Towner looked at her blankly.

"It's made out of quartz crystal." Callie's eyes searched the room, looking for a way to demonstrate. She grabbed a rubber spatula. She lifted the greens out of the bowl, gently placing them on the cutting board, and began to draw the spatula around the outside rim of the bowl just as Gail and Sally came back with another load of dishes. Callie smiled to herself, knowing full well that the two women were about to find her as "weird" as they found Rose. *Good,* she thought. Maybe it would end their gossip.

All the women stopped when they heard the sound. It started with a soft ringing, then built in volume until it circled the room, filling the air with its clear tone.

As the sound faded, Callie turned to look at Towner, who was staring at the bowl. "Wow." Towner shook her head. "I always thought it was a salad bowl," she said after the tone had faded to silence. "I found it in the pantry after Eva left me the house."

Callie laughed for the first time since arriving in Salem. "It is definitely *not* a salad bowl. I'm a music therapist, I should know."

"Gail, could you go to the pantry and find another bowl for the greens?" Towner asked. "Hopefully one that doesn't sing." Gail nodded, looking grateful to escape. Sally scurried after her.

"You're a music therapist?" Towner looked interested.

"Yes," Callie said. "I work at a nursing home in Northampton, and I have a private practice out there as well."

"I've heard good things about music therapy," Towner said. "I think they're using it at the Brigham. To help with surgical patients and palliative care."

"That's traditional music therapy. Which is what I was trained to do. The bowls are a little different. A little more 'alternative.' "

"I'd say Gail and Sally think they're quite alternative."

Callie laughed.

"Hey, I promised John I'd give you a ride over to the station to pick up your car. If you can wait until I finish the salad . . ."

"That's all right," Callie said. "You're busy. It's not too far. I can walk."

"You sure? I don't mind doing it."

"I'd like the fresh air, actually." Her head still ached; the ocean air would help.

"Good enough then," Towner said, turning back to the salad.

Callie was good at sizing people up, which was why she didn't choose to have a lot of friends, especially female friends. She was definitely more comfortable with men. She blamed it on the nuns, who dealt in subtleties she'd never quite understood—doling out advice that walked the line between truth and fiction, saying it was for her own good, their de facto answer for everything.

But Towner was direct, matter-of-fact. The same way Rose used to be. And there was something else. She didn't ask a lot of questions. She just seemed to understand some things without being told. Callie appreciated it.

"I'm going to visit Rose," Callie added. "I hope that's allowed."

"I think it's expected," Towner said. "Ask for . . ."

"Do you think she'll be there today?"

"Rose?" Towner looked at her strangely. "Why wouldn't she be?"

"I'm sorry. I thought you were going to tell me to ask for Rose's doctor." Callie shifted nervously.

"I was," Towner said, curious. "Did you meet Dr. Finch yesterday?"

"No," Callie said quickly, deciding to be honest. "I guessed what you were going to say. I sometimes do that. Sorry."

Towner looked at Callie for a long moment, then continued. "You'll find Zee Finch's offices in the medical building across the street from the hospital. She's been Rose's doctor for a long time."

As she strode down the pedestrian walkway on Essex Street, Callie remembered some of the buildings, though most had changed a great deal. Salem was both familiar and strange to her. At Riley Plaza she passed the newsstand and glanced at a headline from *The Salem Journal:* HAS THE BANSHEE STRUCK AGAIN? Below it was a photo of Rose, the same one she had seen on the news broadcast: Rose on Derby Street with her cart, an angry expression on her face, her wild white hair trailing behind her like a shroud.

Callie found her car at the police station just as she'd left it, and drove to the hospital, taking a back entrance to avoid the reporters still camped by the front door. She made her way to Rose's room, nodding to the guard and steeling herself for what she would see. The first thing she noticed was that the restraints had been removed, and a woman was rubbing Rose's wrists to help restore their circulation.

"Are you Dr. Finch?"

The woman turned. Zee Finch was in her midthirties and had natural auburn hair, though it was already losing its vibrance. *She dresses like a doctor,* Callie thought. Not in the blue scrubs she'd seen in the corridors, though, but in a tasteful silk dress and jacket.

"I am," Zee said.

"I'm Callie." She stopped short of reciting her last name. "Rose's niece. Sort of."

Callie caught Zee taking a quick glance at her palm. Towner or Rafferty must have briefed her. "Any improvement?" Callie asked.

"At least she's no worse," Zee countered. "I suspect she's experiencing a dissociative reaction to complex trauma. She suffered that once before."

Callie didn't have to ask when.

"Talk to her while you visit," Zee said as she prepared to leave the room. "All appearances to the contrary, there's a very good chance that she's aware of what's going on around her."

"What should I talk about?" *How I thought she was dead?*

"Well, nothing too disturbing," Zee said with a wry smile.

Callie nodded. "Until yesterday, I hadn't seen her since that night."

"Why don't you tell her about your life since then?" Zee suggested without missing a beat. "The good things. Catch her up." She made some notes on Rose's chart. "I'll be back to see you tomorrow, Rose." She reached into her jacket and handed Callie her card. "I'm at Yellow Dog Shelter three mornings a week and the tearoom most afternoons. If you have any questions or concerns about Rose's care, you can call me anytime."

"Thank you," Callie said and followed Zee to the door. She watched the doctor stop to consult with the nurses and then walk toward the stairway. Callie took a deep breath and then pulled the guest chair closer to Rose's bed. *Talk to her.* As a general rule, Callie was a listener. Except when she was working, she wasn't comfortable with the sound of her own voice. She'd learned to hold back, to assess people's attitudes about her before talking with them. But this was Rose, and Dr. Finch said it might help. Wasn't that why she'd come?

She sat and faced Rose. "The nuns told me you were dead. That all of you were killed that night." *Oh God, was that really the first thing that came out of my mouth?* "I'm sorry. I mean . . . I just said that in case you're wondering why I never tried to contact you." She took a deep breath, then exhaled slowly before she spoke again. "The nuns sent me away from Salem. Until now, I've never been back."

Rose didn't move. She didn't blink. Her bloodshot blue eyes stared straight ahead.

"The morning after . . . what happened . . ." Callie didn't want to say "the murders." Not if Rose could hear her. "I was so scared. The nuns from St. James's found me—and they sent me to a group home in western Mass. I told them over and over that you saved me. Did you know that? I told the police, too." *Nothing too disturbing. How could she tell her life story and not include anything disturbing?* She paused, then started again. "The nuns have been good to me. They got me the job I have now at a nursing home. They convinced me to go to college. You always told me I had to go to college. Remember? I went to U Mass. I started as a music major. Remember you telling me I was musical? You always used to tell me that when I was little. Then I switched to music therapy and then went on to grad school for an MA."

As she told her story, Callie realized how randomly she had fallen into her own life. There were causes and effects, certainly, and there were decisions. But sitting in this hospital room, she was reminded that the only thing you could be certain of in this world was change. Yesterday Rose was dead. Then Rose was alive. Now Rose was alive, but in a vegetative state.

Callie watched her stare blankly at the ceiling.

For the longest time, she had believed it was All Hallows' Eve that killed her mother and the others. The nuns said it was the one night each year when evil prevailed without God's intervention. They also said that bestowing a blessing without a priest—as Rose had done— was a terrible transgression. And even worse was the fact that the women had called themselves Goddesses. That was simply intolerable to God, the nuns said. It was why he looked the other way, allowing them all to receive just punishment for their arrogance.

Callie slammed on the mental brakes. *Can't I think of anything that isn't morbid?* She was tempted to start lying, to weave a story threaded with friends and joy, but she refrained; banshees and talking trees aside, the Rose that Callie remembered always wanted the facts and had taught Callie never to settle for less than what was true. Even so, after all that had happened, she'd never thought to challenge what the nuns had told her about the night of the murders.

Callie left the room and made a call on her cell, leaving a message at the nursing home, saying she wouldn't be back until further notice, then leaving another message for her private patients on her voice mail, referring them to another therapist she knew from school. She had money saved and could afford to take time off. She'd start visiting Rose daily if it could make a difference. Callie was glad she hadn't reached anyone directly—she didn't want to speak to any of the nuns now. God knows what she might have said. Callie had a reputation for saying things she shouldn't. She'd learned in therapy this was a defensive measure against the fear she'd experienced growing up. She had been working to change it. So far, she hadn't had much success.

Though it probably wasn't necessary, Callie left another message at the apartment in Amherst that she'd been sharing with a changing cast of grad students for the last few years, letting them know she'd be away for a bit. She didn't know any of them well. Though she rented a bedroom there, Callie often didn't come home at night. She'd had a number of boyfriends, but all of those relationships were short-lived, disposable. No one would call out the National Guard if she went missing for a day or two.

She went back into Rose's room, sat down, and continued her story, trying with everything she had to keep it positive.

"Remember when we used to sing that song, Rose?" Callie began a

Gaelic tune that Rose had taught her. A lullaby from Rose's Irish grand-mother that she'd sung to Callie each night when she went to sleep.

The nurses' shift changed, and an aide came in to adjust Rose's position in the bed. "I'm glad to see someone's visiting her," the aide said. "I'm sure it's helping."

"I hope so," Callie said.

The aide stopped what she was doing. She was staring at Callie. "I know you."

"I don't think so."

"Could have sworn . . ."

Callie stared back, as silent as Rose, hoping the woman's conviction would fade before she could place Callie.

She'd been to the Salem library many times with Rose. It was one of their favorite spots to spend an afternoon. The front steps had been too steep for Callie then. She remembered Rose slowing her normally rapid pace, smiling as Callie cautiously giant-stepped her way to the top, Rose holding the heavy wooden door for her to enter. Today, Callie adopted Rose's usual pace, taking the stairs easily and opening the door herself. Though the faces were different, the old brick building had changed little since she was a child. The librarian looked up when she saw Callie enter, then went back to her computer. Callie picked up the day's copy of *The Salem Journal* as she passed the desk.

The library smelled of books and radiators, the same musty smell she'd once loved. She looked ahead toward the children's wing and was seized with an urge to enter, to sit in one of the old overstuffed chairs she had once shared with Rose and look through the illustrated pages of *Treasure Island* or the first book of poetry Rose had read to her: *A Child's Garden of Verses.* She remembered one of her favorites:

> *All night long and every night,*
> *When my mama puts out the light,*
> *I see the people marching by,*
> *As plain as day, before my eye.*

She couldn't remember the rest of the poem or its title. She wanted to go into the children's room and look it up. Instead, she approached the research desk. A middle-aged man in a bow tie and starched shirt looked up. "May I help you with something?"

"Where would I find archived copies of this paper?" She held up *The Salem Journal*.

"What year are you looking for?"

"Nineteen eighty-nine," she said, hoping he would not make the connection.

If he did, he showed no sign. He directed her to the microfiche room. It was off to the side, hidden by a few stacks of books. It didn't have any windows, just a set of jaundiced fluorescent lights embedded in the ceiling. There were four wooden tables with a fiche reader on each. An aide sat off to one side in front of a wall of filing cabinets.

"She's looking for the *Journal*. Nineteen eighty-nine," the bow-tie man said.

"What month?" the aide asked Callie.

"Late October, early November."

The aide directed Callie to one of the tables. "Do you need a demonstration?"

"No," Callie said. "I'm all set."

Before she started looking at the fiche, she read today's *Salem Journal*, the one she had grabbed on her way in. The article about Rose was disturbing, as she'd known it would be. The town was angry and upset and reacting to the fact that the police had not arraigned Rose for the crime on Halloween, or even determined if a crime had been committed. It was very clear that this incident reminded too many people of the crime they believed Rose guilty of in the past.

It took Callie a while to locate what she was looking for on the microfiche, and when she finally found it, she immediately wished she hadn't. A local paper usually concerned with street closings and firemen's musters, *The Salem Journal* seemed to have reveled in being the go-to source for morbid rumors and innuendo, reporting that was far beneath, it seemed to Callie, the standards of a more reputable paper. Day after day, article after article was filled with the grisly details of what had happened that night. One even contained graphic photos of the lifeless bodies, throats slashed, being pulled from the crevasse: the victims bloodied and almost unrecognizable. Callie had never seen these photos. One more thing the nuns had kept from her, though this time she was grateful. As she looked at the images, she could feel her body going into shock, her hand throbbing and then numbing.

The articles were less sensational than the photos, but there was an undercurrent, a subtext to the reporting Callie couldn't quite define. It was straight news—matter-of-fact, the way news should be but often wasn't these days, but the things they chose to focus on were more morbid than she might have expected. Callie read them several times, but nothing stood out as wrong. They reported the events, the time, the place, the facts, a direct contrast to the photos. If the photographer had been shocked by the image he recorded, the writer was not. Journalistically, the story was absolutely correct, but the focus seemed odd.

After she finished the articles from the week following the murders, she went on to read the follow-ups from the next few months. As time passed, more and more editorial opinions emerged. Some speculated that the young women were part of a Satanic cult. Some said they were in a recreational sex club or ran an escort service. One article detailed theories on the manner in which their throats had been cut, suggesting a box cutter or straight razor as opposed to a knife. Callie had to go outside to get some air after she read that one. It had taken her a while to drum up the courage to go back and read more.

Everyone seemed to have a theory. One article featured a photo of the wound on Callie's palm with the caption A MODERN-DAY MIRACLE? There were several photos of the victims, the girls they called the Goddesses: Olivia Cahill, Cheryl Cassella, and Susan Symms, her white albino skin even paler in death than it had been in life. It was reported that trophies of skin and hair had been taken from Susan's body during the murders.

But there were also pictures taken before the murders, and these were the ones that really touched Callie. It had been so long ago, and Callie had been so young that all she had of them were traces of memory; she'd forgotten what they actually looked like. The first shots were of Susan and Cheryl. *They're younger than I am now,* Callie realized. *And so beautiful.* When she got to the photo of her mother, she began to cry. Strangely, when she let herself think of the Goddesses, she always had the most trouble picturing her mother. Olivia had been distant, somehow, had kept herself apart. The image Callie conjured when she thought of Olivia was ethereal, a dark-eyed beauty with vague edges that never quite sharpened into focus. But the photo in front of her wasn't distant or ethereal: the backlit image on the microfiche stared back all too humanly, and Callie knew her mother immediately. The wild dark hair. The gypsy eyes. Part dark angel, part something else. But it was her expression that Callie recognized. Defiant. Challenging. A survivor. "Mess with me," it said. "I dare you."

It was the face that Callie saw every morning in her mirror.

As she finished the final article and shut down the fiche reader, the memory of that night came back to her complete and with the precision of a pinpoint.

"This is really the place?" Cheryl asked as they pushed through the thick brambles of Proctor's Ledge. Her voice didn't sound like her own. It was thicker, her speech slower. "You're sure?"

"Positive," Rose declared, adjusting her tortoiseshell glasses and looking back at the younger women she was escorting.

"But the witches are going up to Gallows Hill," Susan slurred, rubbing her hands as if she was cold.

"The witches are wrong." Rose stopped and looked from Susan to Cheryl, then back to Olivia. "Despite its name, Gallows Hill is not where our ancestors lost their lives." She did not take her eyes off them as she spoke; instead she stared as if seeing through them. "What's wrong with all of you tonight? You know the history!"

They shifted uncomfortably.

"I thought you were going to stand me up again like you did in July," Rose grumbled.

"We're here just like we said we would be," Olivia replied.

"Late, drunk, and wearing revealing Halloween costumes." Rose shot

a look at Susan's low-cut costume, more Playboy bunny than Alice in Wonderland inspired, with rabbit ears that perfectly matched the color of her snow white hair. "This is how you honor our ancestors? I hope you took time out from your party schedule to pack your belongings."

No one answered.

"I'm serious. I want you out of my house tomorrow."

Rose herself was wearing black for the solemn occasion, her long brown braid tucked under a cap that looked vaguely Puritan. "This is a new low, even for you," she said to Olivia, who was dressed as the Mad Hatter with dark skintight trousers, a top hat, and a black coat with tails. "And as usual, we're waiting for Leah."

The young women exchanged guilty looks but said nothing.

Rose gave a dismissive wave of her hand and turned uphill. "Let's pick up the pace and hope that Leah can catch up." She pushed through the brambles, moving higher on the hill into a thick patch of dying brush, its branches dense and dry, snapping back like rubber bands as each of them passed.

"You need a damned machete to get through this stuff," Cheryl muttered under her breath.

Susan stumbled, then stifled a cry.

"Shhh," Cheryl warned.

"Hurry up," Olivia whispered, taking her daughter's hand, pulling her along.

A branch cracked behind them. A squirrel ran across their path, scrambling up a nearby sumac, then onto the branches of a taller tree, leaping from limb to limb in an effort to escape. Callie's eyes followed until the squirrel disappeared into the darkness, leaving only the sound of the wind moving through the tangled trees.

When they finally reached the clearing, Callie stopped short. Her mother tugged at her hand, but the girl refused to budge.

"What now?" Rose turned back with a huff.

The light from the full moon behind the branches cast veined patterns across their faces. Just ahead of them, the crevasse dropped into dark nothingness. Callie recognized the place from the stories Rose had told her over and over. This was where it happened, the pit where the bodies were dumped after the execution.

"I'm scared," Callie said.

"It's okay," Olivia answered. "There's nothing here to be afraid of." She tried to hurry the child to catch up with Rose, who was standing now at the rocky edge of the crevasse, waiting for them. Callie wouldn't move.

"No," she said, her voice shaky, almost inaudible. She gazed past her mother to Rose. "I want to go home, Auntie Rose."

"Oh, honey." Rose came over and leaned down, bringing herself to Callie's eye level. In the moonlight, she could see the little girl's tear-streaked face. "Your mother's right, there's nothing here to be afraid of. Not anymore."

Callie looked doubtful.

"Is that why you were crying?"

Callie shook her head no and seemed about to offer another explanation when Olivia spoke up. "She wanted to go trick-or-treating, but I told her we had to come here instead, that you were going to kick us out of the house if we didn't show up."

The remark was supposed to make Rose feel guilty.

"Was that before or after the adults-only party you took her to?" Rose retorted.

Olivia removed her Mad Hatter cap but said nothing.

"It was a costume party," Callie said, trying to help her mother. "I got to be Alice in Wonderland."

"I can see that," Rose said softly. "You make a very pretty Alice."

"I want to go home now," Callie again insisted, fresh tears forming. "Please don't kick us out."

Rose shot a look at Olivia. She leaned down, bringing her face close to Callie's. "Sweetie, don't you worry about that tonight. Tonight is the special night you and I talked about. Tonight we are going to do something important that is long overdue: We are going to say a prayer and consecrate the ground where our ancestors were hanged and buried." She smiled tenderly. "Can you tell me the name of your ancestor?"

"Rebecca Nurse?"

"That's right," Rose said, patting the girl's cheek.

"Let's do this already," Cheryl said.

"We can't start until Leah gets here," Rose said.

"Leah isn't coming," Olivia blurted.

"What do you mean, Leah isn't coming? This is our last chance to do this. We've been planning it for months!"

Another look passed among the three younger women.

"What are you not telling me?"

"She isn't coming, Rose," Cheryl confirmed, swaying and worrying the tail of her dormouse costume.

"Explain yourselves," Rose said.

"We don't need to explain ourselves," Olivia snapped. "You're not our mother."

The minute she said it, Olivia regretted the words. Rose was clearly seething.

Behind them, more branches cracked.

"What the hell?" Cheryl turned as two more squirrels scrambled out of the brush, one running directly across Susan's foot, causing the March Hare to shriek as the creature went scrambling up a nearby elm.

It was colder here in the clearing, and Callie started to shake. Rose removed her dark jacket and draped it around the girl's shoulders, creating a long cape over the blue dress and white pinafore.

"Can we just get on with it?" Olivia asked. "I've got to get her home."

Rose considered. "For the child, yes."

The women gathered, forming a circle at the edge of the crevasse, just as they had practiced. Rose raised her arms to the heavens and cleared her throat. "Mother Mary, we know our prayer circle is not complete, but we pray that our intention and our strength will overcome any absence. Hallow this ground, dear Mother, in the name of our five ancestors who died here on July nineteenth, 1692. Bless it for all nineteen poor souls who were hanged that terrible year and for the one pressed to death. All innocent victims of government-sanctioned murder. Mary, in your name and in the name of your son, our Lord, Jesus Christ, bless the souls of our faithful departed." She fingered the first petal of her old wooden rosary, the one with a carved rose instead of a cross. "Elizabeth Howe," she said, turning to Susan and moving her fingers to the second petal.

"Susannah Martin," Susan said. In the moonlight, her skin looked even paler than usual.

Everyone turned to Cheryl.

"Sarah Wildes," Cheryl said as Rose touched the third petal of her ro-sary and then moved onto the fourth as Olivia and her daughter, still hold-ing hands, spoke in unison, with Rose joining the chorus. "Rebecca Nurse."

Rose moved her fingers to the fifth and final petal. Hearing a whisper of words on the wind, Callie spun around, but there was no one there. Rose looked around as if she had heard something as well. Then, the wind stilled and the world went silent as Rose spoke the name of the final ancestor: "And Sarah Good."

"Amen," the women chorused. Rose began to chant, an old Irish prayer with a Celtic melody. It hung in the air and moved among the knotted trees that surrounded the clearing, seeming to untangle their branches as it passed. For a moment, everything was suspended in time and ether. Callie looked up and saw a vision of the hanging tree that had not been there just moments before, the one Rose had told her stories about. She saw the victims left dangling from the limbs where they were executed, displayed for all to see, a gruesome warning, the wages of sin. She stared as, one by one, their bodies were finally cut down and dropped into the pit below, each falling slowly, as if through water. She closed her eyes tight to block out the vivid image her imagination had conjured.

"Let us say the Lord's Prayer now," intoned Rose.

"Our Father . . ." they began in unison.

What happened next happened quickly. The prayer stopped, and the world fell silent. Callie opened her eyes, but the moon had passed behind a cloud, leaving only the stars as dim illumination. Rose was standing in the same place, directly across from her, still clutching the rosary beads, but she was no longer reciting the Lord's Prayer. Her mouth was open, yet no speech came out. The only sound was a loud and desperate sucking. In shock, Rose stared at Susan, who was on the ground, facedown, a pool of crimson spreading on the dead grass that surrounded her.

Cheryl rushed forward, turning her friend over, revealing a deep, ugly gash on her neck.

Olivia screamed as she was seized from behind, torn away, and dragged toward the crevasse, letting go of her daughter's hand forever.

Before Callie had a chance to protest, someone grabbed her by the arm.

"Run!" Rose screamed. *Callie felt herself pulled backward, her legs responding only in an effort to stay on her feet.*

It was Auntie Rose who had spun her around and was now pushing her forward on the path. *"That way!"* *Rose said, and the two of them ran together as fast as they could until they found a clump of dense undergrowth. Rose shoved Callie into the thicket, scratching her skin on the thorny branches until she was in the middle of a nest of twining vines.*

"Stay here. I'll come back for you!"

"But Mommy—"

"Don't make a sound!" *Rose hissed.*

Callie's eyes were wide with terror. *"Don't leave me!"* *she begged in a whisper.*

Rose pressed the wooden rosary into the child's hand. *"Here. Hold this! Close your eyes and keep them closed until I come back for you! And pray!"*

In an instant, Rose was gone.

Callie closed her eyes and clutched the rosary as tightly as she could until her palm was stinging, and she could feel the blood running down her fingers from where the carved edges of the rose petals pressed into her flesh. She tried to remember the rosary prayers Rose had been teaching her, but they had vanished into the darkness along with her mother and the other women she called family. She heard a wailing sound, low at first, then growing louder and more shrill, pitching higher and higher until it sounded like the screams of a wild animal. It was unearthly, a sound of both agony and power.

She waited for what seemed like forever, until the sound faded to silence and the darkness finally gave way to morning light. Feeling the warmth of the sun filtering through the branches, Callie opened her eyes.

No one ever came back.

CHAPTER SEVEN

November 9, 2014
SALEM

*A few influential Salemites are calling for DNA evidence
to be gathered, not from the body of William Barnes, who
died on October 31, but from the three women nicknamed
the Goddesses, murdered in 1989, a case in which Rose
Whelan was once considered the primary suspect.*
                                                    —*The Salem Journal*

HE'D BEEN LOOKING AT THE PHOTOS OF THE GODDESSES
all morning. Six boxes of evidence had arrived from the archives, and
he was expecting seven more. He hadn't officially reopened the case,
but he'd already opened the boxes and pored over their contents, staring at a Polaroid of Olivia that was curling at the edges.

Callie looked just like her mother: black curly hair, blunt cut and
shoulder length. Brown eyes so dark you almost couldn't distinguish
the iris from the pupil, the only feature that played against the angelic
porcelain of her skin. Olivia's beauty had been legendary, as was her
reputation and those of the other "Goddesses."

The resemblance between them was profound. Good thing Towner
had told her not to use her last name, he thought. Though Callie's
name hadn't been published in the newspaper accounts of the murders, a lot of the locals remembered the Cahill surname.

The files said Callie's father was a musician Olivia had met in
New Orleans, but no name was listed, and Callie said she had never

known who her father was. Olivia had come to Salem to trace her family tree, which dated back to the witch trials. There had been gossip that she'd practiced a little witchcraft herself down in New Orleans, though there had never been anything to back that up. Her behavior in Salem, as well as that of the rest of the girls, had certainly been bewitching, though more for seduction than for spells. Just one example, he thought, of why the women dubbed the Goddesses were so hated here. They were all beautiful girls, but they behaved more like men than like respectable young ladies.

He'd spent most of the morning watching and rewatching the tape of Callie's questioning sessions. They were remarkable, really. She was so young, and she had so clearly loved Rose. She told the same story no matter how the investigators tried to poke holes in it: Rose had tried to save them all, she said over and over. Her answers never wavered. If he'd been harboring any suspicion at all that Rose was guilty, Callie's testimony had convinced him of her innocence.

The evidence backed him up. Yes, Rose had been at the scene of the murders. Yes, she had been covered in the victims' blood. But she had no defensive wounds on her, and the final victim, Cheryl Cassella, had put up quite a fight. Rose had no weapon. She didn't have the "trophies" that were taken from Susan Symms's body: a slice of skin from her forearm and a shock of white hair, skin still attached, cut from her scalp. Whatever Rose had seen that night had permanently unstrung her. It was no wonder she'd concocted a crazy story. She'd definitely dissociated. He'd seen other victims of severe trauma cope in similar ways.

When Jay-Jay called to tell him Callie was on her way in, Rafferty stashed the evidence box behind his desk. She had told him about the vision at the library, and she'd come by almost every day this week, telling him random things she remembered. Asking questions. Today, he had a question for her.

"What about this Leah you mentioned yesterday, the one you were waiting for who was supposed to be part of the blessing? Was she one of the Goddesses?"

"I don't know."

"Did you remember her last name yet?"

She shook her head. "Sorry."

"She didn't live with you?"

"Not that I remember . . . I do remember how tense Rose was that night waiting for her to show up. I told you she'd been threatening to kick us out of her house."

"Yes." He'd heard it before, and Callie had confirmed it yesterday. She'd told him everything she remembered, and her memories were quite detailed, but there were definitely gaps.

"This time I don't think it was a threat. She made us pack. I remember her telling my mother we had to move out the day after Halloween. Which was why we had to do the blessing that night. I think she really meant to throw us out."

"Why that time and not the others?"

"I don't know. They had parties sometimes, when Rose was at work. I told you that."

He nodded.

"I think it might have had something to do with the parties. I know she didn't like it, that people at work were telling her about it. The neighbors, too. They kept calling the police. The cops were there all the time. 'Enough is enough.' That's what Rose kept saying. It was really getting to her. And then this thing with Leah. Whatever that was."

"Do you think Leah was the fifth petal, Callie?"

"What do you mean, the fifth petal?"

As Rafferty asked the question, he'd been sketching a five-petaled rose on a legal pad. Now he turned it around so she could see it. It looked just like the scar on her left palm.

He'd told her yesterday about something he'd found in the files, something Rose had alluded to after the murders when she was finally lucid enough to be questioned. She'd said that the girls were all petals of the rose. She was referring to that rosary necklace she'd handed to Callie. She said each petal stood for one of the five who were executed in July 1692, and that the petals corresponded to their descendants as well.

"I know you and your mother were related to Rebecca Nurse."

"So was Rose," Callie said.

"Right. I knew that. And I've accounted for Cheryl and Susan. But then I go blank. According to your memory, Rose also spoke two other names that night: Elizabeth Howe and Sarah Good."

Callie thought about it. "I'm pretty sure Rose was related to more than one of Salem's executed."

"What makes you say that?"

"Rose told me she was. She said that's why she got interested in the witch trials in the first place. Because she found out she was related to more than one who was put to death."

Rafferty remembered hearing that a number of people in this area had more than one accused or executed relative. Towner said it was why people here weren't as interested in the whole history as the tourists seemed to be. They'd had enough of it. Their relatives had lived it. Evidently, it was the opposite for Rose.

"So Cheryl and Susan are two petals of the rose," Callie said. "And my mother. And me. I would guess the other one is Rose."

"Maybe," he said. "But if you and your mother and Rose are all related to Rebecca Nurse, wouldn't you all be on the same petal?"

"Maybe."

"And if Rose was related to more than one of Salem's executed, her name may be on another petal as well."

"That makes sense."

"Since she spoke two other names that night, I'm thinking one of them might have been for her other relative and the other for Leah, who was supposed to be there."

"Okay," Callie said, going along with his logic.

"If you remember her last name, let me know. Or if you come up with anything else."

"That's all?"

"Pretty much," he said. "But I'm sure there will be more. I know where to find you."

"As in *don't leave town*?"

"Yeah." Rafferty laughed. "One more thing . . ." He reached into his desk and pulled out an old Polaroid of her mother he'd found in the file, one taken before the murders. He slid it across the desk to her. "You look a lot like her," he said.

"I know," she said, still shocked by the resemblance.

"I don't think not using your last name, as my wife suggested, is going to be enough. I think you'd better dye your hair as well."

"Really?"

"The less familiar you seem to people, the better. If you're right about Rose's innocence, then there may still be a murderer out there. And now you're back in town: the only eyewitness who's even remotely reliable. You could be in danger." He stood.

She handed the photo back to him.

After she left, Rafferty watched the tape again. She was a brave girl, especially for someone so young. Though she was upset—they kept asking the same questions over and over—she never cried. Instead, she stared blankly at the camera, clearly in shock, her hair disheveled and her bandaged hand placed carefully on her lap, palm oddly angled and facing up, as if it were disconnected from her body. Even in that early photo, Callie had looked remarkably like her mother.

He thought of his own daughter at that age and felt almost like crying himself. And from what he'd heard from Towner about Callie's life since the murders, it hadn't been an easy one.

He was almost relieved when Jay-Jay interrupted to tell him the assistant district attorney was on the phone. But any trace of relief disappeared when he heard the word *exhumation*.

"They're going to exhume the Goddesses?" Towner gasped as she read the morning paper.

"They're going to try."

"You're not going to let them do that, are you?"

Normally, Rafferty would have welcomed any shot at DNA evidence when he was trying to solve a crime. This was a triple murder. If it had happened today, there'd be no question about whether to do DNA testing. Hell, he would have insisted. Even twenty-five years later, it wasn't a bad idea, although he knew that actually getting any clarity was a remote possibility. Testing was expensive and time consuming, and, in the case of exhumation, it required a judge's order.

Still, in this case, the thought of testing made him very nervous. Rose had lived with the victims, and their blood was found all over her. If there was any DNA left after the bodies had been autopsied and prepared for burial, it was likely to be Rose's. And the exhumation was being requested by people who wanted to see her charged. He hadn't yet reopened the case, and already people were circulating a petition. This was a witch hunt.

But Rose's words the night of the murders and the conversation he'd had earlier with her kept coming back to him. "Do you think, inside, every one of us is a killer?" And the line that followed, the one she'd repeated when Porter arrested her. "The lesser of two evils." That was the one that bothered Rafferty the most. Had Rose thought about this? Was she talking about what had happened so many years ago on Proctor's Ledge? Or was she talking about Billy Barnes? Had she considered hurting him, or was she, like Towner and Ann Chase and several other people he'd met since his arrival in Salem, able to get glimpses of events before they even happened?

He wanted to see the rest of the physical evidence before he determined his position on DNA testing. If the physical evidence was as complete as it should be, the testing might not be necessary. As soon as he got back to his office, he would place another call to the archives to hurry the process.

Rafferty put down the newspaper and ran his hand through his hair.

"A lot of people in town are calling for DNA testing. The boy's death and Rose's . . . involvement in it have incited all sorts of panic. People want answers."

"Which people?" Towner asked, pouring him a second cup of the secret stash of coffee she kept in the tearoom just for him.

"Mainly Helen Barnes," he admitted. "She's already gotten a large number of signatures on a petition."

Helen had persuaded some of her neighbors from the McIntire District to sign, as well as a few folks down in Washington Square. But it was the signatures from people in the less affluent neighborhoods that bothered Rafferty most, the ones from the Point and Boston Street. Many had recently emigrated from the Dominican Republic and Haiti, where black magic and witchcraft were something older people still feared. The fact that Helen's petition had accused Rose of being a witch wasn't helping. "This thing with Billy Barnes has reminded people too much of the past, and it's unfortunate for Rose."

"Do you think they'll go ahead with it?"

"Too early to say. I wouldn't. Not until we see all the other evidence. But a judge will make the final decision, not me."

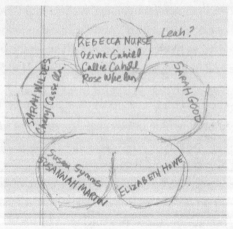

Towner kept glancing at the legal pad on which Rafferty had sketched the five-petaled rose. Each petal held the name of one of the women executed in July 1692. Sharing that same petal was the name of the descendant who had come to honor them that terrible night in 1989. Olivia, Callie, and Rose shared a petal with Rebecca Nurse, Susan with Susannah Martin, Cheryl with Sarah Wildes. The other two were not yet filled in.

Towner pointed. "Wouldn't that one be Rose?" She pointed to Elizabeth Howe's petal. "Didn't Callie say Rose spoke a name that night?"

"Rose spoke three names that night: Elizabeth Howe, Rebecca Nurse, and Sarah Good. One of them presumably belonged to Leah, who didn't show up."

He penciled in Leah's name, not on a petal but just above the sketch.

Rafferty looked at his watch, then stood and took his dishes to the sink.

"Have you told Callie about the petition?" Towner asked, following him.

"Not yet. Though she'll probably read about it in this morning's gossip rag just like everyone else in town."

"That could be disturbing."

He considered. "She's tougher than you think." Now Rafferty looked at his wife. "Actually, Callie reminds me a little of you."

"Really? In what way?"

"She was traumatized. She only has pieces of a child's memory, very vivid ones, but there are gaps. The history is different, of course. But, I think, like you, she's a survivor."

"Let's hope she's better at survival than I was."

Rafferty shuddered to remember what Towner had been through. An abuse victim as a child, she had experienced a trauma lengthier than Callie's, and it had taken her a long time to recover. But, in her recovery, she'd found her life's purpose, to help those who'd suffered similarly. Rafferty was filled with admiration for his wife's bravery. Her struggles and her determination to overcome them had turned her into a strong and confident woman.

Rafferty kissed Towner and headed for the door. "Let's see what happens with Rose before we worry about the exhumation. There are a number of steps that have to be taken before any judge would order it. And even if Rose does come out of her trance, she isn't getting out of the psych ward anytime soon. I'm hoping this whole petition thing will have blown over by then."

Callie pulled over when she saw the street vendor outside the gate of Greenlawn Cemetery. White chrysanthemums. The perfect flower. She used them in her meditation classes to stimulate the heart chakra.

She bought four of them, placing one on each of the graves: for Susan, Cheryl, and Olivia. She'd bring the last to Rose. The markers were simple. Just unpolished granite with each of the women's names carved into the stone. The nuns at the group home had told her that Catholic Charities had paid for the gravestones but wouldn't bury the Goddesses in the Catholic cemetery, choosing the town one instead. They'd said it was because the Goddesses weren't Catholic—another lie, since Olivia had been. Callie didn't know about the others. All she knew was that, at Rose's insistence, each of the Goddesses had learned the Catholic Lord's Prayer, the one without "the kingdom, the power, and the glory" at the end.

Given what she'd learned recently, she suspected there was more to the story than she had been told, probably something to do with the "hubris"—that's what the nuns called it—of the women thinking they were qualified to perform the blessing at the site of the execution. "Only a priest can consecrate the ground of the Salem witches," one of the older nuns at the children's home in Northampton had declared, "although I don't think any priest would agree to do it."

Callie looked at the chrysanthemum she'd saved for Rose, her eyes tearing up. She recalled Halloween nights when the same old-school nun had locked the doors to the home against "evil spirits." The children hadn't been allowed to trick-or-treat. The doors weren't unlocked until the following morning, All Saints' Day, when "God opened the gates of Heaven, and all the souls came down to rid the earth of darkness from the night before."

This morning, standing at her mother's grave, Callie felt the kind of aching loss she'd had little time to feel as a child. She let the tears fall until they stopped. Callie said her own kind of prayer, not to any almighty power but to the women whose graves she was visiting. "Please help me bring Rose back," she said. "I need her as much as she needs me."

She'd tried music therapy with Rose, just basic stuff played on her cell phone. It had no effect. Today, she'd talked herself into a corner after she arrived at the hospital, telling Rose stories about grad school and even her apartment in Amherst. She was quickly running out of material.

By the time she remembered to put the last white chrysanthemum in water, she'd waited too long; one of the petals had dropped and drifted to the bottom of the glass. A single petal. That had meaning, didn't it? What was it? If you dropped a single chrysanthemum petal into a glass of wine, it would yield a long and happy life. A life of ease. Someone had told her that, maybe it was Rose herself. Callie took a long look at Rose's blank expression. Her life had been anything but one of ease. Callie said a silent prayer that this would change for the better.

She walked to the window. With the trees bare, she could see the ocean. Just a hint of horizon that stretched taut, then disappeared behind a far hill.

What could she say to Rose that would make her better? Every story she'd started this morning led to a horrible dead end she couldn't share, a reminder of that night on the hill. The white chrysanthemum was a symbol of truth, yet she couldn't tell the truth to Rose, not all of it. It was so hard to stay positive when she talked about her life. The only solution was to talk about something wholly different. But what?

Looking down, Callie was surprised to see Rose's *Book of Trees* on the windowsill. She was certain it hadn't been there yesterday. She had seen it on an earlier visit in an unlocked cabinet with the rest of Rose's belongings, but apparently someone had taken it out, and now it sat open to where Rose had drawn a winter branch, its bare spines extending across two pages. Callie flipped through, seeing more of the same. The journal was all drawings, pencil sketches of trees in different seasonal stages: fully leafed, then sparser, then bare branches covered with snow.

Realizing how invasive she was being, Callie closed the journal. Pissed off that someone else had been looking through Rose's things, she approached the nurses' desk. "Someone has been looking through Rose's belongings. Do you know who?" Callie demanded.

"Don't accuse me," the nurse said.

"Well, it was somebody." *An aide? The guard at the door?*

The nurse turned back to her computer monitor. "Take it up with her doctor," she advised.

Callie realized she should have been more diplomatic. But seeing Rose's belongings disturbed, her privacy invaded, had plugged into an old issue.

The same thing had happened at the children's home. Periodically, the nuns rifled through the children's belongings, searching for contraband: candy when they were little, drugs later on. Callie's first foster father had searched her belongings the same way. For what? she'd always wondered.

Callie went back to Rose's room and opened the cabinet to see if anything else had been taken. Rose's beat-up down jacket and her black pants were neatly hung, her battered running shoes lined up on the floor. Her little grocery cart with the wheels was half folded and stuffed into the back of the narrow closet with her other meager belongings still inside. Nothing appeared to be missing. Callie buried the book in Rose's cart, covering it with a ratty sweater that needed cleaning and both of Rose's shoes. Then she locked the cabinet, pocketing the key. If—*when*—Rose woke up, Callie would unlock it, but, for now at least, Rose's private belongings were protected.

She couldn't talk any more. Not today.

Instead, she decided to meditate. When she was working with a difficult client, she often led her patient in a guided meditation. She wished she felt confident enough to lead Rose this way, but she didn't.

So Callie closed her eyes and began a silent meditation, sitting at Rose's bedside and picturing her own body filling with water and then slowly draining from her head downward. Others she knew complained that clearing their minds was difficult, but Callie could slip into the meditative state like a second skin. She sometimes taught meditation to students from the university, in addition to sound healing. Truth be told, she preferred this state to real life. Here, there were no barriers for her, and it was easy to travel, to merge with others and see what they saw, to understand what they were going through. Here, all beings were one, something that was difficult to explain to students. It had to do with openness and intention. But first you had to rid yourself of impediments and create an emptiness that would allow you to accept such a merger.

She allowed her focus to linger on every area where she felt a blockage: the crick in her neck from sleeping on Rose's mattress through the tightening of her throat and chest muscles from swallowing tears. When she imagined the water streaming down her arms and out her fingertips, movement slowed from a steady flow to a drip. She could feel the scar on her left palm. And then through closed eyelids she saw a shadow darken the room and felt a chill wind creep through the dying leaves of a nearby tree and move close, jolting her. She opened her eyes.

Too-bright hospital lights. Outside the window, it was no darker than before. The lone oak on the hill across the parking lot was the same.

That was weird.

Callie closed her eyes again and resumed her meditation, taking things back a step, to the elbows. She imagined the liquid draining downward and out through her fingers. This time there was flow, and the rest of the exercise went smoothly. There were no more blockages, no shadows, no further impediments to the meditative state.

She rubbed her hands together and placed them on top of Rose's.

She opened her mouth but didn't sing. Instead she breathed a silent Om. Her intention was to merge herself with Rose and to discover Rose's home tone, the frequency her body was most comfortable with, the one that would become her healing modality. Everyone had one note of the scale that was home for them; sometimes Callie had to listen hard to discover it. When she was able to merge through meditation, the tone often played through her, moving through her fingers, then upward and out her mouth, expressed in a clear healthy tone as if in song.

She'd accomplished this type of bond before—she had a talent for emptying herself of herself when someone was very ill or when she sensed a misdiagnosis, and then joining with them. Empathetic healing sometimes accompanied this type of embodiment.

But today nothing happened.

Rose wasn't easy to inhabit. Callie kept stopping and starting, completing a series of deep breathing exercises before she felt the familiar falling feeling and recognized the scent of oranges that always accompanied a merging.

For Callie, the sound she heard when she meditated—she dubbed it "the music of the spheres"—was akin to a gentle sea breeze. As she went deeper, the sound grew more complex, revealing additional layers. On particularly successful days, it became a series of harmonics in which she could hear all the sounds of nature in gentle concert.

Today, she heard nothing. Instead, as she approached the place Rose inhabited, all sounds ceased. It wasn't silence so much as it was nothingness. The visuals she experienced changed as well, moving from a brightness that lit from within to a darkness that surrounded everything. In the space Rose inhabited, it wasn't frightening. Or painful. It was simply empty.

Empty.

All the time Callie had been telling Rose her life story, she'd feared that the negativity of the narrative would be upsetting. She'd even worried that the simple shock of hearing her voice for the first time in twenty-five years might be making Rose worse. But now she knew that this wasn't the case. Despite what Zee Finch had said, it was clear to Callie, as she released herself from her trance, that in the days Callie had been talking, Rose hadn't heard a single word.

Callie climbed the steps to Towner's house. It was late afternoon and the tearoom was closed, but Towner was there as usual. Callie was surprised to see Zee still sitting at one of the tables, sharing a pot of tea.

"Join us," Towner said with a smile when she saw Callie. She took a cup and saucer from one of the other tables and set a place.

"What are you drinking?"

"It's called Difficult-Tea," Towner said.

"It was named for Towner when she was a teenager," Zee explained, grinning.

"Very appropriately, I might add," Towner said. "It's a blend my grandmother, Eva, used to make: black tea with cayenne and cinnamon, and just a hint of cilantro."

"Sounds terrible," Callie couldn't help saying as she collapsed into a chair. Her hands were shaky. She placed both of them palms down on the cool table in front of her.

Towner laughed. "It was meant to be."

"I think it's pretty good," Zee said. "But people either love it or hate it."

"How about something herbal? To calm your nerves," Towner suggested, already heading over to the pantry, where the canisters of tea were stored.

"Am I that obvious?"

"You just came from the hospital?" Zee asked.

"I did." Callie picked up a spoon and turned it over in her hands, looking at it instead of Zee. "Nothing's working." She sighed. "And someone has been going through Rose's things. I found her *Book of Trees* on the windowsill. It wasn't you, was it?" She put down the spoon and looked at Zee.

"It wasn't me," Zee said. "But I'll certainly speak to the nursing staff about it."

"I spoke to the nurse at the desk," Callie said. "I'm afraid I annoyed the hell out of her."

"Was anything missing?" Towner asked.

"I don't know," Callie said. "I put the book away and I locked the cabinet." Callie showed her the key she had pocketed.

"Good idea."

Towner came back to the table with another teapot, smaller this time and covered with painted roses. "Let it steep for a minute," she said, setting it down in front of Callie.

Callie put her hands around the teapot to warm them.

Zee looked at Towner and then back at Callie, passing the plate of scones that had been on the other side of the table. Callie waved them away.

"Not hungry for sweets? That's never a good sign," Towner said.

"I'm frustrated. I don't see any improvement, and I don't know what to do."

"There's nothing to be done, besides what you're already doing," Zee said. "The idea is to bring her back, to form a connection of some kind. And you are doing that—you are talking to her every day. You won't really know it's working until she wakes up."

"That's the problem. I don't think she's hearing me."

"What makes you say that?" Zee asked.

Callie shrugged. Something kept her from revealing the darkness she'd felt inside Rose during her meditation. "I'm a music therapist. I'm supposed to be a healer," she said instead.

"Supposed to be? You sound doubtful," Towner said.

I've always been doubtful about my healing abilities, Callie thought. Despite many positive results, her embrace of New Age methods was undercut by a small seed of doubt instilled by the nuns she'd grown up among. They had hired her to work with their patients at the nursing home, and even though in her worst moments she worried it may have been only because they felt bad for her, she knew it meant they had a base level of confidence in her abilities, at least some of them did. Even they'd had to acknowledge there were healers in the Bible; Jesus himself was the best example. But Callie's "gifts" were always spoken of as if the word were in quotes, as if they had a dark origin and might end up doing more harm than good. This doubt was the reason she never moved beyond the nursing home and a few private clients. People at the end of life were safe. She could usually help them, and if she couldn't . . . Well, then at least she could ease their way.

Towner was still looking at her, waiting for comment.

"Being a healer is an odd thing to announce, especially in front of Rose's real doctor."

Zee looked at her curiously. "It hasn't been long enough to know whether or not you're helping." She stood and began to gather her belongings. "I've got to get out to Yellow Dog. I missed them this morning," she said, looking at her watch. "Just keep doing what you're doing."

"The other time Rose was in this state, she was this way for a year," Towner said.

"I know. I'm already out of stories," Callie admitted. "I can't possibly do this for a year."

"No one expects you to," Zee said.

Towner lifted the lid of the teapot and checked the brew, then poured a cup.

There was a long pause as Callie sipped. "Thanks," she said. Then, looking toward the pantry, she asked, "Towner?"

"Yes?"

"May I borrow that salad bowl of yours?" Sound itself didn't seem to have any impact on Rose, but *vibration* pulled in another sense entirely. It could be *felt*. It was worth a shot.

"You mean the singing bowl?" Towner asked. "Would you like the rubber spatula, too?"

"Yes, please."

Zee looked confused. "Are you planning to cook something up for Rose?"

"With your permission."

CHAPTER EIGHT

November 10, 2014
SALEM

*In the community that made up Salem, nineteen people
were executed, as well as two dogs. Samuel Sewall, a
judge for the Court of Oyer and Terminer, was known
to have kept a diary for forty years. The diary is blank
for the summer of 1692. One popular conclusion among
researchers has been that Sewall's omission was due to
"willful amnesia brought about by the collective guilt
from which the entire city of Salem still suffers."*
—ROSE WHELAN, *The Witches of Salem*

CALLIE WAS UNFAZED BY THE LOOKS ON THE FACES OF
the nurses at the psych ward desk when she passed by carrying the
bowl and spatula. The officer guarding Rose's room looked up at her
suspiciously. "What are you planning to do with that?"

The nurses had not passed him the word. "I'm going to make
some music," she said. "I have permission."

He looked doubtful but let her pass.

Callie did a quick scan of the room: Nothing was out of place;
no one had interfered with Rose's things. Good. She set the bowl on
Rose's bedside table and then moved the table to the middle of the
room, to center it as best she could within the four walls.

After striking the bowl to create a vibration, she slowly drew the
spatula around the rim until the sound built and the bowl began to

sing. She kept circling until the ringing grew loud enough to ripple the surface of the water in the pitcher by Rose's bedside. She could see the tiny waves in the half-empty IV bag that hung by Rose's bed, and she could feel the rolling sensation as the ellipse formed and began to move around the room. There was only one window. It was a small one and high up, barely interrupting the expanse of wall. With the door closed, the sound was contained by the four walls of this square room, playing off their smooth surfaces, creating what felt like an eternity of sound. She imagined she could see the sound moving, see the colors it created as it passed over and through Rose's still body. For just a moment, she thought she saw Rose shiver, and then, as quickly as a blink, Rose's body went still again as the door opened. Standing there were the day nurse and the aide. Behind them, the officer stood tentatively.

"Come in or go out," Callie said to them as the sound began dissipating. The nurse and the aide stepped inside, but the policeman went back to his post, closing the door behind him.

Callie once again pulled the spatula around the rim, and this time the bowl was primed. The newcomers watched openmouthed as the sound built until it was almost unbearable, then circled the room once more. Callie put down the spatula and watched Rose. She could feel the scar on her palm begin to throb where she had held the tool. Unconsciously, she rubbed it, never taking her eyes off Rose.

The shiver she had seen earlier, if that was what it had been, did not return. But the vibration continued for a long time, longer than Callie imagined it could, and far longer than the first time, before the door had been opened. Neither the aide nor the nurse moved until the sound had faded and disappeared.

The aide spoke first. "What is that supposed to do? Is it meant to heal her?"

"It's intended to balance her," Callie said, without turning away from Rose.

"Fascinating," the nurse said, not meaning it.

She went back to the front desk; the aide remained, looking from Callie to Rose and back. Finally, she turned and walked out.

Callie could see no sign that the shiver she thought she'd seen earlier had been real. Rose appeared exactly the same. "Come on, Auntie Rose," she whispered, as much prayer as command. "Come back to me."

She walked over to the door and closed it again, sealing the room.

Once again, she began to play. It took a while for the vibration to build, but when it did, Callie could feel it, not only in her fingers but in every bone and muscle.

She played until her wrist throbbed and her back muscles ached from bending over the bowl. Then, just as she was about to give up, she saw the shiver again. She circled the rim once more, forcefully, leaving a trail of rubbery dust around the edge of the bowl. She joined the sound with voweled tones, creating a shifting harmonic as it moved up and down the scale: *om, ah, ee.* Finally, her voice found Rose's home note, weak though it was, and held the tone. The volume circled and built until it was so loud, Callie had to will herself not to cover her ears. At its peak, she stopped and stood perfectly still, letting the sound fade to an extended silence, a stillness sound healers consider sacred.

Rose blinked. Callie stared at her as the silence held, wishing someone else was with them to bear witness. "Rose?"

Rose coughed once. Then, looking straight ahead, she began to speak.

"I am a cipher."

Callie stared.

"I carry no weight, no worth, no influence. I represent nothing. I do not exist."

It was as if Rose were speaking to someone—or something—beyond the realm of sight. Then, slowly, she sat up in her bed, tripping an alarm that had replaced the restraints. The aide and the nurse burst into the room, pushing past Callie as they hurried to Rose's bedside. "Careful," the nurse said, holding Rose to support her. "Let me help you."

Rose pulled back as if stung.

"It's okay," the nurse said. "You're okay."

Rose hissed at the nurse, pointing a witchy index finger. "You turn away when you pass me on the street." The guard was now standing in the doorway. Rose turned to the aide. "You run from me when you should embrace me."

The aide took a step backward.

"But remember this as you flee: You brought me into existence. I am not the cause, I am merely the effect."

The aide stepped back, and the nurse let go of Rose. "I'm going to call Dr. Finch."

The policeman stayed by the door, as if nailed there.

Rose turned to look at Callie, staring for a long moment. Then, slowly, her eyes filled with tears and she reached for Callie's hand.

PART TWO

PART TWO

CHAPTER NINE

November 15, 2014
Salem

It's outrageous that she hasn't been charged.
It's time for this town to ditch that witch.

— @Truthseeker247

RAFFERTY CHEWED AN ANTACID TABLET. SINCE ROSE'S awakening, he'd given up his usual four cups of coffee and had started living on this stuff, sometimes forgetting to eat until the end of the day. The news had traveled fast, HIPAA laws be damned, and some-one had shared it with the press. It could have been his own guard for all he knew. At any rate, someone had talked, telling people the crazy pronouncements Rose had made. Now he was fielding several angry calls a day from good citizens wanting to know when he was going to charge her for what had happened to the boy and for the Goddess Murders twenty-five years ago. Propelled by Helen Barnes's petition, more and more Salemites were in favor of exhuming the Goddesses. It was ghoulish.

He'd expected seven more boxes of evidence from the archives, but only six had arrived this week, bringing the total he now had to twelve, all neatly sealed and labeled from 1 of 13 on up. Number 9 was missing. He'd called daily to remind them that he was still wait-ing for it, had even gone down to the archives himself to locate the missing carton, but it was nowhere to be found.

The deeper he looked into the evidence, the more people he found who were implicated. The girls who had died that night had many enemies with motive—angry wives, jilted lovers, righteous moralists. It was as frustrating as having no suspects at all. If there was any information to be found about Leah, the one he'd begun calling the fifth petal, it wasn't in any of the boxes he'd received. The other missing element was the clothes the girls were killed in, the costumes they'd evidently worn to the party that night, the ones Rose had objected to. The police would have kept the clothing as evidence, checking it for bodily fluids, blood, semen, hair. The costumes were undoubtedly in the missing box. Maybe DNA-testing the existing physical evidence would be enough to satisfy the mob. He made another call to the archives.

He truly detested the idea of the Goddesses' exhumation. If they dug up those poor girls, and there was enough left of them to test, he'd wager Rose's DNA would be all over them; they'd lived with her, for God's sake. Which meant things could easily get serious for Rose, especially since so many people *wanted* her to be guilty. In the best of all possible worlds, they'd find nothing in the remains. He'd looked it up. The rate of corpse decomposition varied greatly, depending on environmental factors, dampness of the soil being the biggest variable. But if the deterioration was minimal, then they could find DNA.

Just yesterday afternoon, he'd had to send two cruisers to Salem Hospital because a gang of middle school kids were shooting a BB gun at what they believed to be Rose's window. They'd caused an active shooter lockdown that crippled the surgery center for the rest of the day. Add to that the online posters who enjoyed venting anonymous judgment on a woman they'd never met . . . He had a real problem on his hands, and it was growing.

Through Towner, who was becoming close to Callie, he'd heard that Rose was having good and bad days. She was in and out of lucidity, sometimes making perfect sense, sometimes ranting about the banshee. For the most part, he'd kept his distance from the hospital unless he had official business there. He'd accompanied Barry Marcus to visit Rose soon after she regained consciousness. Unfortunately, she'd been more out than in that day. The minute Barry was introduced as her lawyer, she'd said: "The banshee jumped into me on the night of the Goddess Murders. It's taken everything I have to keep her from killing again."

"You need to get out of here," Barry had said. Then he'd opened the door and held it for Rafferty to exit.

Truth be told, Rafferty was grateful to be dismissed. He'd heard too much about the banshee and Rose. People were already calling him daily and acting as though the banshee were real. *If, as Rose Whelan herself insists, it was a banshee that killed the Goddesses, and that banshee jumped into Rose, then Rose is the killer!* Such was the logic of public opinion. He'd waited for the attorney outside that day. "Well, there's little doubt as to what her defense will be," Barry had said when he finally exited Rose's room. "If any defense is needed, considering there's no evidence of a homicide. Can't you hurry the kid's toxicology report along?"

They already had the results of the autopsy, but it hadn't told them much. Billy Barnes had died of a cerebral hemorrhage. It didn't point to Rose in any way, but it also did nothing to tamp down the crazy rumors about Rose that were circulating. *The banshee's scream made the kid's head explode!* was the first online post Rafferty encountered. The toxicology report would tell more about what had really happened. But it was going to take a while.

Rafferty wasn't in as much of a hurry for the reports as Barry was. He knew Rose was protected from the rumors and an inflamed public as long as she was in the hospital. She was off the streets, warm and dry, sleeping in a bed and eating regular meals. And it gave him time.

Rafferty leaned back in his chair and contemplated taking another antacid. He was more worried about Callie at this stage. He'd heard some gossip: She was being touted as a healer, the girl who had awakened Rose from her trance. No one was talking about who Callie Cahill really was—yet. As far as he could tell, the only rumors that were circulating at this point were of the miraculous healing performed with a "magic" bowl. But it was only a matter of time until people started to recognize her and remember. He needed to get further into his reinvestigation of the Goddess case before the damned exhumation could go forward. Finding something that was missed the first time was the only way to keep both Rose and Callie out of the public's crosshairs.

Rafferty was at his desk when the tox report finally came in. He read it through twice, just to make sure he understood the ramifications.

There had been late season thunderstorms all morning, full-on hail that had dented some of the cars at the station and sent the ubiquitous news crews scrambling. It was the first bit of amusement Rafferty had enjoyed since Rose's hospitalization and the media circus that followed. Though it was still pouring outside, he pulled on his raincoat and headed to the hospital.

"Hey, Chief!" some reporter yelled from across the parking lot. "You gonna give the okay to dig up those Goddesses?"

"No comment."

Rafferty shook the rain from his coat on the threshold of Rose's room. He nodded to the guard, wondering again if one of them was the source of the leaks to the press. He'd grilled them both about it, but neither admitted guilt.

Rafferty opened the door. Rose was sitting up in her bed. Callie, Towner, and Zee were sitting with her. He cleared his throat, and all of the women turned to him. "I've got news," he said. "The autopsy is complete. We knew Billy Barnes died of a cerebral hemorrhage, but the toxicology report indicated there were large amounts of both cocaine and heroin in his body."

"That's good news!" said Towner.

Rafferty shot his wife a look, and she quickly tried to redeem herself. "Well—not for him. I mean for you, Rose."

Rose looked confused.

"You didn't do it, Rose," Rafferty said. "You are not responsible for the death of Billy Barnes. The mix of drugs likely caused the hemorrhage."

Rose started to speak. "But I . . ."

Rafferty held up his hand. "Don't say a word. There's no banshee. You didn't explode his brain by screaming, and please stop suggesting you might have. He died of a drug overdose. This is over now. Just concentrate on getting better."

He quickly said his good-byes and excused himself, dismissing the guard at the door on his way out. Then he headed back to the station to deal with the fallout. As the door closed, he heard Towner inviting Callie to the upcoming fund-raiser for the Yellow Dog Island Shelter. *Good,* he thought. *Callie can have my ticket.*

CHAPTER TEN

November 22, 2014
SALEM

*Unfortunately, there will be one family in Salem who
will not be celebrating Thanksgiving. "There is little to
be thankful for this year," Helen Barnes said. "William's
mother is so grief stricken that she has put her house
on the market, a house that has been in the
Barnes family for almost three hundred years."*

—*The Salem Journal*

"YOU SURE THIS IS A GOOD IDEA?" CALLIE ASKED. THE
color on the L'Oréal box was a very light blond. "Is it even going to
take?" She gestured to her dark curls.

"Time will tell," Towner said, putting the shower cap over Callie's
head and removing her gloves. "You probably should have gone to a
colorist."

Callie had to laugh. "Nice time to tell me." Rafferty had her too
worried about being recognized to go to a local salon, so she'd asked
Towner to do it.

During the hair dyeing process, Towner had been running back
and forth from the tearoom to the coach house. She was a waitress
short today: One of her regular girls whose children were in foster care
had been in court all day, trying to win them back.

"I'm not a big fan of foster care," Callie said. She'd already told
Towner she'd been fostered more than once, never successfully.

"The first time was the worst. The father sent me back to the group home and left me on the front steps with a note pinned to my chest."

Towner stared at her. "No way."

"Cross my heart," Callie said.

"What did the note say?"

"You don't want to know what the note said," Callie said, remembering.

Towner waited.

"It was a biblical quote. Proverbs 5:5. Are you familiar with Proverbs?"

"Not really," Towner admitted.

"Her feet go down to death; her steps lead straight to the grave."

"Oh my God," Towner said. "Please tell me that didn't happen."

Callie did her best to shrug it off. "It really did. I honestly think the man didn't know I could read.

"There were three or four more foster homes after that. Some with a lot of kids, and not much discipline or attention, the parents fostering just for the money they could make from the state. The last one was when I was a teenager. The mother worked two jobs outside the home, but the father paid a lot of attention to me. All the wrong kind."

"Jesus."

An hour and a half and two showers later, Callie was down in the tearoom trying to catch a glimpse of the back of her head with the hand mirror Towner was holding out.

The effect was striking, with little contrast between the dye's pale color and her porcelain skin.

Towner held the hand mirror up for her approval.

Callie looked at it. "I definitely don't look like myself," she said. For a moment, she felt a chill. Callie looked like the memory she'd had of Susan, with her white, white hair and pigmentless skin. "Are you sure tonight's a good idea?" The fund-raiser was just hours away, and she was having second thoughts about going.

"Don't worry about it," Towner said. "Most of the patronesses are so old they can't see five feet in front of them anyway . . . God, look how great your eyes look."

Towner held the mirror up again, and Callie looked. Well, at least the eyes were hers and not Susan's pink ones. They seemed almost black. She looked like the negative of a black-and-white photo from the thirties that Olivia had once clipped from an old magazine.

Ignoring the Closed sign on the door, a woman pushed her way into the tearoom, where Callie and Towner were sharing a late afternoon pot of Difficult-Tea, and dropped the papers she was carrying down in front of Towner.

"Marta, this is Callie," Towner said. "Marta's running tonight's event."

"Nice to meet you, Callie," the woman said, looking at her curiously.

Marta was dark eyed, attractive, and stylish, though not exactly pretty in any classic sense. She looked familiar in a New England way, a type Rose might have referred to as "a handsome woman." *Commanding* was the word that came to Callie.

"Callie recently moved to Salem."

"Why would anyone in their right mind want to do that?" Marta smiled at Callie.

Callie hesitated. She knew the question was rhetorical, but it was a question she might be asked again more seriously, and she hadn't thought far enough ahead to have formulated a response.

"Oh, come on, Marta, you moved back," Towner teased.

"Only because my mother was dying."

"Oh, I'm sorry," Callie said, remembering the loss of her own mother.

Marta dismissed her concern with a wave of the hand. "It was a long time ago. I'm just saying, why would anyone move to this dismal place if they didn't have to?"

I did have to, Callie thought but did not say. The way Marta was looking at her was making Callie uncomfortable. Reflexively, she touched her new hair.

Marta gestured to the papers she had placed in front of Towner.

"Will you please sit down and join us?" Towner said. "You're making me nervous hovering like that."

"Only for a minute." Marta laughed, taking a seat at one of the lacy table settings.

Towner held up the teapot, but Marta waved it away. "I've got to get back to make sure the hotel doesn't screw up the seating list."

Towner examined the guest list Marta presented. "Impressive."

"We're essentially sold out."

"As usual, thanks to you," Towner said, then turned to Callie and explained, "this evening wouldn't happen without Marta."

Marta shrugged off the compliment.

"She's kind enough to chair the event every year. She's also one of the best fund-raisers around."

"If I were half as good at making money for myself as I am for charity, I'd become a 501(c)(3), fund my retirement, and go back to where I came from."

Towner laughed. "I don't think that's allowed."

"More's the pity," Marta said.

"Where did you come from?" Callie asked.

"Manhattan."

"She came back because of her mom, but she stayed because she missed New England so much." Towner smiled.

Marta groaned, gathering up the papers she'd placed in front of Towner and putting them into her leather shoulder bag. "People like Towner make this place tolerable, at least. I'll see you tonight. Will you be there, Callie?"

"She's my plus one," Towner said.

Marta laughed. "I'll bet Rafferty's relieved to be off the hook."

"You know it." Towner laughed.

"I'll see you both tonight." Marta headed for the door, reaching it just as two older women were trying to come in. "The tearoom's closed," she said, pointing to the sign posting the hours. "Come back tomorrow." She waited while they turned around and slowly descended the stairs. Unable to hide her frustration at their slow movement, Marta couldn't help rolling her eyes at Towner.

"She's interesting," Callie said.

"She is that."

With its mirrors and gilt, the banquet room at the Hawthorne Hotel reflected Old World elegance. Towner and Callie walked the length of the room, stopping every few moments so people could either greet Towner or introduce themselves to her.

After dyeing her hair, they had talked again about how Callie wanted to be introduced. "Pick another last name," Towner said. "Something you can remember."

Callie picked O'Neill, which had been the name of her first foster mother, the one who died.

"This is my favorite fund-raiser," a local dowager in a long-sleeved crepe dress with a too-low neckline said to Towner. "May must be so proud of you!"

"I'd like to think she is," Towner replied graciously.

Callie followed in Towner's wake, smiling when greeted, shaking hands when introduced. Towner had told her about May Whitney, the family matriarch who ran the shelter on Yellow Dog Island. Evidently their relationship was strained, partly because of history and partly because May had left Towner doing most of this fund-raising work. May was known for her skills with a six-gauge shotgun and for being as antisocial as they come. "I don't believe she's stepped on the mainland for the last five years. So both the organization and the hosting of this event fall to me," Towner told Callie.

"That's a lot of work for one person."

"I don't do everything myself. I have a group of volunteers to help. And, of course, there's Marta. If it weren't for this fund-raiser and the money the women earn making Ipswich bobbin lace, the shelter would have closed a long time ago. When you see the work they do out there, it's definitely worth it. Any complaint I have about this event seems ridiculously selfish."

"There must be at least two hundred people here tonight," Callie said, looking around to see if she was dressed appropriately. She'd purchased a simple black sheath with thin shoulder straps for the occasion, and Towner had complimented her on it, but she wasn't sure.

Some people seemed as if they'd come directly from work, but most of the older women had dressed more formally, looking as if they'd donned a lifetime—or at least a few marriages' worth—of accumulated jewelry for the occasion. The room sparkled with diamonds and the light refracted from the crystal chandeliers and candlesticks on each table.

Even though she was dressed nicely, Callie felt awkward in this crowd. Most people glanced quickly at her and then resumed their conversations. But she noticed a few women looking at her strangely, their eyes lingering as if trying to place her. Was she being recognized? Many people here were certainly old enough to remember Olivia.

Callie was relieved when the master of ceremonies asked people to take their seats. Towner hurried Callie to a table near the stage. A handsome young man in a dark suit who'd been sitting next to a distinguished looking middle-aged woman stood politely at their approach. Their eyes locked; her steps quickened. *This fund-raiser just got a lot more interesting.*

"Emily, Paul, we're so delighted to be seated with you tonight. I'd like to introduce you to my friend Callie O'Neill. Callie, this is Emily Whiting and her son, Paul. Emily and her husband, Finn, run the Whiting Foundation. They do some of the best charitable work in New England. Emily is the shelter's biggest supporter. She never misses one of these dinners."

"So nice to meet you, Callie," Emily said, extending her hand. Emily's dress was far more understated than the others Callie had seen and far more elegant, a winter white cashmere with a matching waist-length jacket. Her hair was shoulder length and deep brown, with just a few streaks of grey at the temples. Callie noticed the emerald ring on her right hand, a simple platinum and diamond solitaire on her left.

Callie shook Emily's hand, then turned to Paul. Something about his sandy hair and startlingly blue irises made her wonder where she'd seen him before.

He held Towner's chair first, then Callie's. She sat, still gazing curiously at him. His eyes were amazing. She always noticed people's eyes. *Windows to the soul.* She felt like laughing at her use of the old cliché.

"Callie is the music therapist I told you about," Towner said to Emily.

"Ah, the one who awakened Rose Whelan," Emily replied.

Callie detected skepticism in her tone.

Towner spoke over her: "I told Emily about the singing bowl and the music therapy. And about the effect it had on Rose."

"Do you know Rose?" Callie asked Emily.

"No, I've never had the pleasure," Emily said. Without pause, she turned away from Callie and focused on Towner. "Where's Rafferty this evening?"

"He donated his ticket to Callie."

"Generous."

"More like relieved." Towner laughed. "You know he hates these events. You look very lovely tonight. I take it that means the drug trial is agreeing with you."

"All credit goes to Chanel and La Mer, not the chemo. I don't think Finn is going to make it, either," Emily said. "He sends his regrets. As well as the foundation's checkbook. And I have a far more handsome escort, don't you think?"

Chemo, Callie thought. She wondered what kind of cancer Emily was fighting. She didn't look exhausted, the way some of the chemo patients Callie treated did. By the way Emily had gazed at her son, Callie knew instantly that the woman was crazy about him. *The perfect son,* Callie thought, *the solace of every woman who has ever tried and failed to mold the man she married.* As soon as the thought occurred, she chided herself for thinking in stereotypes. She had no idea who Finn Whiting was or what his relationship with his wife was like.

Callie was only half listening to their conversation. It was clear that Emily would rather talk to Towner, which was fine, good in fact. Callie didn't enjoy making small talk, especially if she had to work at it. Instead, she kept stealing glances at Paul, who was easily chatting up two cougar types on the other side of the table. She could smell their too-strong musky perfume from here.

How do I know him?

Feeling her eyes on him, Paul turned. "You're staring at me."

"I am not." Callie laughed, both embarrassed and amused to be caught.

"Did I spill wine on my shirt or something?" He looked down at his shirt, then, finding nothing, he flashed a smile, waiting for her to explain.

"I know you from somewhere," Callie said.

"Isn't that supposed to be my line?"

"Ha, you're quite the charmer, Mr. Whiting." She smiled back at him. "Seriously, have we met?"

"I don't think so," he said, now looking at her with amusement.

She shook her head. She wasn't great with names, but faces were different. She'd seen him somewhere. Hadn't she?

"If I'd met you, I'm sure I'd remember," Paul said, holding her gaze. "I've been living in Matera since last January. So, unless we met before that or in . . ."

"Italy," Callie said.

"Yes," he said, surprised. "You know Matera?"

"Never heard of the place."

"Okay," he said, drawing out each syllable.

She considered telling him that she had always wanted to go to Italy, but it would have been a lie. She didn't tell him the truth, either: that she often knew what people were going to say before they spoke. The same way she sometimes knew what was going to happen just before it occurred.

"Red or white, miss?" The waiter offered Callie wine.

"She'll have the red," Paul said.

He obviously didn't have the same talent anticipating answers. "White, please," Callie clarified.

"The red is much better, trust me."

"Red is a little too bold for my taste."

Paul caught her subtext immediately. Grinning, he held up his glass, toasting her. "Suit yourself."

She took a sip and immediately made a face.

"Told you so." Paul laughed.

"What did I miss?" Marta rushed in, grabbing the empty seat beside Emily; she was older than Emily, but not by much. Unlike most of the women in attendance, Marta wore no jewelry at all, not even a wedding ring.

Paul started to stand again, but Marta motioned him to sit.

"You didn't miss a thing," Towner said.

Back at the tearoom, Towner had introduced Marta and Callie only by first names. Now, as she looked at tonight's program, Callie saw Marta's last name.

"Hathorne," Callie said. "Any relation to Nathaniel?"

"He's Hawthorne, with a *w*," Marta said, after an uncomfortable pause. "And yes. A different branch on the same family tree. Which also includes the hanging judge from the Court of Oyer and Terminer, I'm afraid. The embarrassment of which is what prompted young Nathaniel to change the spelling of his name."

It was a much longer explanation than Callie had expected and had the feeling of a rehearsed speech. This must be a frequently asked question.

Marta signaled to a waiter and pointed to her glass, never taking her eyes off Callie.

"The difference between their side of the family and mine," Marta continued, this time less rehearsed and more conversational, "is that we have a great deal more fortitude and daring. But we who dared to keep our original spelling would have missed a great commercial opportunity in the story of Hester Prynne. We wouldn't have seen the tragedy in that tale. Each of us would have worn that scarlet letter as a red badge of courage."

Paul choked on his wine. His mother shot him a look.

A long silence followed. Callie realized that, beyond the literary references, Marta had made some kind of inside joke, and that she'd missed it. Not an uncommon occurrence for Callie, given how she'd grown up. She was relieved when the waiter came to take their dinner orders.

The meal was as expected, with a choice of roast beef, salmon, or chicken, but the salad course was served at the end, European style. The dinner conversation settled into predictable small talk, learned from years of etiquette classes and cotillions. Callie felt lost.

Fortunately, the inside jokes stopped. Paul asked the usual "Where did you grow up?" questions most people asked when meeting for the first time.

"New Orleans first," Callie said. "Then Northampton, Mass." She didn't mention Salem.

"That must have been a big cultural adjustment."

"I was very young when we moved. I don't remember much about Louisiana."

The waiter put down dessert plates, a combination of chocolate mousse and madeleines. Paul waved his away. "I'll have a brandy instead, please."

The waiter looked as if he were about to protest but then caught Marta's eye. She nodded.

"Certainly, sir," he said.

"Would you like something?" Paul asked Callie, his hand touching her forearm. "Brandy, or something else?"

"I'm all set," Callie said.

Paul's hand lingered for a long moment before he removed it and continued the questions. Where had she gone to school? How had she decided to become a music therapist? And what the heck was music therapy, anyway?

She tried to match him question for question, but he was far better at the dance. At one point, Callie noticed the two perfumed women glancing in her direction. Then they fell immediately into an animated conversation. What were they saying about her? She was relieved when the auction began.

The first item up for bid was a painting, a fishing shack at the water's edge donated by Racket Shreve, a much-admired local artist.

"It's beautiful," Callie commented, noting the play of light and wind on the water of what looked like an early version of Salem Harbor under a moonlit sky.

Paul concurred. "Shadow and light."

"Two hundred, do I hear two fifty?" the auctioneer barked. "Two fifty, do I hear three?"

The bidding closed at more than a thousand dollars. The next item offered was a small painting by H. L. Barnes, a historically accurate rendition of one of the merchant vessels that had sailed out of Salem during the 1800s. This painting brought even more.

The third painting was much smaller than the other two. Callie had noticed it displayed on the way in. Smartly, Marta had set up the auction items just inside the entrance to the ballroom, so you had to pass by them on the way to your table. Callie had admired each of the three paintings as she passed. While the first two were beautiful, this one had stopped her in her tracks, though she wasn't sure why. It was an old portrait done in oil, a beautiful woman with an owl on her shoulder.

"This painting was donated from the collection of Ann Chase. Artist unknown. Titled: *Minerva, Goddess of Wisdom, Medicine, and Music,*" the auctioneer said. "Note the owl sitting on her shoulder. As we all know, the owl is a symbol of wisdom."

The auctioneer held up the portrait for viewing. But it was a far smaller painting than the other two, and difficult to see, even from the front tables. As a result, the bidding got off to a rough start.

"Do I hear a hundred dollars? Come on, people, a hundred dollars is a steal for a beautiful painting like this."

Finally someone held up a paddle.

The auctioneer went on, getting the bidding to $190 before it stopped.

"That's ridiculous," Paul muttered, raising his paddle and speaking loudly. "Five hundred dollars."

Really, Callie thought. It was a beautiful painting, but five hundred dollars, without blinking an eye?

"Sold." The auctioneer quickly handed the painting off to his assistant, gesturing in Paul's direction, and moved on.

Several high-ticket items followed: a week at a New Hampshire summerhouse was snapped up. A New York foodie weekend complete with a breakfast *very near* Tiffany's inspired a hot bidding war; a wine tasting and food pairing for ten at a local restaurant hosted by the Whiting family's sommelier had people in a frenzy.

Emily Whiting didn't bid on any of the items. Callie kept a rough tally in her head, and, when the auction ended, she estimated the evening had raised more than $50,000 for the shelter.

The assistant approached the table, breaking into a smile when she saw Paul. She held out a clipboard for him to sign and a credit card receipt. "I'll hold her for you at the back table," she told him and smiled flirtatiously. "You can pick her up on your way out."

"Oh, bring her to me, please," he said. "She's too pretty to sit at the back table all by herself."

The girl blushed and headed off to fetch the painting.

Callie was shaking her head.

"What?"

" 'She's too pretty to sit at the back table all by herself'?"

"She is."

"That's the cheesiest line I've ever heard."

"Not as bad as 'I know you from somewhere.' "

Callie laughed.

As the bidding concluded, the audience applauded. Marta rose from her chair and headed to the podium.

"What? You're not speaking this year?" Emily smiled at Towner.

"Very funny," Towner said. Reading Callie's curious look, she added, "Public speaking is not my forte."

"Public anything," Emily joked. "It runs in the family."

"What does that mean?" Callie asked. She was tired of not being in on the joke.

Emily smiled. "Towner's family tends to shy away from public forums. May Whitney hasn't left her island for, what is it now, five years?"

"Almost," Towner said.

Marta said a few words of greeting, thanking people for coming out on such a rainy night, thanking them for their ongoing support. Then she lowered the microphone and moved closer to it, softening her voice as well until all residual conversation ceased, leaving only the occasional clink of cup on saucer.

"My message this evening is brief but to the point. Twenty four-teen has been a challenging year for the shelter financially, as you all know. Yellow Dog Island usually shelters about fifty women annually. But this year they have seen a hundred percent increase in guests."

There was an audible gasp from the crowd.

"The reentry program that Towner Whitney runs at Eva's Lace Reader Tearoom has funded itself and is able to provide some money for the shelter. But we need more help. Hard times can bring out the worst in people. Abuse increases as employment falters. Violence is on the rise." She paused and took a breath, then smiled at the audi-ence. "For most of us, times have greatly improved in the last few years . . . For *most* of us. But not for everyone. There's a growing number of people out there for whom the economy has not improved. Nor have their lives. We need to remember that. You know the work we do out there, and you know what we need from you. Your pledge cards are on the table. Thank you."

"Short but sweet," Emily said as Marta sat down at their table. "Well done."

When she saw the pledge card, Callie was embarrassed not to have brought her checkbook. "I'll contribute tomorrow," she said quietly to Towner.

"Don't be silly," Towner said. "That's not why I brought you." Towner raised a glass to Marta. "For all of your help this year," she said. "We couldn't have survived without your fund-raising skills. We don't thank you nearly enough."

Slowly everyone raised their glasses and toasted Marta.

Everyone sipped except Marta herself.

"You're not drinking?" Callie said.

"One doesn't drink when one is being toasted," Marta said.

Callie quieted. Emily noticed her embarrassment and turned to her conspiratorially. "One doesn't drink, and one doesn't ever clink," Emily said to Callie. "Nor does one ever toast with water. Oh, the many things right and proper we've learned from Marta! They could fill a book that would rival anything written by Emily Post or Miss Manners."

She said it with a smile, but Callie noticed an edge to her tone.

Marta took the cue and didn't say anything else but, instead, turned her attention to Callie. She was staring at her intently.

Callie shifted uncomfortably in her seat, trying to look away, but she could feel Marta's eyes on her the whole time.

"I meant to tell you, Callie. The Whitings and Marta are next-door neighbors," Towner said, to fill the awkward pause. "Their family histories go back generations, all the way to the Salem Witch Trials."

"Marta moved back to the 'provinces' a few years ago," Emily said, her air quotes showing she was still annoyed by Marta's rude correction of Callie. "She's far too sophisticated for us. I'm sure we bore her to distraction."

"Not at all," Marta said, recovering her composure and smiling sweetly at Emily. "Actually, I find Essex County both exciting and rather decadent."

Before Emily had time to reply, Towner tried to redirect the conversation. "Callie recently moved here," she explained to Emily and Paul. "Though we don't yet know if she'll be staying."

"I'll be staying for a while at least," Callie said.

"Marta's mother left her a beautiful First Period house," Towner said. "Marta, you should show it to Callie."

"I'd be happy to," Marta said.

Towner continued, turning to Callie. "You really should see the place. Emily and Marta always host a holiday house tour to benefit local charities. Combined, the properties have buildings and outbuildings from five different architectural periods, though Marta's 1630s saltbox and Pride's Heart are the only two opened for the public to tour."

"What is Pride's Heart?"

"Pride's Heart is the Whitings' mansion in the very 'heart' of Pride's Crossing," Marta indicated with air quotes of her own.

"It's really quite remarkable. The land is part of the town of Beverly now but was once considered Salem. It's picture perfect over the holidays. We go to Thanksgiving dinner at Pride's Heart every year," Towner said.

"You should join us this year," Paul said. "Mother, don't you think Callie should join us for Thanksgiving?" He wasn't looking at Emily but was keeping his eyes on Callie and grinning. He was playing with her.

"You really should," Marta chimed in quickly. "Emily's Thanksgiving feast is legendary in these parts."

Callie saw a look pass between Towner and Emily.

"You'd be more than welcome," Emily said.

"I appreciate the invitation, but really I don't even know if I'll be here on Thanksgiving—"

"You'll love Pride's Heart," Towner added.

"Come for the weekend," Paul said. "Towner and Rafferty always do."

"Don't you go to see May on Thanksgiving?" Callie asked Towner.

"We go out to Yellow Dog Island for a few hours first, but we always arrive back in time for dinner," Towner said, in a coaxing voice.

"It's a very generous invitation, but I'm not sure . . ." Callie said.

"Oh, you must come," Marta said, jumping in. "I'll pick you up myself."

"Wow," Callie said, not quite certain whom she should address but choosing Emily. "Can I let you know in a day or two?" The minute she posed the question, she heard her mistake. Rose had corrected her almost daily. *You can, but you may not.* Now Callie corrected herself: "I mean, may I?"

"Of course," Emily said. "Take your time. And don't let my son talk you into something you don't want to do."

"I'd like to," Callie said. "Really. I just need to check my schedule." She knew she sounded both inane and rude. *What person doesn't know whether or not they have plans for Thanksgiving when it's less than a week away?*

Marta excused herself and went to speak to a woman a few tables over.

"Let us know," Emily said, managing a smile, then turned back to her son. "I think we'll be heading home now."

Paul took the cue and stood to hold the chair for his mother.

"Nice to meet you, Callie," he said, sounding as if he meant it.

They said polite good-byes, and this time Emily seemed sincere. "Very nice to meet you, Callie. I hope we see you again."

As Paul hurried to retrieve her coat, Emily handed Towner an envelope. Towner opened it and gasped. Callie could see the amount of the check: $300,000.

Towner was clearly stunned. "Thank you," she said.

"You're very welcome."

Paul helped his mother on with her coat, then offered his arm. "I hope you'll consider joining us, Callie."

Emily took her son's arm, and they walked slowly toward the exit.

"What in the world was that all about?" Callie asked Towner as soon as she was sure everyone else was out of earshot.

"What do you think it was about?" Towner laughed. "I'd say from the invitation and from what I know of him, that Paul Whiting is interested in you."

"I picked up on that pretty quickly." Callie laughed. "But what was all that . . . other stuff?"

"Other stuff?" Towner feigned innocence.

"What was going on between Marta and Emily? Air quotes. Subtext and innuendo. I felt like I was at a new staging of an Albee play."

"Oh, that. Well, there's some history there." Towner laughed again. "Come to Thanksgiving, and you'll find out more, I'm sure."

CHAPTER ELEVEN

November 27, 2014
THANKSGIVING, SALEM

*The deeds of witches are such that they cannot be
done without the help of Devils.*
—*Malleus Maleficarum*, 1486

"WHAT DO YOU NORMALLY CHARGE PER SESSION?" TOWNER
asked Callie. "I want to pay the going rate."

"No, no, it's on me. They've invited me for the weekend." Callie
glanced at the gift certificate Towner had prepared to present to Emily
as a hostess gift of sorts. It entitled her to *one music therapy session with
Callie O'Neill.* Callie was still wondering if she should have accepted
the spontaneously issued Thanksgiving invitation, though it had been
followed by Emily's handwritten one the next day. When Towner had
asked her to do a treatment on Emily, she'd asked about the cancer.
"How bad is it?"

"It's bad. Metastatic breast cancer. Stage four."

"Damn," Callie said.

"She said they used music therapy on her after her first surgery, so
she knows what it is. Emily's fairly traditional, though. I might hold
off on the singing bowls."

"That's fine," Callie said. They were two different treatments, really.
Traditional music therapy involved three elements: the music, the patient, and the therapist. Sound healing with the bowls, on the other

hand, worked directly on the patient, removing the middleman. And even if Emily Whiting was open to it, Callie's full set of bowls was still in Northampton; all she had here was Towner's salad bowl. "But I'm not taking your money."

"I'll see you at Pride's Heart," Towner said, leaving a check on the table anyway. "Wish Rose Happy Thanksgiving for me when you see her later."

Rose was fully dressed and sitting at a table by the window, sketching the tree that sat on the hill across from the hospital parking lot.

Callie flashed on a memory of another Thanksgiving, at Rose's house on Daniels Street.

Callie was sitting with everyone at the table, sketching a turkey wearing a Pilgrim's hat that Rose found quite amusing, when a pounding on the door interrupted them. Olivia excused herself and went outside to talk to the uniformed policeman standing on the porch. The other women watched them through the window. Callie could hear her mother and the man arguing. Rose stayed seated.

As the argument escalated, Callie started to cry.

"What's the matter, sweet girl?" Rose asked.

"Is he going to take her to jail?"

"No," Rose said. Then, to Susan and Cheryl, "Though jail might do the whole lot of them some good."

The memory took Callie by surprise.

"What are you frowning about?" Rose asked, pulling her back to real time.

It took a moment for Callie to regain her composure. She made herself smile. "That's very good," she said, pointing to Rose's drawing. She looked out at the hill where the single oak stood in winter silhouette. Rose wasn't drawing the entire tree; rather she was rendering an impressionistic suggestion of it in light and darkness, the branches and twigs weaving over and under as it moved across the page. "It looks like lace."

Rose turned to look at her. "What else do you see?"

Callie gazed at the sketch. In the negative spaces between the branches, Rose had placed a series of check marks.

"What are those?" Callie asked.

"You tell me. What do *you* see?"

"Just some marks."

"Not people?"

"People? No. Where do you see people?"

Rose pointed to the spots she had marked. "You don't see anyone at all?"

"No," Callie said.

"Good," Rose said, and then shushed Callie and leaned in toward the window. "She's singing to us."

"Who is?"

"That oak." Rose scrunched her face in concentration. "Listen."

Callie could not hear anything through the closed window. "What song is she singing?" she whispered. Over the past two weeks, she'd found that agreeing with Rose's more fanciful statements kept her talking; challenging them could shut her down.

"That Thanksgiving song," Rose said. "You know it."

Callie started to sing: "*We gather together to ask the Lord's blessing* . . . Is that the one?"

"That's it!" Rose said, excited.

"It's the only Thanksgiving song I know. I didn't hear it from the tree," she confessed.

"I know that, silly girl," Rose said playfully, reminding Callie of the old Rose. *Silly girl* had been one of Rose's nicknames for her when she was little. *Silly girl, sweet girl, sweetie, honey,* all pet names, and all uttered fondly, always followed by a pat on the head or a kiss on the cheek.

"And just how do you know that?"

"Because you're singing it in a completely different key." Rose laughed. "And you should know that your singing was flat."

"You know that's not true."

Rose smiled.

It had been Rose who'd once told Callie she had perfect pitch, something Callie later found out was true. Perfect pitch was something they'd recently discovered was genetic. It must have come from her father, the musician. Olivia couldn't sing a note.

"Tell me more about the trees," Callie said. "I know they talk to you. What else do they say?"

"Did Dr. Finch tell you to ask me that?"

"No. Has she been asking you the same thing?"

"For years." Rose sighed, closing her journal.

"And what have you told her?"

"I haven't told her anything. She wouldn't understand."

"You've talked to Towner about the trees."

"Towner's different. She's one of us."

"What does that mean, 'one of us'?" Callie sat forward in her chair.

"You know."

Callie shook her head. "I really don't." *But did she?*

"I'm pretty sure Towner could hear them if she listened."

"The trees?"

"Only the oaks."

"What do they tell you, Rose?"

"A lot of things."

"And they sing. Better than I do, evidently." Callie smiled.

A shadow crossed Rose's face.

"Sometimes."

"Towner says you are documenting all the oaks in Salem. That you think they can lead you to the current location of the old hanging tree and to the missing remains of our ancestors."

"They will."

"Is there a connection between the oak trees and the banshee?"

"There has always been a connection."

"What is it?"

"It's a long story." Rose sighed.

"I like your long stories." Callie remembered sitting at Rose's feet, listening to myths and fairy tales she'd never heard before or since, epic stories Rose seemed to make up as she went along.

"You have to go to Thanksgiving," Rose said.

"I have time."

Rose seemed reluctant, something Callie had never seen before. Finally, taking a deep breath, she began. "It was an oak tree who was her jailer."

"The banshee?"

Rose shook her head. "She wasn't a banshee then, she was a goddess."

Callie nodded. "Got it."

"The goddess's captors imprisoned her in the tree, stealing her power, as well as that of the oak, and changing the nature of both. When she finally escaped, she had turned."

"Turned?" Callie repeated. Rose had used the word *turning* in her written confession to Rafferty. Was this where she'd gotten the expression? "What do you mean by 'turned'?"

"Imprisonment changed her nature, as it tends to do. She 'turned' from a goddess to a banshee."

Callie considered Rose's own imprisonment. After she'd gotten out of the state hospital, she'd never been the same. She had "turned" into a different person. Was Rose talking about herself? Hadn't she told Rafferty that she, herself, was a banshee?

"The banshee hid in the tree's upper branches, sending her mournful cries on the wind to herald death. When she was finished with the Old World, she voyaged to the New, on a sailing mast made from the bloody trunk of the stricken oak, landing in Salem in 1630 with the second wave of Puritans. It was a difficult voyage and only a handful of the passengers and crew survived. She nested in the rigging of the cursed ship and whispered doom on the chilling winds, then followed it with blame. When the crops failed, when the savages bloodied the border settlements, her winds whispered tales of devils into the ears of sleeping Puritans. The whispers built into wails and then to shrieks. As the snows came, the shrieks were heard in every home in Salem Village, turning neighbor against neighbor. When she took her final revenge, it was the oak who paid the most dearly. For they didn't burn those condemned as witches in the New World as they had in the Old, they hanged them from the branches of the sacred oak."

Callie stared. Rose had spoken as if the words were memorized, a combination of poetry and fairy tales. It was disturbing.

"You don't believe me," Rose said.

"You . . . surprised me, that's all."

"You asked a question. I answered you."

"I never heard that story before," Callie said, quite certain Rose had never told her anything like this.

"There's a lot you haven't heard." Rose considered her. "You don't like the story."

Callie reached for something neutral to say. "It sounds like the kind of story you were dead-set against when I was a child."

Rose looked at her curiously. "What do you mean?"

"I mean the kinds of superstitious beliefs that got our ancestors hanged as witches. You're an academic, Rose. You know better."

"I'm not speaking of witches, I'm explaining the banshee."

"And why is this banshee—this evil thing—a woman?"

"She's a diminished goddess. Trapped by the priests who made her small, imprisoning her and stealing her powers."

"And a devil?"

"Not a devil, no."

"But evil. And female."

"Yes, but not in any human sense. She was once a goddess. So of course that's female. After her imprisonment, she turned into something else entirely."

"The banshee."

"That's right," Rose said. "Look at me. And you'll see her."

"You're a banshee?" Callie said without disguising her disbelief.

"Rafferty told you . . . You know that I am."

"I don't accept that, Rose."

Rose grabbed Callie's hand urgently and held it tight. "The banshee isn't a woman in any traditional sense. She represents the change. The *turning*." Rose held eye contact as she spoke. She squeezed Callie's hand and leaned forward. "Do you understand?"

Callie shook her head.

"It's important that you understand."

"I'm sorry," Callie said. "I really don't." Rose's eyes were the most focused and intense Callie had ever seen. "I'm trying, but I just don't get it."

"You will," Rose said. The proclamation sounded like something between a warning and a curse. "Go," she said, dropping Callie's hand and turning away. "Go to your stupid dinner. I don't want to talk about this anymore." Then, blinking her eyes, pointing a finger at Callie, she spoke again, in a voice that was nothing like her own: "God will give you blood to drink!"

Rose's voice echoed off the walls.

A chill ran down Callie's spine. Unlike the unfamiliar story Rose had just told, Callie was certain that she'd heard this phrase before. She waited for Rose to say something else, something that would give her a clue, but Rose was pulling away, turning inward. Her eyes had taken on the same emptiness Callie had seen when she first arrived.

Callie had accepted Marta's offer to drive her to the Whitings'. But she hadn't expected to leave Rose so soon, so she sat in her car in front of the tearoom and called Zee. "I think I may have set her back," she admitted, telling Zee what Rose had said. "I wish I hadn't pushed her about the banshee—I don't know what got into me."

"You didn't do anything wrong," Zee reassured her. "She has these outbursts. You witnessed it yourself, the day she woke up."

"She said something different that day."

"She has catchphrases. *Ciphers. Courting the strike. Blood to drink.* She's used that phrase before. When I asked her about it, she said those were the words the banshee spoke to her before the murders."

For a moment, Callie felt as if she couldn't breathe. God, was that where she'd heard those words? The night of the murders?

Zee was still talking, but Callie had lost track of the conversation.

"Are you still there?" Zee asked.

"Yes. Sorry. My phone must have cut out," Callie lied.

"Look, I wouldn't worry about it. I'll stop by the hospital tonight and sit with her. You enjoy the holiday."

Callie sat in the car for a long time after she hung up. Her mind was reeling. "Stop," she said aloud to herself. Marta was due any minute, and Callie couldn't be a nervous wreck when she showed up. Why had she said yes to this invitation?

"You'll be okay," Towner had told her earlier when she expressed doubts. "Pride's Crossing may be just over the bridge and only one town away, but it's a world apart."

Callie took a few deep breaths to center herself. Better.

She turned on the radio. The Thanksgiving song she had sung for Rose was playing.

Marta's Volvo was even older than the one Callie drove. She pulled into the driveway and reached across to open the door. Callie grabbed her suitcase and put it in Marta's backseat.

Marta looked at her for a long moment, as if taking her in. "Happy Thanksgiving," she finally said.

Immediately, Callie noticed that Marta was dressed more glamorously than she had been at the fund-raiser. The neckline of her green velvet dress was cut low, and she wore a simple gold cross dangling into her cleavage, creating an intentional focal point. Her black hair, pulled back severely the night of the fund-raiser, hung straight and shoulder length. She wore red lipstick and had shadowed her eyelids a smoky grey.

Callie hadn't wanted to wear her dress to the hospital, so she'd packed it, intending to change at the house, as Towner had said she was planning to do.

"Thanks for picking me up," she said.

"I'm glad to do it."

They both fell silent. It was a beautiful day. Along Salem's North River, the view began to open up, and by the time they crossed the Beverly Bridge, there was water everywhere. Harbors merged and stretched inland, speckled with empty moorings. To the right of the bridge, most of Salem Sound was visible: from Marblehead north toward Gloucester and Rockport, to the border islands along the horizon. Lighthouses dotted the shore. Even with the windows up, Callie could smell the salt air.

After the bridge, Marta turned right and followed the coastline north. The sun sat low on the horizon as they drove past stately old oaks and maples standing guard over the mansions of a grander era. The bare trees cast long shadows as the sun filtered through them to the water, reflecting back intermittently in blinding flashes.

"Will Mr. Whiting Sr. be there?" Callie asked, glad to have thought of something to say.

"Finn? Yes, of course. The entire family will be there. And a lot of guests as well. It's a big, traditional Thanksgiving feast: everything from pottage to cheese, not soup to nuts as the usual saying goes. In this case, most of the nuts will be seated around the dinner table."

"Oh, really?" Callie was amused.

"There are a few characters . . . the privileged kind."

Callie instantly regretted accepting this invitation. She wasn't in the mood for a party, especially after what had happened at the hospital. And she dreaded the thought of the kinds of people who were likely to be the Whitings' guests. She forced herself not to think about it. Not right now.

"All very nice people," Marta said, reading her. "Emily can be a bit of a snob, but you'll get used to her."

"The Whitings talk only to God?" Callie joked, remembering a poem Rose had taught her to recite, saying the words aloud.

> *"And this is good old Boston,*
> *The home of the bean and the cod.*
> *Where the Lowells talk only to Cabots,*
> *And the Cabots talk only to God."*

"That was the Cabots, not the Whitings," Marta said, sounding annoyed. Then, recovering her composure, she pointed. "But Henry Cabot Lodge used to live right over there, through those trees."

Callie squinted in the direction Marta was pointing. Even with most of the leaves gone, the trees were so thick it was impossible to glimpse the legendary mansion that lay beyond them.

"Just follow my lead if you don't know what fork to use."

"That's right. I forgot you were the expert on etiquette." Callie didn't mean it as sarcastically as it sounded.

Once again, a scowl crossed Marta's face. "That was Emily taking me down a peg, putting me in my rightful place in the social pecking order."

"Oh God," Callie said. "Is that what she's like? Can we just turn around now? I'll treat you to a nice meal at the Hawthorne."

Marta laughed. "You'll enjoy yourself. I saw the seating chart this morning. You're next to Paul. I think he reconfigured Emily's classic arrangement. Usually she's got her darling boy seated right next to her. I don't think Emily has noticed the switch, but there'll be hell to pay when she discovers it."

Callie said nothing. Now she really wanted to turn around.

They passed a train station. Callie read the sign: PRIDE'S CROSSING. The name said it all, she thought, wondering what illness she could feign to convince Marta to let her out here so she could take the train back to Salem. Marta put on her blinker and turned right. They drove down a long gravel driveway that was tunneled by two rows of mature elm trees, the afternoon light streaming through their web of branches.

"The grounds here were designed by Frederick Law Olmsted," Marta said. "It takes four full-time groundsmen to maintain them."

"Beautiful," Callie said, meaning it.

"Impressive, isn't it? That's one of the last rows of standing elms in New England."

The driveway turned as it approached a massive stone house, the line of elms giving way to rhododendron and mountain laurel. As they drove on, the view opened up to reveal a seascape that stretched past the border islands east toward the British Isles. Finally, Marta pulled up in front of the house. To say that Pride's Heart was impressive was a gross understatement. It was a Georgian-style mansion that stretched over almost an acre of oceanfront land. The style was very British, making it clear to Callie that the Whitings had never fully left their ancestry behind.

A uniformed butler came out to greet them, and Marta handed him her keys. Callie started for her overnight bag. "Leave it," Marta said. "Darren will have someone take it to your room."

They approached the front door, and Darren held it open for them. As soon as they entered, a housemaid took their coats and directed them to the library.

At the far end of the dark mahogany-paneled room, an attractive middle-aged man with greying hair sat at a huge partners desk. He was talking on the phone and stood when he saw Marta and Callie, gesturing that he'd be right with them.

He ended the call and walked over to them, kissing Marta on the cheek. "So glad you could join us. Don't you look lovely in your green dress."

"Callie, this is Paul Finnian Whiting," Marta said.

Finn looked at Callie and then shot a quick look at Marta, before taking Callie's hand. "Finn," he said. "So nice to meet you, Callie."

Callie felt his charm immediately. And though Emily Whiting was an attractive woman, it was evident her son's striking good looks came from his father's side of the family, except that Finn's eyes weren't deep blue, like Paul's. Callie couldn't name the color of Finn's eyes, though he held eye contact more than long enough for her to get a good look. They were odd, really: mostly brown, with a darker ring around the edges, and a few flecks of green and blue. He wore glasses with frames that reflected the same combination of colors and lenses with a magnifying effect that made his long lashes look even longer.

"Emily will be down in a minute," he said. "Meanwhile, may I get you two a drink?"

"I'll have my usual," Marta said.

"Callie?"

"Sure," she said. "What are you serving?"

"Anything you can name."

"I can't name much, I'm afraid." When it came to drinking, she was a lightweight. She didn't get silly; she didn't confuse her words. Instead, she became exceedingly quiet. The social skills she had, which were limited at best, were overrun by self-consciousness.

"I'm having an Old-Fashioned," Marta said. "If that helps."

It didn't.

Finn caught her confused look. "Whiskey, sugar, bitters, lemon, orange, and a cherry on top," he said.

"Sounds delicious," Callie said.

"Far too delicious." Marta smiled.

"An Old-Fashioned sounds good to me," Callie heard herself say. *What in the world am I doing here?* she wondered. The house was designed like a movie set, not a real home. Everything looked like old money. Callie could feel herself scowling as she looked around the library at the leather-bound collections; the marble and mahogany double partners desk was almost as large as any bedroom she'd had growing up.

The door opened, and young Paul entered. "Callie O'Neill," he said, surprised, before breaking into a wide grin. "So nice to see you again."

"Drink?" Finn asked his son.

"I'm driving," Paul said. "I have to run an errand to Salem."

"On Thanksgiving?"

"He has to go to Ann's for an hour or so. He cleared it with me weeks ago," Emily said, sweeping into the room.

Her hair was beautifully done, her navy silk dress and shoes perfect, but there was a weariness in her face. As soon as Emily smiled, though, the weariness disappeared. She kissed Marta on both cheeks, European style, then turned to Callie, extending her hand. "I'm so glad that you could make it, Callie. Did my husband offer you a drink?"

Finn held up the Old-Fashioned he'd just finished mixing.

"Paul's team is helping to restore the rock churches of Matera," Emily explained to Callie. "Ann Chase is helping Paul with research."

"Is that what they're calling it these days?" Finn said.

"I'm running late, and I know you want me back ASAP," Paul said, as he shot his father a look.

"Damned right," Finn said. "You know, Callie, a few years back there was a program called Ditch the Witch. I gave them a huge donation."

"Not from the foundation!" Emily was horrified.

"Yes, from the foundation. I considered it urban renewal."

Marta smiled. It was clear she had heard this kind of banter before.

"All those witches running around casting spells on our young men." He held Callie's glance for a long time.

"That's not true," Emily said.

"It is true," Finn said. "Your son is obviously bewitched enough to be leaving us on Thanksgiving."

"Just for an hour," she said. "You've been on the phone longer than that today."

"An hour, a week. It's straight to the devil after that." Finn looked at his son, who wasn't taking the bait. "The devil has once again been raised in Salem."

"Some would say the devil never left Salem," Marta said.

"Witches don't worship the devil," Paul said. His tone had the good-natured edge of an ongoing discussion. "They're Celtic Pagans in Salem; they don't even believe in the devil."

"That's exactly what they want you to think," Finn said, wagging a finger.

"Oh, I seem to remember you having a bit of interest in all things Celtic yourself, back in the day." Marta smiled.

"These days I'm into all things Celtic." Finn laughed, changing the hard C to a soft one. "I'm a big basketball fan," he said to Callie.

"Have you met Ann Chase, Callie?" Marta asked. "Salem's most famous witch?"

"I haven't. Isn't she the one who did the painting you bid on?"

"The witch paints now, too?" Finn said. "Is there any end to the talents of that woman?"

"It was part of her collection," Paul said. "She didn't paint it."

Callie saw a look pass between Marta and Finn.

"If you haven't met Ann, you should go along with Paul," Marta said. "Ann's hosting her yearly open house today. She's quite something."

"Would you like to come along?" Paul asked. "You'd be more than welcome."

Callie saw Emily tighten her lips. Her smile was beginning to look like a grimace.

"But I just got here," Callie said, with a nervous laugh. "I don't want to be rude."

"Oh, go," Marta cajoled. "Besides, I have some foundation business I need to speak to Finn and Emily about before the party starts."

"Go right ahead, dear," Emily said, recovering her composure. "We'll all have a few drinks in your absence and be much more polite to each other upon your return."

"This is a bit awkward, don't you think?" Callie said as Paul held the car door for her.

"What is?"

"All of this. Marta pawning me off on you."

"Don't be silly. I'm delighted to have your company."

Paul helped her into the old MG, its windows open, and then walked around to get in and start the engine. Callie struggled with her seat belt. "It sticks a bit," he told her, and reached over to free it, pulling the belt out and buckling it in one quick motion, his arm brushing against her, sending a chill she hadn't expected. They headed back down the magnificent driveway.

"Your father certainly seems to disapprove of the woman we're going to see," Callie said. "I'm guessing that's part of the reason we're going."

He grinned. "If only it were that simple."

"I guess nothing is that simple," she said.

"You'd be right about that." Paul pulled the car onto Route 127 and gunned the engine. By the time she rolled her window up, any chance Callie'd had of keeping her wild hair tamed was swept away by the wind and damp salt air.

The MG crested the Beverly Bridge and Paul turned left, taking the back streets along the harbor into downtown Salem.

Ann Chase lived down by Derby Wharf in a yellow house on Orange Street. It was the same part of town where Callie had lived with her mother and Rose and the Goddesses.

They parked and got out of the car. Callie noticed a plaque on the side of the house: 1727.

"It was once owned by an arresting officer for the court," Paul remarked. "Not long after the hysteria ended. Ironic that a witch lives there now. But that's Salem."

It was a small home. The door was open, and, as they walked in, Callie first noticed the huge fireplace, which took up most of one wall. There was a fire burning, fragrant with herbs and pine, with a cauldron full of hot mulled wine that hung from its lug pole. The house smelled the way real estate agents want houses to smell, Callie thought. Like apple pie and cookies.

It was crowded. There were several young women in the living room, dressed in variations of black, some serving food and drinks, some standing around chatting. In the far corner, standing next to a man dressed as a pirate, was a towering redhead in a long purple crushed-velvet cape. It might have been the way the floors tilted, or it might have been her stature, but Callie realized that all paths and all eyes led directly to her. Feeling their presence, Ann Chase turned to face them. She looked Callie over seriously and then looked at Paul.

She broke into a slow grin.

Ann walked over, kissed Paul on the mouth, and extended a hand to Callie.

"Have we met?"

"If I'd met you, I'm certain I'd remember," Callie said. It was almost exactly what Paul had said to her the night they met, but the meaning was completely different.

Ann laughed. "Let's get you something to drink."

She led them to a smaller L-shaped room, low ceilings with sparse furniture: a rocking chair, an antique spinning wheel. On the far wall, herbs were drying over its fireplace, and on the facing wall were the portraits: dark oil paintings made darker by time. There were depictions of gods and goddesses and other Wiccan imagery: Pan,

Bacchus, Samhain fertility beasts, expertly lit and hung sixty inches on center like a gallery show.

"Ann is a collector of sacred imagery," Paul said. "Her collection has become almost exclusively Celtic, which is why she donated the Roman painting, but you'd be surprised how many of the same images occur in early Christian art." He pointed to some of the pictures. "Sacred fish, trees, crosses. All Pagan symbols that were later appropriated by the early Christians."

"Interesting," Callie said, looking more closely at a painting of a harp. It appeared to be made from the branches of a tree. The title read: THE FOUR-ANGLED MUSIC.

"What's this?" Callie asked. "A tree?"

"Uaithne. The Oak of Two Blossoms," Ann said. "It belonged to one of the Celtic gods and was stolen by his enemies. But the god had bound the music, and the harp would not play until he commanded it. When he called to it, the harp sprang to life, killing nine of his enemies with the music it made."

"I thought harp music was supposed to be comforting!" Callie said. She'd been considering learning to play, or at least getting some recordings of harp music for her practice. There was evidence that the harp could play vibrational tones that had a soothing effect on both humans and animals, though the human ear could not detect them.

Paul noticed the discomfited look on Callie's face. "Ann knows quite a bit about Irish mythology," he said. "As well as sacred imagery. She's helped identify many of the images we're finding in the rock churches we're restoring in Matera. Contrary to my father's remarks, she and I are actually doing some research here."

Among other things.

Ann looked at her and broke into a grin, as if reading Callie's thoughts. She motioned to a young woman carrying a tray of drinks. "Help yourselves."

"What's in it?" Paul asked.

"Eye of newt," Ann answered. Then she said, "Seven-Up, cloves, Hawaiian Punch. And just the tiniest sprinkle of fairy dust."

"Will we fly?" Paul asked. He took a glass of punch and handed one to Callie.

"Not unless you've ingested something earlier from Mummy's medicine cabinet."

"Not today," Paul replied.

"So," Ann said to Callie. "Tell me about yourself."

"There's nothing much to tell."

"Oh, I'm certain that's not true."

"Why don't you tell me about yourself first?" Callie said. The last thing she wanted to do was talk about herself to this woman.

"Oh, I'm just your average little witch, from your average little town. Let's try this another way." Ann took Callie's right hand and held it while looking into her eyes.

Luckily, it wasn't the hand with the scar. Callie felt the warmth from Ann's hand travel up her arm.

"You're a healer," Ann said. "There's a strong connection with music. And a stronger one with Salem, I see."

"Callie's living in Salem," Paul volunteered.

"Only for the past few weeks," Callie said. She fought the urge to reveal that she'd lived here before, but she couldn't escape the feeling that Ann knew who she was. If she did, she said nothing.

"You have a prodigious gift. It scares the hell out of you . . . as well it should." Ann started to drop Callie's hand, then held it for a moment longer, a strange look passing over her face. "You've suffered a great deal of loss. And, oh my dear, much worse."

She looked at Callie as if to say, *I know exactly who you are. You're not fooling anyone.*

Callie pulled her hand back, but it dropped limply to her side. It seemed to take a moment for Ann to shake something off, but, when she regained her composure, she took Callie's hand back and held it in both of her own until, slowly, from the fingers up, Callie's sleeping arm began to awaken.

"What the hell?" Callie demanded. Her whole arm was tingling.

"Parlor tricks," Ann said. "As well as being rude and invasive, I did a little binding spell on you. Please accept my apologies."

A binding spell. She'd heard the phrase before, just as she had heard the curse Rose had uttered earlier. Once again, she had no idea what it meant.

"We'll talk later," Ann said. "When there aren't so many people around." Other guests arrived, and Ann moved off to greet them.

"Not if I can help it," Callie muttered.

"Don't worry, we're not staying much longer," Paul said with a laugh.

They finished their drinks and Ann returned, carrying a package she handed to Paul. "Herbs for Mummy," she said. Then, so quickly Paul didn't notice, she slipped a small packet to Callie. "Use it," Ann whispered in her ear. "It works."

Ann turned and walked away, her purple robe floating behind her.

Paul checked his watch. "We should head back now," he said.

Callie was still shaken and didn't question him as he guided her back to the car. She looked at the packet in her hand. On the side was a scrawled note: *Put these herbs under your pillow each night to stop the evil spirits from invading your dreams.*

Callie stared at it, then at the package Paul had placed on the console between them. She picked it up and smelled it. "Weed? The witch is a weed dealer?"

"She's the intermediary. She gets it from the pirate. For medicinal purposes only."

"Oh sure." Callie laughed. "That's what they all say."

"It helps my mom with the nausea from the chemo."

Callie was silent then, suddenly touched by the errand.

CHAPTER TWELVE

November 27, 2014
THANKSGIVING, SALEM

With his unquestioning acceptance of spectral evidence,
Cotton Mather was largely responsible for both the scope
and the duration of the witch hysteria of 1692.
—ROSE WHELAN, *The Witches of Salem*

"WORKING ON THANKSGIVING DAY?" RAFFERTY SAID, REC-
ognizing the assistant district attorney's number as he picked up the
phone. "Should I be worried?"

"Right back at you, Rafferty. I was planning to just leave you a
message."

"What message?" Rafferty's tone was suspicious.

"I'm hearing a lot of noise about this thing with Rose Whelan,"
the ADA said. "I have a petition here in front of me, signed by almost a hundred people who want to reopen the Goddess Murder case.
Helen Barnes and some of her friends have reportedly been calling the
governor."

"Great," Rafferty replied. He'd told only a handful of people he'd
been quietly investigating the case. The last thing he wanted was to
make it official.

"And there's something else."

"What's that?"

"They told him that you're biased and slowing things down because Rose lives with you. Is that true?"

"No! Not exactly," Rafferty clarified. "Eva Whitney left Rose a tree in my wife's—our—courtyard when she died. Rose sometimes slept under it. Before she was hospitalized this last time." He took a breath. "And Towner gave Rose a room over the tearoom. She almost never used it, though."

There was a long silence.

"What about Rose's niece?"

Rafferty said nothing.

"She's been visiting Rose at the hospital. Isn't she living with you now?"

"Technically, she isn't related to Rose."

"But she *is* staying at your house?"

Rafferty didn't answer.

"This doesn't look good," the ADA said.

"No, it doesn't," Rafferty admitted. He was more upset that people were beginning to question who Callie was than by the implied accusation of bias.

"Let me talk to a couple of people and see what they think. I'll get back to you. Happy Thanksgiving."

Rafferty hung up the phone. *No good deed goes unpunished,* he thought. He shouldn't have dropped by the station; he should have gone straight to Yellow Dog Island with Towner. It was Thanksgiving, for God's sake. What had he been thinking?

There was nothing he could do about his history with Rose. And nothing new was going to be resolved over this holiday weekend. At the moment, that was about all he felt thankful for.

Out on Yellow Dog, Rafferty had to wait for one of the women to lower the ramp so he could get to the island. It was May Whitney's policy to pull up the ramp for security, since boaters were often eager to explore these border islands. The last thing they needed out here was unwanted visitors. To say the women at Yellow Dog Shelter were paranoid was an understatement, but they had reason to be. Though the place was considered a safe house, every so often an abuser was successful in locating his escaped partner, and the resultant rage had consequences the women here knew only too well.

Rafferty understood the need for security. Still, it seemed odd today, since they were expecting him. Usually, when they knew he was coming, they would leave the ramp down. Something was going on. He'd have to remember to ask May about it.

The women were gathered in the red schoolhouse, a place usually reserved for the lace makers, who would sit in a silent circle as they worked, their pillows in their laps, passing bobbin over bobbin. On those days the only voice heard—aside from the occasional call of a seagull on the wind—was that of the reader, often May Whitney herself, who would stand in front of the room reciting what she called "random acts of literature." The most damaged women, the newbies, wore lace veils. The veils hid their identities, but they also did something else, something better. Looking at life through the handmade lace provided a different perspective. It filtered reality by making the ordinary beautiful.

Today, the place was bustling. The circle of chairs had disappeared, and tables lined the room for the annual Thanksgiving brunch. Rafferty looked at the women and felt bad about his earlier lack of gratitude on this special day of thanks. By the time you landed on Yellow Dog Island, you'd left everything familiar behind except life itself. The abusive spouse, certainly, but everything else as well, including your extended family and your daily life. And yet, they were all celebrating, thankful to be here and safe. This year, he noticed that the children's table was set with more places than ever.

"The ones who have children do the best," May had told him once, after he'd been called to the island to fend off a husband who'd managed to locate his estranged wife. "It gives them reason to hope," she'd said. She'd been carrying a loaded shotgun, just in case the police didn't arrive in time. "Something worth fighting for."

He wondered. That day, as he'd cast off with their father in handcuffs, the man's children had stood at the top of the ramp crying. *The ones with the children do the best,* he'd thought, as he piloted the vessel away. Maybe. They were safe from abuse. Which was the point. But the children still looked so sad, as they watched their father being taken away from them, maybe forever. The next night he'd seen May's lights: two lanterns in her window, the signal she'd use when she needed to relocate people. *Two if by sea.* May and her network moved women and children to other safe houses when things looked dicey— part of what May called the New Underground Railroad, a network of safe houses up and down the coast. Seeing those lights, Rafferty had understood that the children and their mother would leave the island and become new people in a new place.

Now Rafferty watched as the women who were currently staying at the shelter walked in groups, back and forth between the schoolhouse and the big house, carrying platters of food. Towner had arrived on the island earlier this morning to help with the brunch preparations. Each year his wife closed the tearoom on Thanksgiving Day, and every year it saddened her, because it left the women who worked there at odds. Most had lost contact with their families, and the holiday reminded them of this wound. Almost every one of them had started out on Yellow Dog Island, then gone on to work at the tearoom when they were ready to rejoin the world. Each of them was welcome today—the women would have celebrated in their honor—but the island wasn't someplace they wanted to return to. They just wanted to move on.

Which was exactly how Towner felt about the place. She loved May well enough. And she did everything she could to support the shelter. But coming out here was difficult for her. Too many bad memories. Towner had grown up here, the victim of an abusive father, who had blinded her mother, leaving her brain-damaged as a result of one of his rages. The trauma Towner had suffered was the reason May did the work she did, and why Towner helped her. Still, coming out here, even to visit May, was difficult.

But if Towner hated to come to Yellow Dog Island, May hated to leave it even more. Except for this yearly Thanksgiving brunch, the two women communicated only via e-mail and cell phone. As soon as it was over, Rafferty and Towner always went directly to the Whitings' Thanksgiving dinner, and then Towner would spend the rest of the weekend at Pride's Heart trying to recover.

Rafferty had no blood family on Yellow Dog Island, but he saw far more of the place than Towner did; there was always something going on that required police attention. He and May were uneasy relatives. Her rescue methods, though effective, were often illegal. She was not opposed to using firearms to protect the women and children she sheltered, and, though she'd deny it if questioned, more than once she'd fired a warning shot across the bow of the police boat as it approached her island. He understood that most of what she was doing was necessary; he secretly applauded her efforts. But as a cop, he wished he never had to deal with her.

He walked against the crowd to find his wife and see what he could do to help.

"And *I* told *you* I'm not comfortable doing that!"

He could hear Towner's raised voice the moment he entered the old Victorian that had been May's house for as long as anyone could remember. He found the women in the kitchen. Towner stood, red-faced, her hands on her hips, looking every bit the petulant child she had once been under May's care.

May sighed and turned back to her dishes. "Have it *your* way."

Towner pushed past him and out of the house.

"I don't know why she still comes out here every year," May said to him, shaking her head. May's long curly hair was pinned on top of her head with chopsticks, but it still escaped its confines. Though her expression was calm, it was a practiced look. The pitch of her voice had risen by several notes.

"You know why she comes. You insist on it. You're the only family she's got left." Rafferty gestured out the window toward a burned-out house at the far end of the island. "Why don't you get rid of that place?" As if he hadn't suggested this to her a hundred times already. That place, or what was left of it, was full of sadness and ghosts.

"You think it's that simple? What, I just call someone and presto? Or we put on hard hats and tear it down? This is an island, Rafferty. Things aren't that easy out here."

Rafferty didn't dispute the fact. Nor did he remind her that they'd accomplished other, far more difficult tasks over the years. He'd offered to demolish the house himself, but May had refused his help. She was holding on to the wreckage of the burned-out old building. As what? A reminder of the worst time of Towner's life? She'd lost someone she loved very much in that fire.

"Out of sight, out of mind," he said.

May glared at him.

"Seems like everyone's a little tense out here," he said, trying to lighten things up.

"It's Thanksgiving, Rafferty. What do you expect?"

"What about the heightened security? You trying to move someone?"

"You know better than to ask me that," May said, turning away from him.

He left May and found Towner where he knew she would be: standing on the hill overlooking what had been her childhood summer home.

"You want to go?" he asked, as she buried her head in his chest. "We can go right now and be at Pride's Heart before she even notices we're gone."

"No," she said, forcing a smile. "I'm okay. I can stay. But only if we can sit at the kids' table."

"Done. You can even have crayons."

CHAPTER THIRTEEN

It is Shown that on Account of the Sins of Witches,
the Innocent are often Bewitched,
yea, Sometimes even for their Own Sins.
—*Malleus Maleficarum*

CALLIE AND PAUL PULLED INTO THE DRIVEWAY AT PRIDE'S Heart just in time to see Rafferty and Towner emerge from the woods beside the big house.

"How was Yellow Dog Island?" Callie asked as she got out of the car, glad to see familiar faces. "Did you have a good visit with May?"

"It was fine," Towner said too quickly. Rafferty rolled his eyes and shook his head.

"We just docked at the boathouse," Rafferty said, eager to change the subject. "We've got my Whaler tied up behind the big boat. Is that all right?"

"Perfect." Paul shook Rafferty's hand and hugged Towner. "So glad you could join us."

"Wouldn't miss it," Towner said, turning to Callie. "You're just arriving? I thought Marta was picking you up."

They walked together toward the door, Rafferty and Paul in front, Callie and Towner lagging behind, just out of earshot.

"Paul took me for a little ride," Callie said.

Towner lifted an eyebrow. "A ride, huh?"

Callie shook her head. "Tell you later."

Paul beat Darren to the front door, opening it and holding it for them to enter, then directing them all to the library. Other guests had arrived during the time he and Callie were gone; servers were circulating, offering hors d'oeuvres and champagne, but, Callie noted, Finn was still playing bartender.

"Ah, Paul and Callie, you're back!" Finn called, speaking much more loudly than when they'd left him. "With Towner and Rafferty! Come on in and join the usual suspects."

After they greeted Emily, Paul said he had to go back to his car, he'd forgotten something. "Walk with me," he whispered to his mother. "I have something for you."

Callie realized that he'd left Ann's package behind, probably to hide it from Rafferty. She looked around the room and recognized several of the better-known guests: a bestselling author, a middle-aged man who had once played second base for the Red Sox, and Archbishop McCauley from Boston. She felt completely underdressed.

"I'd never have come if you'd warned me it was this fancy," Callie said quietly to Towner.

"Which is exactly why I didn't," Towner said. "It's time for us to change into our prom gowns." Her tone was light, but Callie could tell it was forced.

They quietly left the library and reentered the main hall just as a new guest arrived in a full-length mink coat, which she insisted on keeping rather than handing off to one of the maids. Callie and Towner watched the woman compel the maid to follow behind her as she headed into the party.

"I guess she'll take it off after everyone sees it," remarked Callie.

Towner smiled and started up the stairs. "Come on, I'll show you to your room. Emily told me she's giving you the one right next to ours."

They made their way to adjoining rooms, stopping at Callie's first. An antique canopy bed stood by a window that looked out on the water. Across the room was a sitting area with overstuffed chairs facing a deep fireplace, a single log burning and crackling. Callie's bag had been unpacked, her dress steamed and hung.

"Was everything in this house designed to look like old money?" whispered Callie.

Towner looked at her with appreciation. "Astute observation."

"Every piece of furniture I've seen so far is an expensive antique, but it's all . . . too perfect. You can tell that a designer arranged everything just so," Callie said. The furniture didn't match; the designer hadn't made that mistake, but the pieces were too similar. True inherited money tended to show a mismatch of pieces far more random than this.

"Do you have a design background, Callie?"

She shook her head. One of Callie's foster mothers had been an antiques dealer. "One of my better foster homes," she said.

Towner waited for her to continue. She didn't. "You are full of surprises."

"I shouldn't have said anything," Callie said. "It just seemed curious, that's all."

"Finn Whiting comes from a family of farmers. The money you see here was made generations later, illegally. His grandfather was known for running rum and guns. He built Pride's Heart just before he died. The original 1600s house was over there." She pointed toward the woods. "Still is, though it's part of Paul's boathouse now. When the grandfather died, Finn's parents inherited his money and furnished the place with the best antiques from the auction houses of Boston, New York, and London."

"I guess crime does pay."

"For a while. Finn's father lost the rest of the fortune in a bad business deal. He died young and penniless. But not before he found a wife for his son. One who had the fortune to replenish the Whitings' coffers and the pedigree to take the family legitimate."

"Emily?"

"Emily Sprague of Hingham. *Mayflower* and founding father descended. Not only did her ancestors throw tea into Boston Harbor but the family later made a fortune importing it from China. She's as rich as they come."

"I thought rich girls don't marry poor boys." Callie quoted the movie version of Fitzgerald's classic.

"They do when they look like Finn Whiting," Towner said. "And when there's a shotgun involved."

Callie raised an eyebrow. "Paul?"

"Surprising, huh? Just proves you can never tell about people."

Callie liked the woman more now. It made Emily seem almost human.

Callie pulled her dress off the hanger. "This isn't as formal as what everyone is wearing downstairs," she said. It was the knee-length black sheath she had purchased for the fund-raiser.

"Don't worry about it," Towner said. "You can dress it up with the pearl necklace I brought."

"I couldn't take your necklace—"

"I inherited it from Eva," Towner said, as she headed into her own room. "It's really not my style, but it will look great on you."

Callie put on the dress and played with her hair, pulling it back into a knot and then letting it go again. It was a mess: too curly and just plain wild. And she still wasn't used to being blond. When Towner came back with the pearls a few minutes later, she had already changed into her own dress, a long black cap-sleeved wraparound gown. "God, you look gorgeous," Callie said. Towner's reddish blond hair hung perfectly straight and shoulder length.

Towner smiled, holding out the pearls.

"You sure?"

"They'll look perfect with your dress."

They stood in front of the mirror while Towner fastened the clasp. Then she pulled Callie's hair back off her face and neck, winding it into a loose chignon. "Like this, I think." She held it back. "You'll look great." Towner motioned for Callie to sit at the mirrored dressing table so she could pin her hair for real. "Very sophisticated."

Callie's phone pinged.

Towner noticed the worried look on Callie's face.

A text had come in from Zee: *Rose fine. Awake and eating turkey dinner in her room.* Callie put the phone away, relieved.

"Everything okay?"

"Better now. Rose was having a bad day. But Zee says she's okay. Eating Thanksgiving dinner and giving thanks."

"I'm guessing the thing Rose is most grateful about today is your return."

Callie tried to shrug off the compliment.

"I mean it," Towner said. "She always worried about you."

The remark touched Callie in a way she hadn't expected. Her eyes filled up with tears, and she turned away.

Sensing her awkwardness, Towner changed the subject. "So," she said, "are you going to tell me what you were up to with Paul? Where did he take you on your 'little ride'?"

"What do you know about Ann Chase?"

"Ah," Towner said. "You met Ann."

"She and Paul are involved, I'd say."

"Ann's involved with a lot of people."

"How old is that woman?"

Towner laughed. "She's in her fifties, but you wouldn't know it."

"That's some strong magic."

"You're interested in Paul," Towner teased.

"Not really," Callie lied. "He's probably too young for me."

"He's twenty-five."

"Five years too young."

"Almost twenty-six."

"And I don't like that he's involved with the witch."

"Paul's been sleeping with Ann on and off for years. Ever since he turned eighteen. Nothing serious, but Emily hates it."

"I can understand why. Is he even out of college? He could be her son."

Towner laughed. "Well, he obviously likes older women . . ."

Callie rolled her eyes.

"Ann's actually nice," Towner said, and Callie could tell she meant it. "She's just got enlightened attitudes about sex. Free love and all that. Comes from her neohippie days. I have to say the men in this town seem to enjoy her."

"Apparently."

Towner laughed. "She's really okay. She's helped Rafferty with a number of criminal cases."

"How?"

"She's very intuitive. Psychic. She reads lace, which is why I gave her most of Eva's pieces. She even reads for me at the tearoom sometimes."

"What do you mean, she 'reads lace'?"

"It's kind of like reading a crystal ball, but she uses lace. She gazes into the patterns, and she can see visions. My grandmother Eva used to do it. Ann reads the lace, then tells Rafferty what she sees. Sometimes it helps him figure things out, sometimes not."

"Do you read lace, too? At the tearoom?"

"No," Towner said. "Not anymore. Though I do sometimes have visions."

"Visions. Really?"

"Oh, don't act like you don't know what I'm talking about."

Callie stared at her.

"Salem is full of people who have 'gifts.' Who seem to know things they shouldn't or things that haven't happened yet. You're obviously one of us."

"Us?" Callie wasn't sure how she felt about being outed. "You sound like Rose."

"Takes one to know one. I fought my visions for years." Towner pushed a hairpin into place. "So much so that I almost made them disappear. Now they're more like glimpses. Ann has taken the opposite approach, honing her skills. She's what they call a seer."

"And a witch."

"That, too."

And a drug dealer.

"Medicinal use only," Towner said. "Until the dispensaries finally open up."

"Wow," Callie said. "That was impressive."

Towner smiled. "A bit of proof for the skeptic."

Callie thought about it. "So you read minds?" She'd seen Ann do the same thing this afternoon. It was disconcerting.

"It comes and goes. Some people are easier to read than others. Ann's great at it. She's also renowned as an herbalist. She's developed treatments for mercury and lead poisoning, chelation agents that work with fewer side effects. She's a powerful force in these parts."

"I'd say so," Callie said, thinking about Paul.

"Towner? You up here?" they heard Rafferty call from the next room. Towner walked over and opened the door that connected them. "Wait for us here if you like," she said to Callie. "John only takes a few minutes to get ready, and I know you don't want to go back down there by yourself."

"The wine cellar was once a speakeasy," Finn was telling a group of guests who were waiting to go down in the elevator. He was about to start his third tour of the day, leading guests behind the paneled bar and down the elevator into the cellar. Callie had gotten separated from Towner and Rafferty moments after returning to the library; now she was on her third Old-Fashioned. She should have said no to this last one, but Finn kept handing them to her, not asking if she wanted another. She'd have to stop letting him catch her eye. The way he kept staring at her, she was wondering if he was flirting. She glanced over at Paul, who was engrossed in conversation with a group of wealthy-looking older women.

The truth was, Callie was having trouble with all this ostentation. The Whiting Foundation might fund everything from schools to soup kitchens, but the way the Whitings lived didn't seem right. *Conspicuous consumption* was a phrase the nuns used when they disapproved of people who hadn't taken the same vows of poverty they had. Conspicuous consumption certainly seemed the name of the game in the Whiting mansion. Callie realized she was scowling.

"A bit much?" Rafferty asked, joining her. She noticed he wasn't drinking. Just a club soda with lime.

She should have followed his lead. "A tad."

"Wait until you see their artwork in the dining room. A collection of Dutch Old Masters. I'm told it's about to make the rounds of European museums."

"It all seems slightly obscene," she murmured, staring directly at the woman who'd come in wearing the full-length mink.

"Would you like to see the speakeasy, Callie?" Finn asked, his fingers searching for the hidden elevator call button.

Rafferty had been observing Finn earlier, the way he kept gazing at his own reflection in the wall mirror. *Classic narcissist,* Rafferty thought, though he had to admit that most people found Finn Whiting charming. What wasn't charming was the way he also seemed to be gazing at Callie in that same mirror. *"I'd* like to see it," Rafferty answered, breaking the long silence that followed Finn's invitation.

Paul swooped in, taking Callie's arm. "Come take a walk with me," he said, directing her toward the door. "I haven't had a chance to show you the grounds."

They left the library together and headed across the hall, cutting through the kitchen and into the butler's pantry. "First rule," Paul said, taking her half-empty drink. "Never try to keep up with my father. The man's got an iron liver, and he's just getting started."

She blushed. "Thanks for the warning."

He emptied her drink down the copper sink. Then he poured two mugs of coffee. "Cream? Sugar?"

"Black is good," she said.

He gave her a mug and then led her outside through the pantry door, holding it open for her. It was a warm day for November, but it was still chilly outside. He took off his jacket and held it out to her. "Unless you want me to go back for the mink? We could find some red paint to splash on it in the barn."

So he had overheard her. "I shouldn't drink."

"Everyone should drink," he said. "Though probably not the way my father does. If it weren't for alcohol, none of this would exist." He looked around. "Which I'm sure would devastate you."

"You make me sound like a horribly judgmental person," she said.

"Do I?" His words feigned innocence, but his look was playful.

They walked up the gravel driveway. She could smell the woodsmoke from the chimneys. As they approached the stables, some dogs ran out to greet them. Hunting dogs that looked as if they'd just emerged from the Currier & Ives print she'd seen in the library.

"Be careful of Jasper there, he'll steal that right out of your hand. He has quite a coffee habit."

Callie held her cup high and laughed as the dog jumped for it.

"Leave it, Jasper," Paul said, and the dog reluctantly stopped and fell into step behind them, with a look that was at once disappointed and ashamed.

Callie noted the dog's expression and spoke for him in a sad and goofy drawl, propelling her voice until it seemed as if Jasper were saying, "I don't have a problem. I can quit anytime I want."

"Ventriloquism?" Paul looked amused.

"One of my many talents."

"Is that part of sound healing?"

"It could be. If it saves your dog from his addiction."

"It sounds as if my dog is in heavy denial. How'd you learn to throw your voice?"

She sighed. Towner's assertions about her "gifts" were still fresh in her mind. "I've always just been able to play with sound."

They passed the stables, which were empty.

"Do you still keep horses?" Callie asked, happy he hadn't probed further.

"Mum isn't riding much these days. She boards her horse at Myopia Hunt Club now. The last bastion of snobbery for the horsey set," he said in a voice meant to mimic hers.

"I didn't say it."

"I beat you to it." He laughed.

She saluted him with her coffee mug. He really did have a devastating smile.

They walked in silence for a few minutes, their steps crunching on the gravel driveway, Jasper peeling off, tracking a scent that enchanted him. "Come on, I'll show you where I live when I'm home," Paul said, cutting to their right.

Callie recognized the spot as the one from which she'd seen Towner and Rafferty emerge earlier. Tall pines stood in rows as if they'd once been planted for harvesting as Christmas trees and then abandoned to grow. She saw the long path winding through the trees disappearing into the fairy-tale darkness of the woods.

She took the first step into the woods, and a twig broke under her feet. The sound paralyzed her. A squirrel scurried up a nearby pine. She willed herself not to panic but couldn't move.

"Come on." Paul faced her, smiling, holding out his hand. He took her mug and put it down on a nearby tree stump.

She managed to step onto the path, not taking his hand. Her heart was beating too fast.

He turned and walked ahead.

She wanted to turn back, but she knew she was being ridiculous. Instead, she stayed a few feet behind him on the narrowed path, forcing herself forward while dodging tree roots, stepping on soft moss and pine needles. She'd been in this kind of place before, among far more twisted trees in the most terrifying moment of her life. Where the hell was he taking her, and why had she followed? Suddenly, the path steepened and arched downward. He turned back and took her arm instead of offering his. "Careful," he said. "Watch your step here."

She hesitated.

"It's okay, I've got you." A hand on her arm, the other on her hip, he lowered her slowly to the ground. "There," he said as her feet touched earth. He paused ever so slightly before he released her, bringing them close enough to feel his warm breath on her face. He smelled like salt air and sage. He stepped aside, and the view opened up to a hidden cove. The sloping lawn and deep unmowed grass that swept toward the ocean looked like a receding wave. Callie immediately thought of the Andrew Wyeth painting *Christina's World,* the girl sprawled on the grass, the houses on the hill behind her.

The first building Callie saw had the look of a small lighthouse with a narrow observation tower. It was built into the side of a red granite ledge; a main level sat on the grassy land, and a lower story was on the beach underneath, just feet from the water's edge. The lighthouse towered another four stories from the main floor, becoming glass as it ascended, more church spire than warning light. The second building had all but disappeared into the landscape, the roof on the same angle as the hill's slope, its color a camouflage of rock and sea grass.

"Come this way," Paul said, leading Callie over a pebbly path, across more red granite, and around the back of the house to a half-hidden door on the ocean side of the building.

At their approach, a huge seagull raised itself and hung on the wind, dropping a quahog on the rocks below in an effort to break open its shell.

They entered the house in the side of the hill. Callie could see that it was designed with all of its windows on the ocean side. Paul opened the shutters to the sunset. Even in the half-light of impending dusk, the place seemed made of silvery water and golden sun.

The first things she noticed were the brass compasses and an old-fashioned diving helmet. They looked like they belonged in a steampunk exhibit. Then, in the center of the large open room, she was surprised to see what looked like another house: it was only one room, with a large walk-in fireplace similar to the one she'd seen at Ann's, and it had leaded-glass windows that were opened.

"This was the original house," Paul said. "Built in 1640. My great-great-grandfather wanted a larger house but didn't want to disturb the historic value of this one, so he simply surrounded it. It's the kitchen now."

Callie had to duck a little as she passed under the low beam. "Sixteen forty, huh?"

"It was home to one of Salem's accused witches."

"One of your family members, I assume?"

"I'm afraid so." He smiled.

Paul led her through the small room and out the other side, ducking so as not to bump his head on the ceiling beam. The far door led back into the main room, revealing more steampunk gadgetry.

"My grandfather was a bit of a collector. He spent a fortune on this stuff, among other things. Come on, let's catch the sunset," Paul said, walking her through the living room and up a spiral staircase to the glass tower.

At the top of ninety steps was a tiny octagonal room with 360-degree views. All of Salem Sound was visible, as was much of the North Shore from Beverly to Manchester and south to Marblehead Light. Straight ahead were the border islands: the Miseries, Baker's, Children's, and Yellow Dog.

"That's Norman's Woe," he said, pointing to a tiny speck of rock in the far distance, three towns away.

" 'The Wreck of the *Hesperus.*' Longfellow."

"You know the poem?"

"I do."

It was one of her favorites.

It was a breathtaking view, with the sun setting over the land west of Beverly Harbor, its reds and oranges flaming as it dropped. Paul and Callie watched as the eastern sky deepened and melted into water, the spreading darkness building above and below the horizon until, as it slowly erased its dividing line, the sky blackened, and the stars became visible.

She could feel Paul close behind her in the darkening room, breaching the personal space she usually protected.

There was usually one thing men wanted from her, and, generally, it was the same thing she wanted from them. She didn't have relationships per se but a series of short-term boyfriends. She liked the dance, the approach/avoidance of attraction. But relationships were far too complicated. Her therapists called it a fear of intimacy. Maybe it was. Callie thought of it as something more positive. Quick hits, no entanglements, that was her philosophy. Was that what Paul Whiting wanted, too? She was pretty sure it was. *Just turn around and find out,* she thought. It would be easy enough to turn.

Something stopped her. She didn't step away, nor did she turn to face him. Instead, she kept her eyes on the horizon for several minutes until the sun finally disappeared.

"They'll be looking for us," Paul said, finally, breaking the spell.

There were no lights on the stairway, and as they descended they moved into complete darkness. "Wait here," he said.

His footsteps echoed on the metal stairway, dulling as he walked across the wooden floor. Finally, Callie heard a pop and a rush of sound and saw old gas lamps flicker to life. He came back and took her hand for the final few darkened steps. The gaslight filled the main room with a warm glow. As she moved into the space, she noticed the desk in the corner; his laptop was open, his books and papers spread all over. Above the desk was the painting of Minerva he'd bought at the auction.

"Oh, this is where she ended up," Callie said.

"Goddess of Wisdom. I figured she'd help me in my work. She's also the Roman goddess of music," Paul said. "Which should interest you."

"And medicine, I remember. Wisdom, medicine, and music?" Callie said, recalling the auctioneer's description. "That's quite a workload. I hope the owl is helping." She squinted at the painting. "He looks a bit sinister up close."

"In many cultures, the owl is the portent of death."

"Like the banshee?"

"Kind of. The name for owl in Scottish Gaelic is Cailleach, the crone aspect of the triple goddess, which is sometimes thought to be connected to the banshee. But that's Celtic mythology," he said, "not Roman."

Callie took another look at the owl. "I wouldn't want those eyes staring down at me every day."

"The owl gets a bad rap. She's really a creature who can see what others miss. Some may be deceived, but she never is."

"She?"

"Oh yeah." Paul nodded. "The owl is definitely female."

Callie could see the bedroom through the French doors, his unmade bed. He noticed her looking at it. His cell phone rang. He removed it from his pocket, glanced at the number, and turned off the ringer. She could see the Salem phone number, Ann's name flashing. The house phone rang next.

My, she is persistent!

This time Paul picked up.

"Hello, Mother."

Emily said something, and he answered, "Absolutely."

He hung up. "We've been summoned." Then, doing his best impression of an English butler, "Dinner is served."

Outside, a blanket of fog fell on the cooling water and settled in for the night.

CHAPTER FOURTEEN

November 27, 2014
THANKSGIVING, PRIDE'S CROSSING

> *Religious suffering is, at one and the same time, the*
> *expression of real suffering and a protest against real*
> *suffering. Religion is the sigh of the oppressed creature,*
> *the heart of a heartless world, and the soul of soulless*
> *conditions. It is the opium of the people.*
>
> —KARL MARX

THE CAVERNOUS DINING ROOM WAS ILLUMINATED ONLY by candlelight, casting a halcyon glow on every dark wood surface. Sterling silver sconces circled the perimeter, taking Callie back instead of forward in time, from the gaslight of Paul's boathouse to the tapers of an even earlier period. Candlestick holders of gold, silver, and bronze dotted every available surface, a hundred tiny flames casting overlapping circles of gilded light. Soft music played—strings, both violin and harp—and muted the accompaniment of the foghorns from the distant harbor.

As soon as everyone was settled at the table, three strapping young waiters appeared and stood silent, a magical presence ready to anticipate everyone's needs. Just as Marta had predicted, Callie found her place card next to Paul's. If Emily objected, she showed no sign. She smiled across the table at her son.

Archbishop McCauley said the blessing. It was not a biblical verse but a traditional Thanksgiving poem, "Fire Dreams" by Carl Sandburg.

> *"I remember here by the fire,*
> *In the flickering reds and saffrons,*
> *They came in a ramshackle tub,*
> *Pilgrims in tall hats,*
> *Pilgrims of iron jaws,*
> *Drifting by weeks on beaten seas,*
> *And the random chapters say*
> *They were glad and sang to God."*

Callie could see that the poem summoned the ghosts of memory for her hosts. Suddenly, she saw what they were remembering as she surveyed the table, and, for a moment, there were more people in the room than the guests and silent waiters. Callie stared as time shifted and history revealed itself: Finn's eyes were cast down and looking to his left. Next to him sat his dead father, now young again. He had the same dimpled chin and a mischievous grin. The scene altered and Callie saw Finn's father's part in the early, shadier family business, collecting money from bars in Dorchester.

Another shift, and they were back at the table. She smelled the pleasant doggy odor before she spotted the beloved dog, not Jasper from this afternoon but one they had loved and lost, a black and white springer spaniel, lying underneath the table, at his master's feet, and another sitting next to him, a golden retriever. Finn sat at the head of the table, looking every bit as regal as the Celtic gods Callie had seen in Ann's gallery. In the space between Finn and Emily was Paul's paternal grandmother. Callie turned to Emily, and her history was as clear as if it had been written: DAR aunties, cotillions, and then college and a hasty marriage that came with Catholicism, a religion she'd never embraced. She also felt Emily's illness, lurking in shadows the candlelight couldn't reach.

Callie looked at Marta, and another portrait emerged. Her face was softer. Her eyes sparkled with innocence and youth. She was much younger, a teenager, sitting on the pier in front of the boathouse, dangling her feet in the water. A young man sat facing her, his back to Callie. Was it Finn? His hair was lighter but had the same thickness and wavy texture.

"Excuse me," Paul said to Callie, pulling her out of her visions. "I couldn't hear what you said."

"Nothing," Callie said, waving him away, unaware that she had spoken aloud. What *had* she said?

She glanced around the table, seeing everyone as they were—no one was staring at her. Good. Then the waiters approached bearing oysters and caviar and began serving.

"All right, now that everyone is here," Emily said to her son, "tell our guests what you've been doing in Matera." Her speech was more animated than Callie had noticed before, but her eyes were a bit bloodshot. "We're lucky. We have him home until February because they have to do some work on the rock church he's been restoring. Some water damage or something they have to clean up before he can go back to Italy."

Paul smiled, waiting for her to finish.

"As most of you know, Paul is doing his Ph.D. dissertation on his work restoring the ancient churches in Matera," she said to her guests, then proudly turned to her son. "Go ahead, tell them what your team is finding over there."

"It's a joint venture between my adviser at Harvard and the Vatican, with grants from the Italian government. Basically, we're restoring the frescoes in some of the rock churches," Paul said, addressing the table. "So far we've discovered several ancient paintings of Jesus, one of Mary, and a number of symbols common to many religions around the world."

"Have you switched your focus to archaeology, Paul?" the Mink Woman asked.

"I'm still focusing on art history and comparative religion, but I'm specializing in ancient religious symbols and relics. I work with archaeologists to interpret what they uncover."

"That sounds fascinating," Mink Woman said. "Your mother said these were rock churches, right?"

"I've heard about those rock churches," Rafferty said. "Aren't they actually caves? There are supposedly hundreds of them."

"There are," Paul said. "All hand carved out of *tufo* stone. They say St. Peter preached in those caves."

"Really," Rafferty said. "They date back that far?"

Paul nodded. "Matera dates back even further. The Sassi district was the site of a prehistoric troglodyte settlement. It's one of the oldest continually occupied spots on earth."

"The *tufo* dries tears," the archbishop said. "Isn't that the phrase?"

"It is," Paul said, sounding excited. "They think it has other healing properties as well; it's rumored that the early Christians performed ceremonies there using methods taught by Jesus himself."

"What kind of healing?" the Mink Woman asked. "The laying on of hands?"

"Sound mostly," Paul said. "Different tonalities and durations. Chanting was probably a big part of it."

"That sounds like what you do, Callie," Towner commented.

Everyone at the table turned to look at Callie as the archbishop asked, "What is it you do?"

"Callie practices sound healing," Towner explained.

"As in 'Music hath charms to soothe a savage breast'?" McCauley asked, taking a spoonful of soup.

"I'm trained as a music therapist," Callie said. "But sound healing is a little different. It removes the therapist from the equation. The sound works directly on the patient. I often use singing bowls in my practice."

"The bowls are better for healing than for salad." Towner winked at Callie.

Paul said, "You use salad bowls to heal people?"

"Ignore her." Callie laughed. "I use bowls made of quartz crystal. I have one for each chakra. They vary in size and tone."

The archbishop looked confused. "I don't understand. They make music of some kind?"

"Are they like the small brass ones used in Tibet for meditation? You rub a wand around the perimeter to get the tone?" Paul asked.

"Exactly," Callie said, more pleased than she'd admit. Then he grinned and she knew: It was the smile. Not the perfect blue eyes or the sandy brown hair. The smile—just a bit crooked on the right side— was what got him the girls.

"One of them brought Rose Whelan back from a catatonic state," Towner offered.

"We don't really know what brought Rose back," Callie said quickly.

"I'm afraid I'm still not following," the archbishop said.

The waiters took the soup bowls and replaced them with nuts, celery, and olives.

Paul dipped his index finger in his water glass, and then drew it around the rim of his wineglass until it created a vibrational tone. "Like this?"

The Mink Woman gasped. "Don't hurt that beautiful glass."

Paul hesitated.

Emily dismissed her concern. "Don't worry. That crystal is almost unbreakable. It's been in my family forever." She motioned for Paul to continue.

Once again, he drew his finger around the rim until the tone became clear and strong.

"That's a G note," Callie said. She looked at the archbishop. "It's associated with the throat chakra; the tones are thought to have a soothing effect on the corresponding energy center of the body. So, if you had bronchitis, for example, I might use the G, and also an F to treat the heart chakra, which rules the lungs."

"And this isn't normally part of music therapy?" Marta asked.

"Not traditionally, no. Sound healing is a new approach."

"Not so new if St. Paul used it in the caves of Matera," Emily said.

"St. Peter," Finn corrected.

"What'd I say?"

"St. Paul," he said, smiling at her slip.

There was goose, and venison, and every food that might have been offered in New England during the first Thanksgiving feast. And Paul had been right about the pace of the alcohol. There was endless wine, a different vintage with each course. Callie followed his lead and sipped slowly.

Eventually, though, the talk turned to Rose.

"Rafferty, got any inside information about that Halloween murder up on Gallows Hill? I've been seeing quite a bit online about it," Finn asked the police chief.

"Talk about the stuff of fiction . . . the woman who killed him claims to be a banshee," the author said.

"She didn't kill him," Rafferty said quickly. "The kid died of a cerebral hemorrhage brought on by a drug overdose."

"Still," Finn said. "It's got the Salem websites going crazy. The comments sections are really heating up. They're calling for exhumation of the bodies of the girls who were killed decades ago. Seems like they're dying to finally pin it on that woman."

"What?" Callie said. She'd heard there was a petition going around requesting DNA testing. She'd seen it in the paper. But she had no idea people hated Rose quite so much. She could feel Towner watching her reaction.

Rafferty looked as if he were about to take Finn down, but Towner shot him a look and interjected, "There's no evidence Rose had anything to do with those murders. There never has been."

"Why not do DNA testing on them? It's the only way to know for sure," Mink Woman said.

"Not necessarily," Towner answered. "They could find DNA on the bodies from anyone with whom they came into close contact, before or during the murders. Isn't that right?" She turned to Rafferty. From his scowl, it was clear he didn't want to talk about it.

"How can they find any DNA twenty-five years after the fact?" the archbishop asked. "Won't the bodies have decomposed?"

"Some physical evidence could survive," the author chimed in. "Their hair, for instance. And if the murderer left a hair or something like that . . ."

"I heard they were buried in their Halloween costumes," Mink Woman said. "That no one paid to embalm the bodies. Wouldn't some of the clothing have survived? There could be DNA found there . . ."

"They weren't buried in their costumes," Rafferty said.

"Well, there wouldn't be much left if they didn't embalm them."

Rafferty didn't take the bait, but he held up his hand to stop the conversation.

"Dear God!" Emily said. "Let's drop the subject. And find something less gruesome to talk about."

Not for the first time, Callie was grateful for Emily's rescue. Her hand shook as she reached for her fork. How could this be happening? The thought of the town digging up the bodies of her mother and the others filled her with a panic she couldn't rid herself of. Why hadn't Rafferty told her they were seriously thinking of exhuming them? She could feel his eyes on her, as well as Towner's. She reached for her wine and took a deep swig.

There was a long silence, and finally Finn acted on Emily's cue. "What's the other news from across the bridge? I heard that my friend Mickey Doherty has opened two more haunted houses," he offered.

"Oh, I love Mickey Doherty," Emily said, encouraged by the new subject. "He's such a funny man."

"Anyone who makes a living as a pirate reenactor is okay by me. It's the creative economy at work," Finn said.

"I hear he opened a new side business tracing tourists' ancestry back to the Salem Witch Trials," Towner said.

"He's made that a business?" Emily seemed surprised.

"Sure. Six degrees of separation and all that. I'd bet a good number of tourists can find a connection if they look back far enough. The same way anyone whose family has been around here long enough does," Paul said, turning to Callie to explain.

Finn nodded agreement, adding for Callie's benefit, "Many people whose families have been here for generations have accused witches in their families."

"Some who've been here for generations have both accusers and accused," Marta said, looking directly at Finn.

"Marta has both," Emily explained. "Goodwife Hathorne was both at various points during the hysteria. She's related to Rebecca Nurse, too, if I'm not mistaken."

Callie looked at Marta. Rafferty, too.

"No, not Rebecca Nurse," Marta said. "But there were others on our family tree as well as on the Whitings'. Take it back far enough, and we could all be accused of communing with the devil."

"You're not clinging to that erroneous mythology," Finn said to Marta. "You still think the devil was raised in Salem?"

"Not personally, no," Marta said. "But even most of the accusers came to believe that they were wrong about the accused, though they still believed that the devil had been raised. They came to think the entire episode was a 'delusion of Satan.' A misdirection of sorts."

"What does that mean?" Paul asked.

"The devil is a known trickster," the archbishop offered.

"Be careful what you say, Father," Finn warned, turning back to Marta. "You Protestants are pretty free with your labels. We are Catholics, and Catholics *were* the devil to these people. Catholics and Native Americans. And don't forget the poor Quakers. They used to hang them on sight as agents of the devil."

Marta shrugged. "This isn't my belief system, Callie. I'm just telling you that they thought he was on the loose. Only not in the places they had searched.

"The stage had been set with the Catholics for a long time," Marta said. "Back in England, Catholics did the persecuting and executing, mostly of Puritans. So deep hatred and a desire for revenge was carried with the Puritans on their ships to the New World."

"After the Reformation, England wasn't the best place for Catholics, either," Finn said. "Mistakenly convinced that the New World was the place to avoid religious persecution, my Catholic family headed over on the third voyage of the *Mayflower*. We landed in Salem to find it populated by Puritans, the people who hated us most. The Whitings quickly hightailed it out of Salem Town and over to what is now Pride's Crossing. Even so, they had to practice their religion in secret. There weren't any clergy nearby, as preaching Catholicism was a hanging offense."

"Pride's Crossing was where all the outcasts ended up," Emily said.

"Still is," Paul joked.

"But you said your family was Puritan," Callie said to Marta.

"But Marta's family had been suspected of witchcraft once before," Emily said. "Isn't that right, Marta?"

"How nice of you to mention that again." Marta smiled at Emily, then turned to Callie. "Even though they were related to one of the hanging judges, under the circumstances, my family thought it best to create a bit of distance from the center of town."

"The same way my family did," Finn said.

"But Whiting's wife and Hathorne's widow ended up accusing each other," Paul said. "And they both landed in jail."

"The Salem courts were willing to hear an accusation by a Catholic?" McCauley sounded shocked.

"By then, everyone was accusing everyone, and no one was safe. The Puritans thought the devil could be anywhere. Things were out of control and everyone knew it. But it was the end of the trials, so no one was hanged. The Court of Oyer and Terminer had been dissolved, and spectral evidence was being questioned. It all came to a close when the governor's wife was accused."

Callie was becoming more and more uncomfortable. The talk of exhumation had triggered the darkness from her past; her deepest fears were curling around her and trying to join her at the table: the murders, the nightmares, that ever-present thing . . . She took another gulp of the wine a waiter had just refilled.

"What about banshees? Aren't they agents of the devil, too?" Mink Woman asked.

"And we're back to this," Emily said, frustrated.

"According to Church history, banshees originated as paid mourners," Archbishop McCauley explained. "A leftover from the Pagan religions. The more mourners a family could afford, the higher their stature. When the early priests went to Ireland, they banned the practice. The mourners were mostly women; they wore their hair long and uncovered, which was forbidden at the time. And the keening was otherworldly. The banshee myth originally comes from those women. The priests outlawed keening, making beggars of the mourners."

"They let them starve?" Mink Woman had the grace to sound horrified.

"No, but the women had to rely on the charity of the Church to survive."

A shadow crossed Marta's face. "Lovely."

"It made for easy converts. And that was the point," McCauley said. "I'm not condoning the behavior any more than I do the proselytizing missionary programs of any organized religion."

"And that's all there is to the banshee legend? Some ostracized women who were converted?" Mink Woman was clearly disappointed.

"The story I've heard is that they were part of the pantheon of Celtic goddesses, diminished by the early Christian clergy," Paul said.

It was very similar to the story Rose had told Callie just this afternoon.

"Well, that might be true," acknowledged the archbishop. "The priests certainly wanted to rid the Celts of their Pagan practices. I do know that some of the original families who hired the mourners claim they still exist. The Church might have tried to erase or even absorb early beliefs, but they often persisted, or reemerged as something else. In this case, a portent; the banshee became something from the spirit world predicting death."

"But they've never been considered human, have they?" Towner asked, repeating something Rafferty had said earlier.

"Not that I know of," the archbishop said.

"I've heard them referred to as spirits who predict death," Mink Woman said, making a moaning sound.

The baseball player followed with *Twilight Zone* music.

Towner glanced at Rafferty as if he might have something to add, but he said nothing.

"But surely, human or spirit, no one believes they're killers," Towner said.

"Do you think, inside, every one of us is a killer?" All eyes turned toward Callie as she spoke.

"What?" Towner asked.

Callie was unaware she had spoken the words aloud, and they shocked her. She had no idea where they came from or what they meant, but she could feel Rafferty's eyes on her, staring. *Great, now I've got the chief of police suspicious of me.* "Nothing," she said. "Sorry."

It was almost midnight by the time they finished dinner. Finn herded everyone back to the library for port and cheese. Callie found herself at the rear of the group and stumbled at the threshold. "You're tired," Towner said. "I don't think anyone would mind if you skipped the port."

"I am tired," Callie said, catching Towner's subtext immediately.

"I assure you, I won't be far behind," Emily said, joining them. "It's lovely having you in our home, Callie. We'll meet in the morning." She smiled. "Not too early, though. We girls need our beauty sleep." She sounded sincere enough, but her expression and her words seemed at odds.

"I'm heading home," Marta said.

"Do you need Paul to walk you through the woods?" Emily asked, just as her husband came back to round up stragglers.

"I can walk you," Finn said.

"No one needs to walk me home." Marta's tone was clipped. "My car is still right outside."

Callie excused herself, thanking everyone and saying good night. She was vaguely aware of the eyes on her as she started up the stairs. She tried to walk without holding the railing, but it was difficult. She hoped she hadn't embarrassed herself too much during dinner. Towner had been right to give her an excuse to leave the group.

She made her way back to her room. It was warm and softly lit, her bedclothes were laid out, and a fluffy robe had been placed next to them. She wasn't just tired. She was exhausted. And drunk. She undressed and put on her nightgown, thinking of how she had promised to meet Emily for their session the next morning. She hoped she wouldn't have a hangover. As she was putting her dress in the closet, she knocked her jacket off the hanger, and something tumbled to the floor: the parchment envelope Ann had given her. "Put these herbs under your pillow each night to stop the evil spirits from invading your dreams." Callie scoffed out loud.

Not bloody likely.

She glanced out the window in time to see Paul's car pull out, and she watched as he went down the driveway, stopping just momentarily before turning left toward Salem. Off to see Ann Chase, she assumed.

She sat on the bed and exhaled, reclining onto the pillows and staring at the packet. The room was warm. She shook the herbs and then brought the envelope to her nose and sniffed it. It smelled like hemp. How appropriate. And something else. Anise. It wouldn't help her sleep. Nothing ever did.

At least meditation would relax her. She sat on the bed and leaned back against the pillows, letting herself sink into a trance. It was something she did every morning and again every night. But tonight it wasn't working. The smell of the herbs was too strong.

Callie tossed the envelope into the fireplace and watched it begin to burn, gasping when it suddenly exploded into flames. A bolt of pure light shot across the room, barely missing her as it grazed the couch across from her bed without leaving a mark. It extinguished itself as quickly as it had flared, putting out the fire as well, leaving the room in total darkness. The sound of the wind screaming down the chimney sounded like Rose's banshee. In the distance, Callie swore she could hear the bells from St. James's Church ringing . . .

No one had come back for her. All night long, she had done as Rose had told her to do. She did not open her eyes, and she didn't come out of her hiding place. Her fingers were clenched around the rosary, hurting her palm, making it bleed and sting. But now she felt the late fall sun warm through the leaves of the hedge, and she could hear the church bells ringing, carried on the wind. Slowly, she pushed through the bushes and made her way downward through the tangle of trees, following the gravel path until she came to the crevasse.

At first, she believed they were alive. The movement of the trees, as the wind played their branches, created a hypnotic rhythm, and, for a moment, their stilled bodies seemed to dance, the blood from their wounds pulsing with the rhythm of her own heart. The scent of impending weather was on the east wind. The music of the spheres played a mournful requiem through the tangled branches, and, finally, it was the music that made her understand what she was seeing.

It was her mother and the goddesses. And all who had come before. Salem's accused and executed. This was a blood grave.

CHAPTER FIFTEEN

November 28, 2014
Pride's Crossing

Those hanged never admitted to witchcraft.
Those who confessed were spared.
—Rose Whelan, *The Witches of Salem*

THE GIFT CERTIFICATE TOWNER HAD CREATED WAS propped up on the glass table of the orangerie where Callie had agreed to meet Emily this morning. It was a room of glass, full of light and ocean breeze. Potted citrus trees lined south-facing windows, their scents perfuming the ocean air. "I'm sorry my son is being so rude this morning."

"How so?" Callie asked. She was exhausted from her nightmares; still, she noticed how yellow Emily's skin looked in the morning light.

"He appears to have spent last night in Salem." Emily glanced out the window at the expanse of unseasonably green lawn, and Callie followed her gaze. "He's not a very good host, I'm afraid. He invited you; he should be entertaining you."

"He's been quite entertaining so far," Callie said, cutting the line of conversation short. She suspected Emily didn't like her any better than she liked Ann Chase. The reminder that Paul had spent the night with Ann made Callie remember part of her dream: the bells, the hypnotic rhythm of the trees—and that packet of herbs bursting into flames. Or was that part real?

"You don't have to do this," Emily said, indicating the gift certificate. "This . . . music thing."

"I understand you've tried traditional music therapy before?"

"After one of my surgeries."

"And did it help?"

Emily shrugged. "Not a great deal."

Callie took a long look at Emily in the natural light. "Your color looks off."

"My liver is failing. Which means they'll take me off the chemo. And my husband won't rest until he finds yet another treatment I don't want to endure."

"Do you meditate?"

"I can't do yoga," Emily said, raising her brows. "My bones are too brittle."

"I was thinking less of yoga postures and more of a seated relaxation exercise, if you're open to it."

"I guess so." Emily shrugged.

"Let's have you sit there," Callie said, pointing to an overstuffed chair in the corner.

Emily walked over and sat primly on the edge of the chair. She had the air of someone who was humoring a fool.

Callie put on some soft music: Bach cello solos.

"Yo-Yo Ma," Emily said.

"Good choice?"

"We shall see."

"I've had some favorable results with it." The cello was the perfect balance of odd and even harmonics. Bach's compositions had the opposite effect, with the music spaced at even intervals, something that never occurred in nature. But Callie liked Bach. His key changes often served to highlight particular energy blockages in a patient. And, in Callie's opinion, there was no better expression of Bach's cello music than Yo-Yo Ma's. Callie adjusted the sound levels, turning up the bass slightly. She pulled a small pillow off the couch, gently placing it behind Emily's head while encouraging her to sit back. "Better?"

"Yes."

"Any pain or discomfort anywhere else?"

"No."

"Okay then. Close your eyes and listen for a few minutes." The piece always reminded Callie of water. "Let it wash over you."

She'd recently heard Yo-Yo Ma interviewed. He said the Cello Suite No. 1 in G Major was all about flow. She took Emily's hands and placed one on her lap and the other on the arm of the chair, palm up. Then she stepped back and watched. After a few minutes, Emily settled back into the chair. Instead of speaking, Callie began singing harmonic sounds: a third, a fifth. Then she closed her eyes and began to sing random tones, trying to find the home note that would vibrate at the core of Emily's being. Unlike Rose's home note, Callie could easily determine Emily's; it was still very strong. But people need a balance of all frequencies to ground them. As with many people who've become ill, it was clear to Callie that Emily was missing some of them. By singing different notes, using an open vowel sound, Callie was able to fill in the missing tones.

The effect on Emily was subtle but immediate. Callie watched her muscles loosen, saw her sink even deeper into the chair.

"How do you feel?" Callie asked.

"All right," Emily said.

"Good. Let's stay with this, then."

Yo-Yo Ma continued playing Bach, and Callie stopped singing as the notes descended. She watched the music take Emily with it. As the cello notes began to climb again, Callie harmonized with them a second time, visualizing the song carrying Emily over water. Emily's breathing slowed, and Callie could see her truly relax into the chair. Outside the room, the waves broke rhythmically on the granite ledge below, creating their own counterpoint.

Callie sat in the chair opposite and quickly fell into her trance state, resting there for just a moment before letting her breathing sync up with Emily's. The scent of oranges deepened, and Callie recognized the falling feeling that often accompanied the merging; she let herself go with it. She searched for the cancer, sought the inevitable catch in her breath where the music skipped, snagging itself on the rougher edges of illness. The chest was clear. If there had been cancer there before, it was gone now. She moved through Emily's body once, then again. It might not be cancer she was feeling but it was something, and it was in the liver. Two patches. One was green, the same green as the lawn just outside the window, and the same texture. Centered in the green was a patch of brown, and beyond it a much darker object she couldn't make out. As Callie tried to decipher its meaning, the music shifted from the Bach to a melody that was dissonant and much louder. Organ music? It reminded her of church. No—the opposite of church. The sound jolted her out of her trance, her eyes snapping open. The organ music disappeared, and Bach was back.

What the hell had just happened?

She was relieved to see that, whatever it was, it had not affected Emily, who still sat with her eyes closed and her hands where Callie had placed them. Her muscles were slack, and her face seemed to have softened. Callie turned off the music and opened the window wider to the ocean below, taking a few deep breaths to compose herself. It was a warm day, and the sun filled the room with light. The only sound for quite some time was the waves moving against the rocks.

Finally, Emily opened her eyes.

"How do you feel?" Callie asked. The color had come back to Emily's cheeks, and her expression was far more relaxed.

"The same," Emily said. "No change at all. How long have we been here?"

"Not too long," Callie said. "A little over an hour."

Emily looked surprised. "Well, at least the music was lovely."

It was fine with Callie that Emily wouldn't acknowledge the improvement. It wasn't uncommon for a patient not to notice subtle change. "You should rest now," Callie said. She needed to rest, too. She often picked up released energy during healing sessions, and usually she could shake it. But this session had been weird. What was it she'd seen? Or heard, for that matter? "Do you want me to close the window?"

"No," Emily said, dismissing Callie. "Leave it open. I like the fresh air."

"Oh, good," Paul said, coming in the front door as Callie was getting ready to head up the staircase to her room. "I've been looking for you. Towner and Rafferty had to leave early. Something about Yellow Dog Island."

Callie was surprised by the change of plans. "Are they okay?"

"I think so. They just wanted me to let you know."

"Oh," she said, wondering what she was supposed to do now. Was she still supposed to stay for the weekend? Were they coming back?

"Let's go for a ride."

She frowned. She really needed time to herself. "I'm tired."

He looked skeptical. "You can't be tired. It's only noon."

"I need rest after a session."

"You look quite rested to me."

"Wish I could say the same," Callie said, looking him over. "Rough night?"

"What?" He feigned an innocent look.

"Your mother thinks you're rude."

He laughed dismissively. "My mother thinks I'm perfect."

Callie shook her head, smirking at him. "That's not what she said behind your back."

"Come on. Let me redeem myself." He smiled.

That smile!

"And there's something I want you to see."

"What?" she asked, suspicious.

"It's a surprise," he said, taking her arm and leading her toward the still-open door. The old MG was parked outside the house.

She stopped at the door. Maybe getting out for a ride would clear her head. She'd been seeing odd images ever since she arrived at this house. And hearing even odder sounds. The sound of the wind last night . . . She shivered to remember. It would be good to get away. She'd go for that reason, no other.

Paul opened the passenger door for Callie, then walked around to the driver's side and climbed in.

At the end of the long gravel driveway, he turned right onto Route 127, taking the road that hugged the shore north toward Gloucester. It was a beautiful ride, alternating between woodland and ocean expanse and dotted with the biggest houses Callie had ever seen. It seemed so familiar. Had she taken this ride with her mother when she was a child? Doubtful. Her mother hadn't owned a car, at least not that Callie remembered, although she did have a brief memory of someone driving. Still, the shore road was familiar in a way that surprised her, each curve revealing a framed glimpse of something she had never seen before yet somehow knew would be there.

They passed through Pride's Crossing, Beverly Farms, and Manchester-by-the-Sea. After Magnolia, with its wooded canopy, they crossed into Gloucester. Paul turned right, down a side road that hugged the shore, then took a left into an empty parking lot. He pulled the car to the far side under a large oak tree and turned off the engine.

"Here we are," he said, reaching across to open her door, then walking around the car to meet her.

He led her down a steep stairway, past a large house on the left. The stairs continued downward, steeper as they descended. He took her arm.

"What is this place?"

"Hammond Castle," he said.

As they reached the bottom of the stairs, she glanced to her right, catching her first glimpse of the Gothic structure. She stopped short. It was an image she'd seen for years in a recurring dream. She knew what was beyond the doors: the great hall with its rose window and the huge organ that echoed so loudly it made her cry. She'd always assumed the vision had originated in the fairy tales Rose read to her each night, stories of gods and goddesses and kings and battles.

She dropped Paul's arm.

"Callie? Is something wrong?"

"I've been here," she whispered.

"Oh," he said, sounding disappointed. "Well, we can go back. The castle is closed for the season anyway. It won't open for tourists again until April."

"I'm confused," she said. "Why are we here?"

"I didn't actually bring you here to see the castle. I brought you here to see something else. But if you've already been—"

"We don't have to leave," Callie said to him. "I'm just having déjà vu." She smiled, regaining her composure. "Show me what you brought me here to see."

Paul turned left, away from the castle, leading her down into a courtyard with tall stone archways, each framing a stunning expanse of ocean. He took her arm again and turned right, directing her down more steps until they were on the lawn in front of the great house. It was the same green patch she'd envisioned earlier on Emily's liver, the same brown spot as well, which she now recognized as a dry patch in the middle of the sloping lawn. Beyond it lay the shadowy object she'd tried so hard to focus on in her treatment of Emily, something she now realized was a small island of rocks a few hundred feet out.

"That's Norman's Woe," Paul said, pointing to the rocks. "Where twenty died on a schooner called *Favorite*, when it ran aground in a terrible storm with a woman lashed to a piece of the wreckage."

" 'The Wreck of the *Hesperus*,' " she said, relieved. "You mentioned it the other night." The lines of the Longfellow poem that Rose had recited so often came back to her. She flattened her palms against each other in front of her waist, left hand fingers facing right and right hand fingers facing left, one up and one down, just as Rose had taught her to do, and began to recite, with old-fashioned pauses and inflections:

> *"The salt sea was frozen on her breast,*
> *The salt tears in her eyes;*
> *And he saw her hair, like the brown sea-weed,*
> *On the billows fall and rise.*

> *Such was the wreck of the* Hesperus,
> *In the midnight and the snow!*
> *Christ save us all from a death like this,*
> *On the reef of Norman's Woe."*

"I didn't know you were an elocutionist as well as a ventriloquist," Paul said, amused.

"I told you I was talented," she said, offering a little curtsy as Rose always insisted she do after a recitation.

"Very polished. Any other talents I don't know about?" He grinned.

"You'll just have to wait and see," she replied and smiled back.

She took a long look at the rock that had become so famous. "It's smaller than I imagined," she admitted. Once, on a day when she particularly missed her mother and Rose, Callie had looked up the poem. She'd discovered that Henry Wadsworth Longfellow had taken some liberties with the victim, changing her from an older woman to the captain's beautiful young daughter. She had been tied to the mast of the ship in an effort to keep her from drowning, but her ending had been even more tragic. When the girl was found, she was frozen to death and still tethered. "It's difficult to imagine a ship running aground there," Callie said.

"Don't be fooled. It's treacherous. The reef is submerged. At least twenty ships have run aground on these rocks, going all the way back to 1630. One of the first Puritan ships went down there, which is an epic story in itself. And then there are the suicides."

"Suicides?"

"A number of them. Marta Hathorne's father, among others. Jumped right into the churn."

"Marta Hathorne's father—" The way Paul had put it sounded a bit cold.

"You've got to see this," he said, changing the subject and hurrying her to the other side of the castle, across the great lawn and onto a granite ledge. They climbed out as far as they could, then sat down on the rocks. She realized it was the same perspective on the view she had seen during her meditation with Emily. She felt relieved at being able to place it. Things often happened to her this way, occurring out of time sequence. It wasn't just things that people were about to say, it was images, too; she saw things in visions before they happened in real time. She thought of it as a kind of reverse déjà vu. Over the years, she'd become fairly accustomed to this oddity.

They sat on the rocks for a long time. The sun was hypnotic. Callie watched for a while, then, still unable to see the treacherous reef below the surface, she looked at the sky, watching the tiny puffs of clouds moving slowly from west to east, letting the warmth settle in. She could feel herself beginning to doze, and she didn't fight it.

"And who might you be, little girl?" A woman in red was standing over her, leaning down. She wore a beaded mask.

Callie was standing in the middle of the castle's ballroom. Organ music reverberated from the adjoining hall, and the high ceiling echoed the sound, giving the room a churchlike ambience that stood in stark contrast to the masked and costumed partiers who filled the room. "I'm Alice in Wonderland," Callie said.

"Do you know who I am?" The woman's hair was multicolored: gold, blue, and several shades of red. "I know you," she said.

"The Queen of Hearts?" Callie asked, hoping she was wrong. That was who Leah was planning to dress as, and she wouldn't be happy to see her costume taken by someone else. Callie looked around. Leah was nowhere in sight.

"No, not the Queen of Hearts, but that's a very good guess. Come closer and I'll give you a hint." The red woman pulled a hand mirror out of her bag. "Mirror, mirror on the wall . . . Can you finish that one?"

"Who's the fairest of them all?"

"That's right. Now you know who I am."

"The Wicked Queen," Callie said.

"I have another name," the Wicked Queen said. "Can you guess it?"

"You're not nice," Callie said, remembering all the renditions of "Snow White" that Rose had read to her, from Grimm to the original Celtic version, called "Gold-Tree and Silver-Tree." The fairy tale never ended well for the Wicked Queen. Why would anyone choose to be her?

"I can be nice." The Wicked Queen laughed. "As long as you're not Snow White."

"I'm not Snow White! I told you already, I'm Alice!"

"So you are," the Wicked Queen said, leaning down and offering a sniff from her chalice. It smelled like licorice, Callie's favorite candy.

Callie sniffed. "Is it poison?" she asked, remembering the poisoned apple.

"Of a sort." The Wicked Queen laughed. "But it's a good poison. It's called the Green Fairy."

"I like fairies," Callie said. Rose sometimes told her stories of fairies in Ireland. Callie leaned in, trying to take a sip, but the Wicked Queen pulled the chalice away.

"She's five years old, for God's sake!" said her mother, rushing over to grab the chalice as Callie reached for it.

"I could repeat that right back to you, Olivia," the Wicked Queen said. "What are you thinking, bringing your child to a party like this?"

"We're leaving," Olivia said.

"Not yet," said Cheryl the Dormouse, who seemed to simply appear. She spoke quietly so the Wicked Queen wouldn't hear. "We have to meet him first. And I have the car."

"I'm late, I'm late, for a very important date," Susan, the March Hare, sang with excitement. She, too, just seemed to appear out of nowhere.

The Wicked Queen shot her a disapproving look.

"We're late to meet Rose," Olivia reminded her friends.

"Rose can wait," Cheryl said. "This won't take all night."

"It might," Susan said, loudly, knowing the Queen was listening. She giggled. "I mean, if he's anything like last time."

"It has to be all of us together," Olivia said. "And Leah isn't here."

"Just because Leah did something stupid doesn't mean we all have to suffer."

"There are rules," the Dormouse said. "And Leah broke them first."

"Rose told us to stop."

"Well, Rose isn't here, either," the Dormouse said. "And she's kicking us out of her house tomorrow, so she no longer has any say in the matter. She's not our mother."

The Dormouse started upstairs and the March Hare followed, calling over her shoulder to the Wicked Queen, "Maybe you'd like to join us?" And then she said, "Oh no, I forgot, that would never work. Dad just wants us."

"Don't do this," the Wicked Queen said. "Think about the child for a change."

The two disappeared, and Olivia lifted Callie and took her into an adjoining but empty hall. She placed her on a chair that felt like a throne. "Stay here," she ordered, "and don't move. Don't talk to anyone. And for God's sake, don't drink anything!"

Before Callie had a chance to speak, Olivia disappeared up the stairs to find the others.

Callie stared through the glass door to the front lawn, where a group of guests had gathered. It was a moonless night, and Callie couldn't tell land from sea. The chair was hard and hurt her back. Someone began to play chords on an organ. The sounds were ugly and too loud. They hurt her ears. Tears came to her eyes, but she sat mute and obedient, her hands over her ears. Had her mother left her? The chair seemed larger now and growing taller. The organ had eyes and an enormous scowling mouth. Its pipes had become teeth.

Callie climbed down from the chair and started for the stairway, passing other guests as she moved. As she entered the great room once more, she saw the Wicked Queen talking to another woman in a similar red costume. Leah was crying, and ranting, and choking on tears. The Wicked Queen was trying to comfort her.

The Wicked Queen spotted Callie. Leah did, too.

Her eyes were wild. "Where are they?" Leah demanded. She was angrier than anyone Callie had ever seen. "Tell me where they went!"

Callie pointed to the stairs.

Leah started up the stairs and Callie made to follow.

"Stay down here with me," the Wicked Queen said, smiling sweetly. Callie shook her head and followed Leah.

The stairs were steep, and Callie had to move slowly. When she finally reached the landing, the corridor was long and dark and every door was closed. She walked slowly, pausing to listen. At the last door, she heard their raised voices crying and Leah shouting accusations. It was scary out in the hallway. She could hear the Wicked Queen and her friends' voices echoing up the stairs.

She pushed open the door, and the shouting rushed into the hallway.

"You betrayed me!" Leah yelled at the girls. They were all there: Cheryl, Susan, and Olivia. In the center of the room was a bed surrounded by red velvet curtains. The man on the bed was trying to calm Leah, who had stopped yelling and was now sobbing. "Dad," Leah begged. "Dad, please." She went silent when she saw Callie, then fled the room, revealing the full profile of the man on the bed. Callie stared at him: She had never seen a

naked man. Then she looked past him and saw Susan, who was naked as well, the White Rabbit costume at her feet, her pale skin sparkling in the candlelight. The man stared at Callie, freezing her in place.

Then, slowly, wickedly, he smiled.

The blood started slowly, dripping down the walls in thin ribbons of scarlet. It thickened, surrounding everyone, and the ribbons turned to waves, spreading across the room, pooling at the feet of the White Rabbit. The only one untouched was the man on the bed. Cheryl tried in vain to cast a circle, spinning clockwise and pointing with her index finger, quickly pulling Callie inside its protective barrier. But it didn't stop what was happening, and the blood kept coming.

"What are you doing?" Olivia demanded.

"Binding," Cheryl said. "For protection."

"It's too late for that now," Olivia said.

The blood rose higher and higher, and still the man kept smiling his Cheshire cat grin. Callie tried to run, but his blue eyes held her in place. She recognized them immediately. They were Paul Whiting's eyes.

Callie screamed and jolted back to consciousness.

Paul was leaning over her. She gasped, scrambling out from under him.

"I'm sorry! I didn't mean to scare you," he said. "I think you were having a nightmare."

It was no mistake. His eyes were the same eyes she'd seen in her dream.

"I'm sorry," Paul said again, now alarmed. "Your eyes were open. I couldn't tell if you were awake or asleep."

She stood up, willing herself to let go of the horrible images, but they were impossible to shake. "I've got to get out of here," she said, backing away from him.

"Did I do something wrong?" he asked, confused.

Try as she might to think of a rational explanation, she was at a loss. All she wanted was to get away from him as quickly as possible. She was both frightened and embarrassed. There was no way to hide it.

They didn't speak as they hurried back to his car.

"I'm sorry I brought you here," he said as they drove away. "It was Ann's idea. She told me there was something that she thought you needed to see."

"Excuse me?"

"Last night. Ann said she'd had a vision. That I needed to bring you to see Norman's Woe."

Callie didn't reply. She wasn't scared anymore. Now she was angry.

They drove back to Pride's Heart in silence. Callie was out of the car and heading for the butler's pantry door before Paul turned off the engine. As she was reaching for the door handle, she saw Marta at the sink, holding one of the crystal glasses from yesterday's dinner and looking at it curiously, then, as if deciding something, she smashed it on the side of the sink, jumping back as it shattered, as if immediately regretting her impulsivity. She pulled a small splinter of glass from her palm, and a tiny trickle of red ran down her fingers.

Blood. Callie forced her eyes shut against the image she'd seen on the wall of the castle, an image that was now forming on the pantry wall. When she opened her eyes, the image was gone.

"What was that?" Finn's voice echoed from the kitchen.

"I broke one of Emily's glasses." Marta seemed at once surprised and worried.

Finn came into the room. "Are you okay?" He looked at the shattered pieces first, then examined her hands. "You've cut yourself."

"I'm okay," she answered, pulling her hands back, then turning to see Callie framed by the doorway, not moving, her face pale. "But she's not . . . Callie, what's the matter?"

Callie looked around. "Did Towner come back?"

"They're not coming back," Marta said. "Has something happened? Where's Paul?"

"I'm right here," Paul said, catching up.

"What's going on?" Finn asked his son.

"I have to get back to Salem," Callie said. "Does anyone know when the next train runs?"

Finn looked at Paul, waiting for him to offer. When Paul said nothing, he said, "My son, of course, will drive you." He was looking at Paul curiously. "Won't you, Paul?"

"Of course," Paul answered flatly.

It was the last thing either of them wanted. But Callie had already made a scene. She went upstairs and gathered her belongings, her hands shaking as she quickly stuffed everything into the overnight bag. At the last moment she looked around the room for the packet of herbs, wondering if she had really thrown them into the fire or if that, too, was part of this nightmare she seemed to have been experiencing since she arrived. It was nowhere to be found.

She carried her bag down the stairs, and Paul put it in the trunk. This time he didn't go around to open the door for her, nor did he reach across to help with the seat belt. They sat in the driveway in strained silence for a long time before he started the engine.

"Are you going to tell me what's going on?"

"I couldn't even if I wanted to."

Paul turned the radio on, raising the volume and erasing any possibility of further conversation. John Hammond's cover of Robert Johnson's "Come On in My Kitchen" was playing. She closed her eyes, letting the music consume her, as they sped south. The air was cooling. She tried to relax, to let go of the earlier memory, but it was impossible.

Leah. She hadn't known the answer when Rafferty asked the question, but she knew it now . . . Leah had definitely been in deep with whatever her mother and the two other goddesses were doing.

She remembered the red dress Leah was wearing as the Queen of Hearts, part of the Alice story they were all playing out that night. Callie shivered as she remembered the last view of her mother, Susan, and Cheryl, lying at the bottom of the crevasse, those same fanciful costumes soaked with blood. She'd spotted her mother's Mad Hatter top hat first, then she'd seen the bodies.

Callie forced herself to breathe, feeling the chill of the deep blue waters of Salem Sound reaching ever eastward in the icy Atlantic.

CHAPTER SIXTEEN

November 28, 2014
SALEM

That there is a Devil is a thing doubted by none
but such as are under the influences of the Devil.
—COTTON MATHER, *On Witchcraft*

RAFFERTY PULLED THE CRUISER INTO HIS DRIVEWAY AND parked. The graffiti that had been sprayed on the oak tree was still visible, bleeding through the paint Towner had used to cover it. He got out of the car feeling as if he'd worked a double.

Rafferty had gotten May's call this morning. His suspicions had been right. They were trying to move someone, but it hadn't happened. There had been a tip, something that led May to believe the woman was in danger, and the tip had been right.

Rafferty still didn't know the extent of May's network. It was better that way, she said, and on that point he agreed. If he were ever questioned, ever called to help in a missing person search for a woman who'd escaped an abuser, he could only tell them what he knew. The less he knew about their network, this New Underground Railroad, the better for all concerned.

Still, Towner knew a lot. Right now, she was on her way to a safe house with the woman, who had only escaped because May had held off her ex with her six-gauge until Rafferty arrived and took him into custody.

He wanted to call Towner but knew better. He couldn't ask any questions, and she wouldn't give him any answers. He only hoped the transfer had occurred without incident. They couldn't hold the guy. Not for long. And even though he knew it wasn't logical, that the man didn't know where Towner had taken the woman, Rafferty still wouldn't relax until his wife called in.

He had gone straight from Pride's Heart to Yellow Dog, and then immediately into meetings, one right after the other. The first was the one he attended every morning before work: In all his years of sobriety, the single thing he'd learned for certain was to "keep coming back." The second had been an awareness meeting over at the Methodist church to which he'd taken Jay-Jay, though, in Rafferty's opinion, Jay-Jay was far from ready; he wasn't close to hitting bottom yet. He'd been drunk on the job a few weeks back—that was why he'd ended up on the desk, a punishment Jay-Jay hated. Even so, he'd kept drinking, and most mornings he was so hungover, he didn't want to talk, which was unusual for Jay-Jay, who generally talked too much. He was skinnier than usual, which meant he wasn't eating right, and he was more disheveled, though that was harder to tell since Jay-Jay had never been particularly well groomed. He had all the classic signs. And he had the family history. Both his father and his brother were drunks.

So today Rafferty had told Jay-Jay his story, or at least part of it. How guilt had kept him from sobriety for a long time: guilt about what his drinking had done to his daughter and his first marriage. How he still struggled with it every day. "Guilt is the enemy of sobriety. One reason you don't get better is because you don't think you deserve to," he'd told him.

Jay-Jay had listened but said nothing.

Rafferty's cell rang, and he breathed a sigh of relief when he saw who it was.

"You okay?"

Towner said she was, thank God. "I'm just heading back now."

They wouldn't discuss it further.

Rafferty was so lost in his thoughts as he walked down his driveway that he almost bumped into Callie and Paul Whiting. "What's wrong?" he asked, reading their faces. The look on Callie's was fear.

"Nothing," she said, walking past him and into the house.

"Something you did?" Rafferty asked Paul.

"Evidently, though I have no idea what."

Paul looked guilty and even a little bit angry. Rafferty had always thought of Paul Whiting as a good kid. Still, Paul was male and appeared interested in Callie. Anything could have happened between them. Maybe it was just the day's events that had triggered the suspicion. But there was something . . .

Callie's words, or rather Rose's words, spoken by Callie at the Thanksgiving dinner yesterday, had gnawed at him all day. "Do you think, inside, every one of us is a killer?" Had Rose said those words to Callie? Had she told Callie what she knew to be true about him? Rafferty doubted it. What troubled Rafferty was that he had been thinking about Rose's words just before Callie uttered them. Callie hadn't seemed to direct the words at him, and when he'd looked to her for some sign that she knew what she was saying, he hadn't seen any. Still, it was odd. Could she read him the same way Towner sometimes could?

"What happened?" Rafferty asked.

"I took her to see Hammond Castle," Paul said. "The grounds and Norman's Woe. I had reason to believe she'd like to see it."

That's probably the last place she'd like to see, Rafferty thought. He'd read the files. He knew the Goddesses had attended a party at Hammond Castle just before the murders and that Callie had been with them. He'd asked her about the party, though he'd never said where it had been held, but she'd just looked at him blankly. "I don't remember any party."

Three of the tearoom waitresses walked up the steps, talking quietly among themselves. Rafferty and Paul exchanged a glance and moved out of the way to let them pass.

"I should probably go," Paul said.

"Sounds like a good plan," Rafferty agreed.

He watched Paul drive away. He fought the urge to find Callie now and question her, but he made a mental note to do it soon. Whatever she had seen or remembered had obviously been rough on her.

It had been a rough day all around. As Rafferty and Jay-Jay had exited the meeting, Helen Barnes from the McIntire District had blocked their way. She was out walking her springer spaniel. As upstanding and traditional as Helen appeared in public, Rafferty was aware of another side of her: Helen was the president of a secret sewing circle. He knew of at least two of these groups; the first was formed after the witch trials. For a number of years after the hysteria, women hadn't been allowed to gather in groups in Salem. If they'd wanted to get together, they'd done so in secret, and, though no longer necessary, that tradition had continued until this day. Not that there was anything necessarily illicit about these groups. Towner said they funded several charitable organizations, Yellow Dog Island included. But the secrecy still made people nervous. They were so secretive that if Towner hadn't told him about the circles, he never would have known they existed.

Despite Helen's clandestine gatherings, from what the ADA had told him the other day, she had no qualms about urging the commonwealth to exhume the bodies of the Goddesses. "Rose Whelan is a damned Satanist," Helen had declared this morning, refusing to let Rafferty and Jay-Jay pass. "She was one back then, and she's one now. You don't want to do anything about it, but there are plenty of people around here who will."

"Watch what you say, Helen," Rafferty said.

"The so-called Goddesses were all related to Salem witches," Helen replied.

"There *were* no Salem witches," he reminded her. "There were innocent people who became the victims of unfounded hysteria." Rafferty hoped Helen would catch his subtext.

"Well, witches are everywhere now!" She gestured to the Witch House across the street, one of the town's last remaining buildings with direct ties to the trials. As she spoke, two costumed neowitches walked past the historic house. "You can blame Rose Whelan for them all!" Helen said. Her dog picked that moment to squat.

"She's not a witch, she's a banshee," Jay-Jay said, trying to help.

Rafferty shot him a look.

Helen started to move along. "Pick it up," he said, pointing to the pile.

She glared at him.

"If you'd rather a fifty-dollar fine, I'll be more than happy to give you one," he said, patting the dog's head. He watched as she searched her jacket pocket for a plastic bag and bent over to pick up the mess, frowning.

"We're going to dig them up. Every last one of them," she promised. "It's going to happen, and there's nothing you can do to stop it."

Callie tried to make sense of the vision she'd had at Norman's Woe. Walls didn't bleed, for God's sake. And logically, she knew that the man she'd seen could not have been Paul, and that she owed him an apology for her rude behavior. But his eyes had been terrifying.

The sun was blindingly bright off the water as she walked from the tearoom to Derby Street, taking a left at the harbor. At Daniels Street, she turned right, looking for the grey-shingled building.

The hippie house where they had all lived together was boarded up now, a huge contrast to the row of 1700s restorations that were its neighbors. A bright orange Condemned sign was posted on the door. The front steps had collapsed, and graffiti covered the shingles: Words that looked like Latin and the number 666 were scrawled across the base of the front door and repeated every so often along the clapboards.

Callie walked around to the side of the house that faced the harbor, ignoring the No Trespassing signs. There was trash in the overgrown yard. The porch she'd once played on hung crazily off the side of the building. She looked around to make sure no one was watching, then grabbed hold of the only support post that looked substantial and climbed up. She moved tentatively along the porch, fearful of causing its collapse, and carefully made her way to the windowed door that led to the front room where she had always slept. She peered through: It was messy, either with remnants of the last tenant or from squatters. She looked for the mural, which was what she'd come to see. An older man, Henry, had painted a portrait of the Goddesses; he was a friend of Rose's, and she had given him permission to paint the mural. Callie remembered how upset Rose was at what Henry had painted on the wall, even though Callie remembered it as a beautiful picture.

Callie was hoping to see Leah's image, hoping the image would help her remember more about the woman who she thought had probably become Rafferty's main suspect, the *fifth petal of the rose*. But the entire portrait was gone. Someone had painted the wall white, though it was an old job and starting to yellow. Had it been Rose? She'd certainly been upset enough at the girls to repaint that wall herself. The tension between Rose and the Goddesses had been building all that summer and into the fall. Rose hadn't approved of their behavior; Callie remembered that. She'd thought they were setting a bad example for Callie. Once, Rose had lost her temper so badly, yelling and calling the young women out for all sorts of offenses, that a neighbor had called the police.

Callie now remembered that the police had also been called to the house before the party at Hammond Castle. Rose had screamed as they left in Halloween costumes, telling them they were being "cheap and disgusting," and reminding them they had committed to other plans for the evening. Rose had followed them out to Cheryl's car, yelling as they loaded up. "Pack your things. I want you out of my house tomorrow!" When they'd pulled away, Olivia had shouted, "We'll meet you at the hill, Auntie." The police cruiser had arrived just as they were turning the corner.

Callie climbed back down from the decrepit porch, in time to see a neighbor coming out of one of the nearby houses to get her mail.

"I'd keep away from that house if I were you," the woman said.

Callie didn't recognize her; the woman hadn't lived on Daniels Street back then. "I'm just looking around," Callie said.

"That house is cursed. A Satanic cult once lived there."

Callie stared at her in disbelief.

"It's true," the woman said. "The cult's leader was just arrested. They call her the Salem Banshee. My neighbors tell me she murdered everyone in that house. Even a little girl." The woman grabbed her mail. "The whole place is evil," she said and walked back into her own house, a historically perfect saltbox restoration that fronted the harbor.

Shaken, Callie cut through the side lot to the street behind. As she passed the back of the house, she saw more graffiti on the rear facade: the image of a black rose, its petals withered and drooping, leaves curled and dried. The thorns had life and color, though: Their tips were red and dripping with blood. Callie recognized it as the image that Towner had been trying to erase from Rose's tree in the courtyard. The rose contained a written message. Along its stem someone had scrawled the words *Death to the Banshee!*

Callie dialed Rafferty's cell twice. He didn't pick up.

She marched down Daniels Street to Derby, turning left, walking fast, rage and disbelief alternating with each step. She almost knocked over an old woman with a cane. The woman turned, gave her a quick look of recognition, then stepped out of the way. Callie wasn't quite certain where she was going until she found herself on Orange Street.

She pounded on Ann's heavy front door. There was no answer, so she walked back down Derby Street to the Shop of Shadows on Pickering Wharf. Ann Chase was on a ladder arranging a flying display of Christmas stockings filled with candy, the image of a witch on a broomstick embroidered on each one. A sign proclaimed: BEFANA DELIVERING GIFTS TO THE CHILDREN OF ITALY, THEIR TRADITIONAL EPIPHANY CELEBRATION.

Ann turned as soon as the door opened. "Callie."

"You told Paul Whiting to take me to Norman's Woe." Callie couldn't calm herself, and now a group of young witches, who'd been decorating the front of the store, looked at her with concern. "Why the hell would you do something like that?"

"It's all right," Ann said to her staff. "Get back to work." She motioned for Callie to follow her, passing several reading rooms adorned with heavy curtains, and heading to the office.

"Tell me what's going on."

"People think Rose killed every one of the Goddesses . . . including the little girl who lived with them."

Ann looked surprised. "Who thinks that?"

"Probably everyone!" Callie said, entering Ann's office.

Ann looked doubtful. "That's not true."

Callie's phone rang then; she checked the number and picked up when she saw Rafferty's name.

"Hi, Callie. What's up?"

"You have to do something."

"What's happened?"

"I don't know," Callie said, trying to hold back tears. "I don't know what's going on. They think it was some kind of Satanic cult."

Hearing Rafferty's voice, Ann took the phone from Callie's hand. "Can you please come over here?"

"Ann?"

"Yeah."

"What's going on?"

"I don't know. Can you just get over to my shop, please?"

All the imagery Callie had seen at Norman's Woe swirled in her brain, and the Wicked Queen's words echoed in her ears. "Why did you make him take me there?" she asked Ann, sounding childlike.

"I thought—I had a vision when I was looking at the lace—it told me there was something there you had to see," Ann said. "My intent was not malicious."

"I don't believe you."

Ann did not tell Callie that—in this moment—she looked every bit the child that Ann had seen in the vision: a young girl in a blue pinafore, blood dripping from her palm as she stood staring over the edge of a deep ravine.

"Rose didn't kill anyone," Callie insisted. She sipped the tea Ann had made to calm her down, and sat in the sling chair next to Ann's desk.

Rafferty sat behind the desk in Ann's usual spot. Ann lingered in the doorway, not quite certain whether to stay or go.

"Tell me again why you wanted Callie to go to Hammond Castle," he asked Ann, calling her in.

"I didn't actually send her to the castle, I sent her to see Norman's Woe."

"Why Norman's Woe specifically?"

"I thought there was something there she needed to remember."

"And was there?" Rafferty turned to Callie.

It was clear Callie didn't want to talk in front of Ann.

"I'll be in the shop," Ann said, exiting through the beaded curtains.

"There was a costume party at Hammond Castle the night of the murders," Callie said. "I guess that's the party you asked me about."

Rafferty had read about the party in the files and knew the Goddesses had been guests. Witnesses had documented that there was some kind of altercation between the girls and some other woman that night, someone wearing a red dress. But from what he could tell, the police hadn't taken that account seriously and hadn't investigated further. Which shocked him. The more he learned, the more it seemed like the cops would have been perfectly happy to blame the murder on Rose and move on.

"There was a woman in a red costume," Callie said. "Two women, actually. One of them was dressed as the Wicked Queen from 'Snow White.' The other one was Leah."

Rafferty looked at her. "Leah."

She nodded.

The files had, not surprisingly as he was discovering, made no mention of a Leah anywhere.

"I remember her now. She was at the party." Then, recalling it only as she spoke, she said the name. "Leah Kormos."

"That's her last name, Kormos?"

"Yes," Callie said, as it came back to her. "That's the name. She *was* one of the Goddesses. But they had some kind of falling-out."

Rafferty had left the folded-up yellow paper back in the office. He'd already penciled in the other names of the Goddesses on the petals with their corresponding ancestors: Olivia/Callie, Rose, Cheryl, and Susan. Leah's first name was penciled in above. Now he typed her surname, Kormos, into his phone.

That Leah shared her first name with Rafferty's only daughter had been something that had been difficult for him to reconcile. He felt better knowing her last name. From now on, he could say her full name and remove any mental connection.

"I think so." Callie struggled to remember. "I remember she was around for a while, and then we didn't see her anymore. They had some kind of argument."

"Over that man?"

"Maybe, I don't know."

"What about at Norman's Woe?" he asked again.

Callie looked at him blankly.

"Was there something about Norman's Woe that was important to what happened that night?"

"I don't know."

"Did something happen on those rocks?"

"I don't know. Nothing I remember."

"Think about it. Is there any connection?"

"I don't know," Callie said, exasperated. "The only connection I can think of is that Rose made me learn the poem about it when I was little," she offered, trying to make sense of all that had happened. " 'The Wreck of the *Hesperus*.' That's all I can think of. She used to make me memorize poems. But that wasn't the night of the party, that was before."

"But you'd never been there. Before the party."

"I don't think so. I don't even remember seeing Norman's Woe the night of the party. All I remember is the castle."

Rafferty called Ann back in. "Ever heard of a girl named Leah Kormos?"

She shook her head. "No."

"She was evidently one of the Goddesses."

"I don't know the name."

"But you obviously know who this is," Rafferty said, gesturing to Callie.

"Callie O'Neill," Ann said.

"Ann, come on . . ." Rafferty said.

Ann said nothing.

"Tell me again why you sent Callie to Norman's Woe. You sure it was the rock and not the castle that you meant her to see?"

"I'm not sure at all. There might not be any significance beyond the general location," Ann offered. "It's possible for my visions to incorporate images from two different time periods," she went on, as if she knew exactly what Rafferty was talking about. "It happens. We all know time isn't linear."

"We don't all know that," Rafferty said. "Not all of us believe in magic."

"Nonlinear time isn't magic. It's physics. Quantum mechanics. It's Heisenberg's uncertainty principle writ large. Each observer has his own frame of reference for time. It's also math if you want to get technical about it."

Ann had adopted what she called a "philosophical perception of time." Something about the spontaneous absorption of light that Rafferty didn't understand at all.

He turned back to Callie. "What else did you see? Before you had the dream memory."

"Nothing," Callie said.

"What did you and Paul talk about?"

"Just the rock itself."

He waited.

"It has a submerged reef."

Rafferty nodded.

"Paul said a lot of ships have run aground on those rocks."

"That's common knowledge," Ann offered.

"What else?"

Callie thought about it, remembering. "Paul said there were a number of suicides there, too. That Marta Hathorne's father was one of them."

"He worked for the Whitings back in the day," Rafferty said. "I heard he was blamed for a bad business deal that cost the Whitings their fortune. That that's why he killed himself." General opinion had been that Hathorne had been a scapegoat. Everyone knew it had been that way for generations, going all the way back to the witch trials, the Hathornes and the Whitings blaming each other for anything that went wrong in their lives. "Let's get back to the party. You said it was a masked ball?"

"Yes. A fairy-tale ball."

"So there was an orchestra?"

She didn't remember any music. Just the dissonant chords from the organ. "I don't know. Maybe there was."

"Was there anyone else you recognized? Besides your mother and her friends?" he asked. "What about the man on the bed? Did he have a name?"

He caught her hesitation.

She took a breath. "I think they were calling him Dad."

"Dad?" Rafferty repeated, just to make sure he'd gotten it right.

Callie nodded. "I think so."

"That's *really* creepy," Ann said.

"Tell me again. Everything you saw at the party."

She repeated what she'd told him: the masked costume ball; the Wicked Queen, who'd given her a whiff of a green drink that smelled like licorice; how mad Olivia had been at the woman. She told him how Leah had come in, angry and ranting, how Callie had followed her upstairs to the bedroom. "She was screaming at them, saying they betrayed her."

"With the man on the bed," Rafferty said.

"Yes."

"Someone they were sexually involved with."

"Yes." Callie was struggling with the image. "I remember it now. I remember when it happened. I went up the stairs, and I heard them yelling at each other."

"Sounds like this Leah character should be your main suspect," Ann said to Rafferty.

"I didn't know what they were doing with him or why the man was naked."

"You never saw them doing that kind of thing before?" Rafferty said.

"Then you'd be one of the only ones in town who didn't," Ann said.

Rafferty shot her a look.

Ann shrugged. "It was common knowledge," she said again.

"She was five," Rafferty retorted. "Your mother and the others . . ." Rafferty said, as gently as he could, not knowing how much she'd heard of the rumors. "The Goddesses had a reputation for being"—he searched for a word—"seductive."

"Very seductive," Ann added. "They made a sport of it. Sometimes a competitive sport."

"I've heard some of this. But a competition . . ." Callie stared at her. "You're kidding."

Rafferty nodded. "That's the way people remember it."

Callie looked to Ann for verification.

"Hey, no judgment here. I thought they were cool." Ann smiled sweetly.

Callie wanted to smack her.

Rafferty's phone rang. "Let's take a five-minute break," he said, walking outside.

Callie looked around Ann's office and at the shop behind: Labeled spells in little envelopes lined the walls, one for lost love, another for wealth, one that treated male impotency. Beyond the packaged spells were canisters of dried herbs, with labels that sounded witchy: wolfbane, eye of newt. Potions obviously designed to relieve the tourists of their dollars, Callie thought. Crystal wands were in a display case and handcrafted witch's brooms hung from the ceiling. And then there was the lace, all kinds of lace: dream catchers, doilies, random pieces of half-finished work. Callie watched a young woman seated in the hallway dressed in black holding a piece of lace up in front of a customer, gazing into it the way she'd seen wizards in old movies gaze into crystal balls. The girl looked as if she could read the lace. Callie squinted at it, trying to see what the girl was looking at.

When they reconvened, Callie told Rafferty about the portrait painted on the wall, the one Rose hated. How Callie had been to the house to see if it was still there, but it had been painted over.

She told him again about the argument at the party that night, how Leah had come in looking for the others and had followed them upstairs and argued with them, how, in Callie's vision, there was blood running down the walls.

Then she remembered something else about the dream. She turned to Ann. "Do you think they were witches?"

"Who?" Ann asked.

"The Goddesses," Callie said.

"Why would you ask that?" Ann asked.

"One of them was trying to do something in my dream. Drawing a circle on the floor of the bedroom," Callie answered. "She said something about binding."

"A binding spell?" Ann asked.

"Like you did on me," Callie said.

Ann considered.

"It was for protection, though," Callie said.

Ann shrugged. "Binding spells are usually for protection."

"Were they witches, do you think?" Callie asked again.

"Were they?" Rafferty asked Ann.

She shrugged again. "I've heard they thought their Salem ancestors were 'real' witches. Not just victims of hysteria, but practicing witches. Which was a dangerous and, frankly, silly thing to believe. There were rumors that one of them was a frequent visitor to the Left Hand Path."

Rafferty knew that the Left Hand Path was a shop the city had been trying to shut down at the time. The owner had been a vocal practitioner of black magic, the kind of stuff Hollywood loves. But the other witches in town had lobbied to get the place closed down after it was rumored that the owner had been sacrificing animals and using their body parts in her rituals. Witches had been relatively new to Salem when Rafferty first arrived, and if they were going to make a permanent home and be welcomed by the community, they felt it was important to keep their reputation clean. Even Ann, with her practice of grey magic, had toned things down in an effort to be embraced by Salem. She'd even started a foundation: an antidefamation league that helped educate the public about the witches' harmless religious practices.

"I never knew if the rumors were true." Ann shook her head. "Everyone was doing a little magic back then, reading the tarot or using a love potion. But even if they were doing an occasional spell, the Goddesses weren't real witches by anyone's standards."

"Why not?" Rafferty asked.

"Well, they obviously weren't solitaries, and they weren't in any coven. And they weren't very good at it, were they?" She turned to Callie. "That spell, if it even was a spell, didn't protect anyone, did it?"

Callie bristled. The remark was true, but coldhearted.

Rafferty said, "I read the files. There was another argument that night, a bad one between Rose and the girls. Rose followed them to their car; there was a lot of yelling in the street. A neighbor called the police. Callie, do you remember why they were fighting?"

"I think so. It came back to me at Rose's house. She had learned something really bad about them. They were mad at someone for telling her. In the car, they talked about getting revenge. Whatever it was Rose had been told, it caused the worst argument I can remember. But I told you, the neighbors were always calling the police," Callie continued. "The police were always coming to the house for one thing or another." She thought for a minute. "They searched that house, right?"

"After the murders? Of course," Rafferty said, watching Callie carefully. He had seen the report: they hadn't found anything worth noting. But with one box of evidence still missing, he really couldn't be certain. He didn't elaborate; it wasn't something she needed to know right now. His cop's instincts were telling him there was something she wasn't saying, something she was holding back.

"What about the blood? You said there was blood running down the walls," Rafferty said.

"That was part of the dream," Callie answered. "Not a real image."

"Do you think it was the blood from later that night? There was a lot of blood spilled on Proctor's Ledge."

"I don't know," she said. "It might have been. But I think I may have conjured it . . . from something Rose said to me yesterday."

"What was that?"

Callie hesitated. She didn't want to make more trouble for Rose.

"Tell me."

"When she was upset yesterday, Rose shouted, 'God will give you blood to drink,' " Callie admitted, waiting for Rafferty's reaction. "Zee said Rose heard someone say it on the hill the night of the murders."

Rafferty bristled. He'd never heard this bit of information. Doctor-patient confidentiality would forbid Zee from sharing it with him, but confidentiality could be ignored in the face of imminent danger. Of course this wasn't exactly imminent. The danger had passed twenty-five years ago.

"Did you hear the statement the night of the murders?"

"I don't think so," Callie said nervously. "I know I've heard it before, but I don't think it was that night. I've been racking my brain trying to figure out what it means."

"I know what it means," Ann said.

"You do?" Rafferty turned to her.

"You could have heard or read it anywhere; it's very famous. It's a quote from Sarah Good, one of the accused witches. She said it when she knew she was going to hang. There's more to her speech than that, though that's the part most often quoted. You can look it up."

"Did Rose say who uttered the quote that night?" Rafferty asked.

Callie hesitated. She didn't want to answer in front of Ann. But Rafferty was waiting. And this was important. "Rose says it was the banshee."

Rafferty had offered to give Callie a ride back to the house. They sat in silence as the cruiser pulled out.

"So much for keeping my identity a secret," Callie said. "Ann obviously knows who I am now."

"I'd say she's known for a while," Rafferty said. "You have to admit, she was pretty helpful with her insights."

Callie wasn't so sure.

"I know going to Hammond Castle was difficult for you, but it might have triggered a memory that could be very helpful in discovering who killed your mother and the others. Is there anything else you remember?"

Callie replayed the vision and lingered on it for a long moment before speaking again. "They were arguing about Leah Kormos at the party before she got there: my mother and Susan and Cheryl. My mother said it was against the rules to go to the man upstairs without Leah; that it had to be all of them together. Cheryl said the rules had already been broken, that Leah was the one who had broken them."

"Rules? What do you mean? They had rules?" Rafferty asked.

"Evidently."

She was silent for a long time. "I think Ann might be right. I think Leah Kormos might be the killer."

They didn't speak again on the ride back to the house. Callie looked out the window, thinking about the eyes that had stared back at her from the bed. She shivered.

Rafferty pulled the cruiser in next to her car and shut off the engine. He turned to her.

"So what else aren't you telling me?"

"Nothing," she lied.

"Callie," he said, holding her gaze. "I've been a cop for a long time." She sighed.

"Every memory you have gets us one step closer to finding your mother's killer."

"This wasn't a memory. It was a dream." Callie shook her head. "I have no illusion it was real. It's just not important."

"Why don't you let me decide what's important?"

"It was a weird party."

He waited. When she didn't reply, he prompted her. "What about the guy on the bed? This . . . Dad."

She shivered.

"Tell me about him again."

A blush was creeping into Callie's cheeks.

"What didn't you want to say in front of Ann?"

"Look, I already told you I don't know if any of this is real—if there was even a man—or a room—that night! And the man I saw on the bed . . . it isn't possible he was in the room."

"Why not?"

Callie took a breath before continuing. "Because the man I saw on the bed was Paul Whiting."

Rafferty said nothing as she got out of the cruiser and unlocked her car door. Finally, he leaned out his window. "That's the reason you were so angry with Paul when he dropped you off earlier?"

Callie nodded, feeling the color burning in her cheeks.

"You realize he wasn't even born until later that year."

"Yes."

"I think you owe that young man an explanation. And probably an apology."

She had to knock on the boathouse door several times before he opened it.

"What the hell?" He looked annoyed. Then, seeing who it was, he stopped, staring at her.

"I lied to you," she said.

"What?"

"I lied to you about who I am."

Callie guessed that there was only a small window of opportunity before Ann told him the story, if she hadn't already. But that wasn't why she was telling him. Callie really wanted it to come from her. After she told him, there was something equally important she had to do. But first things first.

"My name isn't Callie O'Neill, it's Callie Cahill." She looked at him for signs of recognition. He stared at her blankly. "I was the little girl who survived the Goddess Murders."

He stood framed by the doorway, looking at her as if he wasn't quite sure what he was hearing. Finally, he stepped back and opened the door to let her in.

Two hours later, on her way back to Salem, she stopped at CVS and bought herself a flashlight.

CHAPTER SEVENTEEN

November 29, 2014
SALEM

*I am no more a witch than you are a wizard, and if you
take away my life, God will give you blood to drink.*
—SARAH GOOD, 1692

RAFFERTY SAT IN HIS OFFICE STARING AT SARAH GOOD'S words. Ann was right, it was a famous quote, and often taken out of context, which made Good's curse seem more threatening. In some ways, her accusation was typical of the hysteria; she was outspoken and definitely an outsider. She was also in debt from a first marriage, something her second husband (also her accuser) inherited. But what struck Rafferty most about Sarah was the fact that her young daughter, Dorcas Good, was also accused. Four years old at the time she was arrested, the child sat abandoned and neglected in Salem Jail for several months, long after the execution of her mother. After she was finally released, she was never the same, and had to be cared for all of her life.

In different ways, the story of Sarah Good and her daughter reminded him of the Goddesses. He thought of Olivia and Callie, of course. The wronged mother, the daughter who suffered after her loss. He also thought of Rose. Dorcas Good, whose real name was Dorothy, was mentally ill like Rose, an affliction blamed on her lengthy incarceration under horrendous conditions. When she was finally released, she was broken, in much the same manner that Rose had been broken. Neither was ever the same again.

Rafferty noted the similarities. But he found no real connection, other than the obvious one: the date of Sarah Good's execution, July 19.

Though the records kept of the Goddess Murders were sketchy at best, he did know that the women had been on Proctor's Ledge that Halloween intending to honor their ancestors: five of Salem's accused who had been hanged together on July 19. Callie had confirmed that story. He knew that each of the Goddesses had been related to one of the five. If each represented one petal of the rose, then one of them had to be related to Sarah Good.

"God will give you blood to drink." Sarah Good's curse was evidently a catchphrase of Rose's, something she'd been saying since she got out of the state hospital. Did she really hear it spoken that night, or was that, along with her insistence that a banshee had done the killing, another of Rose's delusions?

It might be a dead end, but it was worth following. One of the Goddesses had to be related to Sarah Good. But which one?

He sat with all the reports, testimonies, and crime scene photos spread out in front of him, sifting through them piece by piece, trying to find anything he might have missed.

He erased the penciled-in names of the Goddesses from the sketch of the five-petaled rose, listing them, instead, to the right side of the image. Now he tried a different approach, inking the names of the five executed that he had penciled in before: Rebecca Nurse, Sarah Wildes, Elizabeth Howe, Susannah Martin, and Sarah Good. Those names he was sure of. He'd checked the spelling of each name online, then double-checked with Salem's records, mentally noting which towns they were from—all of which had once been part of Salem—and their ages. With the exception of Sarah Good, who was thirty-nine, the women executed on July 19, 1692, were much older, ranging in age from fifty-seven to seventy-one. Some were homeless or nuisances to the community: indebted, outspoken, or otherwise troublesome. It made him think of Rose.

He inked in the Goddesses' names under each of the corresponding ancestors he was certain of, crossing out the names from the list below as he went. Under Rebecca Nurse, he inked Callie, Olivia, and Rose. Assuming Callie's recollections of the night, and who'd spoken which name, were correct, he continued, inking the name Susan Symms on Susannah Martin's petal and Cheryl Cassella under Sarah Wildes. Callie had recalled Rose telling her that she was related to more than one of Salem's executed, and since she had recited the name of Elizabeth Howe that night, he'd initially assumed she was Rose's other relative. But Callie had told him that, after determining that Leah Kormos wasn't coming to the ceremony, Rose had also reluctantly recited the name of Sarah Good. Callie had assumed that was the name meant to be spoken by the absent girl. Maybe, but not necessarily. Rafferty penciled Leah Kormos's name under Good's, placing a question mark after it. Then, looking at it again, and knowing Rose had also recited that name, he went back and penciled in Rose's name as well, also followed by a question mark. Sarah Good could be Rose's second ancestor, after all. With Elizabeth Howe's name, he penciled in the names of both Rose and Leah, both followed by question marks. Finally, with his pencil, he crossed both Leah's and Rose's names off the list.

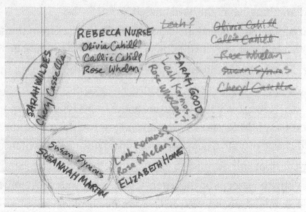

He held up the sketch and looked at it. The ink had a good psychological effect, as if he'd actually figured something out, though he didn't really know any more than he'd known before. The drawing was still as confusing as this case had become.

Despite Callie's recollection that the police were there "all the time," he could find only three times on record when the police had been summoned. Twice when Rose and the girls had loud arguments, including the night of the murders, and once when an anonymous female caller complained about underage boys coming and going "at all hours."

He contacted the archives, once again requesting the missing box of evidence, number 9. If there were more police reports, more records of officers being called to Rose's house, that's probably where they were.

He flipped through some of the pages of handwritten comments about the women. The town gossip was so profuse it bordered on obsession. They had made a lot of enemies, breaking up marriages, threatening the moral code of a city already infamous for its rigid Puritan standards. The speculation of Satanism was brought up several times in the witness statements, though, when questioned further, none of the witnesses had any basis for their claims or any evidence to back up the accusations.

The victims: Olivia Cahill, Susan Symms, and Cheryl Cassella. He had backgrounds on all of them, along with lists of living relatives. None had come from a stable family, and each had left home at an early age. Cheryl had come to Salem in 1987 at seventeen because her mother, a bitter divorcée, told her there was a real Salem witch on her father's side of the family. She met Rose at the Center for Salem Witch Trials Research, where Rose helped her find her ancestor who was executed on July 19, 1692. She moved into Rose's house on Daniels Street a few days later. Though Ann had claimed otherwise, rumor had it Cheryl had been briefly involved with one coven, studying the Craft, or at least learning a few spells.

Susan was an albino originally from Miami, teased and bullied all of her life, until her family moved to Marblehead, and she discovered her connection to the accused witches (again at the center). When her father was transferred, Susan stayed behind, moving into Rose's house. According to witness statements, it was Susan who first became fixated on the idea that Salem's accused really were witches— with supernatural powers—a belief that certainly alienated her from

Rose. Hers was the body that the trophies were taken from the night of the killings; Rafferty looked at the photos of her missing skin and hair.

Callie's mother, Olivia, was the most unusual. According to Rose's account, Callie and Olivia had arrived from New Orleans on Halloween when Callie was three. Olivia had been drawn to Salem because she knew she was related to one of its accused and had always felt as if she had magical powers herself. Almost out of money, she and Callie had been sleeping on the common until Eva Whitney had taken pity on mother and child, giving Olivia a job waiting tables in her tearoom. When she heard that Olivia was related to Rebecca Nurse, Eva introduced her to Rose and the center. "You three are long-lost family," Eva told Rose. Rose asked Olivia and Callie to call her Auntie Rose, and a connection in blood and spirit was made. Within a week, Olivia and Callie moved into Rose's house.

In the short time Rafferty had known Callie, they'd never really talked about her mother. He knew she had visited Olivia's grave, but beyond that he hadn't known how much Callie remembered about her mother. Not her behavior, certainly. He'd seen the shock on Callie's face when their provocative encounters were described by Ann. According to the files, Olivia had been involved with many men in Salem. And possibly some underage boys, or so some of the witness statements had suggested. Rose had evidently argued vehemently to get her to stop this—she'd argued that with them all. That was not just witness hearsay, it was public record. Rafferty thought Rose was probably the only voice of parental reason any of them had.

According to all accounts, the girls, who'd started to call themselves the Goddesses, began to see that they had power over the men in Salem. They believed their powers had been passed down through the generations—from their witch ancestors.

He wished he'd known Rose back when she was in her prime. She'd taken in these young women who had no place else to go. She had obviously helped raise Callie. Though her cause on behalf of Salem's accused had taken some quirky turns, it seemed a noble one. She had devoted her life to seeing justice done for the victims of the trials, and he gave her credit for her fortitude. As life's purposes went, it was certainly better than the more selfish drives most people followed, himself included.

There was nothing in the Goddess files about Leah Kormos, the one he and Callie had conjectured was the fifth petal. He needed to know more about Leah. The one who had broken the so-called rules. She had possibly been seen arguing with the Goddesses, accusing them of betraying her. She should have been a suspect. But the trail ended there.

Rafferty searched the local phone directories for the name Kormos, trying several different spellings, since Callie had likely never seen the name written out. He found a few listings and called. No one had heard of Leah.

Then he called Barry Marcus. "I need to talk to Rose."

"What about?"

"I'm looking for someone. A suspect. Someone who might actually take the focus off of Rose for a change."

They met at the hospital. Barry was fifteen minutes late, so Rafferty waited in the corridor. When they entered, Rose was sitting in a chair writing in her journal.

"Well, isn't this a surprise?" she said, closing the journal and standing to greet them as if they were houseguests.

"Rafferty has some questions for you," Barry said.

"Okay," Rose said, slightly more tentative at the thought of interrogation.

Rafferty gestured for Rose to sit back down and took a seat himself on the heater in front of the window. "Did you know a girl named Leah Kormos?"

Rose stared at him for a long time but said nothing.

"Callie told me she was one of the Goddesses."

"Yes," Rose said.

"You remember her?"

"Yes," Rose said.

"Did she live with you?"

"No," Rose said.

"Not on Daniels Street with the others?"

"No."

"Wasn't she one of the Goddesses?" he asked again.

Rose shifted in her seat. The word made her uncomfortable.

"Isn't that what they called them?"

"I've told you already, the goddess was diminished. The goddess turned." Rose was starting to hyperventilate.

"I think that's enough," Barry said.

"Okay," Rafferty said. "I'm sorry, Rose. I didn't mean to upset you. I just need to find this girl. This Leah."

Rose turned away.

Barry held the door for Rafferty, when Rose called after him.

"I think she lived in the dorms."

Rafferty waited for Rose to add more details, but she had gone silent.

He searched the 1989 records of the local colleges and universities, Salem State first, then Endicott, and other local schools. He was about to start searching prep school rosters when he found her registered at Montserrat, an art school. On scholarship and living in a dorm, she was there for the spring semester in early 1989. Her grades were good. She'd evidently registered for the fall semester but never came back after summer vacation. Looking for her home address, Rafferty requested more information, marking the request as official police business. It was against the school's policy to give out home addresses, they said.

"Get permission, or I'll get a court order," he told them.

Rafferty stopped at Mickey Doherty's pirate shop on his way to Ann's. Mickey was in full costume and holding court with a group of middle-aged women.

"I need to talk to you," Rafferty said, too abruptly.

"Never a good sign for a pirate when the chief of police wants to talk to you," Mickey said with a laugh.

The women scattered.

"This better be good," Mickey said. "Those were paying customers."

"I'll just bet," Rafferty said.

Now Mickey looked worried.

"Relax. I'm not here to talk about your side business," Rafferty said. "It's your new business I'm interested in."

"You want me to look up your family tree? You're more likely related to one of the accusers than one of the accused." Mickey managed a laugh.

Rafferty ignored the comment, handing Mickey a list of names he'd written on a legal pad.

"What's all this?"

"Names I want you to look up."

The information Rafferty handed Mickey was spotty at best. But it included the Goddesses' full names as well as the names of their parents. And, of course, Rose. The only one he didn't have full information for was Leah Kormos. "I want you to tell me which one of these women was related to Sarah Good."

"Sarah Good, huh?" Mickey looked over the paper, then up at Rafferty.

"Can you do that?"

"For a price."

"How about I don't *become* one of the accusers and arrest you?"

"Sounds like fair market value." Mickey nodded.

"Start with that one," Rafferty said, pointing to Leah Kormos.

"Aye, aye, Captain," Mickey said. "But you're going to have to get me more information than just a name."

"I'm working on it," Rafferty said.

Rafferty walked out of Mickey's store and across the wharf to Ann's Shop of Shadows. It was just 7:00 P.M., and Ann was locking up. "I sense this isn't a social call," she said when she saw his expression.

"I need you to tell me everything you know about the Goddesses," he said, ignoring her comment. He didn't do social calls with Ann. Not since that night a few years back. It had been a mistake, and it had clearly been his fault. When he'd tried to apologize, she'd shrugged it off. "It never happened," she'd said. They hadn't talked about it again.

"Didn't we just do this? I didn't really know them. Everything I know is hearsay."

"I want to hear what you say without Callie Cahill around."

She held the door open, and Rafferty walked inside.

"They weren't Satanists, were they?"

"Of course not. They called all witches Satanists back then. Though I don't think they were witches, either, not exactly. As I said before, they weren't solitaries, and they weren't studying with any of the covens in town."

"Where did they learn things, then?"

"If the rumors are true, maybe at the Left Hand Path. That store had a big selection of books on every kind of spell imaginable. The best around. We all bought books there. I thought it was a shame when they closed, but that's just me. It was a great resource. As I said before, magic was getting popular here back in the eighties. Everybody had a bit of leftover hippie in them, especially in this city. We all believed in magical powers: We conducted séances, read tarot, believed in astrology. My Wiccan friends and I worshiped the Goddess. But those women . . . they believed they *were* the Goddess."

"Wasn't that a nickname someone gave them?"

"I always heard it was one they gave themselves."

"From what I've read, they were pushing a lot of boundaries."

"That's an understatement. Sex is power, and they knew it. Men followed them around like puppies. The girls seduced them, and some would say they took advantage of them. Sometimes separately, often all together. It was a game."

"Do you know about the 'rules'?"

"What rules?"

"Callie said they had a set of rules. Evidently for seduction."

"If there were rules"—Ann shrugged—"I never heard about them. I heard a lot of other fascinating things; they were very open about what they were doing. You could ask the 'victims' if they knew about rules."

"The victims?"

"That's what the locals called the men: victims. That's not in the files? Every once in a while, the girls would 'take' a man, someone having trouble at home. He'd be gone for days, ignoring his work, his family. Eventually he would drag himself home to his wife, sick and exhausted. I know the Goddesses swore it gave them energy. Maybe that was a rule?"

"Do you know the names of any of these so-called victims?"

"I don't," Ann said. "And even if I did, I'm not sure I'd tell you." She looked at him for a long time. "I believe in discretion."

An awkward moment passed.

Rafferty regrouped. "The sexual revolution was long over in 'eighty-nine, and yet some of the accounts I've read, the condemnation of these girls, it reads as an overreaction, as if it happened in the 1600s."

"It's the same overreaction it was back in the 1600s . . . fear."

"Fear of infidelity? Of the devil?"

"Yes, both maybe. And something else. A number of cases of heterosexual HIV were diagnosed on the North Shore right about that time. The sexual revolution might have brought sex out of the prover-bial closet, but AIDS made it lethal. Someone started a rumor that the Goddesses were spreading it."

Rafferty ran his hand through his hair. "Were they?"

"I doubt it, but it was easy for people to believe, and that's all that mattered. They needed someone to blame. It certainly didn't help with their reputation around town." Ann looked at him curiously. "I thought this case was closed."

"Cold, not closed."

"Are you pursuing something new? Since this thing with Rose?"

He didn't answer.

"The trouble with those girls started the minute they decided they'd inherited special powers from their ancestors, the women who were all hanged on the same day."

"Why?"

"Think about it. It's a short step from believing the accused had supernatural powers to justifying their hangings and the atrocities they suffered while awaiting execution. Those condemned women were not witches in any sense of the word. They certainly never 'signed the devil's book.' Which—for the record—has nothing to do whatsoever with any witch I've ever known. The Salem accused were Puritans."

"And subject to Puritan laws."

"Exactly. Thank God those laws changed, but, in some ways, not much else has. The accused were usually women, sometimes elderly. There's speculation that some were mentally ill. Or homeless."

"Like Sarah Good."

"Yes."

"And Rose."

"And once you start demonizing groups of people, when you make them the *other*, you can justify doing just about anything you want to them, can't you? Look at history if you don't believe me."

Rafferty got the call as he was driving back to the station.

"There's been a break-in at that condemned house on Daniels Street," Jay-Jay said, explaining who'd called it in. "Do you want me to send a car, or are you still down in that neck of the woods?"

"I'm here," Rafferty said, U-turning as he spoke.

"You need backup?"

"Nope. I got it."

Rafferty didn't climb the decrepit porch to get in; instead he jimmied the front door. Callie looked more surprised to see him there than he was to see her. "I figure we've got about ten minutes until our friend across the street calls 911 again and Jay-Jay sends the backup I told him I didn't need," he said. "You still want to look around?"

Callie looked a lot like a teenager standing in front of him, staring at her shoes.

"Am I under arrest?" she asked.

"Not yet," he said. He turned on the flashlight he was carrying, which was about a hundred times more powerful than hers. There was nothing in the front room except a few old McDonald's bags. The kitchen was empty: both sink and stove removed, copper pipes ripped out of the wall, probably stolen. It looked as if someone had started to sweep but abandoned the project, leaving a pile of debris in the corner: It had a network of cobwebs running from it to the handle of a base cabinet and down to the floor.

In a back bedroom closet was a dead water rat.

"Oh God," Callie said, stepping back quickly to get out of the closet. As she shifted, her foot pushed through a rotting floorboard, and she nearly fell.

Rafferty caught her by the arm. "You okay?"

"Yeah. Thanks," she said, still shivering from the sight of the rat.

"Be careful," he said. "A lot of these boards look rotten." He shone his light up to a damp-looking patch of plaster in the corner. "Water damage." He pointed the beam back at the floor in an effort to identify other rotting boards.

Rafferty shone the flashlight into a crack between floorboards, then stepped over the rotting one to retrieve an envelope that had fallen in. Shaking the dust from it, he turned it over. "To Dagda from Morrigan," he said, reading aloud. "Are those names of Goddesses?"

Callie shook her head. "I don't think so," she said. "I don't remember hearing them before."

"There's something else," he said, squinting. He brought the flashlight in closer, making the envelope translucent and revealing a faded lipstick kiss.

"A love letter maybe?" she said, and it triggered a memory. "My mother and the others used to receive 'love letters' from their . . . 'friends.' Sometimes I'd recite them."

"Love letters?"

She nodded. "Rose gave me elocution lessons. She made me memorize, too, and I'd perform poems in front of my mother and the others. In the elocutionist's pose." She indicated one hand poised over the other, palm up against palm down at chest level. "At the end I had to curtsy."

"Sounds adorable."

"It was meant to help me gain poise in front of an audience. Not sure the poise thing worked, but it did help me learn to read."

"And the love letters?"

"Rose worked nights at the center. Most people came in to do their research after work or on Saturdays. When she was out, my mother and the Goddesses had me recite passages from love letters. I'd struggle with words I didn't recognize. They found it hilarious."

Callie could feel herself blushing as she remembered the words she'd had to sound out, words she was all too familiar with now.

"I didn't have to take the elocutionist's stance when I was reading those letters, but they did insist on the curtsy at the end."

She remembered the Goddesses giggling and whooping throughout the reading, but it was the curtsy that sent them over the edge. They would laugh until they couldn't breathe, then they would be silent catching their breath, and one of them would start to giggle and they would be off again. Callie had counted these times as happy ones, with all the Goddesses together and herself as the center of their attention. Now, as she recalled more of the context, she had a different feeling.

She could see Rafferty's quick look of disapproval before he covered it. "But you don't recall any of them being called Morrigan?"

"I really don't," she said. "Is this a clue?"

"I don't know," Rafferty said. "It might be, Nancy Drew."

A beam from headlights moved across the walls, lighting the room as the backup cruiser pulled up out front. Rafferty looked out the window to see the neighbor coming over to talk to the officers Jay-Jay had predictably dispatched.

"Let's get out of here," Rafferty said. "Before we both end up in jail."

He ushered Callie out the back door, then left by the front himself, stopping to talk to the policemen and the neighbor before getting into his car, giving Callie time to get away unnoticed. Then he drove around the corner and pulled up next to her, opening the passenger door. "Where are you parked?"

She pointed up toward the common.

"Come on, I'll give you a ride."

Montserrat College of Art called the station the next morning with Leah's last known address.

The three-decker where she'd lived in Beverly was long gone; he'd found a condo development in its place. He'd talked to one of the neighbors. "The kid was a runaway," he said. "She was in school, I think, but then she came home. She didn't stay long. She and the father never got along."

The man couldn't remember when Leah ran away, but it certainly hadn't happened before the murders, Rafferty knew that much.

The father had died a long time ago, the man said. "Lung cancer. There was a younger sister, Becky. She moved away. Had a kid. Last I heard she was living in New Hampshire."

The man didn't know where, said he'd heard somewhere that the guy had run off, leaving her a single mother. He hadn't found anything online, but Rafferty had recently found a copy of Leah's birth certificate at the town hall in Beverly, though the original had been handwritten and was almost illegible, and he couldn't quite make out the parents' names. He'd managed to locate the father's name from online real estate records, then had found his birth certificate; he was born in Beverly, his parents having come over from Greece just after the war. Rafferty found nothing on either the mother or the sister.

He dialed Mickey from his cell.

"Greece, huh? Then it's probably not the father's lineage we're looking for. Plus it's really hard to trace records back to Europe."

"Give it a try."

"Get me the mother's records."

"I'm working on it."

On his way back to Salem, Rafferty stopped at the Beverly Police Station on the off chance that someone had been looking for Leah and had filed a report. He spoke to a detective he knew, another transplant, who had moved north from Connecticut. When Rafferty mentioned the name Leah Kormos, he thought he noticed one of the older cops shoot a quick look at his buddy.

It took a while for the detective to locate the records. "She was a runaway all right. Disappeared into thin air."

"When did she disappear?"

"Let's see," he said, looking at the screen. "It says here that she was reported missing on November fifth, 1989."

CHAPTER EIGHTEEN

December 1, 2014
SALEM

> *Witchcraft comes from carnal lust,*
> *which is in women insatiable.*
>
> —*Malleus Maleficarum*

THEY STOOD AT THE "FOUR CORNERS OF THE CIRCLE," each woman holding a candle representing east, west, north, or south. As he sat on the bench watching them at the far end of Derby Wharf, the wind was off the ocean and the candles kept going out. Rafferty had seen this ceremony performed before. Ann named it "calling up the seas." Once it was drawn, you couldn't penetrate the circle, not without cutting an entrance of some kind, a metaphorical door to pass through.

"Circles don't have corners," he'd said when she'd tried to explain the process.

"Don't be so literal," she'd replied.

"What would happen if I just walked in?" Rafferty had asked. "If I just stepped inside to say hello?"

"At the very least you'd break the spell," she said. "That's the best-case scenario."

"And the worst?"

"You'd be exposing those inside—and probably yourself—to some danger. Inside the circle, you are protected. By the gods and goddesses you've invoked to join you."

"And outside?"

"Outside are the ones you didn't invite. Fairies and impish creatures. And they can be a jealous lot. They love to crash a party."

Rafferty had listened with the amused detachment of a nonbeliever. Even so, today he kept his distance and waited until the ceremony was over and the circle had been uncast before talking to Ann. He watched until she pointed with her wand, undoing the circle counterclockwise or, as he'd once heard her refer to it, "widdershins."

"Three times in one week?" she said, spotting him waiting for her as she and the witches walked back toward shore. "People will start to talk."

"Raising the sea again? The climate change people will be all over you," he replied.

"Just the opposite, actually. It's a spell called Time and Tides. It's meant to turn back both. As a *cure* for climate change."

"And is it working?"

"Time will tell," she said.

"I thought time didn't exist," he answered.

"Linear time doesn't exist," she grouched. "Enough. What do you want to ask me *this* time?"

"I need to know more about goddesses."

"Goddesses in general or those poor girls from 1989?"

"In general. You have a particular goddess you worship, right? From a specific group?"

"My coven has chosen the Celtic pantheon, though it more or less matches the Greek, Roman, and Norse ones. We worship all of the gods and goddesses from our group, each of us choosing one with whom we identify. Mine is Danu, mother goddess of water and war."

"Isn't that a contradiction in terms?"

"Not at all," Ann said. "I can handle her. But you do have to be careful who you choose, and remember that, by calling down your goddess, you are summoning all of her powers. Which is why we discourage novices from making the choice too early." She sighed.

"I know you don't believe in this, so what's your real question, Rafferty?"

He got to the point. "Do you think the 1989 'Goddesses' might have had a special goddess they worshiped, a goddess named Morrigan?"

Ann suddenly looked interested.

"Is she one of yours?"

"She's Celtic, yes, but she's not someone to emulate."

"Is it Morgan le Fay?"

"No, completely different derivation. The Morrigan comes from the Gaelic. Loosely translated as the Phantom Queen."

"That sounds ominous."

"It also means 'terror.' She's a powerful lady. I'd stay away from her."

"What about Dagda?"

"Dagda is a god, not a goddess. Legend says he trysts with Morrigan on Samhain."

"Hold on a minute," Rafferty said, pulling out his phone to take notes.

"I have a particular interest in Dagda," admitted Ann. "He is a good god. Either Danu's father or her son."

"That's quite a wide range of possibility."

"It's all in the interpretation." Ann shrugged. "This has something to do with those girls?"

"Maybe," he said. "It was a random name written on an envelope—"

"Probably not random," she said. "But not good, either."

She thought about it before speaking again. "Some describe the Morrigan as a triple goddess in the usual sense: the maiden, the mother, and the crone. Others say she's three sisters: Nemain, Macha, and Badb."

Rafferty handed his cell to her. "Spell those for me, please."

She typed in the names, handing it back to him.

"Pronounce them again?"

Ann spoke slowly, highlighting each syllable: Ne-main, Ma-cha. She stopped before she got to the last one.

"And this one?"

"Badb," she said, looking as if she'd just realized something. "Which, in some parts of Ireland, is the same thing as this." She typed it slowly, then turned the phone so he could see. B-E-A-N S-I-D-H-E.

He looked at it, trying to sound it out. "Bean what?"

"Banshee."

CHAPTER NINETEEN

December 10, 2014
PRIDE'S CROSSING

> *I am a cipher. I carry no weight, no worth, no influence.*
> *I represent nothing. I do not exist.*
> —ROSE'S *Book of Trees*

"PAUL AND I ARE FRIENDS. WE'RE NOT SLEEPING TOGETHER, if that's what you're wondering, Mrs. Whiting."

"Yet that's what everyone in Pride's Crossing is thinking," Emily said.

Callie watched Emily look around the boathouse. Paul's research papers for his dissertation were spread all over the table. There were scattered photos of images found in the rock caves and some open reference books. On the computer screen was an article on the cave restoration that his adviser had written and Paul had contributed to for *National Geographic.*

"At least you're still getting some work done," Emily said to Paul. She turned to Callie, her face pinched. "And you still have a job and an apartment in Northampton?"

"Would you like me to leave, Mrs. Whiting? Is that what you came to say?"

After Callie had confessed and apologized to Paul, they'd started meeting for coffee every day at the Atomic Cafe in downtown Beverly, since Salem was becoming more and more problematic for Callie. There had been several incidents in Salem, and people were beginning

to recognize her. One confrontation at the hospital had particularly
unnerved her. On her way to visit Rose, Callie had been followed into
the stairway by an older man, who'd stepped in front of her, blocking
her way.

"I knew it wasn't true." He had leaned in so close she'd felt his
breath and seen his eyes filling up with tears. "I knew you'd come
back to me."

She'd let Rafferty know about the man.

She'd heard from Towner that Rafferty had been called on the
carpet for his "bias" toward Rose, and the fact that Callie was living
at their house was fanning the flames. Around town, more hateful
graffiti about Rose kept appearing, one adding Callie's name. Someone had thrown a rock through a window at the tearoom. Reporters
were harassing her. She suspected it had been Ann who'd passed the
word—she was the only one besides Rafferty, Towner, and Paul who
knew her identity for certain—but Towner said no, that Ann wouldn't
do that. Callie wasn't so sure.

A few days later, Towner had come to her. "I'm so sorry to have to
do this, Callie, but I need you to find another place to stay." Towner's
concerned expression reflected her words. "Rafferty's always been
worried about your well-being in Salem, and frankly I'm worried about
his as well."

"I understand. I'll find another place." The truth was, Callie had
already been looking online for other places to stay. "You've gone way
past the call of duty by putting me up."

"Thank you," Towner had said, adding, "please don't stop coming
for tea. I love seeing you. You're like the daughter I never had. There's
just some trouble with you *living* here."

Callie still visited Towner for tea, but far less often. She stopped
going to the cemetery altogether. Now, when she visited Salem, it was
almost always to see Rose. She drove around to the back side of the
hospital and used a little-known entrance. She'd also begun looking
at short-term sublets in Beverly not far from Pride's Crossing.

When Paul had heard what was going on, he'd invited her to stay
at his boathouse. "I'm leaving for Italy sometime in February," he'd

said. "Then you can have the place to yourself. Meanwhile, I'm happy to share."

"Just as friends, right?"

"Of course. I didn't mean to suggest otherwise."

He'd turned away as soon as he said it, which probably meant he'd had something else in mind, so it was good she'd brought it up.

He'd generously given her his bed, and for the past three days she'd slept in it while he camped on the couch in the tower's reading nook. With the exception of the first night, it had gone smoothly.

"You sleep with your eyes open, did you know that?" he'd said the next morning as he handed her a cup of coffee. "You were doing it that day at Norman's Woe, and again last night."

"You were watching me sleep?" Callie, horrified, had put down the coffee.

"No. I mean yes. Just for a few minutes. I heard you talking and sort of moaning, and I came down to see what was wrong. I thought you were having another nightmare."

Waking memories, that's what her psychologists had called them. The nuns had called them visions, another reason they'd found her frightening. Sleeping with her eyes open had been one of the things that had scared them about her. For a short time, she had even sleep-walked, which had made the nuns start locking her inside her room every night, fearing her escape. Her dreams were vivid, if disjointed, and she'd often awakened in a cold sweat, unable to get back to sleep until sunrise. For the most part, the dreams were snippets of memories from the night of the murders, details that came back unbidden and unwelcome.

"You didn't think to wake me up?" she'd asked Paul, incredulous.

"By the time I got up the stairs, you had stopped moaning."

"But you watched me anyway."

"Yes," he'd said, holding her gaze. "I did." There was a definite sexual undertone.

"Well, stop it." She'd scowled at him.

Now Emily's disapproving expression mimicked her own that morning. It was clear Emily didn't believe Callie and Paul were just friends.

"I'll go if that's what you want," Callie said. She was getting used to being asked to move on. She tried to sound sincere, but her tone had an edge.

"Not necessarily."

"Then what's the point of this visit, Mother? Callie is trying to help Rose. And whomever I have as a guest is none of your business."

"Given that this is still my house, and you're still my son"—Emily frowned—"I'd say it's very much my business."

"Callie was accosted in Salem a few days ago. Did you know that?"

"No." Emily's tone was tentative.

"Well, she was. You may not realize this, but everyone in Salem seems to have picked up on it. Callie was the little girl who survived the Goddess Murders."

Paul had already explained to Callie that Emily hadn't moved to Pride's Crossing and married Finn until a few months after the murders. Just months after that, Paul had been born. They hadn't been in town when the murders happened, but they knew about them. Everybody did.

"Oh my God, Callie. I had no idea. I'm so sorry." Emily stared at Callie as if trying to understand the full implications of what she'd just heard. "My God, what you must have gone through."

"She apparently looks enough like her mother that Rafferty and Towner don't think she should be staying in Salem."

"What happened? Who accosted you?"

Callie looked at Paul, who nodded.

Callie related the story about the older man.

"'I knew you'd come back to me'?" Emily repeated. "What does that mean?"

"I think he believed I *was* my mother."

"Then she got several calls from *The Salem Journal,* trying to persuade her to do an interview about the murders," Paul interjected. "They wouldn't leave her alone. And someone broke a window at the tearoom. She can't stay in Salem now. So please, I don't want you coming in here and telling her she can't live in Pride's Crossing, either."

"If you'd be quiet and listen for a minute, you might give me half a chance to say what I came here to say." Emily turned away from her son and spoke directly to Callie. "If you're going to be our long-term guest, Callie, I'd like you to stay in the main house."

"For the sake of appearances?" Paul asked.

"Not entirely." Emily took a long breath, as if reconsidering, before she continued. "I would like you to treat me," she said. "With those . . . bowl things."

Callie had marked Emily's expression from the moment she'd entered the boathouse. She'd believed she had been witnessing disapproval; now she realized she was seeing something else. "You're in pain."

"Yes," Emily said.

Paul's face softened.

"Is this something recent?" Callie wanted to know.

"It's been intermittent. Until recently."

"What does Dr. Hayes say?" Paul asked.

"Nothing he hasn't said before."

Callie thought for a long moment. Truth be told, she'd be relieved to get out of the boathouse. The whole place smelled like Paul: soap, sweat, and some kind of spice she had smelled at Ann's shop that day she'd told Rafferty about her memory of the party. She hadn't been as attracted to anyone as she was to Paul Whiting in, well, ever. It would be too easy to just walk up those stairs at night . . . not long ago, she would have. But ever since the waking memory she'd had at Hammond Castle, the vision of the naked man with Paul's eyes, and Ann's description of the Goddesses' seductive behavior—she'd been more and more uncomfortable with her own sexuality. She'd never realized how much her behavior mirrored the Goddesses'. Intentional seductions followed by one-night stands with no attachments. A preference she'd always thought of as her own had now become something else. Was she unconsciously mirroring the behavior she'd seen as a child? The idea was disconcerting at best. At worst, it made her feel slightly ill. She wasn't sure she could trust her own instincts, and in Paul's house, under the same roof, those instincts were screaming at her. And then there was Paul's obvious involvement with Ann. Her mind told her to keep her distance, even as her body was telling her otherwise.

"You don't have to offer me a room in your house, Mrs. Whiting. I'll treat you. I can find another place to stay." Callie's tone had become softer. This whole thing was getting too complicated, and Emily wasn't well.

"Don't be silly," Emily said and smiled at Callie. "I want you to stay with us."

It wasn't true, and Callie knew it, but it was gracious. And in February, when Paul went back to Italy, she'd have the boathouse to herself. At least until she found a place to live, someplace she could take Rose to when she finally got out of the hospital.

"I'll have to go to Northampton to get my singing bowls."

She wasn't certain, but she thought she read disappointment on Paul's face.

The cold and rain made the Mass Pike slippery. Callie turned up the radio to listen to Amy Black's "Alabama" to distract herself from the confrontation with the nuns that she could no longer avoid. The fact was, she was ready for it. She needed answers. *Why did they tell me Rose was dead?*

The morning the nuns from St. James's had found her, they'd told her they had been outside with all the students when they heard strange cries echoing down the North River. They'd thought at first it was some animal, a cat trapped under the brick building. After the children were led inside, the nuns had searched the property and finally realized the sound was coming from the hill behind Boston Street. They'd found Callie standing, trancelike and silent. The sounds had ceased.

It was a miracle, they'd said, that she had lived, protected by the rosary she clutched so tightly. The mark it left represented not only the five wounds of Christ but the Virgin Mary herself.

The song on the radio ended, and Callie switched lanes, passing a

Massachusetts state trooper car hiding in the underpass. She checked her speed and slowed down.

When the nuns at the children's home in Northampton had found out about the Goddesses and about Rose, they'd changed their minds. The miracle had quickly turned to sacrilege, and they'd begun to watch her with suspicious eyes, looking for something unholy, fearful that whatever had happened on Halloween night had scarred Callie far beyond the physical. "Why was there no figure of Christ on your rosary?" they'd asked her. "Do the petal scars stand for the five accused witches?"

She was so young; she hadn't known how to lie or even to keep quiet about things that might be considered strange. When she'd told them she could see things, images of events before they happened, their fears about her had multiplied. In class, Callie often answered questions just before they were asked, as if she could read them as they were forming in the minds of the sisters. It was uncanny, and she'd sometimes been punished for it and called impertinent or, even worse, accused of cheating. Once, during an oral exam, Callie had given the answer before the question was asked, and had been accused of stealing a copy of the questions from Sister Agony's desk. And there were other things she just seemed to know. Secret things about the nuns that she'd never been told. It worried them.

In self-defense, Callie had taken to eavesdropping on their conversations about her. "Do you think it's witchcraft?" she'd heard one of the older nuns ask, her voice fearful.

"Well, there are seers in the Bible, too," a younger nun had responded. "Weren't the prophets seers?"

"That young girl is no prophet," the older nun had declared.

The order was known as an old-fashioned one, and the children's home was a place where, with the exception of Sister Agony, the more timid and world averse sisters of the order often ended up. When it came to superstition and fear, they were easy marks, not entirely unlike the Puritan citizens of Salem whom Rose had often described to Callie. Group hysteria was easy to ignite, and Callie had to admit she wasn't entirely innocent of lighting that fire. To amuse the other girls, she'd often thrown her voice down a seemingly empty hallway, making one of the nuns turn to see who had spoken and find no one behind her. The young girls had giggled as they hid inside an empty classroom watching one of the more easily frightened nuns shiver, cross herself, and hurry away. It had made the girls admire Callie's mischief, but it hadn't made her popular. The truth was, Callie's history had scared all of them.

Callie checked her speed again as she neared Chicopee, then took the I-91 North exit toward Amherst and her apartment.

Each time the nuns had sent her away to a new foster home, they'd seemed relieved, and every time she'd come back, they'd grown more agitated, studying her for "signs."

Why did I keep getting sent back to them? And why did they allow it? Callie pounded on the steering wheel in frustration, thinking of all the years she'd spent believing she was alone in the world, when Rose had been just 120 miles away. The last time she'd landed on their doorstep, insisting she wouldn't be fostered again, the nuns had told her they'd let her stay because they "loved" her . . . now she knew they'd only done it because there'd been no place else for her to go. She'd often suspected that they also felt tasked to save her soul and make sure she didn't end up like her mother. Or, worse, like Rose. *They must have rejoiced when I went to college.*

There was no one at her apartment when she arrived. Her room hadn't been disturbed. Even though it contained all of her belongings, it still looked as if no one lived in it, which was partly true. Callie had never spent much time here. The bed was always made, and everything was perfectly arranged, a neat and tidy version of postcollege life. The only things that violated the image were the bowls. Four of them were lined up on the dresser; the other three were at the nursing home. She pulled the rest of her clothes from the closet, using them to pad the bowls as she placed them into the Volvo. After she'd cleaned out the room, she left a note for her roommates, telling them she was going to stay on the North Shore for a while and giving them permission to use her room for guests. *Happy Holidays*, she wrote, signing her name.

She didn't plan to wish the nuns happy anything. She was too angry. Part of her wanted to grab the bowls and go, but she wasn't going to do that. She was seething about the lies they had told her. It was time.

She drove to Northampton, parked in her regular spot at the All Saints' Home, and walked inside, nodding to the receptionist, who was on the phone. She walked directly to Agony's office and opened the door without knocking, not bothering to close it again as she entered. The nun was seated at her desk reading, her glasses low on her nose. She looked tired. "Callie," she said with a smile, which quickly faded when she saw the expression on Callie's face.

"Why did you lie to me?"

"What?"

"Why did you tell me that Rose Whelan was dead?"

The prioress got up and closed the door against Callie's raised voice.

"She was the only family I had."

Agony sat down again and quickly folded her hands, the rapid movement summoning a memory. Agony's nickname had come from the ruler she used to punish the girls. It happened so fast you almost never saw it coming. They'd stopped using the old-fashioned punishment the year after Callie arrived, and Agony had taken to folding her hands, holding them in prayer pose until her knuckles went white in an effort to control her temper. Now the nun's order formally forbade corporal punishment, but the ruler still sat on the nun's desk, and Callie remembered its sting. Most of the girls had gotten slapped across their knuckles. Callie had received her lashes across her scar, the stigmata that had become unholy.

Callie watched the prioress's knuckles go white. It was a long time before she spoke.

"How *is* Rose?"

Callie stared at her. "Are you fucking kidding me?"

CHAPTER TWENTY

December 10, 2014
PRIDE'S CROSSING

The music is not in the notes, but in the silence between.
—WOLFGANG AMADEUS MOZART

IT WAS AFTER DINNER BY THE TIME CALLIE GOT BACK TO Pride's Crossing. The harbor was fogged in, the horns wailing mournfully from across the water. In the driveway of Pride's Heart, she ran into Marta wearing a trench coat and leather gloves and carrying a manila envelope.

It had stopped raining, but the ground was still slippery. Callie's foot slid on the wet gravel just as she reached the landing.

"Whoa," Marta said, reaching out. "Need some help?"

"I'm good," Callie said, rebalancing the huge quartz bowl she was carrying.

"Where is everyone? Where's Darren?" Marta asked her.

"It's his day off," Callie said. Emily had told her that when she gave her the key. "I don't know where Emily and Finn are, though."

"Let me at least get the door for you," Marta said, taking the key from Callie and opening the huge wooden door.

The sound of their footsteps echoed as they stepped inside, the bowl picking up the vibration. Callie put the bowl down on the stone floor, and the echo reverberated through the hall.

"That's wild," Marta said. "Is it alive?"

Callie laughed. "I sometimes think it might be."

"I saw more of them in the car. I'd be glad to help bring them in."

"Thank you," Callie said, "but Paul's on his way."

"Oh," Marta said, smiling. "I heard you and Paul were an item."

"We're not an item." Callie laughed. "We're friends."

"Okay," Marta said, clearly not buying it. "Well, anyway, welcome to the neighborhood."

"Thank you," Callie said, not quite knowing what to do next. Without Emily here, she wasn't really sure what the parameters were. "I need a glass of water."

"I'll get you one. Hildy's not here today, but I know where everything is," Marta said, leading her into the kitchen and getting a glass from the pantry.

"Bottled or tap?" Marta asked.

"Either," Callie said.

Marta went to the refrigerator and pulled out two bottles. "Plain or bubbly?"

"Such luxury," Callie said.

"Nothing but luxury here," Marta said, motioning Callie to the kitchen table, then taking a seat across from her, co-opting an old Arlo Guthrie tune and customizing it, singing. . . . "You can get anything you want at Emily's restaurant."

Callie laughed, knowing the tune. "Excepting Emily."

Marta smiled. "Oh, you've picked the right house to move into," she said, her voice concealing a bit of an edge.

The door to the butler's pantry opened, and Paul came in. "How'd it go with the nuns?" he said. Then, realizing Callie wasn't alone, "Oh, Marta." His tone was neither welcoming nor surprised.

"I have some pledge papers for Finn," she said, standing up and preparing to leave. "Will one of you make sure he gets them?"

"Sure," Paul said, taking the envelope. "I'll put this on his desk."

They were on their third trip carrying in the bowls when Paul asked her again. "So what happened with Sister Agony?" He was dressed to help, casual with worn jeans and a blue sweater that matched his eyes. Alice blue, that's what Rose would have called the color. *Azure*, Callie thought. The color of the ocean—though not today. Today the grey sky and ocean had been a moody watercolor wash, and the air tasted of salt.

She gave him a withering look.

"That well, huh?"

"She didn't answer my question, if that's what you're asking."

"What did she say?"

"She claimed they didn't tell me about Rose to protect me, that they wanted to put distance between me and what happened. Evidently, the police questioned me so much I couldn't sleep, or, if I did, I had terrible nightmares."

"Which is well established," he said.

"Agony said they planned to tell me Rose was alive, but then she became a murder suspect, and they didn't want me to 'reexperience the trauma.'"

"It sounds logical, Callie," Paul admitted. "If ill-advised."

"It does. But I don't think it's the whole story."

Paul waited for her to continue, but she didn't. "Let's talk about something else," she said, looking at the bowl he was still holding. "Don't you want to put that down?"

"Not yet. I want to show you something first."

"Seriously?" she said, feigning horror. "I remember the last time you said that."

"Don't worry. This one is my idea, not Ann's."

She hated hearing him say Ann's name.

"We're not leaving the house. This has to do with your bowls." He led her into the library.

Tonight, the room was dark. With the staff gone, there was no fire burning in the massive fireplace. Paul turned on a table lamp, then walked to the far wall and pressed the button that turned the bookcase inward ninety degrees, revealing the hidden bar and the elevator leading down to the wine cellar, the one his father had been boasting about on Thanksgiving Day. Paul put down the bowl, opened the iron grate, and held it for her. "After you." She got in. He picked up the bowl again. "You have something to play this with?"

Callie reached into her pocket and pulled out a rubber wand. Now she was intrigued.

The elevator clanged loudly as it descended. They traveled past three levels of wooden racks filled with dusty bottles. At the first landing, Callie saw a corridor cut into the granite, leading to more racks. The air cooled as they descended. On the second level, another corridor led to a dark hallway with a huge wooden door at its end. At the bottom level, the elevator slowed to a grinding halt. Paul slid back the iron grate, then shoved open a thick glass door, securing it to brass cleats on the wall.

"Wait here," he said. A moment later, the space was bathed in soft light, illuminating the pink granite walls and floor of a huge room, about forty feet in diameter and almost perfectly round. There were no wine racks, no furniture at all except for an old couch against the wall, on which Paul carefully placed the bowl. At the far end appeared to be some sort of water feature. The faint musky smell of salt water and ambergris perfumed the air.

"This is a cave," Callie said, realizing what she was looking at.

"We call it the spa. It's where the bootleggers in our family used to store their hooch when it came down from Canada, before the house was built. It's too damp in this room for the wines, too close to the ocean. Hence the glass door," he said, pointing to the elevator. "If we didn't have that, the salt air would corrode the mechanics."

"Sounds like that's happening anyway," she said. "The grinding noises that elevator makes? My teeth hurt."

"It sounds bad"—he laughed—"but you get used to it. This cave is similar to those I'm restoring in Matera. The houses there are all built on top of hand-carved foundations, sometimes a few rooms, sometimes multifloored palazzi. The families added on to the structures above as they amassed greater wealth. Which is essentially what happened here."

"Interesting," said Callie, looking around.

"This wasn't carved with hand tools, though. Granite is not soft, like *tufo* stone; these are a natural phenomenon. The structuring of the floors and the passageways—what you saw from the elevator—was done later by construction crews."

"The more money, the bigger the house?"

"Exactly. Though the original Whiting wealth was amassed almost entirely from ill-gotten gains."

"Bootlegging," she said. She'd also heard gunrunning.

"Among other things. Cocaine and heroin in the early seventies. We were quite the family before my father married my mother. Thanks to her, fame, fortune, and respectability are our new métier."

Callie walked over to what appeared to be an open well in the stone floor surrounded by a polished wooden rim. She could hear water lapping. "What's this for? Bathtub gin?" Now she could hear the sound of the ocean.

"One would think," he said. "We call it the sea well. Actually, it's an early attempt at a hot tub, for seaweed baths. There's kelp lining the walls, and when the water is heated, it releases its oils."

"Seaweed baths? That sounds kind of . . . slimy."

"It's great for the skin."

"How do you heat the water?"

"There's a gas heater a few feet down that warms the water in the upper level."

"It has levels?"

"It's very deep. The water goes in and out with the tide."

"Are there seats?"

"About three feet down, there's a rim you can sit on."

She ran her hand along the top of the well and then tested the water. Her left hand had been burning since Northampton. Probably from the roughened quartz surfaces of the bowls. Or the encounter with Sister Agony. The warm water and the oils were soothing. "It's quite warm."

"Only when the tide is high." He laughed. "When I was younger, this place was off-limits, so it was, of course, the only place I wanted to go. I used to sneak down here. And I loved the sea well. I got stoned one night and decided to stay in longer than I should have." He shuddered. "Not such a good idea."

"Did you turn into a prune?"

"The tide was going out. Below the pipes and the heater, the walls are slick with kelp. There's no way to climb out. And it's much colder below the heater. I was in there for six hours before the tide came up again."

"Oh God," she said.

"Almost died of hypothermia. And sufficiently scared the hell out of myself. Amazing the things you experience as the body is shutting down. It was like some kind of limbo between life and death."

I can understand that feeling better than most.

"The colder I got, the more I imagined I was dead already, that bony fingers were grabbing me and trying to pull me under. It was lucky I knew that putting up a struggle would just send the blood to my extremities and kill me faster. Otherwise, I would have fought those hallucinations, and I probably wouldn't be here right now."

"God. That's horrifying. Did your parents rescue you?"

"The tide came up, and I crawled out. They hadn't even known I was down there."

"Did you tell them?"

"I made it to the phone," he said, pointing to the house line. "I had to be hospitalized for several days. As soon as they were certain I was going to live, they grounded me for a month and forbade me from ever going in this tub again without their supervision. Which was totally unnecessary. I haven't been in it since."

He led her away from the sea well to the middle of the room. "Anyway, this room, and not the hot tub of horror, is what I brought you to see. The acoustics in here are a lot like those in the healing caves in Matera," he said. He sang a note, and the sound circled the room, vibrating against the granite. She listened, then added a note in harmony, and the echo circled the room.

"The sound is amazing," Callie said, impressed. "We could be inside one of my singing bowls."

"There are veins of quartz running through the granite," he said, pointing to one. "Limestone as well. I think this would be a great place to treat my mother. I'd be glad to set up the room for you." He took the bowl off the couch, carried it to the middle of the room, and carefully placed it on the floor, motioning for her to play.

She hit the bowl once with the rubber wand to prime it, then slowly began to pull the wand around the perimeter. The sound was even richer and deeper than she had imagined.

"This is unbelievable."

She played it again. The sound moved elliptically, circling both from left to right and then from overhead to the floor. She listened, her eyes following the pattern. "It needs to be cut back a bit. The sound is supposed to circle clockwise, but it's moving this way as well." She indicated overhead and along the floor.

"Would a blanket on the floor fix that? Maybe a rug?" Paul said.

She hit the bowl one more time, listening intently, nodding.

"You think it will work?" Paul asked.

"It should work well for her. Your mother's resonant frequency is strong."

"What does that mean, exactly?"

"Everything and everyone vibrates to a certain frequency. Measured in tone and sound waves. If you can match it, the tone acts like a soothing massage on her cells."

"Will that stop the pain?"

"Pain is interesting," Callie said. "It has a particular frequency that's as unique as that of the individual, but our pain receptors can only handle so much information. If we can match the vibration of the pain frequency, making the same sound it makes, the receptors get overloaded, and the pain often just disappears."

"And how do you do that?"

"I listen," she said.

Paul looked at her oddly.

"You think I'm crazy," she said.

"I don't, actually," he said. "There was a sound study done in some of the healing caves around Matera. They were trying to discover the caves' frequency. I didn't know what it meant at the time, but I know they all came out with the same number."

"Do you remember what the frequency was?"

"I think it was ten something."

"That's impressive," she said. "Very low. Ten and a half herz is supposed to be an ideal healing frequency."

"I'm not sure I'm right. I wasn't paying as much attention as I might have." Then he remembered something. "They're using sound in medicine now, aren't they? I know they're breaking up kidney stones with ultrasound. My father had that done just last year."

"They do that by discovering the vibrational frequency of the stone, then pumping up the volume of the same tone, overloading it until the stone explodes."

"Sounds violent."

"It is. And it's the choice of allopathic medicine. Chemo, which targets the specific tumor with a blast of medicine in an effort to destroy it, works by the same sort of violent principle. It battles the cancer. My approach is a little different. First I try to locate the cells that contain the illness. Then I discover what is healthiest about the patient: love, compassion, gratitude, et cetera, and I try to determine the resonance of those healthy emotions. Then I play that healthy frequency back to the cells that are suffering, in an effort to vibrate them back into harmony. They're opposite approaches to sound medicine, but they both work."

Paul looked at her strangely.

"You're skeptical," she said.

"Emotions have corresponding sounds?"

"I'll give you an example," she said. "If you're open to it."

"Sure," Paul said.

"Close your eyes."

Paul closed his eyes, listening while she sang and held a note.

"Anything?"

"You have a very nice voice."

"Thank you. What else?" She sang the note again, holding it for twice as long. "What do you feel right now?"

He hesitated, listening for a minute before answering. "Relaxed. I have to say, it's very calming."

She nodded. "Good. What about this?"

This time she didn't sing but drew the wand around the bowl a few more times, letting the sound build. "What do you feel now?"

"That's calming, too, but more than that. It makes me feel really good, actually."

"That's the universal tone for love."

"Ah," he said.

"See how calming it is when I add this." She played the tone again, then sang a diminished fifth, the tritone or blue note.

"Not as calming," he said, opening his eyes and staring at her. "Agitating, actually."

"That's love in a different form," she said.

"Sex," he said, getting it.

"You got it." Now it was her turn to grin.

"I think I need a drink," he said.

"Sounds like a good plan."

She'd never seen a real speakeasy, hadn't taken Finn's tour of it on Thanksgiving.

She followed Paul up to the second level, which featured the same soft lighting illuminating the racks of wine that lined the walls of the hallway. After walking a long corridor that wound around the elevator shaft like a corkscrew, they came to the heavy oak door she had seen on their way down. Near the top was a tiny hatch that could be opened from the inside to check the identity of those who were entering.

"This was a hot spot during Prohibition. Boats came in at high tide, and customers climbed through a hidden tunnel to get to the bar. My father recently had the whole room done over to house his collection of port—and other exotic liquors. That's why he was giving so many tours on Thanksgiving. He wanted to show it off for the holiday."

"He doesn't enjoy showing off generally?"

"Not all the time." Paul grinned.

"That looks authentic," she said, pointing to the hatch. "Is there a password?"

"Nope. But there probably should be. This is my father's pride and joy."

Paul reached for a large brass key hidden among the wine racks. He opened the door, replaced the key on the hook, and then switched on the lights. The walls inside were mahogany. Around the perimeter of the room were some polished brass steampunk-looking items similar to the ones she had seen in the boathouse.

"The bar was imported from a pub in London."

The only visible stone in the room was the floor, which tilted slightly.

"It feels like we're on a ship," Callie said. She imagined she could feel the rocking motion of the sea beneath them.

"Thank my father. The walls and fixtures came from an old Salem ship, one that served the China trade during the early eighteen hundreds. That table was from the captain's quarters." A decanting candle and bottle sat in the middle; the candlestick holder was bolted down. "That rug was brought back on the same ship after one of its voyages to the Orient."

Paul picked up the decanter, crossed to one of the barrels, and gently opened the spigot. "This is what you missed on Thanksgiving," he said, bringing it back to the table, pouring her a glass of deep red-brown liquid. "A hundred-and-thirty-year-old port. Stolen off a Portuguese ship."

He held a glass under her nose. She took a whiff. It smelled of earth, molasses, leather.

"So the Whitings were pirates as well?"

"Did I forget to mention that?"

She laughed. "Your mother really did clean up your family's reputation."

"Told you," he said. "They dealt in illegal spirits, some ancient brandies, and absinthe when thujone was outlawed here. Prohibition and scarcity create great business opportunities, if you're willing to take the risk, which my family was. How they got seven barrels of antique port all the way across the Atlantic without them being ruined,

I'll never know. And it's pre-phylloxera port at that." He placed the glasses on the table, taking a seat opposite her.

"Thujone? Phylloxera? You're losing me here." Reflexively, she'd been rubbing her palms together off and on all evening. She saw him notice.

"Thujone is the active ingredient in absinthe, and phylloxera was a tiny insect that destroyed the grapevines of Europe in the eighteen hundreds. This port, thank God, predates that tragedy." He looked at her seriously. "There's a reason my father keeps this place locked: Wine lovers have killed for less. They've also tried to counterfeit the stuff."

"Counterfeit port? Never heard of that; another illicit family hobby?"

"Not us that time. That was Marta's father. Some kind of get-rich-quick scheme to sell the phony stuff. But he worked for us and managed to take down our whole business with the scandal."

"I'm not sure I understand the business model."

"If they're lucky enough to find it, the great houses use pre-phylloxera port as a starter for the ports they produce today," Paul explained. "My dad sold two barrels a few years back, and the new blend they made from it sells for a thousand dollars a bottle." He pointed to some cases in the far corner. "Which is how he was reimbursed, of course.

"Go ahead, try it," he said, lifting his glass to her as if to toast.

Callie sipped slowly. It didn't taste at all the way she'd expected. Instead of earthy, it was sweet, with just a trace of maple syrup and honey.

"Marta's father didn't have the real thing but thought he could fake it. The people he sold to knew the difference and exposed him as a fraud, and us by extension."

"Thus the scandal," she said, sipping. Though it was cool in the room, Callie could feel the heat from the alcohol.

Paul shrugged. "The Whitings and the Hathornes don't mix well. Too much history."

They sat for a long time. She asked about his studies in Matera, and just about everything he said intrigued her. He told her the history of the area, and of the Sassi district, where he'd been living. And she found herself watching him speak as much as she was listening to him. When he went behind the counter to get some water, she watched him cross the room. His jeans were worn but tight; she noticed his thigh muscles flexing as he moved. Whether it was the port working its magic or Paul, she couldn't look away.

He poured them each another glass, and then a third. She declined the last one, but he insisted, holding up the decanter. "I can't exactly put it back in the barrel."

Finally, the decanter was empty. He took it along with the glasses and walked behind the bar, turning on the water and waiting until it ran hot. She watched his hands as he cleaned the glasses, placing them carefully back on the shelf.

He held the door for her, turning off the lights as she moved past him into the corridor. She waited while he locked up and replaced the key. Then he led her back down the corridor toward the spa, where the creaky elevator waited. "Can't we go up this way?" Callie asked, pointing to the winding walkway they'd just taken.

"The passageways don't go all the way to the top," Paul said.

"What about that tunnel the speakeasy customers used?"

"Well, that exit supposedly leads down to the ocean, but I've never been able to find it."

"You're kidding."

"Nope. So the only way back is the elevator. It's really very safe," he said, taking her arm as if to reassure her.

They rode the elevator in silence, listening to its moans and rattles. The space was tight, forcing them close together, and she was aware of his breath and body. She hadn't minded on the way down, but she felt self-conscious now.

They stood on the landing at the bottom of the stairs.

"Good night. Thank you for the port."

She started for the steps, but Paul made no move toward the front door. She turned back. They stood facing each other for a long moment, and then he took her left hand. He held it for a minute, turned it over, and gazed at her palm. She had told him about her scar, but she hadn't shown it to him the way she had to Rafferty.

"It's amazing," he said, as if surprised. "Almost perfectly symmetrical. Do you know what it symbolizes?"

"I've been told it's the five wounds of Christ."

"Before that."

"I don't."

"*Rosa rugosa,* the five-petaled rose. It's Roman and was used by navigators to chart their way. It's sometimes called the Rose of Venus because its shape traces the planet's pentagramlike path in the sky. It first represented the goddess of love and later the Virgin." He looked at it for a long time, then looked up at her. "It's beautiful."

She scowled. "Not to me."

He was still holding her hand, running his index finger over her scar as if reading braille. "It's bewitching," he murmured.

"Stop," she said, trying to pull her hand back.

Paul didn't let it go. "Look at it, Callie," he said. "It's a work of art."

Then, keeping his eyes on hers, he lifted her hand to his lips and kissed the scar.

That night her dream images were of Paul. Paul kissing the scar and kissing other places, too—her neck, her arms, her breasts, and torso—moving slowly and deliberately downward. Paul looking up at her with the blazing eyes from her vision. Her desire turning to anger and then to fear, seeing Paul on the bed and blood running down the walls behind him, pooling and deepening and finally threatening to drown them both. His eyes piercing and hypnotic. "Dad," her mother called, and then Leah called, too. And finally, she saw Paul, wide eyed and dead on the cold stone floor, blood trickling from the corners of his open mouth.

By 3:00 A.M., she was agitated. By five, she was up and showering.

It was a cold morning. The fire she'd lit in her fireplace had died to embers, and the large ocean-facing room was drafty. She turned the shower to its hottest setting, fogging the tiles and mirrors. When she opened the door to the bedroom, a cloud of mist swept her into the suite, growing thicker in the colder air outside the bathroom. She dressed hastily and started her morning meditation, but she couldn't rid her body of the electric pulse that had begun the moment Paul kissed her scar.

Dad. She heard Leah's voice again.

Please.

She squinted to focus her eyes, erasing the dream image. Lacy frost etched the window. Beyond the glass, she could see only milky whiteness, growing brighter as the sun lifted itself above the horizon, creating a shapeless luminosity. It was as if a blanket of nothingness had descended on the house, made even lonelier by the moans of distant foghorns. She needed to get outside to clear her head. Putting on her coat, Callie descended the stairs slowly, letting herself out through the pantry door.

The mist was so thick outside it was difficult to tell which way to walk. She couldn't see more than a few feet in front of her. The blank whiteness stretched in every direction now, and, for a moment, she panicked, afraid of stepping over the edge of the cliff and falling into the ocean below. But then she heard the horns again, and the faint sound of waves, and so she turned and headed the opposite way. Pulling her coat tighter around her, she took baby steps until she felt the crunch of stones, then followed the driveway toward the barn, where her car was parked.

By the time she reached the road, the fog had lifted enough to see a few car lengths in front of her. Callie pulled onto the shore road as if in a trance, and instead of turning left toward Salem, she turned right toward Gloucester.

Route 127 wound in and out through misty woods and oceanfront, crossing and recrossing the tracks of the commuter rail, thumping her tires once, then twice, each time she went over them. She drove as if summoned, as if a magnetic pull was taking her north and east toward Cape Ann. The rhythm of driving had a sedative effect; she wasn't sure where she was going, and she didn't care.

She felt the vibration of the train before she saw the red crossing lights and heard the clang of warning bells. Her brakes shrieked as she slammed her foot down, the front bumper pushing against the crossing gate, bending it forward to the point where she feared it might snap. The nose of her car was so close to the passing train that she could see the horrified expression on a woman's face looking down from her window seat.

Long after the train disappeared, Callie sat at the crossing, her breath heaving, both feet pressed on the brake pedal, wondering what the hell was wrong with her.

Twenty minutes later and still shaking, she crossed the town line into Gloucester and pulled into the parking lot at Hammond Castle. This had been her destination all along, she realized. She turned off the engine and rested her head against the steering wheel, trying to breathe herself back to calm.

"May I help you?" An older man slapped her driver's-side window with his open palm, then motioned for her to roll it down.

"I just want to look around—"

"We're closed for the season," he said, pointing to a sign. "And this is private property."

"Sorry," she said, restarting the engine.

"Come back in the spring."

She couldn't shake her nervousness. She felt dizzy as well. She needed to eat something, she decided, so she drove to downtown Gloucester, pulled into a diner near the harbor, and ordered a full breakfast of eggs and bacon, toast, and orange juice.

By the time she finished, she felt better. The fog had cleared, and the sun was shining. Even so, she didn't take the shore route again. She opted for Route 128 and headed over to the hospital to see Rose.

"Stay back," Rose said. Her eyes darted wildly around the room. "She's gotten loose. I don't have her anymore."

The nurses said Rose had spent the whole morning pacing the perimeter of her room. Circling once, twice, then reversing direction as if to undo the circles she had just created. Apparently, Rose had tried, just last night, to escape the confines of Salem Hospital to get back to her oak trees. They'd had to restrain her for several hours.

"Who don't you have?" Callie asked.

"The Sidhe."

Callie looked past Rose—the cabinet that held her belongings had been pried open, the lock broken. Rose's clothing was ripped and shredded. And whole pages of her book were torn out and crumpled. Callie picked one up. Across the top was a sentence she'd seen before, written in caps: *KILL THE BANSHEE.*

"Who did this?" Callie asked.

"The banshee!" Rose said. "She's gotten loose and I can't stop her!"

"I don't understand."

"I had her inside of me. But she escaped. I saw her face. Right here in my room!"

"The banshee?"

"The goddess who turned!"

Rose was shaking. "The creature who killed your mother and the others. She got loose that night, and she killed them all. Then she jumped into me. I tried to hold her there, tried to stop her from killing again, but I couldn't keep her there forever. When I saw the boy, saw the violence he was capable of, and what they could do together, I could feel her bloodlust rising. She wanted to inhabit him. If I hadn't stopped him, everyone around him would have died," Rose cried. "It was the lesser evil."

Both the nurse and the aide were standing in the doorway staring at Rose.

"She doesn't know what she's saying," Callie said, reaching out, trying to calm Rose down.

"I'm going to call Dr. Finch back in," the nurse said and hurried off.

Callie tried to calm Rose, but Rose squirmed away from her touch. "You don't understand! The goddess is out there. She tried to kill me!"

An orderly appeared at the door. "I hear you need help in here." The aide stood behind him.

"No," Callie said. "Stay where you are."

More than her words, she knew it was the sound of her voice and the look on her face that stopped him. Locking him in place with her stare, Callie grabbed her phone and called Zee's number.

"The nurse just paged me. I'm on my way."

She called Rafferty next and reported the vandalism. "Rose says the goddess tried to kill her! Or the banshee!" Callie said. "Someone was definitely here. They vandalized the room. Do you think it could have been Leah? Maybe she saw Rose on the news and came back to try to hurt her."

"Did Rose say it was Leah?"

"No. But someone was in here, that's for sure. There's been a lot of damage."

"Stay there. I'll be right over. Don't touch anything."

The nurse started into the room.

"Stay where you are," Callie warned. "The police are on their way."

CHAPTER TWENTY-ONE

December 11, 2014

SALEM

As his 1693 book, Wonders of the Invisible World, *demonstrated, Cotton Mather felt little remorse for his part in the hysteria. To Mather, witches were a very real threat in the colony he called "the devil's country." He considered them to be "among the poor, and vile and ragged beggars upon Earth."*
—ROSE WHELAN, *The Witches of Salem*

"IT'S NOT LEAH KORMOS'S FATHER," MICKEY TOLD RAFferty. "He wasn't related to Sarah Good. You're going to have to get me her mother's name."

"I'm working on it," Rafferty said.

He'd called several New Hampshire numbers looking for the sister, since the neighbor said that was where she'd moved. Though Kormos was a common surname in the Greek community, there were fewer listings than he'd expected, and he called them all. He checked online real estate transactions for Vermont and Maine as well. Arrest records and tax filings told him nothing. He checked the other Department of Criminal Justice Information Services websites: missing persons, Victim Services, military records, even the firearms registry, but came up short on any family names. He was going on the idea that the sister was using her maiden name. He didn't know her married name.

"Do you want me to start in on the other Goddesses?" Mickey asked. "This research takes a while."

"Yeah, go ahead," Rafferty said. Everything about this case was taking a while.

What hadn't taken him long to discover was who'd vandalized Rose's room. It wasn't Leah Kormos. Though there had been an unconfirmed report of a female doctor visiting Rose earlier in the day, the vandalism had happened later. It was an orderly, not the one in Rose's room when she arrived, but another man with a long record of offenses, his fingerprints all over the ruined property. He was a troublemaker, someone who'd heard the public opinion and decided to do a little damage, not unlike the growing number of people who were writing messages of hate online or gathering in front of the hospital to protest the police's "inaction." The man had an open bench warrant on charges completely unrelated, and was immediately taken into custody and held at the jail in Middleton.

Rafferty had gone to Pride's Heart to give Callie the news. He sat across from her at the partners desk in Finn's study and said, "There's one more thing you need to know, Callie. It's about Rose's release."

"They're releasing her?" Callie sounded horrified. After all that had just happened, the thought made her worry for Rose's safety. Before Rose's recent outburst, Callie had been thinking she should start looking for a permanent place, somewhere they could both live. But this was happening a lot faster than she'd expected. "Rose isn't well enough to be released."

"Her commitment hearing only granted her thirty days. She'll be heading over to the Crisis Abatement Center on Arbor Street as soon as they have a bed."

"When will that be?" Zee had already briefed Callie about Arbor Street. Patients were allowed to come and go during the day but were provided with meals, meds, counseling, and shelter. "There are other options around Salem, but I think Arbor Street is the best," Zee had said.

"Sometime before Christmas," Rafferty said.

"They told me that Rose tried to escape from the hospital again yesterday . . . She's likely to have run-ins with the people of Salem when she gets to Arbor Street." Callie sat silent for a moment. "Maybe I should say yes to that interview they keep asking me to do. Try to change a few of the opinions about what really happened that night in 1989."

"No one knows exactly what happened that night," Rafferty said. "So what would you tell them?"

"I don't know," she said. "I just think it might help to say something on Rose's behalf."

Towner had told him about the interview requests. When Rafferty learned that Callie had refused them, he'd been relieved. Now he was concerned that she might change her mind. "That's a tough call," he said now. "Talking to the press can make things worse."

"You sound like Rose," Callie said.

"You asked Rose about doing the interview?"

"I mentioned that I was considering it."

"And what did she say?"

"She told me not to court the strike."

He nodded. It was one of Rose's catchphrases.

"But I think it might lead to information about Leah. Someone must know something about where she is."

He'd told Callie that Leah, who'd rapidly become his number one suspect, had been reported missing right after the murders. They sat in silence for a long moment.

"Maybe," he said. "Or it could make her go deeper into hiding."

"But if it helps make Rose safer," Callie said.

Rafferty said nothing. He was as worried about Rose's release as she was.

"It's just too soon to release her," Callie said again. "Only yesterday she was ranting about the banshee being loose."

He sighed. "It's a flawed system."

Lately, every official system seemed flawed to Rafferty. They'd talked about the mental health cutbacks, how the state hospitals had closed their doors while the promised local facilities never materialized. The mentally ill often ended up on the streets, like Rose, or, worse, in jail. Which brought him to the criminal justice system, which was even more troubling. Why, in the twenty-five years since a *triple homicide*, was Rafferty the only cop serious about finding the murderer?

The police chief's cell rang. He checked the number and then apologized to Callie. "I have to take this." He stood up and walked toward the window.

It was the ADA. "I wanted to give you a heads-up. We have approval for the exhumation. We dig up the bodies on January twenty-seventh."

"So Helen Barnes wins," Rafferty said, ending the call with a few terse words. It had played out just as Helen had threatened: Her political influence was going to bring the Goddesses back from the grave. Literally. And the timing couldn't be worse for Rose and Callie. He sat back down.

"Trouble?"

"That was the ADA. They're going to exhume the bodies of your mother and the others."

There was a long pause before Callie spoke. "When?"

"The end of January."

"What does this mean, exactly?"

"Unfortunately, *exactly* is not something I can predict. It might mean we find evidence that will lead us to the real murderer. Which would be great. It could mean we find something that implicates Rose. Or it could mean that we'll find nothing."

Slowly, through snippets he was picking up from his detective friend in Beverly and follow-up on the neighbor's story, Rafferty was cobbling together Leah's history. Her mother had died when the girl was fourteen, leaving only her father and a younger sister. After her disappearance, the younger sister, Becky, was the one who tried hard to find her. She was only twelve at the time, and they hadn't paid too much attention to her persistent requests for help. Though they did some perfunctory searching, they hadn't followed it up. The father hadn't tried very hard to find her. She was a runaway, he said, and had always been troubled. They didn't question him further. There was no record of any coordinating efforts between the Beverly and Salem police.

On the way back from Beverly, Rafferty took a detour to Rice Street in Salem.

Tom Dayle, his predecessor, was in the yard, bringing in empty trash barrels. He looked like a man burdened by life, Rafferty thought, bent at the waist and crippled by arthritis and stress. Even the empty barrels seemed a struggle.

"Want some help with that?" Rafferty parked and got out of his car.

Tom looked up. "I'm all set," he said, frowning.

"Can I talk to you for a minute?"

"Is it about the exhumation of those girls?"

Rafferty was surprised. "Wow, word travels fast in these parts."

"That why you came by? To let me know?"

"Nope."

Dayle stopped and looked at him.

"There's a box of evidence missing."

"So?"

"So I thought you might have some idea where to look."

"Did you try the archives?"

"A couple of times," Rafferty said.

"Then I don't know what to tell you."

"What do you know about Leah Kormos?"

There was a long pause before Tom answered. "I don't know anyone by that name."

"She was one of the Goddesses."

"Never heard of her," he said, this time with more conviction.

"She wasn't on the hill that night, but she was at the party at Hammond Castle. The young woman in the red dress that people talked about? The one who had the argument with the girls the night they were murdered? That was Leah Kormos. Not sure how you guys missed that part."

"I've never heard of any Leah Kormos."

Rafferty looked at Dayle for a long time. "Funny that you guys never made that connection. Especially since Leah Kormos is now my number one suspect."

"I'm retired," Dayle said. "I'm not interested."

"Sorry," Rafferty said. "My mistake. You seemed interested enough in the exhumation."

"I'm hoping the exhumation will prove Rose Whelan's guilt once and for all. And finally end all this nonsense." Dayle turned around and began limping toward the house, leaving an empty barrel midlawn.

Rafferty picked up the barrel and followed. "If we had their clothing, we might not need to do the exhumation. You guys did keep the clothing as evidence, didn't you? You wouldn't have been stupid enough to let that go."

Dayle reeled around, grabbing the barrel from Rafferty and shoving it into a corner of the garage. "Of course we kept the clothing. This may not be New York City, like you're used to, but it isn't Mayberry, either."

They stood there looking at each other for a long moment. "Sorry," Rafferty said. "That was uncalled for."

"It's probably in that box you can't seem to find," Dayle muttered.

"Probably," Rafferty said.

Dayle stood looking at him.

"I'm guessing you're not going to invite me in."

"Hell, no."

"Merry Christmas then," Rafferty said and walked back to his car.

Rafferty sat in his car at the end of the dead-end street. He watched as Dayle closed the garage door behind him, then walked into the kitchen, passing the front window of the cape. He saw him pick up the wall phone and dial.

Rafferty pulled the car around, swearing as the cruiser didn't quite make the U-turn, forcing him to back up and pass Tom Dayle's house once again. He slowed his car.

This time he saw Dayle open the cellar door and flip on the stair lights.

Late that same afternoon, Rafferty officially reopened the investigation.

CHAPTER TWENTY-TWO

December 13, 2014
PRIDE'S CROSSING

That these Witches *have driven a Trade of Commissioning
their* Confederate Spirits, *to do all sorts of Mischiefs
to the Neighbours, whereupon there have Ensued such
Mischievous consequences upon the Bodies, and Estates
of the Neighbourhood, as could not otherwise be
accounted for . . .*
—COTTON MATHER, *The Wonders of the Invisible World*

TRUE TO HIS WORD, PAUL HAD TRANSFORMED THE SPA IN
the wine cellar into a healing room, moving the couch into the center
of the cavern and adding a treatment table for massage. He'd cleaned
the floor and polished the wooden rim of the sea well and placed an
Aubusson rug on the granite to mute some of the harsher acoustics,
cutting the floor-to-ceiling movement of energy in favor of the clockwise ellipse Callie had told him she needed. He'd hung a still life of
apples and oranges on the wall opposite the couch and placed small
tables around the perimeter of the room to hold the singing bowls.

Emily and Callie marveled at the work he had done.

Callie had treated Emily upstairs twice. Today would be the third
time, and already she could see signs of improvement. Emily's color
was better, and she had more energy. "You're doing well with this, I
think," she said.

Emily agreed.

When it was clear Paul's mother wasn't going to describe the change, Callie made her way around the room, adjusting the bowls and then testing the four tiny speakers Paul had placed strategically in the rock crevices. She smiled to herself; he was amazingly thorough.

"Ready to get started?"

Emily nodded, relaxing back into the cushions of the couch.

"I've been meaning to ask you how Rose is doing. I heard she's had a bit of a setback."

"She's better, I think. Thanks for asking." Callie didn't elaborate. She didn't want to stress Emily with her worries about Rose's impending release. When she'd visited the hospital yesterday, after hearing about the exhumation, she'd had to enter through Ambulatory Care to avoid the growing group of protesters at the main entrance, who'd also discovered her preferred route inside. These hysterics were carrying signs that said KILL THE BANSHEE or DRIVE THE DEVIL FROM THE WITCH CITY.

"Before we start today, tell me about your experience with chemo," Callie said.

"I stopped it."

"I understand," Callie said. "Do you remember what they were giving you?"

Emily easily recited the names of four different drugs. "The last two were trials my doctor got me into."

"Why did you stop?"

"I felt like I was being poisoned," Emily said.

"You were," Callie said. "In a sense. Or at least the cancer was."

Emily nodded.

"In a way, chemo isn't that much different from sound. The right amount of chemo can heal you, but too much can harm you. Sound waves can be like that, too."

Emily grew thoughtful. "I seem to remember hearing something about the government testing some sound-wave weapon in the desert that was strong enough to cause earthquakes."

That wouldn't have surprised Callie a bit. From what she'd seen of sound healing, she had come to believe almost any effect was possible. Even infrasound, though largely undetectable to the human ear, had been proven to have odd effects on perception and behavior.

"So you decided on your own to stop the drug test?"

"They took me off the last round. Liver damage. But I'd already decided I'd had enough. Much to the disapproval of my family."

Callie didn't express an opinion. Though she could tell that Emily was looking for approval, she'd learned not to comment on something so personal. The truth was, she did approve. The damage she saw on Emily right now seemed more an effect of chemo than one of cancer. But it was difficult to tell how much the chemo had helped before it had taken its toll.

Callie circled the rims of the bowls with a rubber wand, the vibrations building as they began to sing, softly at first, then louder, until they were singing in harmony. As more of the bowls joined in the song, the ellipses the vibrations created overlapped, crisscrossing as they passed over and through every surface they touched, vibrating and opening Emily's chakras, unblocking the energy trapped in her muscles, letting her chi flow freely. Callie joined the harmony, intoning the notes that were the universal vibrations of joy and gratitude, directing them with intention toward the unhealthy cells in Emily's liver, in an effort to resonate those cells back to health and harmony. The volume increased until it filled every space in the room.

Though the session went well, and Callie could see signs of improvement, she felt distracted. Against both Rose's and Rafferty's advice, she had called the reporter and consented to the interview. She had to do something, she told herself, and Rafferty hadn't said it *wouldn't* work; he'd said it *might* not. And to just sit and wait for the harassment to start when Rose was released seemed more like courting the strike than the interview did. Maybe by telling her story, she could change things.

For the sake of privacy, she'd agreed to meet *The Salem Journal* reporter in Beverly. When she finally found a parking space and walked into the Atomic Cafe, he was already sitting in a booth, his micro-tape recorder beside him.

"Coffee?" the reporter offered. "I'm buying."

"Nothing for me, thanks," she said, sitting down and picking up the napkin from the place setting in front of her.

It seemed longer than a month since she'd told Rafferty the story of how Rose had saved her life, how she had gone back to save the others. It was more difficult to tell it today, the feelings all coming back to her at once—including the sick feeling the details created in the pit of her stomach. She was aware that the reporter noticed she'd been shredding the paper napkin as she was speaking. Now she crumpled it and placed it on the table.

"You claim the first victim fell when you were all gathered together," the reporter said. "Is that right?"

"Yes. As I told you, I thought Susan had fainted. Rose was about five feet in front of us, reading the blessing. So she didn't have anything to do with the murders—"

"At the very least, not the murder of Susan Symms."

"Look, Rose saved my life," Callie said. "This is why I agreed to speak with you. I want people to know that she made sure I was safe; that she hid me and then went back to help. She was a hero, not—"

"Stories develop into legends over time, don't they?" the reporter cut in.

"Exactly!" Callie said, relieved that he understood. "I visited Rose's old house and a neighbor spoke with me. She had no idea who I was. She had heard that Rose murdered the Goddesses and then killed me, too. It's amazing how the story has morphed and rumors have become fact. People in Salem need to learn the truth. I was there. What people have come to believe happened that night is total nonsense."

"Do you think fear plays a part in the public's continuing interest in this story?"

"In what way?"

"Well, here's a homeless mental patient who claimed that a banshee killed three vibrant young women. Now she claims that she, herself, is a banshee. In between, she's been predicting the deaths of everyone she meets. You can see why people might be a little afraid of her."

"Tell me what you want, and I'll tell you who you think you are. Tell me what you fear, and I'll tell you who you really are."

The reporter stared.

"Rose used to say that," Callie said. "I think people are always frightened by the things they don't understand."

"You think Rose is misunderstood, Ms. Cahill?"

"I don't think she's understood at all," Callie said.

"Do you understand her?"

"I believe I do. I understand her better than most people. I know for sure she's not capable of what they're accusing her of."

"Does Rose suffer from schizophrenia? She hears voices; she talks to trees. Those are classic symptoms, aren't they?"

Callie bristled. "I'm not qualified to comment on Rose's mental health."

"But clearly she does suffer from mental illness. She's been in and out of state hospitals, and she's now in the psychiatric ward at Salem."

"I'm not qualified to make a diagnosis. And neither are you."

"Fair enough," he said. "But would you agree that Rose was severely traumatized by the events of Halloween night 1989?"

"Who wouldn't be? Rose was our surrogate mother. And then, in one night, she lost everyone. So, yes, I imagine she was traumatized. Wouldn't you be?"

"Were you?"

"Yes," Callie shot back. "But we're not talking about me."

"There's a great deal of interest in you," the reporter said. "And in the Goddesses themselves. Especially now that they are exhuming the bodies. That's a big story. Would you care to comment on the exhumation? What do you think they're going to find?"

"I hope they find evidence that will lead to the arrest of the person who murdered my mother and two of her friends," she said. Without the napkin to shred, she had no idea what to do with her hands and saw him glancing at them. She placed them in her lap.

"Who do you think had motive?"

"I'm not the person to ask. I was five at the time."

"I hear they had a number of enemies."

She stared at him. "I don't know. Like I said, I was just a child."

"Well, they obviously had one," he said. "You have no idea who that might be?"

"They should look at Leah Kormos," Callie said. "She was one of the Goddesses, and she disappeared right after the murders. She's the main suspect, not Rose."

"Was this Leah as promiscuous as the rest of them?"

"Excuse me?"

"They had sex with a lot of men. Some say they considered seduction a competitive sport."

So the reporter had talked to Ann. Callie's dislike of the woman seemed to grow by the day.

"And I've heard their behavior was blamed for the AIDS epidemic that hit the North Shore back in 'eighty-nine."

"You're telling me that my mother and the other Goddesses had AIDS?" Callie said, incredulous.

"I'm not saying I believe it." He shrugged. "But it's what people are saying."

A month ago, she would have hurled all the curses and profanities that came to mind. But anything said in anger could be used to question her credibility, and would make Rose, by extension, look even worse.

Instead, Callie stood and walked out of the restaurant.

That night, Callie's dreams were vivid and disturbing, and then a long forgotten memory was unleashed:

They were all on the floor in the back bedroom; the beautiful mural of the Goddesses decorated the wall.

"How dare she tell?" Susan demanded. "Rose is going to throw us out, that's what she said!"

Olivia sat on a huge velvet pillow. A half-eaten bag of potato chips was propped up next to her, and the last homemade chocolate chip cookie sat on a plate. She passed a spoon and a pint of Häagen-Dazs rum raisin back to Susan. "She won't."

An exotic silk print draped over the ceiling light, forming walls like a tent. The room smelled of patchouli and herbal incense. Except for the junk food, the place could have been a harem room. Like in the stories from The Thousand and One Nights *Rose was reading to her.*

"You weren't there. She meant it this time," Susan said.

Olivia looked regretfully around the room. "We'll find another place to meet them."

"No more underage boys," Susan warned. "News of that has been getting around."

Olivia rolled her eyes. "But that was so much fun."

"It's probably what set her off and made her decide to tell Rose," Susan concluded.

"Anything sets her off lately. Can't we banish her? Fly her out of town on her broom?" Susan plucked a crystal wand off the dresser and waved it around. "Begone!"

"She's a petal on the rose," Olivia said sarcastically. "We need her for the blessing."

"We don't need her. Should we start packing?" Susan asked.

"Rose doesn't mean it," Olivia insisted. "She'd never make Callie homeless."

Cheryl sauntered in with a letter. She motioned Callie to the front of the room. "Time for recitation," she said, exchanging a look with the others. "My sneakiness has paid off. I stole it from her handbag when we were at the center," she bragged.

Olivia's eyes went wide.

"Okay, let's hear it, Callie," Susan said, clapping in delight.

"I'll hold the letter," Cheryl said. The envelope read: To Dagda from Morrigan. *"You simply must do the hands for this one."*

Callie was delighted to be the center of attention. She put one hand over the other, and the Goddesses snickered in anticipation.

Cheryl shushed them. "Go ahead," she said to Callie. "Read."

Callie tucked a dark curl behind her ear and cleared her throat as Rose had taught her to do to quiet the room.

"My Love,

Meet me tomorrow night in our secret place, and I will show you an ecstasy you have never known. Our bodies will be as the god and goddess. I will touch you as the Morrigan touches Dagda, our heavenly tryst unleashing all the powers of the universe, such orgasmic pleasure as only a god and goddess may know. We have waited long enough, my love . . ."

Callie tripped over some of the words, pronouncing them carefully, syllable by syllable: "Dag-da, or-gas-mic. Mor-ri-gan." *The Goddesses' laughter never materialized.*

"I told you she was a hypocrite!" Cheryl hissed.

Susan was outraged. "She tells Rose we are immoral and indecent, and that she should kick us out of her house, and she's doing the same damned thing?"

But Olivia was laughing. "I can see the old witch humping and pant-ing," she said. "Oh, Dag!" She made a twisted expression. "Don't stop, Dag!" She pumped her pelvis into the air. "I can show you the pleasures of the universe, Dag!"

Susan covered her eyes and said, "I won't be able to unsee that!"

"She calls herself a goddess?" Cheryl snorted. "We're the Goddesses."

Olivia turned to Cheryl. "Let me see that letter." She took it and read silently. Slowly. Finally she looked up, grinning widely. "I know what we can do."

"What?" Susan said.

"You want revenge?" Olivia asked.

"Yes!" Cheryl shouted.

"Do you know his address?" she asked Cheryl.

"Please. I even know their secret trysting place."

"Mail it."

"What for?"

"You want to get her back, right?" Olivia asked.

"Absolutely," Susan said.

"Then we have to take him," Olivia said.

"Oh my God," Susan whispered, understanding. *"Yes!"*

"We'll do it," Cheryl agreed. *"To show her who's boss. To show her not to mess with us."*

"And to show him the true power of the Goddesses. Now there's an orgasmic pleasure he's never known!"

"Yes!" Susan echoed.

Olivia held the envelope to her lips and imprinted a scarlet kiss.

"I can't mail a letter addressed to Dagda from Morrigan. With lipstick all over it," Cheryl said.

Olivia sighed and removed the letter from the envelope, which fluttered to the floor. Then she walked to Rose's desk in the hall, returning with another envelope and a pen. She handed them to Cheryl.

"All right!" Cheryl said. *"Let's do this!"*

CHAPTER TWENTY-THREE

December 13, 2014
SALEM

It was fear that diminished the goddess,
turning her from maiden to banshee.
—ROSE'S *Book of Trees*

"THE MAN ON THE BED? I THINK THEY WERE CALLING HIM
Dag, not Dad," Callie said.

The cell connection was fuzzy. Rafferty repeated the name. "Dag?"

"Right," she said.

"Short for Dagda, I'm guessing."

"That's what I think. I had another dream memory last night.
I e-mailed you the contents of the letter that was once in the envelope
we found. The envelope under the floorboards," she clarified. "I remember now. They had me recite the whole thing to them."

Callie waited on the phone while Rafferty pulled up the e-mail.
He didn't comment as he was reading. "That's quite a missive," he
finally said.

"That's why I e-mailed it."

"Is this something that really happened?"

"God, I hope so . . . I'd hate to think my subconscious could come
up with something so cheesy."

He laughed.

"It might not be true," she said. "But it feels like an accurate
memory."

"You've been pretty accurate so far," he said.

Rafferty had stayed home the previous morning, using the Internet to locate every Kormos he could find in the state of New Hampshire, Becky's last known place of residence. He checked not just the southern towns but all the way to the Canadian border. He tried Manchester first, then Portsmouth. Then he started on the smaller towns. After he ended his call with Callie, he was ready to punch in the next number on his list when he heard Towner slam down the house phone. "You finally picked up, huh?" Rafferty asked her. "Did you tell her we're spending Christmas with my daughter?" May had left three messages before Towner had finally answered.

"As we do every year," she replied.

"And yet she persists," Rafferty said to himself. May was adamant that they come out to the island for all the holidays, no matter what plans they had, and Towner was stubborn. He wasn't certain whom he'd give odds to in this battle.

At noon he had to give up on the hunt and headed into the station. A call had come from Yellow Dog Island to his private office line. He wanted to ignore it, but when May had problems she usually called him, not 911. Especially when she was moving women. Rafferty was the only one she trusted to respect their confidentiality.

"What's going on out there?" he asked when May picked up.

"I've got some trouble."

"What kind of trouble?" he asked.

"I'll tell you when you get here," she said.

He picked up his gun. Then his jacket. Going to Yellow Dog today was the last thing he wanted to do.

It was cold on the water; the grey ocean matched the color of the clouds. There was a whole lot more chop than he'd expected, which made it difficult to tie up. May was waiting at the top of the dock, hydraulically lowering the ramp, the float swaying crazily below it until it finally landed and Rafferty was able to secure it to the cleats.

He walked up to join May. At least she wasn't holding the rifle, he thought. Things couldn't be that bad.

"What's going on?" he asked when he reached her.

"Come with me."

Instead of turning right toward her house, May turned left toward Back Beach at the far end of the island, taking the shortcut across what had once been a baseball diamond. The grass was higher here, matted in tangles, and they had to walk single file to stay on the path, which made it difficult to talk.

He could see a group of women standing around the foundation of the old house. They stepped back to make room when they saw him approach.

A few of the stronger women were standing inside the foundation, wearing hard hats and swinging sledgehammers, hitting the standing structure hard and watching it crumble. May motioned to one of them, who took off her hard hat and handed it to Rafferty. "This is what you want, isn't it?" May asked.

He was momentarily speechless. He was relieved that May had finally consented to tear down that wreck of a house. But at the same time, seeing it actually happen brought up some difficult memories of the time he and Towner had separated and she'd moved back into that old house.

"Out of sight, out of mind." May handed him a sledgehammer. "Your exact words."

"She still won't come for Christmas."

"I know," May said, turning and heading back toward the other end of the island. "But it will be easier for her to come out sometime. That's all I care about."

Rafferty worked all afternoon, swinging one of the sledgehammers, and the women took turns with the other. They worked without speaking, the way he'd seen them do when they spun flax or made lace. Debris was taken away in the wheelbarrows they used in the gardens. Rafferty couldn't tell where they were putting the refuse, and he didn't really care. Out of sight, out of mind. He hoped he was right.

By the time it was too dark to see, only a small portion of the far wall of the house's foundation was left standing.

May set up an early dinner for them in the red schoolhouse: beef stew with vegetables from their gardens, and corn bread made from the heirloom Golden Bantam the women had grown over the summer. He noted the jars of zucchini lined up on the shelves in the back room; they'd been canning at May's house and storing up for winter.

After dinner, May accompanied him back to the pier. He was walking like old Tom Dayle, all bent over. "When are you going to forgive her, Rafferty?"

The question took him by surprise. "What?"

She held his gaze. "She came back to you. Isn't that enough?"

"It's enough. It always has been. You're reading it wrong. I don't have to forgive her, because I never blamed her for anything that happened."

"Okay," she said. She looked at him for a long time. "I'll rephrase the question. When are you going to forgive yourself?"

CHAPTER TWENTY-FOUR

December 16, 2014
PRIDE'S CROSSING

*Strange rumors have begun to circulate, including
accusations of disease, witchcraft, and even spectral
evidence (wives have claimed husbands were receiving
nocturnal visits from the Goddesses). "Is this the 1980s,
or are we back in 1692?" Eva Whitney posited when
asked for comment.*
—The Salem Journal, NOVEMBER 15, 1989

THE SALEM JOURNAL ARTICLE, ENTITLED "A MODERN-DAY
Witch Hunt?," appeared the same week Rose was released to the
Arbor Street shelter. It produced the opposite of Callie's desired effect;
just as Rafferty had warned her, it made things worse. Now people
were focusing their fears on Callie, too. And if she'd hoped the article
would lead to information about Leah Kormos's whereabouts, she'd
been wrong. Rafferty hadn't received a single call. The only mention
of Leah had been one post on the newspaper's website suggesting
that Rose had probably killed Leah in some kind of Satanic ceremony.

The details of the Goddesses' sex lives were luridly described, and
Callie's mother and the others came off badly. There was a sinister
undertone, too, as if it had been inevitable that seduction as "competitive sport" would turn deadly.

Though the reporter didn't come out and say the Goddesses were
witches or Satanists—as some Salemites clearly believed—he revealed

that at least one of Rose's family of girls had visited that black magic shop, the one Rafferty had asked Ann about that had closed down.

The article detailed Rose's unwavering belief that she herself was a banshee. "For those of you who have never heard the term," the reporter elaborated, "the banshee is best known as the Irish herald of death."

Along with archived photos of Rose and the Goddesses, *The Salem Journal* included a photo of Callie—a candid shot someone had taken as she entered the hospital. As a result, she was now recognized everywhere she went. Many people openly gawked and whispered, especially at the tearoom and the shelter. She hadn't been back to the cemetery at all. When she and Paul bought a Christmas tree for the boathouse from a Cub Scout troop in downtown Beverly, the den mother stared at them during the entire transaction. As soon as she thought they were out of earshot, she said to one of the other parents, "That girl is either in deep denial or she's one of them."

"Jesus," Paul said when they got back to the car. "That was incredibly rude."

Callie shrugged it off. She wasn't completely sorry she had given the interview. Someone had to speak up on Rose's behalf. The reporter would have done the story anyway; he had tried to talk to the hospital staff, but they'd protected Rose's privacy as the law required. The officer who had been posted outside her door, however, had no restrictions beyond the dictates of his own questionable ethics. He was quoted several times in the article, talking about Rose's "trancelike state" and her sudden outbursts "like she was possessed or something."

He had also talked at length about "the unearthly sound" of Callie's singing bowl and how "the mystical treatment" had revived Rose. "She's as weird as the old lady, if you ask me."

Rafferty told Callie he had suspended the officer. But the damage was done.

The online gossip was the most incendiary. Protected by anonymity, the commenters on *The Salem Journal* page took the speculation to a new low:

The devil has once again been raised in Salem.
–GOODCHRISTIAN101

Thou shalt not suffer a witch to live.
–LIKESTOSAIL

"That's not even an accurate translation," Paul said, looking over Callie's shoulder at his laptop screen once they were back at his place. "I mean, that last comment."

"Really?" Callie's hands were shaking slightly. The sheer number of posters was frightening enough.

"King James was obsessed with witches. He even attended the first major witch trial in Scotland. As you know, people are terrified of anything they don't understand. That Bible translation, while beautifully poetic, wasn't the best. Many scholars believe that the original word wasn't *witch* but *poisoner*. Poisoning was actually feared more than witches. Until that translation."

"So a mistranslated biblical quote ignited the interest in witch hunting?"

"Yes. That and another bad translation from the original text to German. In the original, nouns didn't have masculine or feminine modifiers, so the word *witch* was considered both. But when it was translated to German, the translator chose the feminine, and witches came to be seen as women. The King James Bible was a product of the Reformation and was based on Martin Luther's version of the text. When the German was translated to English, the association with the feminine carried over. Which led to all sorts of atrocities against women, as you can imagine."

"I don't have to imagine."

Paul nodded. "Sorry." Then he said, "The 1486 bestseller called *Malleus Maleficarum*, which loosely translates to *The Witch Hammer*, added the methodology needed to root out these so-called witches. That book justified horrible persecutions in the Old World and then, much later, in the New. Fear, once again, ran rampant."

"It's still running rampant in Salem," Callie said. "Look at these comments."

"Salem is usually a haven for all sorts of New Age and Pagan practices not accepted elsewhere in this country," Paul said. "People here tend to be pretty open-minded. Which is why this is all so surprising to me. I'm sure it's really only a few people stirring the witch's cauldron, so to speak."

"Helen Barnes and company?"

"Probably." Paul reached over and closed the laptop. He began to massage Callie's neck.

Her muscles were tighter than she realized; she held all her tension in her shoulders. *The weight of the world.*

"I'd like to kick Helen Barnes right in her bony Brahmin ass."

"I'd pay to see that," Paul admitted, moving his hands over her neck and shoulders. "You have knots," he said, surprised.

"Always," she said, leaning into him as his grip tightened. His hands were strong.

"Okay?" he asked, squeezing harder.

"Good."

He targeted the worst spots without being directed, moving from place to place, following the tightness until each muscle began to release. His touch got lighter then, until at last he skimmed his fingers lightly over her neck and shoulders.

"You know what I still don't understand?" Callie said.

"What's that?"

"Every time I hear the word *banshee,* it comes with a different definition. Rafferty said the banshee was a specter sent to predict the death of a loved one to those left behind. Archbishop McCauley said banshees were paid mourners banned by the Catholic Church. Rose says the banshee is human and was once a shrunken goddess trapped in an oak tree, then freed by a lightning strike to wreak havoc on the world . . . So which is it?"

"All of the above," Paul said. "Or none of them."

"That's helpful."

He laughed. "No, seriously, it's all oral tradition. Handed down through the generations. It happens often, many different versions of the same story. That's how most myths are passed along and why the corresponding gods and goddesses of the different pantheons are at the same time remarkably similar and wildly varying in their legends."

He finished rubbing her shoulders. "Better?"

"Much." She sighed, allowing herself to lean back against him for just a moment before standing.

They stood looking at each other for a long minute.

"Thank you," she said.

"Anytime," he answered, not breaking her gaze. She was close enough to feel his breath as he spoke. She knew what he was thinking. She was thinking the same thing.

"Not a good idea," she said.

"No?" he asked, not believing her.

"No. Please, I'd like to just stay friends. Okay?"

"Friends then," Paul said, stepping back and heading toward the kitchen. Even as he did, she wished he hadn't.

But they *were* friends.

And now that the article had come out, it felt even more important to her that they stay that way. Some of the details about her mother and the others had been tough to read, not only because of the murders but because they bore an uncanny resemblance to Callie's own past. There were several young men she'd hurt. They'd followed her, the same way the men in Salem had followed the Goddesses.

And there was something else. Every erotic dream she'd had about Paul—and she'd been having them nightly—ended the same way. She'd wake up sweating, the blankets torn away and tossed on the floor, still feeling him inside her, trying to erase the final image that lingered: Paul dead on the cold stone floor, blood pooling around him. Recently, a woman's voice, one she didn't recognize, had sounded in the dreams. Was it one of the nuns? Whoever it was recited the phrase her foster father had pinned to her: "Her feet go down to death . . ." And sometimes added the one that troubled her even more: "God will give you blood to drink."

"Friends," Paul toasted as he returned, spiking the eggnog he handed her with Napoleon brandy lifted from his father's wine cellar. "Kind of a waste of amazing brandy, but, hey, it will make trimming the tree more interesting."

"It's time to trim already?"

"It is indeed." He took a swig of eggnog.

It was a big tree, and to compensate for the low ceiling where they'd positioned it, he'd had to saw off both the top and the bottom. It looked as if it were growing through the roof.

"We should have put it over there," she said, pointing to the cathedral ceiling in the study.

"It's always been here," he said. "Tradition dictates."

She rolled her eyes. "That's the mantra in these parts."

It really was a ridiculous tree. Paul strung the bubble lights, and Callie plugged them in. As soon as they began their colorful roil, the room felt festive. "I take it these lights are tradition as well?"

"Of course," he said.

He rummaged through some boxes and showed her wooden ornaments carved by his father and grandfather. Then he dug out a seagull figure he'd made when he was a boy. "I have all the family ornaments."

The eggnog was heating her from the inside, and the fire Paul had built was reddening her cheeks. She almost made a racy joke about his possession of the family jewels but stopped herself. "Then what about your parents?" she asked instead. "What do they use to decorate their tree?"

"Interior decorators," he said.

"Of course they do," she said, saluting him with her eggnog. "I would expect nothing less."

"Actually, they hire flower designers. They pick a different one every year for the Holiday House Tour."

"I forgot about the charity tour." She'd seen a poster advertising it just this morning when she stopped by the post office to pick up some stamps. She put down her glass and selected a mercury glass ornament. As she stretched to place it on a high branch, she slipped on her stockinged feet and almost dropped the thing, lunging to retrieve it before it hit the floor. She caught the ornament, and Paul caught her.

"Careful there," he said. "You almost took the whole tree with you."

She saw it wobbling. "I didn't do that—you didn't put the stand on correctly."

"I most certainly did!"

"Paul. The tree is clearly listing to the right, with almost the same slant—"

"The slant was intentional," he insisted, "to match the sixteen-hundreds floors."

"Of course you would say that," she said with false exasperation, taking a seat on the couch.

Paul started to pour them another eggnog, then thought better of it and sat down next to her.

They both stayed silent, watching the bubble lights color the room. He was so close she could feel the warmth of his leg on hers and smell the scent of his skin. She honestly wasn't sure how much longer she could hold out. The brandy was lowering her resistance. She could feel her pulse racing in her chest, her blood flowing, and the faint throbbing that was a gateway to pleasure. If he flashed his killer grin, she was a goner.

Mercifully, Paul stood and moved toward the tree, tilting his head to the side to better assess the angle.

"That's one weird tree," he finally said.

"It sure is," she managed, tilting her head to the same angle to gain his perspective. "I like it."

"I found her in a neighbor's yard this morning," the social worker told Callie the next day when she entered the Arbor Street shelter. "Sleeping under a tree."

"That's not good," Callie said.

The social worker shook her head. "No, it's not. And that's not the worst of it. Come with me."

The social worker opened a door leading into her office, the only room with accessible windows. Several of them had been smashed. Splinters of broken glass were everywhere.

"Rose did this?"

"No," the social worker said. "But whoever did it knows she's here. There were notes wrapped around the rocks they threw, condemning her. The police took them as evidence."

"Do they have any suspects?"

"They said it could be anyone. It's bad enough that people know she's here. But we can't have her sleeping outside anymore. I'm afraid of what might happen to her. We don't think she should be going outside at all, but our policy allows it. If we can't protect her, though, she can't stay here. She'll have to go back or go to one of the other shelters."

"I'm not staying inside. You can't hear the trees inside this place." Rose shrugged. "You can't see them from my window, either."

"You don't understand," Callie said. "They won't keep you here if you're not safe."

Rose was adamant. "I can take care of myself."

"They'll send you back to the hospital, Rose. Or worse."

Callie wasn't sure what she meant by "or worse," but it seemed to profoundly affect Rose. She quieted, her bravado vanishing.

"You have to at least *sleep* inside."

"Okay," Rose said.

Though her meds appeared to be working fairly well—the staff said she'd had no outbursts—Rose confided to Callie that the trees were talking to her more and more. She admitted that she felt compelled to sketch them during the day, and was carrying her *Book of Trees* and her pencils everywhere, drawing as quickly as possible, as each oak on this side of town imparted a new message that took her closer to "solving the puzzle."

"I see you've been sketching," Callie said, trying for something more pleasant to talk about. Something to bring Rose back from the dark place Callie's warning had sent her to. The journal in Rose's hands was almost overflowing. "Can you show me what you're working on?"

She didn't tell Rose that she'd peeked once before, at the hospital. Rose handed over the journal easily. "I've been waiting for you to ask."

Callie flipped through the book. The ripped-out pages had been taped back in place. Rose's new drawings were more intricate, showing every bit of light on bark, every striation of bare branches. In one sketch, she had depicted a torn limb and the pulp beneath, revealing what looked oddly like a human circulatory system, the sap flowing like blood.

"I thought you said the trees were talking to you," Callie said.

"That's right."

"But there aren't any words written in your book."

"Trees don't talk in *words,*" Rose said, as if stating a fact Callie should know.

Callie paged through the book more carefully. She saw limbs, branches, twigs, bare and fully leafed, but no messages that she could decipher. "I can't read any of the messages you wrote," she admitted. "It's beautiful, though. You have a real artistic talent."

She flipped the pages again, and that's when she saw the harp. It was a different rendition of the image she had seen in the painting on the wall at Ann's house, part of her collection of sacred imagery. In Rose's sketch, the harp was clearly made of oak. There were oak leaves coming out of the ends of each string. And what appeared to be a pair of flowers.

"The Oak of Two Blossoms," Callie said.

"You know it?" Rose was delighted that Callie understood one of her drawings.

"It's a harp."

"It's Dagda's harp." Rose smiled at her.

Callie made Rose repeat the name, just to make sure she'd gotten it right.

"He's a Celtic god."

Even before she'd sent Rafferty the contents of the old love letter the Goddesses had had her recite, Rafferty had told her about his con-versation with Ann. How Dagda was one of the Celtic gods, known to tryst with Morrigan—a nickname most likely appropriated by Leah Kormos. The letter, and the plan to "take him," made sense if that were the case, as well as Leah's murderous anger at the party. But now Callie was nervous . . . Hadn't Ann said that the harp's music killed its enemies? Was that possible?

Of course not. It was legend. But it was still bothersome to see the image in Rose's *Book of Trees*.

Rose was disappointed when Callie cut their visit short. Rose tucked her book back into her bag.

"You can't sleep outside, Rose. Whatever messages the trees are sending you, they're going to have to tell you in the daytime. Do you understand what I'm saying?"

Rose nodded. "Don't court the strike."

"Exactly," Callie said.

Callie hadn't been able to reach Rafferty by phone, so she'd gone to the coach house to tell him about the harp. "I don't know what it means, but it *is* something. My gut tells me it's a fairly disturbing something."

Rafferty said he'd talk to Ann about it and asked if Callie wanted to come along.

"I'll wait here, if that's all right with you," she said. The more she liked Paul, the more she couldn't stand Ann Chase. All she could think of was Paul touching Ann, rubbing her neck and shoulders and not stopping there . . . "You know she's talked to the press."

If he knew it, Rafferty didn't comment. "I'll call you if I learn any-thing new."

It was just four o'clock, so she walked over to the tearoom to join Towner and Zee. "I hope Rose really will stop sleeping outside," said Callie, sipping her Difficult-Tea. She'd acquired a taste for it over the past few weeks. "She is required to be in the house by curfew. They can send her back to the hospital if she isn't. Or they'll give her bed to someone who will follow the rules."

"She can't come back here," Zee said to Towner. "Your husband is catching hell because the whole town thinks Rose lives at his house."

Callie stared into her tea. She didn't want to discuss with Towner what people had been posting online about Rafferty, though she suspected Towner knew. Some were calling for his dismissal. Many were calling for much worse. What hateful things people felt free to say when their anonymity was protected. "I need to get a place of my own nearby," she said. "Then Rose can be released to me."

"You need to stay where you are," Zee countered. "You don't understand the toll living with Rose would take on you. She needs to be in a permanent facility, where they can administer her meds and monitor her behavior."

Callie shook her head. "I don't think she needs all that."

Zee sighed. "Denial is a powerful thing."

Callie took a sip of tea.

"Just stay where you are for now," Zee said.

"Besides," Towner teased. "You wouldn't want to leave Paul."

Callie noticed every oak she passed on the drive back to Pride's Crossing. Even without their leaves, they were easy to recognize. Their thick elephant-skin bark stood out. And Rose was right: Oaks did seem to stand alone. While other trees gathered together in groves, the oaks were solitary. Rose claimed that oaks "courted the strike." That their solitary nature made them stand out, and, for that reason, they were more often struck by lightning. Was that true, or another of Rose's delusions? Perhaps it was a more accurate description of Rose than of the trees, Callie mused. Rose had been standing alone for a long time, and her singular nature certainly courted trouble.

"Does anyone know where the phrase *courting the strike* originates?" Callie asked the Whitings at dinner that night. "Are oak trees known for this?"

No one knew the answer, but Finn said, "You aren't taking up Rose's practice of dendrolatry, I hope."

"Dendrolatry?"

"Tree worshiping."

"The oak has a special place in Celtic lore," Paul told her when Finn went after another bottle of wine and was out of earshot. "But don't mention Celtic connections to my father. He equates Celtic beliefs with Satanic ones."

Callie sighed. "History casts a long shadow around here."

They stayed for coffee and dessert. As the maid cleared the table, Emily stood up. Both Paul and Finn stood as well.

"I'm sorry to cut this short," Emily said, "but I'm going upstairs. I'm exhausted."

Emily did look tired. She and Finn had been in Boston all day for appointments with her doctors.

Finn walked Emily to the stairs, then came back to the table.

"How did it go today?" Paul asked his father.

"All right," Finn said. "Nothing terribly new." He walked out of the dining room and into the library. Callie could hear the elevator descending.

"Where's he going?"

"To get more fortification, I expect. That's how he handles difficult days. Let's get out of here before he comes back," Paul said.

"Yeah?"

"I assure you, he won't even miss us."

"Where to?"

"John Pizzarelli's playing at Scullers tonight."

"I heard Pizzarelli play the last time I was in New York," she said.

"Does that mean you do or don't want to go?"

She stood, giving him a thumbs-up. "It means I do."

He smiled. They quietly walked out through the pantry just as Finn came back carrying a dusty bottle of Barolo.

They stayed at Scullers for two sets, then went to an after-hours place back in Beverly, a private smoky cellar club that smelled of weed and sold fancy desserts to those who'd smoked enough of it to require such exotics. Ann and her coven of young witches arrived as they were leaving. Ann kissed Paul hello, lingering before greeting Callie.

"Later," she mouthed to Paul. He laughed but didn't reply.

It took everything Callie had not to punch her.

Paul held the door, and Callie climbed into the car. He went around and got in, starting the engine. The lights popped on, illuminating the tangle of witches with Ann in the middle. Spotlighted, Ann turned and blew Paul a kiss.

"Unbelievable." Callie glared at Ann.

"What?"

"How does she know we're not on a date?"

"We're not?" Paul feigned horror and disappointment.

"You know what I mean. How does she know we're not involved?"

"She knows."

Meaning what? "You *talk* to her about me?" Callie said, seething. Had Paul confided their relationship status to Ann? Or was this something Ann just knew, the same way she intuited all the other personal things she wasn't supposed to know? Callie couldn't decide which idea she hated more.

"What is this, high school?" His tone had an edge.

Maybe not back in high school, but certainly in college. Callie would have relished going head-to-head with Ann Chase over a guy. But not now. "I doubt Ann remembers her time in high school. It was so *long* ago."

It had been a nice night, almost as if it *were* a date, but Ann Chase and her scary entourage had caused Callie's mood to nose-dive.

They drove back to Pride's Heart in silence. Instead of heading to the boathouse, Paul drove her directly to the main house, the tires crunching on the gravel driveway as he braked. The house was dark, the windows reflecting the black sky.

"Thank you for a *lovely* evening." Callie didn't hide her sarcasm. She rifled through her purse. "Damn it. I forgot my key."

"I have a key," Paul said calmly, but he made no effort to give it to her.

She started to open the passenger door. He reached across as if to unlock it, the same way he had that first day, only this time his hand didn't reach for the door but lingered on her shoulder. He pulled her close.

"What are you doing?"

"What do you think?"

"Isn't Ann waiting for you?"

"Shut up."

He kissed her, then kissed her again, his arms tightening around hers. He pulled back until he was looking into her eyes, his lips barely touching hers, his breath sweet from the brandy and chocolate they'd shared at the club.

Immediately a light came on in a third-floor window and then in the hall.

He released her, reaching to open the door. Then he walked around to escort her up the steps, pulling out his key just as Darren opened the front door.

"High school." He sighed, nodding to Darren as he started down the stairs.

"Good night," she said.

At the bottom of the steps, Paul turned and flashed the killer grin.

CHAPTER TWENTY-FIVE

December 17, 2014
SALEM

If coming events are said to cast their shadow before,
past events cannot fail to leave their impress behind them.
—HELENA BLAVATSKY

"I'M SORRY TO TELL YOU, RAFFERTY, BUT IT'S NOT ANY OF them," Mickey said. "It took me a while, but I went through each of their family trees. Twice. Not one of the Goddesses or Rose herself was related to Sarah Good. It has to be this Leah person. Do you have the mother's name yet?"

"I'm working on it."

"You've got to find another line, Rafferty. That one is sounding pretty lame."

No, Rafferty thought, standing in the store, amid holiday decorations, with Mickey in his full pirate regalia, talking about the familial ancestry of the Goddesses was what was lame. Rafferty was frustrated. He'd reached a dead end.

It had been a long day. He'd been down to the storefront on Essex Street where the Left Hand Path had once been located. The whole first floor was deserted now. Though pop-up costume shops, cheesy haunted houses, and psychic reading studios opened here every year at Halloween, no one ever took a permanent lease on the space, and it was showing signs of neglect.

The place had recently been swept clean. There were no clues to be found, and, even if there had been, it would have been difficult to tell what was left from the shop and what was detritus from a temporary Halloween business. He was, however, able to talk with the property owner about the Left Hand Path.

"It was a strange place," the owner said. "The woman who ran it gave everybody the horrors. She used to conduct spells in the back alley, and the noises were terrible."

"I heard there were animal sacrifices," Rafferty said. It was in the police complaints. "That's why the town wanted to shut them down. Is it true?"

"I don't know," the landlord said. "Someone once left a dead cat on the front steps," he admitted. "I remember because I was the one who had to clean it up."

"That must have been pleasant."

"All I know for certain is that the other witches in town took an active part in trying to close the shop. They started rumors that drove customers away, and they kept them up until the owner packed her things and left in the middle of the night. Owed me two months' back rent."

Rafferty had a growing pile of books sitting on the table in his home office. He'd borrowed some on Celtic mythology from Ann and had bought some books on black magic from Pyramid, amid stares from some of the patrons. He could just see what they'd be posting tomorrow. *Chief of police signs the devil's book.*

He'd tried to get all the information he needed online, but what he found was limited and contradictory. Ann told him it was unreliable as well. "If you want in-depth information about Celtic gods and goddesses, Rafferty, you're going to have to open a book."

Luckily she had an extensive library, and Pyramid Books had even more. He'd read the Celtic books looking for more information on Dagda and Uaithne, the killer harp. There wasn't much. Dagda was a prolific god, both sexually and in battle. After one skirmish, Dagda's enemies stole the magic harp. But Dagda had bound the music until he alone summoned it, so the harp wouldn't play. When the god finally called for the harp, legend said it "sprang from the wall, killing nine of Dagda's enemies" on the way back to its master. The story was vague; it never detailed exactly how the "Oak of Two Blossoms" committed its lethal act. When he looked up "The Four-Angled Music," the other title of the painting Callie mentioned she had seen at Ann's house, he found almost nothing; the term was another name for the harp.

He had the books lined up on his bedside table. He'd started reading the ones on black magic. Both Ann and Towner had warned him against spending too much time with those books, for different reasons. Ann said she was afraid it would give him ideas. She was kidding, of course, but you could never tell with Ann. As for Towner, the books gave her the creeps. "Can't you take them to the office?" she asked. "They're giving me nightmares."

Towner was right, the books were a little creepy, especially their covers, which were darkly dramatic. So he'd taken them to his study, where she wouldn't have to look at them. There, he'd finally turned up something useful. In one, *The World History of Black Magic*, in the section on Africa, he'd read a chapter about the magical powers of the "hair of the unpigmented human." It was said to be a powerful ingredient in spells, especially love potions. He thought about Susan's white hair, one of the trophies taken from her body.

Evidently superstitious beliefs about albinos were a problem to this day in sub-Saharan Africa. They led to murders and brutal mutilations. Albino skin was often used by believers to make an amulet to produce wealth and success. Something the ostracized shop owner had sorely needed for her own spells. The second trophy had been a piece of Susan's skin.

When he'd first received Mickey's pronouncement that none of the others were related to Sarah Good, Rafferty had inked in Leah's name on the fifth petal, under Sarah Good's. Now, if he could only find some trace of Leah or her sister . . .

CHAPTER TWENTY-SIX

December 17, 2014
SALEM

The tree is a mediator between the living and the dead.
Where a limb is malformed, where her branches twist
and weave into one another, or where a wound on
bark remains unhealed, all these imperfections are
sacred pathways between the realms.

—ROSE'S *Book of Trees*

"WHAT ARE YOUR PLANS FOR CHRISTMAS?" THE SOCIAL
worker asked when Callie visited the shelter. "Generally, our guests
join their families for dinner . . ."

"Well, I don't know yet," Callie stalled. Towner and Rafferty were
traveling to New York to spend Christmas with his daughter, Leah, so
the tearoom would be closed. And taking Rose to their house, even for
a few hours to cook her a holiday meal, was not an option.

"Rose can come to Pride's Heart for Christmas dinner," Paul suggested, when Callie told him about her dilemma.

"I don't know." Callie imagined Rose in a fancy dress, sitting
through endless courses and telling the area elite about conversations
she had with talking trees.

"Our Christmas dinner is not like Thanksgiving," he assured her.
"It's a quiet meal, just family and a few very close friends."

"Still," Callie said. "We don't know how she'll . . . behave. Maybe
I should take her out somewhere?"

"Where?" Paul said. "Where could you possibly take her that you'd both be comfortable in public together? She's been through enough. You've been through enough. Let's give her a nice Christmas dinner."

"I'm happy to report that Rose has been sleeping inside," the social worker said the following day. It had been raining, off and on, for the last few nights. "Whatever you said seems to have worked. She must feel good to be out of the rain."

Callie smiled noncommittally, and Rose, dressed in dark slacks and the red sweater that Callie had given her during their last visit, grunted. Callie would never say it aloud, but she could understand why Rose had preferred to sleep alfresco. The shelter was anything but inviting. It was a converted industrial space, and someone had convinced them that Aztec white was preferable to institutional green, so the place was almost blinding in its reflective brightness and fluorescent lighting. The big factory windows were too high to allow for any outside views. The small artificial Christmas tree at the far end of the "family room" was the only nod to any of the December holidays, and it was dwarfed by the cavernous space.

"The bed is lumpy," Rose complained. "It's full of marbles."

"It really isn't," the social worker said, smiling. "She's doing well."

Rose rolled her eyes.

When the social worker left, Callie repeated the verdict. "You're doing well."

"I don't know why she always talks about me as if I'm not in the room."

Callie had been wondering the same thing. "Do you want to come to Pride's Heart for Christmas dinner, Rose? The Whitings would love to have you." Paul had already run the idea by Emily. "Can I tell them you'll come?"

"I don't know. It depends."

"On what?"

"What they're serving for dinner, and what I'd have to wear."

"Don't worry about your clothes," Callie said. Rose's concerns weren't that different from the ones she herself had raised about the Thanksgiving invitation. If anyone met Rose for the first time at this moment, she would seem normal. Callie's heart swelled as she allowed herself the thought: *Maybe Rose is coming back.* "It's not formal. You can wear what you have on now. And I'll come by early and do your hair."

"Will they have pie?"

Callie laughed. "I'm sure they will."

Rose smiled. "I like pie."

"So that's a yes? You'll come to Pride's Heart?"

Rose shrugged. "Well, I'm not staying here. That's for damned sure."

"It's a pretty good deal if you think about it," Paul declared, taking a bite of the lobster Newburg that the cook had prepared. "Marta pays no rent and no taxes. The land is maintained by our grounds crew—with the exception of her kitchen garden. All she's required to do these days is participate in the house tour. She could do worse. And she's complaining?"

"I don't know where you got the idea that Marta's complaining," Emily corrected her son. "She's been very gracious about the whole thing."

"As she should be," Paul said.

Finn said nothing but helped himself to another glass of Meursault.

For the last few days, all anyone had been talking about was the Holiday House Tour scheduled for Saturday. Paul had filled Callie in on Marta's backstory. Evidently, the Whitings had owned the land Marta's house was situated on since the time of the witch trials, when Marta's ancestor couldn't pay her incarceration fees. This had been a long-standing sore point for the Hathornes, who had been granted generational life rights to the house itself. There had been various prices extracted over the years for the arrangement, some in the form of labor, some less tangible. In recent years, participation in the house tour was all that was required.

Tonight, as usual, the spacious dining room was lit mostly by candlelight, the sterling chandelier that hung over the center of the room had been dimmed to emit the same simple glow as the candles themselves. Already there were signs of the impending tour. A flower designer from Ipswich and his staff of four had been at work all day, placing arrangements in strategic nooks and on table surfaces. Tomorrow they were expecting another designer, this time from Boston, who had created handmade ornaments for the massive two-story spruce that lay prone in the foyer, surrounded by six humidifiers, all puffing steamy fog through the entryway and into the library. Earlier today, Emily's own team had lowered and polished the sterling chandelier and the wall sconces that ringed the room.

In the midst of all the activity Emily had insisted that both Paul and Callie join them for the last lobster of the season. The Whitings' traps sat just off the rocks, and tomorrow they would be pulled out of the water for maintenance and winter storage.

"The Newburg is very good tonight," Emily said. Darren stood next to her offering a second helping, something she accepted. "My compliments to Hildy."

Callie was happy to see Emily's appetite returning; it was a good sign.

"You'll enjoy the tour, Callie," Emily said.

"I'm looking forward to it," Callie said.

"Did you ask Rose about Christmas?" Paul asked Callie.

"I did," Callie said, turning to Emily. "She said she'd love to come. Especially if you're serving pie."

"What's this?" Finn asked.

"I've invited Rose Whelan to join us for Christmas dinner," Emily said. "Does she have a favorite pie?"

"I don't understand," Finn said.

"Callie has invited Rose Whelan to join us for Christmas dinner," Paul said to his father. "And Rose has accepted. And evidently Rose is fond of pie."

Finn said nothing.

"Hildy makes a delicious mince pie as well as all the sweet ones. Do you think Rose likes savories?"

"I'll ask her." Callie smiled, thinking about her earlier conversation with Rose. She wouldn't agree to come without the promise of pie. Now there would be pies, plural.

"Why didn't you ask me before you invited extra people?" Finn said to Emily.

"It's not extra people. Rose is Callie's aunt. And I'm not in the habit of getting your permission before I invite dinner guests."

"Marta won't want to come if that woman is here. Nor will any of our other guests." He looked not at Callie but directly at his wife.

"Marta Hathorne and any other guests you've apparently invited without informing me are all still most welcome."

"They're not going to feel comfortable with a crazy homeless woman sitting at our table."

"Then you should tell them not to come." Emily rose from her seat, placed her napkin carefully on the table, and walked out of the room.

A few seconds later, Finn stood, leaving Paul and Callie without a word, walking out of the house and slamming the heavy front door behind him.

As soon as his parents were gone, Paul moved to a seat closer to Callie. He wasn't fazed by the scene they'd witnessed.

"What just happened?" Callie asked, staring at Paul.

"Don't ask."

"Where does it hurt?" Callie asked Emily the next morning.

Emily pointed to her right side. Callie played the bowls, targeting the third chakra, to address the liver. Emily was trying to relax into the sound, but she was weak and clearly in pain. She shifted, trying to find a more comfortable position.

It was cold this morning, and Callie had come to the spa early to dial up the thermostat so Emily wouldn't freeze. Emily was late, and, twenty minutes in, Callie had used the house phone to confirm that she was actually coming down.

"She's on her way," Darren said.

Callie was taken aback by the change in Emily's appearance. She hadn't slept. Her hair was uncombed, her makeup not applied. She was holding her right side as she stepped out of the elevator, and Callie had to help her onto the treatment table.

"Hang in there, Emily." Callie played the second chakra, trying to move Emily's energy down and out, the way she had been taught by an acupuncturist she'd worked with in Northampton. It wouldn't budge. There was a sound she wasn't reaching, she could feel it: a note in between the third and second chakras, between the clear E and D.

She began to sing, letting her voice slide downward from the solid E to the E flat and then another quarter tone lower, searching for the place where Emily's pain lurked.

"Oh!" said Emily, and Callie knew she had found it.

Callie sang the note, and the room, with its perfect acoustics, picked up the tone and propelled it. As the sound moved, it broke into fragments that circled the room separately, coming together and then splitting apart again, bouncing off the granite walls; the room itself had become a singing bowl.

Note splitting was something Callie had never achieved before. Still holding the original note, she laid her hands on Emily's right side. The area started to warm and then began to vibrate, first inter-mittently, then more and more steadily.

Callie moved to Emily's feet and removed her slippers. "Send what's hurting you down to me," she said, gently touching Emily's toes. "Let the pain go."

Callie sang, and the fractured tone again circled the room. She felt no energy at all from Emily's feet. Then the strands of sound came back together in a quick burst of energy that was so astonishing it felt the way Callie imagined a lightning strike might; the force of it almost knocked her to the ground. She grabbed the table for support and waited until the tone faded to complete silence before she dared to speak. "Did you feel that?"

Emily was so still that Callie feared she had killed her. Then she opened her eyes and said in breathless amazement, "The pain is gone."

With Callie's help, Emily sat up. She was still too weak to stand so she faced Callie, readjusting the emerald ring she wore on her right hand. She looked up and met Callie's eyes, holding her gaze for a long time.

"Thank you."

Callie had trouble shaking off the energy Emily had released during their session. She tried to meditate but couldn't relax. She took a hot bath, then, finally, a nap.

She dreamed of the hedge bush. She felt herself held captive inside a maze of branches, in a thick liquid that oozed like blood. All of her nightmare images were trapped with her in the abyss alongside the severed openings where tree limbs should have grown. She could hear harp music in the distance, drowned out quickly by another sound.

The piercing scream was so high pitched and loud she could *feel* her blood vessels bursting. When she could bear it no longer, she simply let go, surrendering herself to its power.

CHAPTER TWENTY-SEVEN

December 20, 2014
Pride's Crossing

That the banshee can kill is a given. But any killing done
in anger exacts a heavy toll. The banshee and the dying
become as one. Time shifts, then stands eternal, in the
moment the joined spirits pass between the realms.
—Rose's *Book of Trees*

THE HOLIDAY HOUSE TOUR WAS A CHARITABLE EVENT, and people from all over the North Shore bought tickets and roamed freely through Pride's Heart, invading any space that wasn't roped off.

Finn called the tour a "ladies' event." He and Paul always cleared out early, ostensibly to do their Christmas shopping in Boston followed by dinner at the Harvard Club. Today, they were running late, because Finn was still rifling through things in the library, looking for his glasses.

"You didn't find those yet?" Emily asked, sounding put out. "With your glaucoma, I don't know why you don't keep a second pair."

"I have bad eyes," he said. "I do have a second pair of glasses, but they're simply not strong enough anymore. And you know as well as I do that the glasses don't do a damned thing for glaucoma."

"You're on two medications, but it's still getting worse. You should let Callie treat you with her bowls."

Paul said, "She'd be happy to do it, Dad."

"Not interested."

"Not interested in what?" Callie asked, entering the room.

"No one's interested in helping me find my damned glasses," Finn said.

"You lost your glasses?" She'd always considered them an affectation. Finn had found a designer frame that almost perfectly matched his brown eyes, tortoiseshell with the same flecks of green, yellow, and blue. She'd wondered if he'd had them fabricated expressly for him. It seemed like something he'd do.

"It appears I did. You haven't seen them, have you, Callie?"

"No, but I'll help you look." Callie started checking shelves, the mantel, any flat surface he might have laid them on without thinking.

They all searched quietly and unsuccessfully for a few minutes before Finn gave up. "I'll take these," he said, grabbing his older, weaker pair from the desk drawer. "Let's get out of here before the 'fun' begins."

The two men took their leave, and Callie noticed Finn's eyes looked bloodshot.

Both women followed them into the foyer. The Christmas tree in the front hall towered up to the vaulted ceiling.

"Notice that neither of them is driving," Emily said, pointing to the chauffeured town car that waited outside. "Which is a good thing, considering the condition you'll see them in upon their return. To say they'll be doing a little tippling tonight would be an understatement."

Emily looked so much better to Callie, though everyone including Paul was cautioning her to take it easy playing hostess today.

As Callie admired the tree, the docents and the carolers arrived, soon followed by the staff, who would serve wassail punch to the tourists.

"Have you seen Marta's house yet?" Emily asked.

"I haven't."

"You should. The foundation arranged for it to be decorated by local designers. And the house itself is something to behold. The only change that's been made since it was built was the addition of the saltbox kitchen. And that happened hundreds of years ago."

"I'll see it some other day. I want to help you out with the crowds."

"Please. I feel wonderful. And I have plenty of help. Go. Enjoy a quick look. I'll be here when you get back."

Callie had wanted to let Marta know about Rose coming to Christmas dinner in person, but Marta had caught the flu and declined all visits. Indeed, she'd sounded terrible when Callie had called. "Can I do anything for you? Bring you chicken soup or something?"

"Just let me rest," Marta had said, and Callie had accommodated her. "I'll call you if I need anything."

The call never came.

Today, Callie waited until the tours were in full swing before heading to Marta's house. She walked through thick woods on a path that was almost a twin to the one that led to the boathouse. The trees were older on this side of the property, though, and not pine but deciduous. At the end of the path, she came to the kitchen garden, fallow now, except for the two witch hazel bushes growing near the side door and a leftover pumpkin still attached by its stem that the squirrels were taking apart bite by bite. The rest of the herb garden as well as some small bushes next to the witch hazel were protected with hay against the cold weather to come.

As Callie approached Marta's small house, with its gables and leaded-glass windows, it was easy to imagine herself back in the 1600s. Callie noted the saltbox kitchen with its long slanting roof. She stepped inside. She wasn't tall, yet the ceiling was only a few inches above her head. The kitchen was cozy. The fireplace took up most of the room, herbs and drying flowers hanging upside down on either side and a big iron pot hanging from its lug pole. She'd walked into the middle of a tour.

"The main cause of death for the woman of the house? Can anyone guess?"

No one spoke.

"Kitchen fires," the docent said. "Being a housewife back in the day held many hazards, but the worst were burns, which killed a number of women. And even if the burn didn't kill you, the infection that often resulted might. There were no antibiotics back then."

Callie looked past the assemblage into the next room, where Marta stood, deep in conversation with a man from another tour group.

"Step carefully into the main room," the docent said, making room for Callie. "The house slopes on each side of the center beam here." She pointed to the floor in the middle of the room; it slanted tentlike on either side.

"There's an interesting story about that beam," the docent said. "It was once part of the Phantom Ship."

The group stared at her blankly.

"Has anyone heard of the Black Phantom?"

People shook their heads.

"No," the one man in the room said aloud.

"There were a number of ships that made the journey from the Old World to the New, carrying Pilgrims and Puritans searching for religious freedom. Many of them—financed by the Massachusetts Bay Company—headed for Salem in the early sixteen hundreds, the *Arabella* and the *Mayflower* among them. It was a long trip in close quarters, and many people didn't make it, sometimes dying from smallpox or other contagious outbreaks they had no means to treat. This ship, the *Purveyance*, suffered the greatest losses. All of her registered passengers died of the Black Death, which had wiped out a third of Europe during the fourteenth century and recurred every few generations for centuries. When she finally reached Salem Sound, only the captain, the first mate, and a cabin boy had survived. There were violent winds that day and a following sea that was higher than the stern of the vessel. The captain, who was already sick with fever and boils, overshot the harbor and ran aground on Norman's Woe. Though there were only three left alive, locals swore they heard the moans and screams of the dying all night long. By the time the winds had calmed, and they were able to send rescue boats, not one of them was left."

There was a long quiet as people imagined what the docent had just explained.

Callie was both horrified by the story and amused that the docent had managed, in such short duration, to turn the tour from Christmas festive to Halloween creepy.

"What does that have to do with the center beam?" the lone man now asked.

"I was getting to that." The docent smiled. "The damaged ship was hauled to Beverly Harbor, where it sat for many years. No one dared approach it, for fear of contamination. But resources were becoming scarce in the colonies. England demanded that all good lumber be sent back to London, and the Puritan colonists were left with little they could use to build their expanding settlement. Eventually, the townspeople began to pick apart the old ship, using the wood to build homes here and in Salem Town. The center beam you just stepped over was fashioned from the mast of that ship."

"Didn't the Puritans believe the Black Plague was the work of the devil?" the man's wife said quietly to him.

The docent didn't miss a beat. "The Puritans believed everything was the work of the devil. But necessity dictated that shelter against the harsh New England winters take precedence over fear." She raised her brows theatrically. "At least for a while."

Callie felt her stomach churn the way it had once when she'd gotten seasick.

The docent motioned for the group to follow. In the corner were a spinning wheel and a small table and chair with a biblical primer opened to a children's lesson.

"This is where Mother would spin flax for thread, as the children sat at the table and learned their lessons during those long winters."

"What was Dad doing all this time?" a woman asked.

"In the case of the Hathorne family, the mother was widowed."

A few people murmured words of sympathy.

"Which, at the time, unless you had strong healthy children to help work the fields, would lead to desperation and poverty. In 1692, after the worst winter they'd yet endured, the Puritans began to blame their old standby, the devil. In Goodwife Hathorne's case, she accused the Whiting matriarch of witchcraft," the docent said.

Now the group made less sympathetic sounds.

"Specifically, she claimed the Whiting woman killed her cow by putting a spell on it that caused its milk to sour and then compelled the creature to run into the ocean and drown itself."

Some of the group scoffed.

"Perhaps an early version of mad cow disease attributed to witchcraft," the docent offered. "But then Goodwife Whiting countered the accusation with one of her own. She claimed that Goodwife Hathorne had bewitched her husband, using herbs from the Hathornes' garden."

"That happened in our neighborhood just the other day," a woman deadpanned and got a laugh.

"Both women sat in Salem Jail for a long time, but neither was executed. Eventually, they stopped the executions, and the Court of Oyer and Terminer was disbanded."

"Hanging judges and spectral evidence, that's what Oyer and Terminer should be remembered for," said another member of the tour.

The docent nodded. "After the governor's wife was accused of being in league with the devil, a newly appointed court put an end to the trials, and those in jail were released. But being released was not the same as being free. You had to pay for your jail time, both room and board. Goodwife Hathorne was forced to sell her land to the Whiting family, everything but the house you're standing in."

Marta entered the room at just this moment. "Emily loves that part of the story," she said, rolling her eyes and hustling Callie away from the group. She led her to a small bedroom, saying, "This is not part of the tour."

Marta looked a little thinner than Callie remembered. Probably from the flu. But she didn't look tired, as Callie might have expected. The energy field that Callie sometimes sensed around people seemed stronger than ever around Marta, though her vibration had changed tone. It had always been slightly dissonant; now the dissonance seemed a bit stronger. Illness had a way of doing that to a person. If it had been anyone but Marta, she might have offered to help, but somehow she knew that, like meditation, sound healing would not be a modality Marta would ever embrace.

"Your house is beautiful," Callie said.

"It's sweet and simple," Marta said. "With a no-nonsense New England attitude. Just like its resident."

Callie couldn't imagine describing Marta as either sweet or simple.

"Every piece in here is historically accurate, down to the single 'sleep tight' rope bed in the corner," Marta said. "But I don't sleep in that." She led Callie to an even smaller room, which held two straight-backed chairs and a four-poster queen-size bed with a lace coverlet. "The only anachronism in the entire house," Marta said, indicating the bed, "that you can see, anyway. The regular conveniences of daily living are carefully hidden behind closed doors." She shut the bedroom door behind them, pointing Callie toward one of the chairs. "Watch your head."

The chairs were under a slanted ceiling that housed the structure's only gable, and Callie had to duck to get to them. Marta took a seat on the other chair, pouring a glass of wassail punch for each of them from a carafe on a nearby table. "Everyone thinks the ceilings are so low because the people from the sixteen hundreds were shorter."

"Weren't they?"

"They may have been, but I don't think so. The ceilings were built low to conserve heat."

There was a fire in the bedroom fireplace. Next to it were the regular implements: an iron shovel, a hook and lance to move the logs, and a broom to sweep the embers away. Hanging on a hook was a braided rope that looked as if it were made from the witch hazel branches Callie had noticed on her way in. One of the Goddesses, she couldn't remember which, had told her that witch hazel symbolizes eternal life. "What's that?" Callie asked when Marta spotted her looking at the braided rope.

"That's the switch," Marta said, bitterness creeping into her voice. "My mother said every good New England family has one."

"Was it ever used?"

"Of course. My mother was a big believer in corporal punishment," Marta said, her light tone betraying her disapproval. " 'Spare the rod and spoil the child' was one of her favorite sayings."

Callie grimaced. "I had a nun like that at the children's home. But she used a ruler."

"My mother forced me to braid it myself. Good and tight," Marta added grimly.

Callie didn't hide her surprise. "Why on earth do you keep it?"

"I—" Marta paused. "I really don't know." She walked to the fireplace, took down the switch, and examined it. "I should have buried it with her." With a quick twist of her wrist, she threw it into the fire. "Take that, you old hag."

They both watched as it caught, then slowly started to burn.

"I take it you and your mother weren't close."

Marta burst out laughing. She took her seat. "So, Callie," she said, her mood much lighter. "What's new in the world of Whiting?"

Seeing an opportunity, Callie jumped in. "I hope I'm not overstepping. I want to talk to you about Christmas. Finn said you may not come to dinner if Rose is invited. Is that right?"

"I won't," Marta said. "I'm sorry. But that shouldn't stop you from inviting her."

"I don't want you to stay away. The Hawthorne Hotel has a Christmas dinner. I'll take Rose to that."

Marta laughed again. "Please don't think me rude. I'm simply a person who doesn't want to be associated with any talk of witches and injustice. I had enough of that at Thanksgiving. For a number of reasons, some of which go back generations, as you've heard today. I just don't feel comfortable being in the same room with her, knowing what her beliefs are and how some might construe them."

"Rose is trying to find closure. She wants the bodies of those hanged found so that everyone can move on. When she talks about the oak—"

"I'm not interested in keeping that dark history alive. In any way."

It was rich that Marta—who lived in a museum to the past—claimed she didn't want to keep history alive. Callie wanted to argue the point, to remind Marta of all that Rose had been through. But Marta already knew the story. "I don't want you to miss Christmas dinner because of an invitation I extended," Callie said, an edge in her voice.

"Between you and me, you have no idea how happy I am to use Rose as an excuse not to attend this year."

The remark took Callie by surprise, but Marta quickly softened and changed the subject. "Did you know that Christmas was outlawed in Massachusetts in the sixteen hundreds?"

"Because it was based on the Pagan holiday?"

"Partly that, and partly because the Church of England was pro-Christmas, which automatically made the Puritans vehemently anti-Christmas. My, I am pedantic today. It's one of my greatest flaws."

"I don't think you're pedantic. I do think you're extremely well versed in the past." *Maybe too well versed.*

"Well, thank you for that."

They were interrupted by the docent's knock and entry. "Can you come out here a minute, Miss Hathorne? We need you to answer a question about the spinning wheel."

"Oh, I know quite a lot about spinning and weaving, too," Marta said. She pointed to a plate of Christmas cookies on the side table. "Help yourself. I'll be back as soon as their eyes begin to glaze over."

Callie had more of the wassail punch, took a cookie, and scanned the room. There was an uncomfortable-looking cradle in the corner, hand carved and, in all likelihood, passed down through the generations. She imagined Marta had once slept in the thing. She looked past the cradle to the leaded-glass window above it, and had a clear and disturbing thought: Marta and her family had chosen to live in the dark history of the past for more than three hundred years. They were keeping it alive. With the exception of Marta destroying the switch just now, it seemed as if nothing had ever changed in this house. And, until now at least, no one had wanted to let the darkness out. Maybe now that she'd burned the switch, Marta would consent to opening a window.

Callie looked at the bed, with its lovely lace coverlet, the only thing in the entire house that looked out of place. And then she spotted another thing that didn't belong.

Sitting on the bedside table were Finn's eyeglasses.

CHAPTER TWENTY-EIGHT

December 22, 2014
SALEM

*To the Puritans, anything beyond the western boundary of
Salem Village could invoke terror, for that was where the
savages dwelled. But one could encounter the devil in those
you met in Salem Town as well: In the Quaker heretics
and blasphemers, and in the Catholics.*
—ROSE WHELAN, *The Witches of Salem*

"DOES PAUL KNOW?"

"Everybody knows. It's been going on for the last few years,"
Towner said. "Emily used to look the other way, but these days . . .
Finn and Marta have known each other since they were kids. Everyone thought he'd marry her and end the family feud, but his father
wouldn't allow it because she wasn't Catholic."

They sat across from each other in the tearoom, sharing a pot of
Difficult-Tea. "That seems odd," Callie said. "In this day and age."

"It was odd, and it wasn't really the reason."

"No?"

"The real reason was money. Marta's father was the reason the Whitings lost their business. It rekindled the old family feud. Finn's father
had to refill the family coffers. Marta was not only family non grata, she
was as poor as a church mouse. Emily's not Catholic, either, but they
were happy to look the other way for her money. Of course there was
the not small matter of Emily also being . . . 'in a family way.' "

"You told me as much when I first met her," Callie said.

"I did? How indiscreet of me!" Towner smiled.

"So his relationship with Marta never really ended?"

"Oh, it ended. For quite a while. She didn't live here for a long time. She was down in New York City. I don't think they saw each other again for years. But then, when her mother got sick, Marta came back. From what I've heard, they pretty much picked up where they left off . . . and none too subtly, either."

"That must be really difficult for Emily."

"To say the least."

"Why does she put up with his infidelity?"

A shadow crossed Towner's face. "I think you'll find when you love someone that much, you put up with all sorts of things you never thought you could tolerate, real or imagined."

Callie looked at her friend. "We're not talking about Emily anymore, are we?"

Towner didn't break Callie's gaze, and she didn't answer the question. Instead, she sighed and stood to clear the table.

"There was a time my mother was talking about divorce," Paul said. "But that was before she got sick."

Callie had agonized before bringing up the subject with Paul. But Towner had assured her that he knew about Marta and his father, and, thinking back, some of his less than welcoming treatment of Marta now began to make sense.

"My mother has told me to stay out of it. But it's not always easy," Paul admitted.

Before they'd started talking about Marta, they'd been discussing solfeggio frequencies. Paul had been researching a symbol his team had found in the cave, something the scholars at the Vatican believed corresponded to the ancient solfeggio frequencies, at least from a mathematical perspective.

Callie sometimes used the frequencies in sound healing: solfeggio was an ancient scale of six notes, all of which were pure sound that vibrated at different frequencies: *ut, re, mi, fa, so, la.* This scale eventually morphed into the seven-note musical scale that is used today.

"The scale was used in the early Latin church hymns, for healing and spiritual awakening. Then many of them were mysteriously lost. Only a few remain, but we're interested in finding anything that refers to them. This symbol might."

That the Catholic Church was interested in anything that she was using in sound healing surprised Callie. But she took it as an encouraging sign of the practice's growing acceptance.

They sat and watched the fire until it faded to embers. Paul stoked it once more and brought a blanket from the bedroom.

Lately, they'd taken to making out like high school kids. "Does this mean we're at least going steady?" he kidded her.

She'd never gone steady in high school, never engaged in the "heavy petting" the nuns had warned was a mortal sin. Instead, she'd skipped over that phase entirely. Here, with Paul, she felt as if she were living her life in reverse.

She'd been here almost every evening since their kiss in the car, and, each night, she tore herself away from his hands and lips and rushed back to Pride's Heart before midnight, which Paul had taken to calling "curfew."

"I've got to get back," she said just before twelve, pulling herself away from his embrace.

"Sleep here," he said when she stood to leave.

"I sleep with my eyes open, remember? And I have nightmares."

"I'll make them go away," he said seriously, trailing his thumb across her neck.

She laughed. "Are you going to walk me back?"

"I don't think I am, no."

"Okay." She headed for the door.

He sighed, getting up to follow. "You're killing me, Callie," he said, only half kidding. "I hope you know that."

Hearing his tone change, she turned back. "It's not that I don't want to sleep with you."

"Don't say you just want to be friends."

"No. I can't say that anymore."

"Then what the hell are we waiting for?"

She decided to tell him the truth. Not the whole truth—the horrible suspicion that something awful might happen if she slept with him. Equating sex with death was too Freudian to mention. Instead, she told him, "I don't want to be like my mother."

It was equally true.

"Not much chance of that, I'd say."

"I was a lot like her before we met."

He seemed surprised. "Wish I'd known you then," he tried to joke.

"No, you really don't."

When she finally fell asleep, she dreamed of sex with Paul: wild versions and perversions that left her body flushed and tingling, the blankets damp and clenched in her fingers. The dream ended the way it ended each time, with Paul on the cold stone floor, open eyed and openmouthed, the blood surrounding him growing less red and more purple every night.

CHAPTER TWENTY-NINE

December 25, 2014
PRIDE'S CROSSING

*The Catholic Church embraced December as Christ's
birthday in order to appease the heathens, thereby building
the number of converts to Christianity. For their part, the
Puritans disdained the celebration, which reminded them
not only of the Pagan devil worshipers but of the Catholics
who had once persecuted them in England.*
—ROSE WHELAN, *The Witches of Salem*

"LOVELY DAY," ROSE SAID AS THEY RODE ACROSS THE bridge to Pride's Crossing on Christmas morning. She looked out at the ocean, which seemed to surround them. At least it was warmer than it had been on Thanksgiving. Today it was forty-six degrees.

Emily had offered them her driver, and Callie and Paul had accepted. They'd gone together to pick Rose up from the shelter. Paul had waited downstairs in the family room while Callie braided Rose's wild mane into a single tail, recalling how Rose had once done the same for her. Then it was time to introduce the two most important people in her life. Callie had been worried, but the minute they met, Rose said, "Look at these lovely boots Callie just gave me," and seemed quite at ease. Paul complimented her footwear while ushering her into the car and then climbed in and sat beside her.

"It is a beautiful day," Callie agreed. "Strangely warm for late December."

Paul and Callie filled the rest of the ride with small talk, and Rose was content to listen and gaze out the window, but as they turned into the driveway and she sighted Pride's Heart, Rose grew agitated. When the car made its way around the curve of the driveway, beneath the ancient elm branches, she said, "It's here."

"What's here?"

"The tree."

"Those are elms," Callie said. "Not oaks."

"Not those trees," Rose said, leaning forward in her seat. "It's here. I don't see it yet, but I can feel it. The hanging tree."

Callie and Paul exchanged a glance.

As they pulled up to the front entrance, and the driver went around to open the car door, Rose jumped out and dashed toward the lawn and the ocean beyond.

Paul and Callie scrambled to catch up. By the time they reached her, she was standing near the orangerie at the edge of the cliff in front of the lone oak on the Whitings' property.

"This is it," Rose said, putting her ear to its massive trunk. "It has to be."

"What's going on?" Paul whispered.

"She thinks that's the hanging tree," Callie said.

"I know it is. I saw it floating down the North River in my dream," Rose said, growing more excited. "The North River flows right into Beverly Harbor, and it comes out here."

"This tree was planted by my great-great-grandfather in the late eighteen hundreds," Paul said gently, "before the big house was built, back when he lived at what is now the boathouse. It was never in the North River, Rose."

Rose shook her head. "It's telling me I've come to the right place."

"You *have* come to the right place," Callie said, talking slowly as if to a child. "The Whitings have invited us for Christmas dinner." She looked at the tree, an old and beautiful oak. "Let's go into the house now. We can come back to see this after dinner."

Rose planted herself under the tree. "Thank you, but I'll stay right here."

Callie was speechless for a moment. Until now, she hadn't been overly troubled by the extent of Rose's obsession. "It might be warm for December, but it's still chilly. Come inside."

"You go inside. I'm staying."

"I'm so sorry," Callie said to Emily. Hildy had been holding dinner for Rose, and now it was in danger of overcooking. "I just don't know how to get her to come in."

Since they'd arrived an hour earlier, she and Paul had tried everything they could think of to lure Rose inside. She wouldn't budge. At Emily's insistence, Callie had taken Rose a heavier coat and a blanket.

"I suppose we should just go ahead and have dinner without her," Callie said, trying and failing to look Emily in the eye. "I really don't know what else to do."

"I think we should join her," Emily said. "An alfresco Christmas dinner is something we haven't tried before."

Paul stared at his mother. "Oh, Dad's going to love that."

"As it turns out, Finn is ill and won't be joining us for dinner," Emily said, dismissing his concern.

"What's wrong with him?" Paul asked.

Emily didn't answer. "Put your coats back on and let's go outside."

Paul exchanged a glance with Callie but let the subject drop. With a few brief directions to the staff, the moving process began. The glass and wrought-iron table that stood outside the orangerie was moved under Rose's oak, and four places were set. If the staff thought this was bizarre holiday behavior, their expressions did not give their thoughts away.

Rose wouldn't leave her tree to join them at the table, so they made her a plate and tray and served her where she sat. The table was close enough to engage in conversation, though. Rose said, "How do you do?" when introduced to Emily.

"I'm quite well. It's a pleasure to meet you, Rose."

The meal was much simpler than it had been on Thanksgiving; a crown roast, with wild rice and apples, Parker House rolls, sweet

potatoes, and brussels sprouts. With the addition of Christmas pop-
pers and the party hats and favors they yielded, it almost felt like a
child's birthday party. Without Finn present, Emily did not bother to
say grace.

Rose was the only one who didn't put on her party hat, and yet she
seemed almost amused by the sight of the others at the table. But
she was preoccupied, and soon she retreated to silence, listening to
the tree as if it were telling her something. Not wanting to interrupt
Rose's reverie, they sat quietly, every so often breaking the stillness
with some inane bit of small talk.

Emily kept glancing at the house, as if fully expecting Finn to
make an appearance and growing more and more annoyed when he
didn't materialize. "As I mentioned before, Callie," she said, doing her
best to sound upbeat, "you are welcome to move into the boathouse
when Paul goes back to Italy in February."

"Thank you. That's very kind," Callie said flatly. The last thing
she wanted to do was talk about Paul going back.

"And if Rose would like to stay with you on occasion, I'm sure that
could be arranged."

Paul shot his mother a look. "I'm sure Dad would approve that
plan." He said it as if sincere, but his mother picked up his subtext.

"I think it would be good for all concerned."

Callie said nothing. Luckily Rose was ignoring the entire exchange.

If conversation had been sparse before this remark, now it became
almost nonexistent.

They stayed outside at the table long after dessert, until the sun
had set and it was growing dark. Rose had two pieces of apple pie as
well as a piece of the savory mince.

"I promised to have you back in Salem by six," Callie said to Rose.
"We have to get going."

"I'm not leaving," Rose said.

"You may come back anytime you want, Rose," Emily offered. "I'll
send my driver for you. This can be your tree. I know you already
have a tree in Salem. Now you can have one in Pride's Crossing as
well. You may sit under it as much as you'd like."

Rose considered, looking wary. "Anytime I want?"

"Anytime," Emily said.

"Okay," Rose said, taking the hand Paul extended to help her up.

They hustled Rose into the waiting car, and as they crossed the Beverly Bridge on their way back to Salem, Paul asked, "What did the tree say to you, Rose? I saw you listening."

"They're here," Rose said.

"They're here?" Callie repeated. "That's what the tree said?"

"The missing remains of those executed in 1692?" Paul asked.

"Remains, yes," Rose said, staring out the window, "and their unresting souls."

"That's what the tree said to you?"

"That and something else."

"What else?" Callie asked, steeling herself, not certain she wanted an answer.

"Sometimes the only healing is death."

It took Paul a while to calm Callie down after they dropped Rose back at the shelter.

"I have to acknowledge that Rose is sicker than I thought," Callie said.

"That was always a possibility, wasn't it?"

"Like Zee says, it's denial. And what was that bit about Rose staying at the boathouse? How could that ever work?" Callie asked, confused.

"That was an interesting offer to say the least," Paul said.

Now Callie's mood took a dive. "I don't want to think about you going back to Italy."

"Let's not think about that today."

Neither of them wanted to go back to Pride's Heart right away. Instead, Paul had Emily's driver take them over to Nahant, stopping at the old fort, where the ocean view opened up all the way to the Boston skyline.

They didn't get back until after eight. "Come to the boathouse?"

"I think I'll check on your mother first."

Paul walked her to the door but didn't go inside. "My father's not ill," he said. "He's just being cruel. He wanted Marta to come to dinner, and when she refused, he played sick. He doesn't care how my mother feels about the whole thing. He never has. I'm afraid of what I might say if I run into him."

"I'm guessing it's not 'Merry Christmas.' "

"No, definitely not 'Merry Christmas.' "

Callie found Emily in the orangerie.

"Where's Paul?" Emily asked.

"He went back to the boathouse," Callie said. "He's trying to avoid Finn."

"Smart boy." Emily closed her eyes for a moment. When she opened them, she looked directly at Callie. "I'm not afraid of dying, you know."

Callie was shocked—especially since Emily was doing so much better.

"I don't think we need to talk about you dying."

"Oh, my dear," Emily replied, sinking farther into the downy cushions of the couch. "We both know how this thing is going to end."

With cancer, death was always a possibility. But it wasn't something Callie saw on Emily. She'd been fooled before, of course. There were patients she'd thought she was helping who'd succumbed more rapidly than she'd expected, but Emily didn't seem like one of them. Ever since the day Callie had lifted her pain, Emily had been looking better and better. Today, sitting on the couch, she seemed the picture of health.

"I'll tell you what I am afraid of."

"What's that?"

"I'm afraid of leaving my son unfinished."

" 'Unfinished.' " The word resonated as odd. "I'm not sure I understand."

"Children of privilege," Emily said, "confuse having resources with being resourceful. I'm afraid for my son. I'm not sure he has the . . . survival skills he's going to need. He's a good man," Emily continued. "Any faults he might have come from his youth and privilege. Which is my fault, and Finn's, not his."

That Emily believed she was going to die soon bothered Callie in a way she hadn't anticipated. Somehow, in the past weeks, she'd come to feel really attached to the woman. It was the same way she'd felt about her first foster mother. Callie didn't want to remember how that had ended.

CHAPTER THIRTY

January 27, 2015
SALEM

The oaks take their rest only during the winter months.
Winter is the only time it is possible to forget the loss
of those they loved.
—ROSE'S *Book of Trees*

"I DON'T KNOW WHY YOU'RE SO HAPPY," TOWNER SAID. "A storm this big is going to create more trouble for you than the exhumation would have."

The exhumation of the Goddesses had been scheduled for January 27. Now it was delayed because of heavy snow. When they could reschedule was anyone's guess. *Take that, you old biddy,* Rafferty said silently to Helen. *Maybe Rose does have a bit of magic about her,* he thought. *She's certainly got the weather behind her.*

Rafferty had caught the four o'clock AA meeting at the Methodist church, then picked up Chinese takeout and walked back to the coach house. Towner had already lit the fire and was setting up for s'mores. They had planned to watch a movie Rafferty liked, a rare copy of an old favorite that Towner had bought him for Christmas, but, in the time it had taken him to get home, the electricity had gone out.

"I love a good snowstorm, don't you?" she said.

"I love you," he said, leaning down to kiss her neck.

They'd spent Christmas through New Year's with his daughter,

Leah, in Nyack, New York. Leah had a new boyfriend and now answered to the name Lee.

"I hope you don't mind," she'd said to Rafferty. She'd always been uncomfortable with her name, so different from those of all her friends, the Brittanys and Amandas she went to school with. When she was a kid, she'd looked up the derivation. "Do you know what it means?" she'd demanded. "It literally means 'weary' or 'exhausted.' Plus it's a Jewish name, which would be fine except that we're not even Jewish."

"It's an Old Testament name," he'd explained. They'd talked about it for a long time, with Rafferty explaining how Leah was the wife of Jacob, the mother of seven of his children. His explanation did nothing to appease his twelve-year-old.

He'd had some vacation weeks to either use or lose, and it had been the perfect getaway. After Nyack, instead of going into the city as planned, they'd ended up at a B and B near Sleepy Hollow. The escape had done Rafferty a world of good. It was a romantic week, long dinners by candlelight, no interruptions. On the second day, Towner had taken his hand. "There's something I've wanted to tell you for a long time now," she'd said. "I just never knew quite how to say it. That time we were separated?"

"What about it?"

"I was never unfaithful to you," she'd said. "I never slept with anyone else. I know you thought I did."

There was a lot that still remained unsaid between them about that time. What Towner had told him was the last thing he expected to hear.

"I just thought you should know."

She'd looked at Rafferty curiously. If she'd expected relief on his part, he knew that wasn't what his face was showing. "Thank you for telling me" was all he could manage to say.

They hadn't talked about it again in the weeks they'd been back but instead had settled into the welcome routine of New England's inevitable winter. The snows were late this year, which made some people feel almost giddy, as if they were getting away with something.

Others, like Rafferty, knew this wasn't a good sign. The delay only meant that, when the snows finally fell, they would fall with a vengeance.

Now she laughed and kissed him. "You smell like snow."

They'd both come so far to reach this place. Rafferty had never thought of himself as someone who would end up content, but here it was. He tried to live each day in the present, enjoying their quiet moments together and not thinking too hard about the time they were separated, in an attempt to keep from having his thoughts read by Towner. They had never been as happy as they were lately, and he didn't want to do anything to mess it up.

Still, now that they were back in town, the nagging and persistent dread that it couldn't last had returned. Today he'd had to consciously push it away, which was why he'd made sure he got himself to the meeting. He needed to hear the "one day at a time" stuff again. He needed to believe it.

Rose dressed for the cold, layering every warm item of clothing she owned under her big red coat. The boots Callie had given her for Christmas were not quite broken in, so she added extra socks to pad the heels.

The train had stopped running. It was 3:00 A.M., too late to call for Emily's driver, as she had done a few times in the past weeks. Tonight she would have to walk. Outside, she didn't see any vehicles save the occasional plow on the main streets. As the plows passed, the force of the wind drove the snow back, filling in the pathways behind almost as quickly as they had been cleared.

The wind stung her face as she walked along the North River on Route 1A. She had to lean into it to keep from being pushed backward. Already, several cars had been abandoned, covered in rising snow until they looked like a tiny mountain range along a vast white plain.

When she got to the Beverly Bridge, the wind force doubled, gusting off the open water, and, for a moment, Rose lost her balance completely. Determined, she righted herself and pressed on, leaning forward until her torso was practically parallel to the ground. As the bridge crested at its highest point, the screaming wind faded to an eerie stillness.

Rose felt suspended in time and space.

Whiteness stretched in every direction.

As she descended the downward slope, the wind picked up again, and the momentary calm gave way to a renewed fury. For just a moment, Rose regretted the journey.

When the bridge ended, she stayed to the right on Cabot Street. By the time she reached Route 127, she could no longer feel her feet. The snow turned to sleet, and the road beneath her was slippery. Her fingers ached, so she balled them into fists in the palm of each glove to warm them.

When she finally reached Pride's Crossing, the thick stands of trees provided relief from the sting of attacking wind. By the time she found the Whitings' driveway, the sleet had turned back to snow.

The world was quiet here, insulated, so perfect that it startled her in both its frozen beauty and its white silence. In the glow of solar lights leading to Pride's Heart, Rose watched the snowflakes dance to the faint music of wind through bare elm branches. The lights were crusted and glowing on their windward sides, luminarias lighting her way.

As she walked past the big house, Rose looked in a window of the library and was surprised to see Emily sitting alone by the fire reading a book by candlelight. Rose walked on toward the orangerie; the glass structure was covered with snow, its spiny frame creating a pattern that mimicked the branches of the trees.

When she arrived at the oak, Rose began to cry, her tears almost freezing as they fell to her cheeks. She put her arms around the tree, and its branches seemed to sway forward, reaching for her, the oak pulling her close under the shelter of its heavy limbs.

Rose sat down, leaning her exhausted body against the trunk, disappearing into its strong embrace. She turned her face to the oak's dark and rippled skin, her fingers clasping the bark. She could feel the thrum of life in the tree's scarred beginnings, tracing it back to birth and then to each spring's rebirth, the unfurling light green of every new leaf.

"Mother Mary, hallow this ground," she began to recite, remembering that night so long ago on Proctor's Ledge.

She raised her arms like tree limbs and opened her fingers wide, imagining tiny sprouts of life springing from them: budding, blooming, and greening, then vibrant with color, and finally withering and letting go. She felt her blood-sap cool and slow until she could feel it no longer, and she lay down, resting under the tree, her arms spread wide like the branches of the sacred oak.

From the top of the hill, the Whitings' groundsman spotted the colors: red, purple, deep green, yellow, bright against the snow.

Rose was an island of color in an ocean of white. Her frozen body floated on top of the snow, her arms spread out like angel's wings. She captured motion, as if she were a statue carved at the very moment she moved between the realms. She was beautiful in a way she had seldom been in life: her clear blue eyes looking forward, lips turned up in a smile, and cheeks painted the palest pink. Her long white hair, once so wild, now framed her head like a halo.

"A snow angel," the groundsman told anyone who would listen. "That's what she looked like. A genuine, honest-to-goodness snow angel."

PART THREE

CHAPTER THIRTY-ONE

February 20, 2015
SALEM

*Considered sacred in almost every culture, the oak is
known as a protector. That it was forced to participate in
the killings of 1692 was not only against its nature but an
unforgivable sin, and one from which the tree has
never been absolved.*

—ROSE'S *Book of Trees*

IN FEBRUARY, SNOW FELL FROM THE SKY UNTIL IT INSINU-
ated itself into everyone's consciousness. Piles grew higher and higher
on the ground. Ice encased the tree branches, and, on the few days
the sun chose to appear, it glared with a light more blinding than summer's. At night, everything sparkled and strobed. When the short-lived
annual thaw finally came, the snow and the ice melted and pooled.
Fooled, some of the trees attempted to quench their thirst. When the
water froze again, it split the trees in half.

All over town, people deserted their cars, narrowing the historic
streets even more; vehicles were plowed in too many times to number.
Forced to walk, people slipped on sidewalks, fracturing ankles and
cracking ribs. Old people broke their hips and died of the resultant
pneumonia. One hand-lettered sign on a Salem street corner advised:
PRAY FOR GLOBAL WARMING. That message was crossed out and replaced with scrawling red letters: THIS IS GLOBAL WARMING, ASSHOLE.

"This isn't depression you're experiencing, Callie," Zee Finch said. "This is grief."

Callie looked out the window at the falling snow. *Great, more snow.*

It was all so hard to believe. After Christmas, Rose had seemed to be doing so well. She had come to Pride's Heart to see the tree a few times, and she'd even seemed to make some friends at the shelter, something Callie had never expected. Callie had been able to focus her concern on Emily, and, by the end of January, she, too, had still seemed to be doing fine.

The month with Paul had been a good one as well. They'd started spending more and more time together, settling in for winter as people tended to do in New England, cooking dinners and sitting by the fire. Everything had been wonderful and romantic. Until the night of that first snow.

She still couldn't believe Rose was gone. It seemed inconceivable that after she'd just found Rose again, God had once again taken her away.

Callie had booked a few sessions with Zee; since Rose's death she'd found herself crying at the oddest times. Her nightmares had changed, too: They were a jumble of trees, frozen darkness, and severed limbs harnessed and swinging. Over and over, each limb was cut away, until all that was left of the tree was the trunk itself. Beyond the severed limbs was a vast nothingness that stretched on forever.

But even worse were the memories that had begun to come back unbidden, from the night of the murders:

Susan's fall and the gash on her neck, bleeding into the earth below.

A maze of tangled trees, woven thick and impenetrable.

The blood glazing the dying grass.

The dark heart of the hedge bush where Rose had hidden her.

The pit and their blood grave below.

"How much did you grieve when it happened?" Zee wanted to know.

"There didn't seem to be any time to grieve," Callie said. "I was too scared of what might happen next."

Zee nodded. "And the glimpses of memory you're having now, how do they make you feel?"

"Sad and scared," Callie said. "Very scared." The images were more intense than her nightmares. She started crying again.

"The woman is dead, for Christ's sake!"

Rafferty sat at his desk talking on the phone and lobbing darts at the exhumation order he'd tacked to his bulletin board as a makeshift target. The dart arced too high, looking as if it might miss the target altogether, then dove suddenly at the last minute, finding its mark dead center. "Can't you people let her rest even now?"

He slammed down the phone.

There had been such a great amount of snow over the past few weeks that they hadn't been able to bury anyone, let alone dig people up.

"I can't believe they're still going to open those graves," Towner said later that evening.

Despite Rafferty's protest to the ADA, his attitude about the exhumation was changing. The truth was, now that Rose was dead and could no longer be directly hurt by the results, he was curious about what the procedure might reveal. Increasingly, he wanted to solve this case. He made the mistake of confiding this feeling to Towner.

"I thought you were afraid the exhumation might implicate Rose."

"Rose is dead."

"So you don't care anymore? What about Callie, for God's sake? Didn't you say her DNA is bound to be discovered as well?"

"No one believes a five-year-old girl was responsible."

"They believe a lot of weird things in this town."

"Look, I just need to solve this case, okay?"

Ever since the first snow, Rafferty's tension level had been rising. He'd been reading the online posts, and now most of them were targeting him for the lack of closure to this case. But no one wanted closure more than he did.

"Let's change the subject," Towner said now, reading his expression and seeing where this was headed. "What else happened today?"

Rafferty had to rack his brain to come up with something. "So," he said finally, "have I told you what some of our more industrious citizens have taken to doing to keep using their cars?"

"Do tell," Towner answered.

"They are shoveling out spaces on the street and then 'marking' them: We've seen lawn chairs, buckets full of wood, trash barrels. In the McIntire District, someone set up a bistro table and chairs with two place settings, complete with wine bottles and candles."

"That's kind of funny."

"It is, but God help the interloper who tries to steal a parking space. Last night, Jay-Jay hauled in a guy who'd been smashing windshields and deflating the tires of cars parked in 'his' space. The guy was wielding a sharpened screwdriver, swiping the air like a swashbuckler and bragging, 'I flattened four tires in under a minute!'"

"I can't believe I didn't see it coming," Callie said to Zee, remembering Rose's words on Christmas: *Sometimes the only healing is death.*

"You've got to let yourself off the hook," Zee said. "I was Rose's therapist, and I didn't see it coming, either."

Zee quickly returned Callie to the original reason she had booked the hour. There had been an incident the previous weekend. She'd dropped a coffee cup in the kitchen, breaking it cleanly in two. As she bent down to pick up the mess, she saw the blood, just a few drops of it at first, falling on the floor she'd just wiped. She opened her hands to find her left palm cut, a slice across one of the petals of the rose-shaped scar. Holding her palm under the faucet to wash the wound, she watched the water run red. She pulled her hand out and pressed a paper towel to her palm to stanch the bleeding, but it wouldn't stop. She felt faint and called for Paul, who'd been sleeping upstairs.

"Let me see," he said, taking her hand, which she'd clutched around the towel.

"How bad is it?" she asked, squeezing her eyes shut, unable to look for fear she might actually faint.

Paul was quiet for a long time. When she finally opened her eyes, he was still holding her hand, but he was looking at her with a worried expression. She looked down at her palm. There was no blood, no sign of any wound at all. The coffee from the broken cup still coated the floor, and he leaned down to clean it up. "I think you were dreaming," he said. "Or maybe walking in your sleep."

She nodded. But she hadn't been sleeping, she'd been wide awake. And it wasn't the first time this week that she'd had a vision. Earlier in the week, she'd thought she'd seen Rose, sitting out by the oak where she died. And then, on Monday, there was a far more serious incident by that same tree. She immediately booked an emergency appointment with Zee, fearing that if she didn't get to the bottom of what it meant, her visions could start, like Rose's, to take unhealthy control of her actions.

"Tell me more about these visions."

"I've always had them," Callie admitted. After Rose's death, they'd become more invasive: moments of clarity so extreme that they magnified sights and sounds, rendering them indistinguishable from one another, making everything she perceived seem too loud and vibrant. Her heart pounded so hard she could feel her pulse in her hands, from the scar on her palm to the tips of her fingers. "But they're getting worse. I've never acted on one so impulsively before, never been as out of control as I was that day they started cutting down the old oak."

"Why was Finn cutting it down?" Zee asked.

"He claimed he didn't want to be reminded of what had happened to Rose. And he said that Emily felt responsible. Which she wasn't; I was the one who made Rose come for Christmas . . ."

Zee let the silence hang.

"What I did terrified them all."

The sound of the chain saw had been so loud, so violent—it had felt as if it were tearing through her head. "Stop!" she'd screamed at the groundsman, unable to stand it another second.

He hadn't heard her through the noise. She'd stepped in front of him just as he lifted the saw and lunged, trying to wrest it out of his hands. By the time the saw had gone silent, the pristine snow had been dappled with his blood.

"They all tried to help me," Callie said, shaking as she retold the story. "The man's wound wasn't as severe as the amount of blood suggested, thank God, though he required several stitches in his left arm. Luckily, he didn't want to press charges." She shivered. "The next morning, Paul took me to see what was left."

"Why would he do that?"

"He wanted to show me the growth rings. So I could see that the tree wasn't as old as Rose had believed. I mean it was old, but not three hundred years old. He thought it would make me feel better to know that."

"And did it?"

"No," Callie said. "Finding out—it just negated Rose completely. For all those years she'd been searching, and she finally thought she had found it. And now . . ." She started to cry.

Zee handed her a box of tissues she kept on her desk. "Tell me about the sound the cutting of the tree made."

"I don't want to talk about the tree anymore," Callie said, annoyed. "I want to talk about the guilt I feel. The guilt that Rose's life was wasted—"

"Humor me."

Callie crossed her arms and frowned.

"You said it was the sound that triggered your outburst."

"It did."

"What did it sound like?"

"A chain saw."

Zee waited.

"It was a whining, shrieking kind of thing."

"Did it remind you of anything?"

Callie thought for a moment, then dismissed it.

"What? Don't edit, just tell me what came to mind."

"Trees."

"What trees?" Zee prompted.

"Rose's oaks," Callie said. "All the ones she searched out in Salem before she found this one."

"The images that come back to you, where do they come from?"

"The night of the murders," Callie said.

Zee waited.

"The trees," Callie said. "On Proctor's Ledge."

"What was it about those trees?"

"They weren't oaks. They were just a tangle of branches close to the ground, and we had trouble walking through them. They seemed to be holding us back. And then later the hedge that Rose pushed me into saved my life."

"How?" Zee said.

"I was trapped." Callie felt how the prickly branches had held her. Rose had said not to move, not to make a sound. But she couldn't have even if she'd wanted to. It was as if the bushes had imprisoned her, had put a binding spell on her the way Ann Chase had done on the day they met. "I couldn't move. Not even when the screaming started."

"Who was screaming?"

"Rose said it was the banshee."

"Is that what you think it was, a banshee?"

"I don't know."

Zee looked at her. "Was it one of the Goddesses?"

"I don't . . . I don't think so." Susan's fall had been silent. Her mother had cried out briefly, but that long piercing noise . . .

"What did it sound like to you? The shrieking and whining."

"It sounded like a chain saw," Callie said, making the connection.

Zee sat forward in her chair, holding Callie's gaze. "And where was the sound coming from?"

"I don't know."

"You know."

"I don't!" Callie insisted.

"You know," Zee said again, this time more gently, never breaking her gaze.

Callie stared back but said nothing for a long time.

"Oh my God," Callie said as she finally understood something she realized the nuns must have known all along. "It was coming from me. The screaming banshee . . . it was me."

The nuns were at Vespers when she arrived. Callie sat on the cold stone bench right outside the chapel, where she could hear the last words of the Magnificat, followed immediately by the Lord's Prayer.

The nuns filed out silently. Callie did not meet anyone's eye.

Sister Agony was the last to leave the chapel. At first, she looked surprised to see Callie on the bench. When she caught her expression, Agony's surprise turned to worry.

"What's wrong?"

"Rose is dead. Really, this time." Callie tried unsuccessfully to hold back tears.

"How?"

"She froze to death under a tree."

Agony stared at her.

"It's my fault."

Agony watched Callie carefully, trying to understand.

"She always thought it was a banshee she heard screaming the night of the murders, but it wasn't." Callie began to choke. "You knew all along that it was me, didn't you?"

"Come inside," the nun said, taking Callie's arm and walking her toward one of the wooden benches in the back of the chapel. Callie took a deep breath, willing herself to stop crying.

The old nun folded her hands the same way she had the last time Callie confronted her. This time, though, it wasn't to stop her anger, but to pray. When she finished her prayer, she crossed herself and took a deep breath. "Your screams were heard all night long by the nuns at St. James's."

"They never told me that."

"No, they wouldn't have."

"Why didn't they call the police?"

"That's a question I've been asking myself for a long time," Sister Agony said, her voice far softer than Callie had ever heard it. She wrung her hands together in remorse as she continued. "I believe they honestly thought it was a Halloween prank."

Callie looked at her in disbelief.

"When they finally found you the next day, you were in horrible shape." The nun glanced at the stigmata. "The police only made things worse. You were questioned so much they feared for your sanity. You were an orphan, so Catholic Charities got involved with DCF, and they decided to move you here, away from the investigation. We really thought they would question you again at some point . . . they had every right to, but then Rose started talking about the banshee. We wanted to tell you Rose was alive, but she was clearly delusional, and maybe even a killer. So we decided not to tell you. Which was the second sin of omission committed against you by people who wanted nothing more than to help. But people don't always make the best decisions, Callie. Even with the best intentions."

Callie just looked at her.

"After that you were fostered. The same way we fostered all of our orphans." The nun forced herself to make eye contact but had trouble holding Callie's chilling stare.

Callie made a sound between a laugh and a choke. "Except that I was returned. Because I was *surrounded by death*."

Now the nun held her stare. "You don't remember all of what happened, do you?"

"Please tell me."

She spoke slowly. "Your foster mother died of cancer. Her husband couldn't handle his loss, and he brought you back to us. By that time word of your story had gotten out, and he was a little afraid of you. He was the one who said you were surrounded by death, not us."

Callie recited Proverbs 5:5, the note he had pinned to her shirt. *"Her feet go down to death; her steps lead straight to the grave."*

"Your memory is accurate on that part, though your presentation is somewhat different from the way you first recited it to us."

"I was just a child," Callie reacted.

"You were."

"And you all scared me."

"I'm sorry," the nun said, meaning it. "I've been thinking about this since you were up here the last time. We should have discussed all of this with you at the time. Of course we should have. We honestly thought it was for your own good." She looked as if she might reach for Callie's hand, but Callie straightened, weaving her fingers together in the same angry pose she had so often seen Agony use.

"We are an old-fashioned order. Not new millennium certainly. Some say we aren't even of the twentieth century. There was a lot of fear and superstition surrounding your case, particularly from the older sisters. At first we thought we had witnessed a miracle, an amazing example of Christ's intervention. The hand, once healed, would sometimes bleed for no apparent reason. Some believed that a miracle as well, a holy sign. It took me a long time to realize you were probably cutting yourself; we didn't see such things much back then. Soon after that, the rumors about the murders began to circulate and the stigmata began to raise fears, not only about the murders but about you. You were a strange child, sleeping with your eyes open, sleepwalking. And just knowing things you could never have known. But it was your recitation that terrified everyone. When we returned from mass that morning, we found you sitting on the top step of the children's home. When we asked you what happened, you stood up, as if in a trance, and began to recite that psalm. Holding your hands like this." Sister Agony put one hand over the other in the elocutionist's pose. "At the end of the psalm, you smiled. Then you curtsied."

CHAPTER THIRTY-TWO

And out of the ground the Lord God made to spring up
every tree that is pleasant to the sight and good for food.
The tree of life was in the midst of the garden, and the
tree of the knowledge of good and evil.
—GENESIS 2:9

THEY FLEW OVERNIGHT TO ROME, ARRIVING ON SATURDAY
morning, then immediately took a train to Bari, where Paul hired a
car to drive them to Matera, as no train line ran to their destination.
As they rode away from the coast, the vista broadened, revealing a
painter's landscape of olive groves, vineyards, and the occasional hill
town. The ride took almost an hour. Callie was exhausted from all the
travel, and her mind, blissfully, was an empty canvas, too tired to host
haunting images.

The view narrowed again as they reached the city limits. Matera
looked like other European cities: old architecture contrasting with
new, street vendors, scooters, and automobiles. But then their car
turned, and they began to climb into the Sassi district. The lane narrowed to an impossible width, and the driver shifted to a lower gear.
The look of the buildings began to change: They seemed to be made
of stone and light. *It's* tufo, she realized, the stone she'd heard so
much about from Paul.

Callie rolled down her window. The smells on the wind, the bright, clear air, reminded her of the ocean breeze in Pride's Crossing, but it was lighter here, somehow. The lack of sound was punctuated occasionally by, what was that, music? She strained to hear and then recognized the singing notes of a violin. Someone was practicing scales.

"Do you hear that?"

Paul said, "The violin? Yes."

Now she heard a horn playing. As they passed a building, she saw a sign for a music school.

The driver downshifted again, grinding the gears. The car lurched, bouncing them around. A larger auto passed going the opposite way, its horn bleating, forcing their driver to move to one side and stop his ascent. Images of the present were flooding Callie's mind, as if she were snapping photos to be remembered.

The driver put the car in first gear, sliding backward several feet as he let out the clutch, swearing. Aggressively, he pulled ahead to the top of the hill, scattering ambling pedestrians.

At the summit was a church, construction scaffolding blocking its entrance. Beyond were several palazzi, one restored as a hotel.

"This is good," Paul said. "Please let us out here."

The driver pulled over.

Paul opened Callie's door, and she got out, flexing her leg muscles. Beyond the towering cathedral she could see a deep ravine and, far past that, a hill.

She had never seen light like this or felt the air in such a way. The music had faded. There were no sounds at all now. She could see birds across the canyon, but she couldn't hear their calls. There was something otherworldly about the place, alien and familiar at the same time.

Paul paid the driver. They stood and watched the car descend the hill. A man came out of the hotel, nodded a greeting, then walked across the piazza and disappeared down an alleyway, his footsteps echoing on the stone and then fading to silence.

Paul picked up their suitcases and gestured for Callie to follow him down an alleyway marked Via Riscatto. Stone houses lined its boundaries, their foundations carved into the sides of the hills. Some were occupied, many more stood empty. Callie heard the echoing sound of a hammer growing louder as they approached and then fading again as they made their way past.

They turned left at the corner, and the alley wound downward, the view opening every so often to reveal the colors of the canyon. A dog passed them, paused to drink at a puddle of water, then disappeared up a set of steps.

They stopped at an old monastery that had been turned into a hotel. There were flowerpots by the front entrance and a sign: CASA DEL PELLEGRINO LE MONACELLE. Callie followed Paul inside. A woman was reading a book behind the desk; she looked up and smiled. She welcomed Paul back in Italian, then, hearing him translate to Callie, she changed to English, offering her hand for Callie to shake in the American style.

"Welcome to Matera," she said. Then turning to Paul: "How long are you here for this time?"

"It depends how long it takes to finish the restoration," he said. "I'm not sure how far the team has gotten without me. Probably a few months."

He'd rented Callie a suite for the two weeks she intended to be in Italy.

"Follow me," he said now. "I'll show you where you're staying."

Paul led Callie up a stone stairway to a room that had two levels: The first contained a dark wooden desk and a few chairs, a small sitting room, and a tiny kitchen. On the second level, located up a stairway, was a loft with a bed. Beyond the bed was another stone stairway leading to a blue door.

"Can I collapse here?" Callie asked.

"Not yet! Come with me," Paul said, taking her hand and leading her up the stairs. He opened the door to reveal a private roof garden and a much steeper, crumbling stone stairway leading to the campanile's bell.

"My rooms are just over there," he said. "Right across the courtyard. Ours are the only two suites on the rooftop level."

He led her not toward his quarters but toward the stone steps. There must have been at least forty of them.

"Not more stairs!" Callie said. But she followed him, winded and exhausted, to the top.

The two opposing hills of the Sassi were spread out before them. Callie grabbed the railing for balance and was awed. The hills looked like the figure of a bird in flight. Below, the river wound deep into the ravine. Across the canyon, she could see dark spots on the distant hill.

"What are those dark places?" she asked, pointing.

"Those are entrances to the caves that have been carved out of the *tufo*. Whole families lived in them for generations, until disease and poverty forced the government to empty them. They built apartments to rehouse the people."

Paul pointed out other caves, and soon Callie saw them everywhere.

"Artists have started moving in, and some of the families are moving back as well, despite the hazards of living in constant porous dampness. They missed their homes so much they were compelled to return."

Paul held Callie's hand. They hadn't done more than hand-holding since Rose's death, and Callie was grateful for that. She'd been too depressed, too angry. The last time she'd seen Rafferty, she'd yelled at him. "Find Leah Kormos," she'd demanded. "Lock up the killer."

"I'm not sure she *is* the killer," Rafferty had said.

"Just fucking find her!"

She'd alienated Rafferty certainly, but she couldn't help it. In what world was the police force so incompetent that they couldn't locate a woman given twenty-five years?

She feared her outburst had alienated Towner as well. Their last conversation had been polite but perfunctory.

Despite the sessions she'd booked with Zee, nothing seemed to help.

Paul had been attentive, but he'd also given her space, being there in case she wanted to talk, but not pushing.

"Why don't you drop everything here and come back to Matera with me?" he had finally said.

She'd been surprised. "I'm afraid I wouldn't be very good company."

"I don't care about that."

She'd been skeptical.

"It will help," he'd said. "Trust me. No strings attached."

Emily had agreed. She and Finn wanted to get away as well, to their home in Palm Beach. "Go," she'd said. "Get away from all this death. It'll do you good."

And almost immediately, away from Pride's Crossing, Callie could feel her spirits lifting. Standing abreast of the hills of the Sassi, she understood that part of her revived emotional state had to do with the *tufo* and the company. But the bulk of it, she realized, as she gazed out across the ravine, was that, with the exception of a small orange plant on the balcony of a neighboring palazzo, there wasn't a single tree in sight.

Paul had stayed with her the first few days, walking her around the hills of the Sassi, pointing out landmarks.

He took her to see the rock churches, including the one he was working to restore. There were more than 150 of them in and around the area, carved into the sides of the ravines with primitive tools, places of worship dug into the soft sedimentary stone, revealing the fossils of St. Jacques shells embedded in walls and ceilings that had once been ocean floor. When religion had come out of hiding, visible churches had been built on top, like the houses built over the caves of the Sassi. Paul took her to see a number of these old churches; most had rooms beneath them—sometimes small chambers for the Basilian and Benedictine monks who used them for meditation, and sometimes burial crypts for the faithful who, according to local tradition, were buried sitting up in coffins carved into the *tufo* walls. They'd spent one whole morning exploring the huge and ancient cistern that ran under the Sassi itself. "This is a place where hidden wonders are everywhere," Paul told her.

On the third day, he'd had to get back to work, and he'd left her in the piazza, heading down the hill and into civilization as she headed away from it, deeper into the Sassi, with its hidden stairways and empty shells of houses. She didn't care where she ended up, and so she followed every stairway she could find, until her thighs burned from the climbing and descending. When she was completely lost and exhausted, she turned and headed back.

Every day, she took a new path, and every night, she met Paul in the piazza for a late dinner, holding his hand as they climbed back up the hill to the monastery, where he said good night, then went to his own rooms to record his findings of the day, and she tumbled into bed, too tired to light the candle, undressing by moonlight and leaving her clothes in a heap on the floor.

There were dreams. The same awful ones she'd had before that awakened her from deep sleep, but in this place, the dreams seemed more distant, muted like the light on the *tufo*.

Tonight, she awoke from a dream she couldn't remember. There was no moon. Across the rooftop courtyard, Callie could see the candle Paul had left burning in his window. "In case you need me," he'd told her. The air smelled musty and damp. She watched the flame for a long time, her unclosing eyes dry and itching. Finally, the flame flickered and died, replaced by *the flicker of another brighter candle; a door opened and closed. Rose's house. The back bedroom. Callie watched from her mattress on the living room floor as the men came and went. She could hear their whispers, the faint strains of harp music as the Goddesses welcomed them. The air was hot and smelled of rosewater and patchouli.*

> All night long and every night,
> When my mama puts out the light,
> I see people marching by,
> As plain as day before my eye.

The scene shifted, and Callie, an adult now, stood naked at the front of the bedroom at Hammond Castle, her bare feet against cold stone, reciting the letter from Morrigan to Dagda.

"My Love,"

    Her hands were locked in the elocutionist's pose. Her breasts were exposed.

    "Meet me tomorrow night in our secret place." Cheeks burning.

    "And I will show you an ecstasy you have never known." Heart pounding.

    "Our bodies will be as the god and goddess." Heat moving downward in waves.

    Piercing blue eyes, unable to look away.

    "I will touch you as the Morrigan touches Dagda."

    Paul's eyes.

    "Our heavenly tryst unleashing all the powers of the universe."

    Eyes locked, holding her in place.

Callie jolted awake to find herself standing naked, not in Hammond Castle but in Paul's room, the candle not extinguished but still burning. He lay as still as stone, his bare muscled shoulders above the blankets, his eyes watching her. Though she wanted to turn and run, her hands were still clasped, her feet immovable. Realizing she had spoken the words aloud, she stopped, a shameful blush spreading its heat along her skin. She could not bring herself to recite the next line of the letter, the words far too embarrassing and far from her own. Instead, she remembered its final line, and the words came to her as truly as if she'd written them. Her voice shifted from the lyrical tone of her dream to one of certainty. She spoke each syllable separately and listened to her own voice as if hearing it for the first time. *"We have waited long enough, my love . . ."*

She didn't cling to the dream traces that remained. Instead, she locked her eyes on Paul's, taking one baby step forward and then another, until, finally, she was standing over him. "Another nightmare?" he asked hoarsely.

She nodded. She could see herself in the half-silvered mirror on the wall, looking every bit the pale spirit.

"Make them go away," she commanded.

Keeping his eyes on hers, he pulled back the covers, revealing his naked body underneath, strong and ready.

They didn't emerge from the monastery until long past dinner on Sunday night. The few restaurants at the top of the hill were already closed. Nothing was open in the square, either, and there were few people around. Paul remembered seeing a pizza place down a side stairway and looked to her for approval.

"Pizza sounds great."

The stairway was crumbling, winding another hundred steps down, crossing left over the rooftops of empty buildings, flat for a few steps, then descending again, along the outer rim of the Sassi. Their footsteps echoed on the stone. "There's really something down here?"

"I don't know. I hope so," Paul said, starting to doubt his memory.

Callie had taken to measuring every journey in terms of steps. Five steps down, three up. Descending and climbing. Twenty more steps now, past darkened shells of deserted stone residences.

"If it's not around this corner, I give up," Paul said.

A string of white lights hung over the entrance to the pizza place, a cave that Callie could see served as the foundation for the house that sat above it.

The owner looked surprised to see them so late, but he was delighted when Paul spoke in melodic Italian. The man agreed to serve them, and he led them into a deep chamber carved out of the soft stone, seating them at a table at the far end.

The cave was dimly lit, smelling of pizza and dampness. Sitting across from Paul, Callie found it difficult to look at him directly. She hadn't much experience with what happened *after*; she rarely stuck around long enough to find out. But sex with Paul had been like nothing she'd ever experienced. This had been so intimate, so different—so connected.

Paul took her hand and made her look at him. "Did I make the nightmares go away?"

She had to laugh. "Too soon to say—you didn't exactly let me sleep."

"That was my plan."

Callie ate most of the pizza and didn't protest when Paul ordered another. She was so hungry. She was thirsty as well. They polished off a bottle of Aglianico and another of sparkling water.

The string of lights flipped off as soon as they exited, leaving them in darkness again. He held her hand during the long climb to the top of the hill. By the time they reached Via Riscatto, her thighs were aching. When the path descended again toward the monastery, she was grateful.

He waited while she unlocked her door. Then he followed her inside and up the five steps to her bed. This time they both slept.

It was the first nightmare-free sleep Callie could remember.

The Sunday before she was scheduled to leave, Paul told her he wanted to take her to church.

"Confession?" she asked, nodding her head at the crumpled bed-clothes that surrounded them.

"Just the opposite, actually. I want to take you to the solfeggio mass before you go back."

"Really? There's a mass?"

"I just heard about it," he said. "They're going to celebrate the medieval Hymn to John the Baptist in Latin, composed in the solfeggio scale. It's a healing service."

"Wow," she said. "The Catholic Church is really getting progressive."

"Or regressive," he said. "Depending on your perspective. In any case, people seem quite excited about it."

"Do they do it in one of the caves?"

"No. It's going to be a really big event at a very beautiful old church. The music school is participating as well as some Gregorian monks."

"I'd like to see that," she said. "Or, rather, hear it."

"I thought you might."

The church stood at the top of the Sassi, where the light was brightest. It was one of the earliest churches in the area, Paul explained, built just after Christianity stopped hiding in the darkness of the caves and began to celebrate the mass publicly. They'd built it out of *tufo* high on the hill, and, unlike most of the churches in the Sassi, which were still dark and cavernous, it had long windows, which flooded the entire structure with light.

The sanctuary was crowded. Paul directed her to a seat midway down the long center aisle, where the sound was the best. "It's like being in one of your bowls," he told her.

The students from the music school filed in first; they spent several minutes adjusting their instruments, retuning to the slightly different tones of the ancient scale. When they began to play, the congregants went silent. The sounds of the medieval hymns were echoing off the walls.

Callie had never experienced anything quite like it. She closed her eyes and slipped into an easy meditation. Time stood still as the notes moved across and through each other, creating a tickling sensation inside her head.

It was one of the simplest and deepest meditation experiences she'd come into contact with—and definitely healing. She didn't open her eyes again until they had stopped playing and she could ease herself back into the world. She glanced at Paul, and he took her hand.

If she'd found the music to be healing, the Prayer to St. John the Baptist was sensory on every level. When the monks began to chant the Latin words, the air shifted. The room filled with light as if the sun had emerged from a cloud, and those dreamily calmed by the music just moments before seemed to awaken all at once. Not only was the air vibrating with the tones of the ancient scale, as Callie had expected, but the vibration seemed to bounce off her skin, starting with the scar on her palm, then raising the hair on her arms and the back of her neck, then moving on to the next person, that same tickling bringing everyone to life and tying them together with invisible strings.

She noticed the smell of jasmine first, then of pine, though neither had any logical presence. And just the lightest scent of oranges. She could taste nutmeg and cinnamon on her tongue.

Then something even stranger happened. The white walls, empty canvases just moments before, began to fill with color and pattern, like photos of water crystals she'd seen, or snowflakes, but with color and movement, mandalas being created by the notes themselves. She'd heard about people who could "see" sound, but she'd never quite understood it until now. As the tones shifted, the mandalas—for that's what they were—changed as well, drawing and redrawing their patterns as the music of the spheres—which she sometimes heard faintly during her meditations—absolutely filled the church.

Then, in her mind's eye, she saw Olivia and the others, as they had been on their last night. Dressed in their costumes. So young. Free. Not wise, maybe. Naïve certainly. Unaware of consequences. And she knew something she hadn't known before. They weren't evil. They were full of life. They *weren't* surrounded by death. And neither was Callie.

She opened her eyes. She looked at Paul. He was here, and so was she. They were together. They were both very much alive. It wasn't twenty-five years ago. It wasn't even a month ago. It was right now.

She was leaving the day after tomorrow, but it was the last thing she wanted to do.

"I don't want you to go back," he whispered in her ear. "Stay."

She tilted her head as if to see him from another perspective to judge his sincerity.

"Stay with me."

"Yes."

In the weeks that followed, they began to talk seriously about staying long-term. The restoration was ongoing, and his adviser was talking about several other rock churches in the area that needed restoration and had begun raising more grant money. He'd already asked Paul if he was interested in continuing with the project.

Callie spent her days as she had before, wandering the deserted quarter of the Sassi. She took every winding staircase she came upon, each one revealing a secret treasure or view. Every pathway felt magical, as if it had materialized just as she'd reached it. The brightness of the light and the silence of the stone muted and then erased the past. She began to believe the old saying was right: The *tufo* really did dry tears.

If Paul had seemed as if he'd escaped the pages of GQ back in Pride's Crossing, now he was Indiana Jones. The truth was, his appearance seemed to change a little each time she looked at him, as if he were a shape-shifter, or a chameleon changing color with his environment. She liked him best in this place.

She was so tired at the end of each day that she didn't have time to think, which was a blessing. Most nights, when Paul got back from working, they would meet his friends for dinner or to share a bottle of Aglianico, and then tumble into bed together, their bodies both exhausted and electric. Her nightmares had disappeared; her memory dreams were forgotten.

She was aware that his friends thought she was strange, aware that she must appear so. She didn't speak Italian, and her lone walks through the district did not go unnoticed. Paul confessed they had various nicknames for her: the girl with the rose on her palm, the wandering girl, the girl who's afraid of trees.

In fact, the only tree Callie had looked at since her arrival was painted on the wall of the Cripta del Peccato Originale, the Crypt of Original Sin, one of the few rock churches that had been fully restored. True to her nickname, the first time she saw the Tree of Knowledge, she *had* been a little scared, but she'd quickly gotten over it. She had now visited the Crypt of Original Sin with Paul and his friends twice. The initial visit was to see the tree itself. The second time was to compare the artist's work with that of the frescoes his team was restoring. There was little similarity: The artists' styles and the colors used were very different, so they'd concluded that Paul's restoration and the surrounding imagery were likely of an earlier period.

She had been to the cave Paul was working only once. They'd had to hike down the side of the ravine to get to it; there was no path, no handrail of any kind, and the cliffs were steep. She'd slipped and sent rocks tumbling below. Paul had caught her by the arm just before she would have tumbled after them. A few days later, crews were hired to create a better entrance path and put up a rope railing.

What she had seen of Paul's work had been intriguing; three of the walls had been uncovered, revealing religious frescoes, but the east wall was unrestored. Water runoff from the hill above it had caused damage, and, when the team began to clean it, whole portions of the fresco crumbled away. They'd closed the cave until they could divert the water, which was why Paul had been able to return to Pride's Crossing last Christmas. Though the cave was open again now, it wasn't clear if this wall would ever be repaired. All of the walls had been covered with soot, which had to be removed carefully, but this one was particularly delicate.

"Is this from church candles?" Callie had asked, indicating the layers of filmy smoke residue the crew was so painstakingly removing from the other walls.

"Mostly it's from shepherds," Paul had responded. "They moved in with their animals after Christianity came out of hiding and relocated to grander quarters. Soot from their warming fires did this."

Came out of hiding. *Is that what I am doing?* Callie wondered. *Hiding?* Yesterday she had visited the Church of San Pietro Caveoso, to see its portico of Our Lady of Sorrows sheltering those seeking protection under her cloak. The hooded suppliants looked like faceless children. She'd learned from Paul and his friends that the Sassi had a long history of hiding those not wanting to be found: from those persecuted for their religious beliefs all the way to Hannibal hiding from his enemies. Even the monastery where she and Paul were staying had once provided shelter for women who were running away from something. *Am I running away, too? Probably. No matter, it's working.*

Paul had told her that the Italian government had been giving grants to people who wanted to move into the Sassi district and restore some of the abandoned houses. Not the caves themselves, but the structures built above them, just shells of former domiciles, most standing empty now.

"I could do that," he said. "We could do it together. It would be fun."

He certainly had the skills. He spoke fluent Italian, and his work in the caves had familiarized him with the bureaucracy of permits and government restrictions. "We could live here permanently if you like."

He'd mentioned the idea so casually, as if testing her.

She loved the thought of it. The Sassi was the first place that had felt like home to her. Maybe ever.

They'd taken to exploring the unoccupied buildings, picturing what they would do with this one or that. Callie fantasized about what life in the Sassi would be like. They would live in one of the old houses. Paul would restore the rock churches. And she would learn Italian and get involved with the music school in some capacity, she hoped setting up some kind of sound healing practice.

Today, while Paul worked, she was exploring more of the deserted properties. She hadn't encountered another person since early morning. She was deciding which stairway to climb next when she was alarmed by the sound of approaching footsteps. "I've been searching for you for over an hour!" Paul said, as he turned the corner. "Come with me. There's something you've got to see."

With the new rope railing in place, the hike down to the cave was much easier. Callie could see that they'd hooked up a klieg light at the entrance, creating an artificial sun. The frescoes took on an eerie luminescence; the pietà on the north wall now glowed with a light that seemed to emanate directly from the face of Christ. Paul took her arm. "Over here," he said, leading her to the east wall. "Underneath the first fresco—we found another, an older one."

The east wall, the water-damaged one.

When the workers saw Callie coming, they stepped back to give her a clear view. They were all gathered around, and she could feel their excitement. At first, Callie wasn't certain what she was seeing. Then, slowly, she saw the crisscrossed lines. "It's a tree."

"Not just any tree," Paul said.

It hadn't just been painted on the stone but had been carved into it as well, which accounted for some of the crumbling the water damage had caused. Its roots stretched as far into the earth as its branches extended skyward. The whole image promised to spread out across the entire east wall.

"We think it's a very early version of the World Tree," Paul said. "Yggdrasil."

"Like the tree we saw in the Crypt of Original Sin?"

"No, this is not the Tree of Knowledge. This is the other Garden of Eden tree described in Genesis, the Tree of Life. Also known as the World Tree. You could even call it the Tree of Immortality. According to Norse mythology, Yggdrasil was where Odin hung upside down to acquire the runes of power."

"Wait—you think this is *Norse*?"

"No. We think it's Mesopotamian."

Now she was really confused.

"The Indus Valley image of the World Tree informed a number of religions that followed. Including our Old Testament. The Garden of Eden, for example." He hugged her. "This is where the ancient religions all come together. If we're right, this is really big!"

The tree displayed almost perfect symmetry from roots to branches.

"As above, so below," Paul said. "It's a Hermetic phrase. Ann uses it in her practice of Wicca, but the phrase and its concept appear in varying degrees in almost every culture or religion. Even the phrase 'on earth as it is in heaven,' from the Lord's Prayer, refers to this symmetry."

His enthusiasm was contagious. Paul was in his element; if she thought she loved him before, she was certain of it now.

"This could be one of the oldest depictions on record. My adviser has requested that the Vatican send two of their antiquities scholars here to photograph and study it."

Hearing the news, Emily and Finn sent a congratulatory telegram. They had just returned from Florida, and they said Emily was feeling "renewed."

Paul and the crew hosted a celebration at the Palazzo Gattini Hotel that lasted long into the night, with music and dancing that seemed to grow wilder as the night progressed, with too much wine and some unusual couplings that reminded Callie of a slightly tamer version of Rubens's *Bacchanalia*.

Paul had left the party for a moment, and when he returned, he grabbed her hand, dragging her away from the frenzied crowd and onto a balcony that overlooked the rooftops of the Sassi. He was holding an envelope.

He handed her the letter.

It was from the Italian government. She looked at him, confused. Beyond the official letterhead, she couldn't decipher a word.

"I've been looking into what it would take for us to move in and restore one of the old houses," he said.

"What does it say?"

"It basically says we should start looking."

"Really?"

"You still want to live here?"

"I do."

He smiled. "Me, too." He kissed her. "I love you, Callie Cahill."

"I love you, too."

They chose a house the next day. It was one they'd admired, not far from the monastery. They'd been looking at it for a while. It sat on the edge of the ravine where three stairways came together. From here, they could see the river below and the caves across the canyon. It was just the shell of the old house, and it would take a great deal of work before they could move in, but they could see the possibilities. The location was perfect.

Together, Callie and Paul began to visit all the rock churches, the few that had been restored and the many that were possible. There were years of work here, Callie realized. The thought of it made her happy.

On April 2, they visited the Crypt of Original Sin for the third time. As the one church that had been meticulously restored, it would feature prominently in Paul's dissertation. It was a great example of what was possible.

They stood side by side in the darkness, listening to the presentation as, one by one, lights went on around the cave, illuminating each fresco, finally settling on the one they had come to see, not Paul's Tree of Life from the cave across the ravine but the Garden of Eden's other sacred tree. Callie drew in a breath; each time she saw the Tree of Knowledge, its power intensified. She couldn't take her eyes from the serpent wrapped around its trunk, separating light from darkness, Adam from Eve.

"It isn't the Tree of Knowledge that the Bible describes, per se. A more apt translation is Tree of the Knowledge of Good and Evil. The decision to know the tree is the decision to be responsible for your actions." He pointed to the serpent that wound through the roots. "Original Sin is the dividing line between innocence and responsibility."

Callie was comfortable with the concept of Original Sin, of being born into a sadness, even a corruption, already waiting for you. It seemed to her the way of the world, mirroring the discontent that drove the human condition. That baptism could erase it was something she wasn't sure about. She'd like to think it was true. But perhaps it only obscured rather than erased? The way one fresco obscured what lay beneath. The same way years of smoke from the shepherds' fires had obscured everything.

As she stood before it, the image of Rose's tree in Towner's courtyard came to her, standing silent witness to history. She believed she understood Rose's attachment now. It wasn't dendrolatry, as Finn believed. It was something greater. Humans are rooted like trees, she realized; she hoped that some form of heliocentricity moves us toward the light.

She gripped Paul's hand tighter.

His phone vibrated. He checked the number and exited the cave to get a better connection, motioning for Callie to stay until the presentation ended.

The light of the midday sun was blinding when Callie emerged from the shadowy crypt. She took the stairs slowly, waiting for her eyes to adjust. At the top, she noticed a grove of olive trees. How had she missed them before? She had noticed only the vineyard where they parked Paul's car. She hadn't seen any trees.

She found Paul at the edge of the ravine, the trees and vineyard painting a backdrop behind him. It was an arrangement similar to the ancient landscapes he was uncovering in the caves. She started to tell him this when she noticed he was still holding his phone, but his arm was hanging at his side, and his expression was difficult to read.

"That was my father. My mother died this morning."

CHAPTER THIRTY-THREE

April 8, 2015
PRIDE'S CROSSING

*The banshee wasn't always a terrifying creature. It was
her imprisonment and diminishment that caused the
turning, transforming her into the frightful crone we
finally recognize only as she comes for us.*

—ROSE'S *Book of Trees*

RAFFERTY WAS GLAD TO SEE CALLIE AND PAUL TOGETHER,
though both of them looked miserable. He was sure that Paul felt
guilty for being away when his mother died. He and Towner had seen
Emily and Finn a few times after they came back from Florida, and
she had looked so well that Rafferty had actually found himself wondering if she were in total remission.

He looked at Marta, standing next to Finn. Too close, in Rafferty's estimation. He had never been fond of Finn. The graveside
service was taking longer than Rafferty had anticipated. Luckily, he'd
told Jay-Jay to have them start the exhumation with or without him.
There were still patches of snow on the ground, and the plowed piles
in the parking lot probably wouldn't completely disappear until May.
This was the first day the ground had been cleared enough to bury
the dead—or dig them up—and everything cemetery-related was happening at once.

And, as if it all wasn't awful enough, today should have been the day he took his twenty-five-year chip. Instead, the new anniversary of his sobriety would be tomorrow. Tomorrow it would be two years.

Towner held his arm, joining the prayer responses as required, and trying to hold back tears.

Though it was a nondenominational service, just family and a few close friends, Archbishop McCauley presided. Instead of beginning with the first prayer in the traditional mass of the dead, he ended with it: *"Requiem aeternam dona eis, Domine."* He turned to the group, translating: "Eternal rest grant unto her, O Lord."

"And let perpetual light shine upon her." Rafferty joined in the traditional response, crossing himself as the memorial ended.

"I'm sorry I can't stay for the gathering," he said to Towner as they left the gravesite.

"Everyone will understand," she replied.

He climbed into his cruiser, driving faster than the rest of the cars leaving the property. He didn't want them to get too far into digging without him. Jay-Jay wasn't one to assert himself, and Rafferty wanted to make sure the exhumation team didn't overstep their prescribed duties. Also, he wanted to be certain that curious onlookers were kept at a distance.

He headed out of Pride's Crossing, over the bridge, and arrived at Greenlawn Cemetery. The first thing he saw was a crowd surrounding three open graves.

In direct violation of procedure, the first two pine coffins had been opened on-site, and as he got out of his car, the crew was opening the lid of the last. A photographer from *The Salem Journal* leaned over to snap a shot. "Hey!" Rafferty called out. He raced over to the open coffins, looked down, and felt the surge of adrenaline as it hit him.

All three of the coffins were empty.

Callie hadn't visited her mother's grave since last November. Now, a few hours after the shock of seeing Emily laid to rest, she stood in the fading light of late afternoon staring down into the hole where her mother's body was meant to be. It brought her back to the morning after the murders, when she'd stood at the edge of the crevasse. Everything seemed distorted, and spinning. For a moment, she thought she might faint.

"Who did this?" she asked, trying to regain her balance.

No one answered. Towner took Callie's arm, and no one spoke until they were walking back to the cruiser. "What kind of sick person would do something like this?" Callie demanded.

"Someone who was trying to cover their tracks," Rafferty said.

This day was too much. After Emily's service Paul had started to drink and engaged Archbishop McCauley in a loud conversation about the Church's views on infidelity. The priest had quickly managed to extricate himself, and Finn had said, "You need to learn when to keep your mouth shut, son."

"And you need to learn when to keep your fly shut, Dad."

The place went quiet. Then Paul had walked out without Callie, and she'd gotten the call from Rafferty telling her that her mother's body was missing. "Please don't stop looking for the killer," she asked him now, her eyes filled with tears. "I'm never really going to be okay until we find out who did this." It was the sad truth, and they both knew it. Callie turned and slowly walked back to her car.

Rafferty watched as she walked away. Towner, who had driven over with Callie, waited for him while he spoke to the cemetery caretaker.

Though the ground around the graves didn't look as if it had been recently disturbed, he did notice that about a hundred-foot expanse of lawn around the graves and leading up a nearby hill was a slightly lighter green than the surrounding growth.

"That whole patch was resodded, just before I got this job," the caretaker explained.

"When was that?" Rafferty asked. It couldn't have been that long ago. The kid looked as if he was right out of high school.

"The second week of December," he said. "The guy who had it before decided to retire that week, so I got his job."

"Isn't December a little late for resodding?" Rafferty asked.

The kid shrugged.

Rafferty had just resodded the front yard at the rental house he owned in the Willows. Fall was the best time for planting new grass, he'd learned. Going through a winter gave the grass a chance to properly root itself. Even so, it was usually early and not late fall that was good for grass planting.

"Was there a reason they sodded this whole patch?" Rafferty asked.

The kid shrugged again. "I have no idea."

Rafferty walked back to Towner.

"It's going to be okay," she said, reading his frustration.

"I wish that were true." He was no longer certain that Leah Kormos was the killer. He'd already told Callie that, but now he was even more doubtful. Leah Kormos had been gone a long time, and whoever took the bodies had done so fairly recently, definitely before the first snow fell. Even so, something told him that, if he could find Leah, he'd find the key to unlock the whole mystery.

CHAPTER THIRTY-FOUR

April 9, 2015
SALEM

Tell me what you want, and I'll tell you who you think
you are. Tell me what you fear, and I'll tell you who
you really are.
—ROSE'S *Book of Trees*

THE DAY AFTER THE EXHUMATION, THEY SURPRISED RAF-
ferty with an anniversary cake. The cake thing was a relatively new
AA phenomenon, something someone who'd been in the program in
L.A. had suggested. That's what they did out west, he said. But the
Salem meeting was full of newbies, and they hadn't had a cake for so
long Rafferty had forgotten it was even a possibility. What he hadn't
forgotten for a moment was what day it was or, rather, what day it
should have been but wasn't.

When the moderator brought it in, twenty-five candles blazing,
Rafferty bolted. Ignoring their protests and looks of surprise, he
walked out the back door and down the steps, leaving Jay-Jay without
a word of explanation, not even looking back.

He hadn't taken a chip since the night he picked up, and he hadn't
had another drink since then either, but he had never spoken about
his slip in any meeting, or even told his sponsor, which he knew was
wrong on so many levels. He rationalized his silence: He was chief
of police; he couldn't have people knowing he'd broken his sobriety.
That's what he told himself, but it wasn't true. If this had happened

to someone he'd been sponsoring, he would have called bullshit on the guy.

"Hey, boss, wait up!" Jay-Jay said, snapping Rafferty back into the present. Jay-Jay was out of breath as he caught up with him. "What the heck was that about? You don't like cake or something? Who doesn't like cake?"

Rafferty grunted.

"HALT!" Jay-Jay commanded, and Rafferty stopped, annoyed.

"Hungry, angry, lonely, tired," Jay-Jay intoned, plunging his hands into the pockets of his pants, which were a size too big, and falling into step beside Rafferty. "We're not supposed to let ourselves feel any of those things, and you're all four. If you'd had the cake, you could have at least eliminated one of them."

Jay-Jay had taken to AA with an enthusiasm that was so strong it was almost overpowering. It was the last thing Rafferty would have expected.

"I'm not lonely."

"If you think I'm leaving you in this condition, you don't know me very well."

The truth was, Rafferty knew Jay-Jay LaLibertie a lot better than he'd ever wanted to. "Go back to the meeting."

"You're only as sick as your secrets, you know," Jay-Jay said, quoting another AA mantra.

If you only knew the secret I was hiding, Rafferty thought. He felt sicker about it with each passing day.

His slip had lasted only one day. One night, actually. It had started at a restaurant down on Pickering Wharf at a fund-raiser for Salem's Witches Educational Council, the antidefamation league meant to educate the public about the Wiccan religion and the good works witches do for the community. As chief, Rafferty always had public relations things he had to do, events he was required to attend. He pretty much hated this part of his job. "Just make an appearance," the mayor had told him. "After that, you can sneak away."

It had been the last place he should have gone. But he'd been so distraught after he and Towner had made their separation legally official earlier that day that he wasn't thinking straight. As if it weren't enough that he'd already moved out, she'd felt the need to leave town, relocating to Yellow Dog Island, as if putting the water between them would somehow make the separation final. That night he was expected, and, not knowing what else to do with himself, he'd shown up, realizing the minute he walked in that it had been a huge mistake.

Ann had known something was wrong the minute she saw his face. "What's ailing you?" she'd asked.

"Nothing," he'd said. He couldn't talk about it with Ann. Not without losing it altogether. He walked to the other side of the restaurant, away from the one person he knew could see through him.

When Finn had handed him the green liquid, he'd thought it was punch. Ann was always serving some witchy thing with herbs and something she called fairy dust. He'd questioned her about it the first time she tried to serve it to him.

"It's powdered sugar, for God's sake," she'd told him, laughing. "I know enough not to give you anything stronger."

He'd never told her he was a drunk; she'd always just known. It was one of the many things she knew without ever being told; that ability had freaked him out more than a few times.

"It shouldn't surprise you," Towner had said to him, early in their relationship. "Ann's not only a witch, she's a reader."

"A mind reader?"

"Minds, lace, palms, the bumps on your head. There isn't much that gets by her."

The closest Rafferty had ever come to believing anything paranormal had been the day his mother died, that time he'd heard and seen the banshee. He did believe that some people had intuitive gifts, and Ann was definitely one of them, as was Towner. But he preferred to think of such gifts as scientific, the product of some as yet unmapped part of the brain. Or maybe the nonlinear time theory Ann was always espousing as science. But he'd always flatly rejected the existence of ghosts and specters, though that day he couldn't imagine a time when he wouldn't be haunted by Towner.

He hadn't wanted to think about Towner that night. He'd fall apart if he did. He'd tried to push her from his mind, knowing what a ridiculous task that was. She'd been in his head since the day he met her, and he had no idea what he was going to do now.

He'd taken the drink from Finn and raised it to his mouth. It tasted like licorice only a little bitter.

"What the hell?" He'd realized it was absinthe the moment he tasted it. The Green Fairy. He shoved the glass back at Finn.

"Drink it, for God's sake," Finn said. "She's not worth your pain."

Later, he'd think he'd been staring into the face of the devil himself. He'd taken the drink.

That night Marta had waved to Rafferty from a far corner of the restaurant. He'd nodded but hadn't approached.

"What's Marta doing here?" he'd asked Finn.

"Ann's paying her to raise money for the Witches Educational Council," Finn had said.

That was one of the oddest things Rafferty had heard in a long time: Marta raising money for witches. It was no secret that she hated them and resented it when those living in Salem drew a parallel between themselves and the accused of 1692. "A similarity that didn't exist then and should not exist now," she'd often been quoted as saying.

Still, since Marta had moved back to the North Shore, she'd become the best fund-raiser around. Beyond that, she had some kind of connection with Ann, one Rafferty couldn't figure out. Ann had told him once, "I get most of my herbs from her gardens."

"And what does she get from you in return?"

"I'll never tell."

"I'm guessing it's some kind of love potion," Rafferty had said to Ann. "And we all know who she's slipping it to."

He'd been on his second glass of absinthe before he recognized the falling feeling, the slackening of muscles that had always been so welcome. It was like an old friend, the kind you knew wasn't good for you. There was something comforting about the familiarity, yet something unfamiliar, too, like a stranger hiding in the shadows, someone you didn't want to look at directly for fear of what you might see.

"My family made a fortune from this stuff," he'd heard Finn explaining to another guest. "This is the real thing. Wormwood and all. Thujone intact. Bootlegged from Spain when it was outlawed in France."

Rafferty could have stopped then, but he hadn't wanted to. The blessed blankness had descended, creating the emotional void he'd been craving. More than anything, he'd wanted to be erased. Finn had poured him another glass.

But this glass had brought the opposite effect. With each sip, his senses had heightened. The first was taste. Not only could he taste the blending of herbs but he was able to separate those tastes into component parts: the slight bitterness that faded quickly to reveal the anise and fennel that lay beneath.

Next, his vision had improved, and everything seemed sharper. The colors on Ann's velvet robe had begun to strobe. Finn's face had sparkled in the beam from the light above him.

When Ann touched his arm, the sensation had vibrated his body as if it were a stringed instrument. He'd stepped backward, knocking into a waiter with a tray of hors d'oeuvres. "What the hell is wrong with you?" she'd asked.

He'd seen Marta and her group of friends approaching, and had taken another step backward, almost tripping over another guest standing behind him.

"Let's get you some air," Ann had said. She'd taken his glass and handed it to a waiter, then taken his arm and led him toward the door.

The summer air had only made things worse. As they stepped out of the restaurant, Rafferty had caught the rush of salt breeze from the harbor, and the scent of the sea had flooded his nostrils. It smelled of childhood, of old beach houses on Long Island Sound, and of the ships that had once sailed out of these northern waters. And, whether it was association or delusion, Rafferty could have sworn he smelled the pepper that had once come in on the old ships. The sensation was so strong he'd had to work hard to keep from sneezing.

He'd looked toward Yellow Dog Island but seen only darkness. He was filled with dread, remembering what had happened with Towner only hours before, realizing again what it would mean.

Ann had steered him toward her store, taking him in through the back door to her office, making sure the young witches working in the front wouldn't see him. Behind her office was a room he'd heard about but had never seen, and that's where she'd taken him that night. It looked like a Wiccan bordello, he thought, with its beaded curtains, brass bed, red velvet pillows on the floor, and nature symbols. In the corner was a table with a crystal ball, and around the perimeter hung the lace that Ann used to tell the future. She called this a meditation room, but the men called it something else. Until tonight, he'd never believed this hidden room was real.

"Drink this," she'd said, handing him a cup of herbal tea.

He'd sat shakily on the edge of the bed. "What is it?" he'd asked.

"Consider it an antidote."

He'd thought she meant to the absinthe, and so he'd drunk. For a guy who didn't believe in magic, it was beginning to seem a possibility. His head had spun. He'd felt far too warm, aware of every sensation. The softness of the bed, the brush of Ann's velvet robe as she handed him the tea.

She'd taken a seat across from him, looking at him carefully as if trying to figure something out. "What happened today?"

He'd shaken his head, waving her off. He couldn't talk about it.

She'd watched him for a few minutes longer, and he could tell she was reading him. Seeing what it was he would not say.

"You think your life has ended," she'd said.

"It has," he'd said, meaning it. She'd stared through him, seeing all of it, her expression changing as she took it in.

She'd come over then, and sat next to him on the bed, taking his hand. "I see your future. This is not over."

"The hell it isn't."

"You need to believe," she'd said.

"In what? Magic?"

"If you like."

The idea had filled him with rage. The same violent frustration that had caused him to punch his fist through a wall in the house he'd recently moved back to, bloodying the knuckles of his right hand, now surfaced again, but, instead of striking out, he'd done something that surprised him even more. He'd reached for Ann, pulling her close, his hand slipping under her robe.

She'd stood quickly. "Keep drinking."

He'd obeyed, finishing every drop. His thirst had seemed endless. Putting down the cup, he'd reached for her again, his senses heightened. Just the touch of her skin had sent waves of heat to every pore of his. It was the last thing he would have imagined, yet, at that moment, Ann Chase had been the only thing he wanted.

"Yes," she'd said. "Yes, of course. But you have to wait."

She'd left the room and was gone for a long time. Eventually the lights had dimmed, then went out in the front of the store, and he'd heard her locking up. He'd heard the young witches chatting outside on the way to their cars. And then, when the store was finally quiet, he'd heard something else. It was Ann's voice. Chanting an incantation, a kind of music he'd never heard before, calling in the sounds of wind and water, melding them together until they achieved a kind of low pulsing that beat with the rhythm of his own heart. Hypnotic, it had lulled him. He'd lain back on the bed and waited.

When Ann had come back to him, she'd been wearing a different robe, one that looked like a black silk kimono. Standing before him, she'd let the robe fall and was naked. For an instant, she'd looked just like Towner or, rather, the way he'd always imagined Towner would look before they'd finally gotten together, the prolonged time when she had been only his fantasy. As soon as he'd recognized the vision, it had faded, and pure sensation had swept over him, pulling him into its vortex; he'd let himself go with it, aware that he was not leading, was simply reacting, present and in the moment with whatever spell Ann had just conjured.

It was sex, and yet it had been nothing like sex.

And he'd followed it again and again each time it took him.

Time had shifted. He couldn't tell if it had been a moment or an eternity. It had circled and repeated over and over again, until they'd both collapsed, too exhausted to move, and had finally slipped out of consciousness together on the bed.

Morning had come too early, and Rafferty had awakened as if from a coma. He'd sat up, holding his head, feeling the guilt of everything that had happened.

"Don't do that to yourself," Ann had said. She was already up and dressed, looking fresh and ready for the day. She'd handed him a bottle of water. "Go home. She's waiting for you. And, whatever you do, resist the urge to confess."

To Towner, he'd thought, but had not said. There wasn't much chance he'd ever see her again. Let alone confess.

"To anyone," Ann had said aloud, reading him.

Soon after, the young witches had begun to arrive in the front of the store. Ann had yelled out, said she'd be with them in a minute. "Go!" she'd said, pushing Rafferty out the side door, the way she'd brought him in the night before.

As he'd left, he'd come face-to-face with Helen Barnes, emerging from Peter Barter's flower shop with an armful of snapdragons, carrying the flowers as if they were an infant. She'd met his eyes, then glanced back toward Ann's shop. Rafferty had understood that she knew. Her flowers had suddenly smelled overpowering and funereal.

He'd walked all the way to the Willows, in no hurry to get back to his empty house. He'd sell it, he thought. He'd leave this ridiculous place, and he'd never look back. Go someplace Towner would never be. South maybe. Inland. Away from the cold winters and the smell of the sea. As he'd turned the corner onto Bay View Avenue, he'd spotted Towner sitting on the porch of his Victorian fixer-upper, her long legs folded under her, arms across her chest as if she were cold. How in the world had Ann known that Towner would be there? Towner had looked as exhausted as he felt. She hadn't said anything to him as he climbed the stairs. Instead, she'd stood as he opened the door, walking through ahead of him, not looking back at the sea or the island.

CHAPTER THIRTY-FIVE

May 14, 2015

SALEM

*I firmly believe that the curse of Salem's guilt will persist
until the true site of the hangings is finally memorialized,
a proper blessing is bestowed, and the remains of those
executed in 1692 are finally laid to rest.*

—ROSE WHELAN, *The Witches of Salem*

"HOW DO YOU HIDE A WOMAN IF SHE DOESN'T WANT TO BE
found?" Rafferty had once asked May. "How do you keep her from
sticking out like a sore thumb?"

May hadn't answered him, but Towner had. "You hide them in
plain sight."

"What does that mean?"

"To quote May directly: *Hide like with like.*"

Rafferty still firmly believed that Leah Kormos was, if not the
killer, certainly the person he needed to talk to, if only he could find
her. But everything he'd tried had been a dead end. He reviewed what
he knew about Leah. She was dark, Mediterranean looking. Greek.
Through coordinated police servers and crime databases, he'd been
searching records not just in New England but all over the country,
calling all the Kormos listings he could find in an effort to locate either Leah or her sister, Rebecca. Most of the Kormos listings were in
Massachusetts or New Jersey. He'd talked to a lot of people, but so
far he'd had no luck.

Where would you hide if you really didn't want to be found? he asked himself now. May's words came back to him.

He'd tried every Kormos in bordering Massachusetts towns, but there was no one with the name Leah. Or Becky or Rebecca. And searching on first names was too unwieldy. Then he thought about how his daughter had said Leah was a Jewish name. It was true: Leah and Rebecca weren't traditional Greek names, but they were definitely Old Testament. Maybe their mother, whose name he hadn't been able to decipher on their birth certificates, had been Jewish?

He'd already looked for the father's marriage certificates. There was nothing in Beverly. Now he widened his search, checking neighboring towns. Trying different spellings of the father's last name, he finally found a match in Peabody listed under the misspelled surname Courmos. The mother's maiden name was Rosenfeld, and she'd married Leah's father in Peabody in 1969.

Rafferty searched the name Leah Rosenfeld, first in Peabody and then in all surrounding North Shore towns. He found two matches: The first was a widow in her eighties, and the second was a two-year-old. Neither had any connection to Leah Kormos or to her mother or sister.

He widened his search, looking once again at the Massachusetts border towns, remembering Towner's words: "Hide like with like." Leah may have been part Jewish, but she'd grown up in a Greek community. He didn't find Leah. But, in searching the records for Lowell, he finally found Becky.

First he called Mickey and finally gave him the name he'd been waiting for, and then he headed to Lowell.

She was living in the Greek community under the name Becky Rosenfeld, working in a diner and living in a three-decker that was almost identical to the one they'd torn down in Beverly.

She didn't want to talk to him. She knew what he wanted as soon as he introduced himself.

"She didn't do it," Becky said, putting the cup of regular coffee he'd ordered on the counter in front of him.

"What do you mean?"

"You're a cop. I've been all through this with the cops. My sister didn't kill those girls."

"I'm not accusing her," Rafferty said, taking a sip. Too much cream and too much sugar. "I'm just trying to find her, that's all."

"I've been trying to find her for twenty-five years," Becky said. "No help from any of you."

Rafferty knew Becky had hounded the Beverly Police, who had essentially ignored the girl's efforts.

"Your father didn't try very hard to find her," Rafferty said.

"No big surprise there," she said. "Leah and my father never got along."

"Why is that?"

"I'm not doing this," Becky said, starting to turn away.

"This is difficult for you," Rafferty said.

"Hell, yeah, this is difficult. I lost my sister!"

"And I'm trying to find her."

"For what? So you can arrest her and make yourself a hero? The supercop who solved the case that couldn't be solved?"

"I don't think she did it," he said, keeping his eyes on hers, "but I think she might know who did."

She looked at him as if trying to assess his sincerity. "How are you going to find her, if I couldn't?"

"I found you, didn't I?"

A customer sitting at the far end of the counter held up his coffee cup, and she grabbed the pot to refill it.

She replaced the pot on the burner and turned to Rafferty, who hadn't looked away. "Five minutes," she said, motioning to a corner booth. He took his cup and moved to the booth. She took a seat opposite.

He asked about Leah's history, about her involvement with the Goddesses.

"I didn't know them," Becky said. "I know she had friends in Salem."

"What about magic?"

"Excuse me?"

"Do you know if Leah practiced witchcraft?"

"Oh, please," Becky said, with a snort.

"Were you related to any of the Salem witches, the ones who were executed in 1692?"

"If we were, I never heard anything about it."

"Your sister never told you anything like that?"

"No."

"You really can't tell me anything about her location?" Rafferty finally asked.

"No," Becky said, her eyes filling with tears.

Rafferty could feel her sorrow.

"You still miss her."

"Of course I do." She wiped her eyes. "She's my only sister."

"And you really don't know where she is?" Rafferty waited for her answer.

"I haven't seen her since she got pregnant, and my father kicked her out."

This was news to Rafferty. "Leah was pregnant?"

"Oh, don't pretend you guys didn't know. I was standing right next to my father when he told the police the whole story."

I've been all through this with the cops.

Why was none of this in the files he'd read?

Rafferty drove directly to Rice Street in Salem. He stood on the top step of Tom Dayle's house, ringing the bell for almost five minutes before Tom finally opened the door. He was wearing a robe and slippers, but he didn't look as if he'd been sleeping.

"Do you want to take me down into your basement and show me box number nine, or do you want me to get a warrant?"

The ex-detective slowly opened the door.

Tom had a hard time walking down the cellar stairs. He clutched the railing so hard he was white knuckled, his other hand holding on to the wall as he descended.

Box number 9 was not sealed as the others had been but sat opened on the workbench. Rafferty shouldered past Tom Dayle and reached inside the box, spotting a sheet of paper with big letters scrawled across the top:

THE GODDESS RULES

1. *Never take a man against his will.*
2. *All the Goddesses must be present when we take a man.*
3. *Practice safe sex.*
4. *Never take anyone back to Rose's house again.*
5. *Don't get pregnant.*

Rafferty picked up a photo of the wall mural next, featuring all four girls: Leah, Olivia, Susan, and Cheryl. The artist had captured their beauty and their youth. It was, as Callie had described, a stunning painting, but, as he looked at it, Rafferty immediately figured out what had made Rose so angry. Though the portrait was exquisite, it was the setting that stood out. The artist had dressed the Goddesses skimpily and depicted them lounging on the brass bed Callie had described. They looked like they belonged in a bordello. Rafferty couldn't take his eyes off the photo. In the middle of the bed, dressed in a lacy nightgown that left nothing to the imagination, was the most beautiful of the girls they called Goddesses: Leah Kormos.

It took a moment for Rafferty to pull himself away from the photo. Then he spotted the letters. All made out to the Goddesses, and evidently once tied with the pink ribbon that was still knotted and sitting next to them in the box.

From first glance, he could tell these were the love letters Callie had told him about. That the Goddesses had kept them, had collected them. The smudged lipstick kisses all over the envelopes seemed to illustrate just how young they had been. Something about this touched Rafferty in a way he couldn't quite explain. The number of letters seemed far fewer than the ribbon would have held. To make sure, he slipped the ribbon back over the pile. There was a gap of at least an inch.

"Where are the rest of them?"

"You don't want to know the answer to that."

But he already knew. He'd begun to suspect as soon as he'd talked to Leah's sister. The report of Leah's pregnancy had never been in any of the police records that Rafferty had seen. Nor was it in the database the police had created to track the ongoing investigation. Callie had told him the police were at the house all the time, but there had been only three records of them ever being called. That meant that the rest of the police visits had been purely social calls. The missing letters belonged to them.

"How many officers were involved?" Rafferty asked.

"A lot," Tom answered. "From both towns."

"You?"

"No," he said. "Never me."

"All this covering up because they found out she was pregnant?"

"That baby could have belonged to any of them."

Rafferty shook his head in disgust.

"The force couldn't take the scandal. Even if there hadn't been a child."

Rafferty counted the letters that hadn't been destroyed. There were thirty remaining, every one of the writers a suspect, or at least a person of interest. To say nothing of the cops themselves—even if their letters were destroyed. If he poked this hornet's nest, a lot of people were going to get stung.

"What about the costumes they were wearing?"

"They were the first things to go," Dayle said, looking toward the furnace.

"I said some things I shouldn't have said. And so did my father. Let's leave it at that," Paul said.

They'd been staying at the boathouse since they returned from Italy, and their luggage was still not unpacked. It gave Callie hope each time she looked at it: As soon as they fulfilled their obligations, they would return to Matera. That packed luggage made her feel optimistic.

She hadn't attended the reading of Emily's will. Paul assured her there would be no surprises; his parents had put the houses and grounds into a trust long ago. The surviving spouse would take control, and one day it all would be passed down to Paul. The only things that would be at issue at the reading were his mother's personal items.

But things hadn't gone well or as expected. Paul and his father had had a terrible argument.

"Why do you insist on fighting with him?" she asked, when she heard the story.

He sighed. "At least neither of us was drinking this time." And then he started unpacking, putting his clothes back into his bureau.

Her heart sank as she watched him put his things away, leaving the two top drawers for her. He paused, took a ring off his pinkie, and handed it to Callie.

"What's this?"

"I'd say it's my mother's seal of approval," he said.

Callie had no idea what he was talking about. She recognized the emerald and diamond ring as the one that Emily had always worn on her right hand.

"She changed her will right after we went to Matera. This ring was always supposed to go to the girl I'm going to marry. She left it to you."

Callie stood looking at him. "Are you asking me to marry you?"

Paul managed to smile. "I am."

CHAPTER THIRTY-SIX

May 20, 2015
SALEM

The blade itself incites to deeds of violence.
—HOMER, *The Odyssey*

"LEAH KORMOS ISN'T RELATED TO SARAH GOOD. SHE'S RE-
lated to Elizabeth Howe."

Mickey's news didn't come as a complete shock. For quite a while
now, and certainly ever since he'd talked to her sister, Rafferty had
become certain that Leah was no longer the primary suspect. But if
Leah wasn't related to Sarah Good, if she wasn't the fifth petal, then
who the hell was?

He'd already erased Rose's name from under Good's. He'd made
Mickey recheck the others against their ancestors, not with Sarah
Good this time, but confirming the corresponding names and ancestors now written on each petal. They'd checked out; the positions
were right. Now he erased Rose's name from Elizabeth Howe's petal,
inking in Leah's instead. Finally, he removed Leah's penciled-in name
from under Sarah Good's, but the eraser smudged the paper so badly it
would have been impossible to add another name, even if he had one.
He found an old bottle of Wite-Out in the desk drawer and painted the
petal until it became as white as Susan Symms's albino skin, which
made it stand out even more. Four of the petals now had correct links
from ancestors to women in modern times. All that was missing was

the name of the descendant of the fifth petal, Sarah Good's, which was now more mysterious than ever.

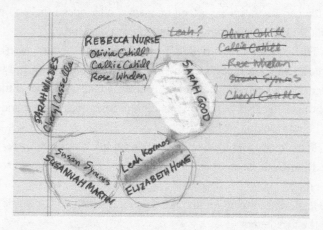

One thing was beginning to become obvious. There hadn't been just one petal missing from the blessing that night on the hill. There had been two people who were absent that night: Leah Kormos and someone else.

"No luck?" Towner said, looking over his shoulder at the blank white petal.

"I'm at a loss," he said, shrugging. "I know each of the girls was related to one of the executed, and that Callie said Rose was related to more than one of them. But Rose wasn't related to Sarah Good, Mickey has already established that."

"I've been thinking about that," Towner said. "I seem to remember hearing that Rebecca Nurse had a sister who was also accused. So I just checked it out online. Actually, she had two sisters who were accused of witchcraft, and one of them was executed. Not on July nineteenth, though."

"Rose never told Callie it was on July nineteenth, just that she was related to more than one of the executed. I guess that means Callie and Olivia were also related to more than one."

"That still doesn't tell you who the fifth petal was."

"There was someone else on the hill that night. Someone who was related to Sarah Good. Was there another Goddess we don't know about?"

Towner was silent for a long moment. "Why does it have to be a woman? Didn't the blessing simply require a descendant?"

"True enough," Rafferty said. It wasn't as if the thought hadn't occurred to him, but that he was hoping it wasn't a possibility. If it were a man, there were so many as yet unrevealed suspects that Rafferty might have to check half the population of Salem before he found the one he was looking for.

He'd already told Callie that he didn't think it was Leah who had killed the Goddesses. "Leah got pregnant, Callie. That was the rule she broke."

He started looking for another suspect. And the place he started was the love letters.

If Rafferty had been moved by the youthful romanticism of the letters when he'd first discovered them, reading them now had the opposite effect. They were very personal, and he found himself embarrassed, so much so that he got up and closed his office door. Each letter contained a description of the sender's fantasy and how the Goddesses had fulfilled it in a way he had never dreamed possible. These weren't love letters per se. They were thank-you notes. That any man had put such personal details down on paper amazed him. That one man had actually signed his letter with his full name was even more astonishing. If the young women weren't witches, they were certainly bewitching.

Rafferty looked up the number and phoned the man who'd signed his letter.

"I spoke to you people about this years ago," the man said.

"We people, as you so politely refer to us, have been replaced by newer people. Which means drop your attitude because you're going to have to talk to us again."

"Okay," the man agreed, put in his place. "But not at my house. I'll come to you." He lowered his voice. "I don't want my wife to know."

The man, Donald Booth, was in his midfifties, a successful lawyer and married for the second time. Once he started talking about the

Goddesses, he became energized, much less reticent than Rafferty had expected.

"It was only one night, but it was the most memorable of my life. It wasn't just the number of them. There was something magical about those girls."

Rafferty didn't react.

"As far as the trouble they caused around town," he went on, "it wasn't the sex. It was the obsession."

"Can you elaborate?"

"The night I was with them, guys showed up at the door twice; each time they were begging to see the girls again, but the girls refused. The thing was, they would only consent to be with you the one time. Then you had to write them a note. Those were the rules. There were exceptions to the one-night thing, I heard, but I wasn't fortunate enough to be one of them."

"Do you know who the exceptions were?"

"I don't."

"What about the two stalkers who showed up while you were there?" Rafferty asked. "Did you know them?"

"I wouldn't call them stalkers," the lawyer said. "I'd describe them as . . . moonstruck. It's difficult to be possessive of four women at the same time."

"Four? Are you sure of the number? It wasn't five?"

"You tend to remember the number when you're being seduced by four women," he said. "Even if you're high as a kite."

"High on what?"

"Pretty much anything we could find," he said. "Grass, X, ludes, coke, scotch. Everything was around in those days. Anyway, you couldn't possess those girls, even if you wanted to."

"Not sure who'd want to take that on," Rafferty said, meaning it.

The man laughed knowingly. "I think those guys just wanted another night with them."

"Is that what you wanted?"

"Absolutely. Why not? I was single at the time. And hey, it was the best sex I'd ever had. But it wasn't just sex. I mean it was, but it was more than that. It was a transcendent experience."

Rafferty paused but didn't comment. "Did you ask to see them again?"

"Several times. But they declined, which was probably a good thing. I might never have finished law school if they had said yes." A shadow of sadness passed over his face. "Terrible, what happened to them."

"It certainly was."

"There's a double standard, don't you think? If men had behaved like they did, a group of them with one woman, it would be called gang rape."

"Are you saying they forced themselves on you?"

"No, not at all."

"Not against your will, then."

"Hardly." The man laughed.

"Then it's not gang rape, is it?" Rafferty saw too much of that these days. Cell phone postings with drunken young women and alcohol-fueled men.

"No, that wasn't the case with the Goddesses. But make no mistake, they were definitely in control." He paused. "At least they were for a while."

"Did you know any of the other men they were involved with?"

He shook his head. "They were actually pretty discreet about their conquests."

Rafferty thanked him, and the two men shook hands. The lawyer started toward the door, then turned back, remembering something. "There was one guy who was at the house quite a bit," he said. "I only know this because I heard them talking about him. He was the one who painted their portrait, the one on the wall. That one might have been a stalker."

"Who was that?"

"H. L. Barnes."

"Any relation to Helen?"

"Her husband."

Rafferty did a double take. H. L. Barnes was Helen's husband? He'd never imagined Helen had ever been married. Everything about the woman said spinster.

"But you won't be able to talk to him."

"Why's that?"

"He's dead."

Rafferty had never been inside Helen's Chestnut Street house. It seemed more museum than home, with chinoiserie and Federal-style pieces crowding every available space. The architecture featured the understated elegance of the Loyalists, in particular Samuel McIntire, whose woodworking defined the entire eponymous historic district. From what Rafferty could tell, nothing but the reproduction rotary phone in the front hall was less than two centuries old. Definitely old money, he thought.

He had been directed to wait for her in the parlor and had been sitting for twenty minutes on a chair that was far too delicate for his large frame, trying not to move for fear of breaking the damned thing.

"It's four o'clock. May I offer you some tea?" she asked, arriving at last, her springer spaniel at her heels. The tray arrived as she spoke.

"Yes, thank you."

She directed her housekeeper to leave the silver service and poured the tea herself, asking how he took it, then handing it to him. He could not get his fingers to grip the delicate flowered cup, and so he held it with two hands, sipping as she did, putting it down on the side table carefully so as not to rattle the saucer.

He had the childish urge to brag to her that he and Towner lived in a more elegant mansion than this one, down on Washington Square, that it was in the Jeffersonian style, had twin marble fireplaces and a hanging spiral staircase, and that if and when he took tea at all, it was at the tearoom, where they brewed a better cup. Nothing she could do to intimidate him would work.

"Your message said you wanted to talk about my husband," she said, her expression pinched.

"H. L. Barnes," Rafferty said. "Until recently, I had no idea you had a husband."

"I suppose you also learned of his demise?"

"I did."

"Then you should know that poor Henry wasn't well. He is the last person I want to speak ill of."

"I would never expect you to speak ill of anyone," Rafferty said. *Yet somehow it seems to happen with regularity.*

"You have questions for me?"

"I have several," Rafferty said, handing her the photograph of the portrait Henry had painted on Rose's wall. Underneath the portrait, he had signed his initials: H. L. B. She looked it over briefly, a pained but not surprised expression on her face. She'd seen the photo before, he realized. She handed it back to him and walked to her desk. "There are different kinds of bewitchment," she said, her tone implying that he, of all people, should understand what she meant.

Rifling through papers in a hidden compartment, she returned with an envelope, stamped and hand lettered. Rafferty could see from the condition of the paper that it had been reread many times. She handed the letter to him. "Keep it," she said. "I've seen quite enough of it for one lifetime."

My Dearest Helen,
*   I cannot go on.*
*   Forgive me . . . Henry*

Rafferty sat for a long moment. "Why in the world did you insist on the exhumation? You must have known it would bring attention back to Henry and yourself—"

"Henry didn't kill those girls."

"I haven't suggested he did. But by insisting we reopen this investigation, you identified yourself and your husband as prime suspects."

"Not my husband, certainly."

"Why not?"

She handed him the envelope. "Look at the date."

The letter was dated October 13, 1989, a few weeks before the murders.

"My husband was a very sick man, Detective Rafferty."

He was surprised by the empathy he heard in her voice.

"That letter was sent from a hotel in Boston. He was kind enough not to take his life here, knowing I would never have been able to stay in the house with the memory."

"I still don't understand your motivation, Helen," Rafferty said. "Why did you call attention to yourself this way? Why cause yourself trouble? As well as a probable scandal—"

"She killed my grandnephew."

"You know that's not true."

"She confessed to the crime!"

"There *was* no crime." Rafferty took a deep breath before continuing. "You know as well as I do, Helen, that your nephew died from a cerebral hemorrhage as a result of narcotics."

Helen sat for a long moment before she replied. "The girls she took in and protected, those so-called Goddesses, killed my husband. Rose may not have done it directly, but make no mistake: Rose Whelan was responsible. My husband had AIDS, Detective."

Rafferty stared at her.

"Given to him by those girls at the brothel Rose Whelan was running over on Daniels Street."

CHAPTER THIRTY-SEVEN

May 25, 2015
PRIDE'S CROSSING

The turning is almost imperceptible. One day you watch
yourself perform a tiny act of revenge. Or you notice an
excitement at the horrors of the evening news. You will be
shocked to find yourself picking up the blade. You will
be far less surprised on the day you finally use it.
—ROSE'S *Book of Trees*

"THEY'VE STOLEN OUR THUNDER," PAUL SAID.

The invitation to celebrate Finn and Marta's elopement arrived as Paul and Callie were composing the announcement of their own engagement. Paul had proposed more formally after his first awkward approach, producing soft music and champagne, and then kneeling, silhouetted by the moonrise over Salem Sound. They would live in Matera as planned. "Happily ever after," Paul had said as he put the ring on her finger. It was a perfect fit.

It had been a magical few days. Then the invitation to celebrate Finn and Marta's elopement arrived.

Paul pretended to shrug it off. "They got married. What a surprise."

It had been less than eight weeks since Emily's passing.

Callie had not been raised with the kind of social protocol that dictated prescribed periods of mourning; still, even she understood that this was scandalous. She could just imagine what people were thinking. Finn and Marta hadn't said a word to them about their intentions. "I just—I don't know why they couldn't have waited," she told him, grasping for something reasonable to say.

"Perhaps she's pregnant," Paul scoffed.

His attempt at humor fell flat.

Callie looked at the invitation again:

Mr. and Mrs. Paul Finnian Whiting
request the pleasure of your company at Pride's Heart
on July 18, 2015, at one P.M.
in celebration of their recent marriage

The accompanying note said that they had left Pride's Crossing several days earlier and that they would be traveling in Europe for the next month.

"Here's the thing," Paul said. "All the land that our family wrested away from the Hathornes in 1692? With one 'I do,' Marta just managed to erase that land grab."

"Paul—"

"You don't understand. All the property is in a trust. All the houses, all the outbuildings. My whole inheritance."

"How can she erase a trust?"

"With my mother gone, my father's now the only trustee—Marta can convince him to dissolve it. People dissolve trusts every day. Or he can sell everything out of it."

Callie shook her head, horrified. "He wouldn't."

"I'm not so sure. At the reading of my mother's will I asked the lawyer a question about the trust. My father said—and I'm quoting him—'You'd better simmer down or I'll dissolve the damned thing.' "

Paul hadn't told her that.

"It's been a difficult time," Callie said, trying to hide her shock. "No one is quite themselves . . ."

Paul made a disgusted sound.

"Why don't we skip the wedding celebration? We don't have to stay here until July. Or we could come back for it. Why don't we just go back to Italy now?"

"And make things easier for Marta?" He was quiet for a long moment. "My mother was getting better, wasn't she?" he asked. "You told me you thought she was getting better."

Callie took a moment to absorb the implication. "She seemed better, yes," she answered carefully. But sometimes a surge of life happened just before the end. She'd seen it at the nursing home many times, only to end up grief stricken. "But sometimes—"

"So maybe Dad and Marta just got tired of waiting, and decided to hurry things along," he said, interrupting her.

She stared at him. "You don't mean that."

They looked at each other in silence.

"I guess not. But I have to tell you, Callie. I want to kill them both right now."

CHAPTER THIRTY-EIGHT

July 15, 2015
PRIDE'S CROSSING

*The song of the banshee varies with the listener. The dying
hear the music of the spheres. Those left behind hear
something else entirely.*
—ROSE'S *Book of Trees*

"YOU'RE DRINKING TOO MUCH," CALLIE ACCUSED. "YOU
need to slow it down."

"You refuse to understand how serious this is," Paul shouted.
"How far back it goes!"

"Paul, I've heard enough."

In the month and a half since they received the wedding announcement, Paul had become obsessed, determined to trace his mother's
death to the land the Whitings had taken from Marta's family so
many generations back.

There had been no talk of returning to Matera.

"You don't get it. Sarah Hathorne's accusation of my ancestor was
cruel and murderous religious intolerance! If the witch trials hadn't
ended, my relative would have hanged."

"I get it! I do. But Sarah would also have been hanged. Your Whiting ancestor made a counteraccusation against Sarah Hathorne, remember?" Callie recalled what she'd heard the tour guide explaining
in Marta's house months earlier. "For the crime of using a love potion
to bewitch her husband. They'd have hanged her as well."

He took a sip of his brandy. "Okay, they might have," he conceded. "But here's the point I'm trying to make you understand." He tilted his crystal tumbler in Callie's direction, not even noticing as a bit spilled over the rim. "Sarah Hathorne was *related* to one of the hanging judges. As a Puritan, things would have gone far easier for her than for my Catholic relative."

Callie stopped short of stating the obvious: History had already proven that Sarah Hathorne had suffered the most. She had gone to jail and, having no means to pay for her jail time, been rendered penniless, losing her land to the Whitings. "It all happened so long ago," she said, to end the conversation. "Who knows what would have happened? Let's move on."

"Move on?" Paul snapped. "I know Marta pretty well, and I guarantee you she'll have us 'moved on' out of the boathouse and off *her* property by Christmas."

"So what? So we'll go back to Italy. It's what we both want. It's what I want anyway."

He didn't comment.

"I'm not sure I know what you want anymore."

Paul still didn't comment. He was too obsessed with his "inheritance" to think about anything else.

Callie hummed the calming tone and counted to ten. Paul wasn't amused, and she hadn't meant for him to be. The tone was as much to calm her fraying nerves as his.

He shot her a look and walked out of the room, slamming the door.

It was difficult to reconcile the changes Callie had seen in Paul in the short time they'd been back. Certainly the loss of Emily had taken its toll. Her absence was felt in every corner of the empty mansion on the other side of the woods, a house Paul had taken to spending time in while his father and Marta were away. Callie could sometimes see him sitting alone in the orangerie, Emily's favorite room.

He looked different, too. No longer was he Indiana Jones. Nor had he returned to the earlier *GQ* image she'd once found so amusing. His jaw was set in a way she'd never noticed; at night, while sleeping, he ground his teeth. He was drinking a lot more than ever before and a lot earlier in the day. The anger she saw building in him with the announcement of his father's recent remarriage was alarming.

She had to admit that Paul was right about one thing, though: Marta *was* taking over. While she was still in Europe, she ordered her kitchen garden to be transplanted from behind her house to the back of Pride's Heart. The new garden was three times as large as the old, and it wiped out a part of the side yard where the dogs liked to play. This enraged Paul. His wild speculation about his mother's death continued.

But Paul wasn't the only one speculating about Emily's demise. Towner had told Callie that when the two met for tea. "There are others who think Finn might have given Emily a little push."

"You and Rafferty don't believe that, do you?" Callie asked.

"No," Towner said. "It would have been a pretty stupid thing to do when Emily was already dying."

It was the first time Callie had heard the words from Towner. With the exception of Emily herself, no one had ever wanted to acknowledge the fact of her impending death.

Finn and the new Mrs. Whiting had returned at the end of June. They arrived at the mansion with huge fanfare. In the days that followed, the packages began to arrive, purchases Marta had made in France and Italy: Florentine gold candlesticks and thousand-thread-count Egyptian cotton bed linens from Rome, a Parisian silver tea service that reportedly had belonged to Louis XIV. Marta had spared no expense when it came to spending Emily's money. Indeed, both Marta and Finn were dressed better than Callie had ever seen them, thanks to a stylist who'd accompanied the couple from Paris to Milan.

Callie had to admit that they seemed happy. Finn looked more relaxed and younger. It took Callie a moment to realize the reason. Happiness certainly played its part. But the greying hair she'd noticed when she first met him had disappeared, replaced by blond highlights. She wondered which one of them had suggested the high-lighting, Finn or Marta. Neither would have surprised her.

Marta's shopping had not been limited to the newlyweds. Presents also began to arrive for both Callie and Paul. Callie received a long black cashmere coat from Milan and a set of golden bangles from Florence. She'd thanked both Marta and Finn. Paul's gifts sat un-opened on the farmer's table.

Marta scheduled a family dinner a few days before the reception was to occur, and, when the evening arrived, Callie got to Pride's Heart first. As she was coming in, the electricians were just leaving, carrying the sterling chandelier that had been in the dining room since the house was built, replaced by a much larger and more ornate crystal and gold one the couple had purchased in Spain. It wasn't ugly by anyone's standards, but it changed the look of the place in a way you noticed the moment you walked in, which, no doubt, was Marta's intention.

When Paul came into the house and saw the new lighting fixture for the first time, he made a beeline for the bar and mixed himself a strong drink. His unsteady gait seemed to indicate he'd already had a few.

The dinner was not illuminated by the huge chandelier but by candlelight, and, by then, Paul seemed a bit more relaxed, intention-ally not looking up at the offensive fixture, but keeping his eyes low. Once or twice, Callie saw him glance at the empty chair his mother had so recently occupied. Marta sat right next to Finn rather than at the opposite end of the table, as had been Emily's custom.

Dinner went smoothly, a simple cold avocado and crab soup, followed by a beef tenderloin roast, one of Paul's favorites, though he barely picked at it, which Marta noticed immediately.

"You don't like the beef?"

"It's fine," he said.

"It's delicious," Callie said, trying to make up for Paul's rudeness.

Conversation was pleasant enough, with Finn doing most of the talking, mostly about their travels.

Callie had to admit that Finn looked good in his new wardrobe. His demeanor was relaxed in a way she hadn't seen during Emily's extended illness. Every once in a while he would pause and smile at his new bride. Well, at least no one could claim she wasn't making him happy.

All went well through dessert until Paul stood and headed for the library.

"Where are you going?" Finn asked.

"I thought I'd go down to the speakeasy and get us some port," Paul answered.

"Not tonight," Marta said.

Finn smiled at his son. "Marta holds the key to the speakeasy," he said. "She's using it as her office."

Paul looked surprised. "Since when?"

"Since we got home," Finn said. "Sit back down. There's something I want to ask you."

Paul stumbled slightly as he lowered himself into the chair.

Marta frowned but said nothing. Finn didn't seem to notice, and he continued, "I wanted to ask you if you'd make the toast at our wedding celebration." He was beaming at his son, as if proud he'd come up with the idea. Marta was watching both of them carefully.

Paul stared at him for a long time before answering. "I think that would be inappropriate."

"What do you mean? It is perfectly—"

"It might be best to rethink your choice, Finn," Marta said. Callie could tell she was seething.

"I don't want to rethink anything. I want my son to make the toast." Finn turned to Paul, waiting for an answer. "So will you?"

Callie tried to catch Paul's eye, but he wouldn't look at her. Instead he looked from his father to Marta and back to his father. "When Hell freezes over."

Paul pushed back his chair and left without another word. Incensed, Finn threw his napkin on the table and stormed up the stairs, leaving Callie and Marta alone.

"I'm sorry," Callie said.

"What do you have to be sorry about?" Marta huffed. "You didn't do anything."

Callie flushed. At a loss for words, she simply stood and said good night.

"May I give you a piece of advice?" Marta said, looking at the emerald ring on Callie's left hand.

"What?"

Marta directed Callie to look out the window at Paul, who was stumbling at the edge of the woods. "He will betray you," she promised. "The Whitings always betray the people who trust them most."

Callie stared at her. "That's not true."

"Oh, yes, it is."

"You were betrayed?"

"I was, many times."

"Well, it looks as if you've ended up getting everything you wanted." Callie came back at her hard.

"That remains to be seen," Marta said, holding her gaze.

"Really, there's more?" Callie stared back at her. She was beginning to think Paul had been right about Marta.

Marta shook her head and sighed, as if to say that Callie was very naïve.

Then Marta forced a smile, and her tone softened. "Look, I know things worked out for me, but it took a very long time. There was a lot of disappointment. A lot of . . . humiliation." She looked at Callie sincerely. "I don't want you to go through what I did. Paul's very spoiled and entitled. You'll have to wait a long time for him to grow up."

Callie could feel her anger rising, her cheeks reddening.

"You're only angry because you know I'm right," Marta said.

If anyone else had proffered this judgmental advice, Callie would have told them off, but Marta and Finn were her future in-laws. Paul had already caused a rift that would be hard to close. Much as she wanted to tell Marta to mind her own damned business, Callie held her tongue. This was doubly difficult because Callie knew that what

Marta had said was partly true. Tonight Paul had certainly behaved in a rude and childlike manner, but under the circumstances, it wasn't hard for her to understand where he was coming from.

"Take my advice," Marta said. "Give him back that ring and run for your life."

CHAPTER THIRTY-NINE

July 16, 2015
PRIDE'S CROSSING

A night terror, an erotic dream, a vision of any sort
wherein the victim claimed to be visited or tormented by
the accused, served to condemn. If one had a complaint
against a neighbor, the accusation itself often became
the most damning evidence.
—ROSE WHELAN, *The Witches of Salem*

"WHAT THE HELL IS THAT?" PAUL MOANED THE NEXT MORN-
ing, covering his head with a pillow.

Callie heard the shrill whine of machinery, too. "I'll find out," she
said, happy for any excuse to get some distance from him. They'd had
a fight when she'd gotten back last night, their first big one. Callie
had tried to avoid it, but Paul had finished off a few more drinks after
storming home and kept following her from room to room, going on
and on about the wedding and about Marta, a continuing loop he'd
been reciting for days.

"I have no intention of even going to the wedding!" he'd said, his
words slurred and angry. He'd ranted about his father and about Marta.

"You're drunk," she'd said finally. "Go to bed."

She'd been relieved when he took her advice, passing out on the
bed. But she was so tense that she couldn't sleep at all. She was still
agitated this morning, both by Paul's behavior and by Marta's words.
She didn't want to talk to either of them today.

Pulling on shorts, she walked through the woods to see what was going on.

"It's an impossible task!" Callie heard a male voice.

"I don't care," Marta was saying. She stood next to a man who was operating some sort of machine. The two were near the remainder of the oak Rose had died under. The rest of the grounds crew was shifting about, looking uncomfortable. "I want it out of here. Remove the entire root and put in grass. By this afternoon." She turned and went back inside.

"This stump grinder isn't strong enough," one of the groundsmen complained.

"I've ordered an excavator," the head groundsman replied.

As if he had summoned it, the huge machine arrived.

Callie stayed to watch, sitting on the ledge by the cliff to keep out of the way. The stump was easily removed as the excavator got to work, but the root proved more difficult. With each dig, the hole the machine created grew larger, but the root was still deeply planted in the earth. It radiated at least fifty feet from the stump.

"This is ridiculous," one of the workmen said. "We'll never get it all."

"She wants all of the goddamned thing removed," the head groundsman said. "If you expect to keep your job, I suggest you follow her orders."

Eventually, Paul came out. He was showered and dressed. "I'm going for a drive," he said.

Callie nodded. "Okay. I think I'll go to the tearoom to see Towner." *And enjoy our time apart.* "This is crazy, huh?"

Paul looked at the root. "No crazier than the whole wedding celebration."

After Paul left, Callie sat in the sun, trying to relax . . . but she couldn't stop staring into the gaping hole, listening to the swearing of the crew as the crevice grew deeper and wider with no sign of stopping. Looking into the blackness, she could see why the taproot was giving them so much trouble. It stretched downward and toward the house and was tangled with another underground root system. When the crew finally tried to pull it out, the earth began to crack, the root slowly splitting the ground as wide as an earthquake might, the crevice expanding all the way across the lawn, sinking the corner of the back steps.

"Stop!" the head groundsman yelled.

"Damn," one of the workers said, shaking his head.

"That's it! Enough! Fill it in. All of it. And then get someone in here to repair the goddamned steps before Mrs. Whiting sees this mess."

The head groundsman went back to his truck and unhooked the chain they'd been using to pull the stump. Callie looked at the root; the knotted mass was as thick as a tree trunk and extended all the way under the house. As she stared, the hole began to fill with water. Was it seawater, seeking its own level? But no, the ocean was at least fifty feet below the cliffs. Even at the highest tide imaginable, it could never rise far enough to fill in the hole. Perhaps the workmen had nicked a pipe?

"Guys?" she called, pointing. They didn't hear her. She left her perch and ran forward. And then she noticed something strange. The water threatening to fill the hole was a deep crimson. It wasn't water. It looked like blood. Rising inch by inch.

"Watch yourself!" A crew member shoved her out of the way a moment before the excavator would have hit her. She hadn't heard it approaching. She could feel the eyes of all the men on her as she quickly walked back to the boathouse.

Once inside, she took a long shower, trying to calm herself. She couldn't quiet her thoughts. Nor could she stop the anger that was building inside her. Why had they come back here? Why hadn't they returned to Matera right after the funeral? Paul was becoming a different person, different from when she'd first met him in Pride's Crossing, and far different from the relaxed, happy guy she'd fallen in love with in Italy.

She dressed and dried her hair. Then she drove to Salem. Just as she crested the top of the Beverly Bridge, a car veered left into her lane. She blasted the horn, but the car kept coming. The driver finally jerked to the right, but not quickly enough. Refusing to brake, she hit his driver's-side door.

They both got out and examined their vehicles.

"You were in my blind spot!" the man said by way of explanation. She handed him her insurance information without a word.

She could tell he knew she'd hit his car on purpose. And she didn't feel bad about that. Didn't even ask if he was injured. It wasn't like her, and it felt odd. Afterward, she drove straight to Towner's.

"Are you okay?"

"Not really," Callie said. "I just had an accident."

"Are you hurt?"

"No one was hurt, thank God. I'm just shaken."

"Sit, have a cup of tea."

As she sipped the tea, Callie was surprised to realize she felt better than she had in a while. Was it the jolt of adrenaline from the accident? It made her feel the opposite of what she might have expected: It was a *good* feeling, strangely calm. Her heart was no longer racing.

"Do you have your dress for the party?" Towner asked. "You want to borrow those pearls again?"

"I'm all set," Callie said. She didn't want to say that if Paul had his way, they wouldn't even be going.

"So how does Paul feel about this whole situation?" Towner asked.

It really was strange how Towner could read her.

Callie shrugged. She didn't want to talk about any of it. "We're both just trying to get through this thing on Saturday."

Callie's cell rang. It was Rafferty, asking her to come to the station. "I have something to give you," he said. "It belonged to Rose."

There was something so pretentious about naming a house. Pride's Heart took it to a new level. Rafferty understood the intention. Someone had decided that, as the largest house in the area, it was the heart of the town, or should be, and had named it accordingly.

He couldn't blame Finn Whiting's ego for that, though he wished he could. The house had been christened long before Finn. He looked at the invitation again. "Pride goeth before a fall," he said to himself, quoting biblical verse.

There was another biblical quote about pride and the heart, he thought, trying to recall it. As a student at Fordham, when he had actually considered becoming a priest, he could have told you both chapter and verse. But now he had to look it up. He searched the web for biblical quotes on pride.

Obadiah 1:3: *The pride of thine heart hath deceived thee . . .*

Rafferty wasn't looking forward to attending the marriage celebration. Ann had told Towner that Marta was planning to have a hundred flower girls serve the luncheon, evidently girls from a school Marta raised money for. No one had said it outright, but it was obvious that she was trying to outdo the previous Mrs. Finn Whiting.

Poor Emily. How had she first found out about Marta? Why hadn't she left Finn? Rafferty rubbed his hands over his eyes. Infidelity. He wished he could wipe the word from his brain. The energy it took not to think about that night, in the hope that Towner wouldn't read his thoughts, was exhausting.

Jay-Jay buzzed Rafferty to tell him Callie was at the front desk.

"Send her in," he said, forgetting until the last moment that the contents of the evidence boxes were spread across his desk and office. He'd managed to find and interview sixteen of the men the Goddesses had been involved with, including two older officers on his own force. He'd had to threaten suspension, but, in the end, they'd cooperated. One suspect led to another, with each adding a bit more of the story, though never enough to solve the mystery. He was able to confirm one thing that proved Helen wrong. Rose's house had not been a brothel. When he asked if the Goddesses ever took money for services rendered, every man replied that they did not. He believed them.

But when it came to who committed the crime, he had no idea whom to believe. The fifth petal of the rose he'd drawn when Callie first arrived now had so many names crossed out and rewritten under Sarah Good's that he'd worn a hole in the paper and had to attach another piece, taping it to the edge and drawing an arrow from the petal to a list of possible suspects that was so long he'd had to fold the paper in half in order to fit the whole thing back in his desk drawer. It seemed everyone had a motive of some kind. Or, if they didn't, then their wives did. Now he had too many suspects, and they were still no closer to locating Leah Kormos. But Rafferty had a nagging idea he wasn't able to shake. If he was right, he might have started more trouble than if he'd left the case alone and the boxes of evidence in storage, as old Tom Dayle had suggested.

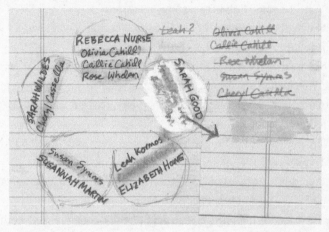

He tried to clean up the papers he'd spread out, but it was too late. Callie spotted the photo on his desk the moment she walked in.

"The mural!" she said, picking up the picture and staring at it. She studied it for a long time. "They were amazing looking, weren't they?"

"They were," he said.

"I remember the painter," she said. "He was a friend of Rose's."

"Was he one of their conquests?" Rafferty asked.

"No, he wasn't one of them. I remember him as a very nice older gentleman. I think . . . well, as I recall him, he was probably gay."

Rafferty had heard this from one of the officers as well. It seemed to be the best-kept secret in town; one of the only people who didn't know it was Helen.

"I'm glad you found this," she said. "I don't have any photos of them."

"Actually, this isn't why I called, though I will gladly make you a copy." He reached down, opened his desk drawer, and pulled out a small box. On the back, someone had written *RETURN TO ROSE WHELAN.*

"I'm not certain why they never gave this back to her, but I am sure she'd want you to have it."

Slowly, Callie opened the box. When she saw what was inside, she started to cry.

It was the rosary.

"Oh," he said. "I didn't mean for it to upset—"

She held up her hand. "No, it's good. I'm fine. Thank you for giving it to me."

She held it in her hand, the five petals fitting into her scar, which had stretched as she'd grown, so the rose that had once barely fit in her palm now seemed miniature. "It's pretty, isn't it?" she asked.

Rafferty nodded. "It is."

She put the rosary around her neck, the same way Rose had worn it. "Thank you," she said again. "This makes me happy."

"You don't look very happy." He hoped he hadn't made a mistake, giving her this reminder of her past. He noticed the ring she was wearing; he knew of the engagement, had already congratulated both of them, but now he said nothing. "You want to talk?"

"It's nothing beyond the obvious," she admitted. "The 'celebration,' " Callie punctuated with air quotes. "I'm happy that you and Towner are coming."

"Looking forward to it," he said, hearing how hollow his lie sounded.

Callie laughed. "My sentiments exactly. As well as Paul's." Then she looked at him curiously. "This wasn't the only reason you asked me here, was it?" she said, fingering the rosary.

"Jesus, what is it with the women in this town? Is every one of you a goddamned mind reader?"

She looked surprised by his outburst but said nothing.

"No," he said. "It wasn't the reason. Not entirely." He hesitated, then pulled out the rules and put the list down in front of her. "Have you ever seen this before?"

Callie stared at the paper filled with girlish writing, titled "The Goddess Rules." "No," she said, softly.

"As I told you, Leah was pregnant," he said. "So we know for certain she broke at least one of these rules. I have a feeling that the man you saw in your dream, the blue-eyed man in bed, the one they were fighting about—I think he might have been the father."

Callie said nothing.

"There's one more question I need to ask. You mentioned in your memory—dream—at Hammond Castle that the woman in red gave you a drink to sniff. This drink, tell me again what it smelled like."

"Licorice," she said. "She said it had fairies in it."

"Could it have been absinthe?"

"It might have been," Callie said. "If one whiff a long time ago can be any judge. Where are you going with this?"

"Nowhere special," he lied. "Probably just another dead end."

"Absinthe." Callie thought about it for a moment. "But Finn's eyes are brown, not blue," she said, feeling a chill pass through her.

"That's true," he said. "And there are a number of places to get absinthe besides the Whiting family, or someone could have procured it from them for the costume party. After all, the Whitings were in the business of selling alcohol."

"Very true," she said, touching the rosary to get her bearings.

"Thanks for coming down."

"That's it?"

"That's it."

As soon as Callie left his office Rafferty went online and pulled up the results of a search he'd done right after Emily died so suddenly. Because it was well known that she'd had cancer, no autopsy had been performed, as was often true in such cases. He'd called her pharmacist, a guy he knew from the program. Rafferty had asked for records of all the Whitings' prescriptions. He'd spent a few days researching each drug. Emily had been looking like a woman in remission up until the day she died, and Rafferty didn't have to be a genius to know there were ways to hasten a cancer patient's demise, if you were so inclined. He'd talked to an ER doctor he'd known in New York, who told him opiates would be the obvious choice, that they would likely have been prescribed to Emily as a treatment for her pain. But the list he'd gotten back from the pharmacist showed no sign of opiates—no sign of painkillers at all. Odd, he thought—especially if her cancer was progressing fast enough to kill her.

But something else he'd discovered was even stranger.

Among Finn's medications were two different treatments for glaucoma. The first drug was latanoprost, which had, in the past several years, become the default treatment for the condition. The second, bimatoprost, had been prescribed initially and did roughly the same thing, but was slightly less effective. *So why was Finn still taking it?* Rafferty wondered. Then, digging deeper, he read about an odd side effect common to both drugs but a bit more significant in the earlier one, something that made the drug popular for an off-brand reason, so popular it was now endorsed by movie stars and marketed under the brand name Latisse: It made the user's eyelashes lengthen and thicken. Finn Whiting was nothing if not vain. He had long lashes, and stopping the drug would halt the effect, which, Rafferty had concluded, must have been why he continued taking it.

But now something else clicked. He scrolled through the list of side effects again. Taking bimatoprost could change the color of your eyes, darkening the irises, effectively turning one's eyes from blue to brown.

He pulled out the drawing of the rose and inked a name he'd penciled in and erased several times before. Then he picked up the phone and called Mickey. "How long do you think it would take to trace the ancestry of Finn Whiting?"

"You're in luck," Mickey said. "I'm already working on it. Though it probably won't be done in time for the reception, I'm giving them their combined family trees as a wedding present."

CHAPTER FORTY

July 18, 2015
PRIDE'S CROSSING

On January 15, 1697, Salem held a day of fasting
in honor of the victims, known as the
Day of Official Humiliation.
—ROSE WHELAN, *The Witches of Salem*

RAFFERTY AND TOWNER TOOK THEIR SEATS; MARTA HAD
seated Ann and Mickey with them, along with Zee and her boyfriend,
Hawk, a rigger on the *Friendship*. The group sat one table over from
the main table, which was set near the edge of the cliffs, twenty yards
from the main house. They were enjoying a clear view of the border
islands and Salem Sound.

"Isn't this the perfect day for a celebration?" Towner said to Ann.

At eighty degrees and sunny without a visible cloud, it was as if
Finn and Marta had ordered the humidity that plagued New England
summers removed for the occasion. They'd had drinks and appetiz-
ers served in the orangerie, then moved the guests outside for the
luncheon. Ann nodded.

"How's old Finch doing, Zee?" Mickey asked. Mickey was seldom
seen anywhere out of his pirate costume. Today, he looked handsome
in a suit.

"Pretty much the same," Zee said. Her father suffered from Parkinson's. "Which is the best we can expect." She looked around. "Does
anyone else think this whole thing is kind of weird?" She tilted her

head at Finn, Marta, Paul, and Callie, sitting at the main table. Finn and Marta looked extremely happy. Paul and Callie seemed miserable.

"Lots of gossip about their hasty marriage around town," Mickey said, as Ann tried to shush him. "I heard one of our staunchest Puritan naysayers, Helen Barnes, say, 'Well, it is very European, isn't it?' "

Fortunately, Helen Barnes was seated at a table on the other side of Finn and Marta, and not within earshot.

"You two are next to tie the knot," Mickey said to Zee.

Hawk smiled. "You don't have to convince me."

"Callie and Paul are next. Didn't you see the ring on her finger?" Zee asked Mickey.

"Seriously, when am I going to see a ring on your finger?" Mickey asked.

"You're such a rude man, even for a pirate." Zee laughed.

"As your uncle, I'm simply looking out for your best interests."

Rafferty said, "Mickey, I have a question for you."

Zee shot Rafferty a grateful look.

"Whatever you're going to ask, I plead the Fifth," Mickey said.

"Relax. I'm not working today. I'm just curious," Rafferty said, looking at Pride's Heart. "You've been sailing the seas a long time. With the family living right here, how did you and your motley crew smuggle anything into the basement? I took a tour of the wine cellar on Thanksgiving, but I didn't see an entrance to the caves below the house."

"You want me to give away trade secrets?" Mickey asked.

"I promise I'll let you turn state's evidence if I have to arrest you."

"I know my rights. There's a statute of limitations on this stuff."

Rafferty smiled. "No, seriously. I'm curious about how you got in."

"*If* anything was still being smuggled when I started working for the Whitings—and that's a big *if*—I imagine the crew, which was certainly not my own crew of merry, law-abiding pirates, would have used the back entrance," Mickey said, pointing over the side of the cliff. "There's a small beach about fifty feet below us. You can only get in when the tide is high enough to tie up. Or so they tell me."

Rafferty had to laugh. "What did you just call them, your *merry, law-abiding pirates*?"

"I did."

"That's a bit of an oxymoron, don't you think?"

Everyone laughed.

"I challenge you to name one of your crew who is law-abiding."

It took Mickey a moment. "Jake O'Brien?"

"Jake O'Brien died six years ago," Rafferty said.

"That doesn't mean he isn't law-abiding, that just means he's dead."

"Doesn't count."

"Okay, okay, give me a minute," Mickey said, really concentrating, "Patch Willis!"

Rafferty cocked an eyebrow. "You're trying to tell me that Patch Willis doesn't have a record?"

"Misdemeanors. And that was a long time ago. Patch Willis has been a respectable citizen for the last ten years."

The fact was that Rafferty hadn't seen Willis for just about that long. "Doing what?"

"He's been the caretaker at Greenlawn Cemetery. He just retired."

Bingo, Rafferty thought. He was already considering Finn his key suspect, but he didn't have enough to go on. The connection between Willis and Finn, as well as Willis's abrupt retirement as Greenlawn's caretaker last December, had certainly given him more. Today might be a celebration, Rafferty thought, but tomorrow morning was going to be something else entirely. He had a lot of unanswered questions for Finn Whiting.

Mickey turned to Ann. "What are we drinking anyway?"

"This is Bordeaux," she said, pouring him a glass. "But I hear we're doing the wedding toast with the port."

"No more of that phony stuff . . ." Mickey said.

"The real thing," Ann said. "The blend that sells for a thousand dollars a bottle."

Mickey looked impressed. Everyone at the table knew he had been part of a group that had poured barrels of phony port into Beverly Harbor, the scandal that had started with a bad business deal allegedly made by Marta's father. Mickey was not much more than a kid when it happened, straight off the boat from Ireland. Costumed as pirates, the group—with the approval of Finn's father—had dumped ten full barrels. The event was as famous in the area as the Boston Tea Party, and had given Mickey license to play the role of pirate ever after.

"There is evidently quite a lot to toasting," Towner said. "No toasting with water, for instance. And you don't toast when someone is toasting you. Marta taught us that the night of the Yellow Dog Shelter benefit."

"I hear that's bad luck," Ann said.

"And never, under any circumstances, should anyone clink glasses."

"Aren't you Miss Manners today." Ann laughed.

"I'm just letting you all know the proper decorum, so we don't embarrass ourselves."

"Who is giving the toast?" asked Zee.

"I hope it isn't Paul," said Mickey. "Look at him—he looks like he's had a few too many already."

Music started playing, and a hundred little girls all bedecked in flowers emerged from the orangerie. They wore long pastel flowered sundresses and daisies in their hair. Each had a corsage of yellow rosebuds on her wrist and carried a plate of food.

All the guests oohed and aahed at the adorable children. The girls were serving the main course, lobster risotto adorned with flowers.

"The flowers are from Marta's new garden," Ann told Towner. "Yellow roses, orange nasturtiums, violet pansies. And for all you cynics and snobs, yes, this adorable procession of young girls assures coverage by *The Boston Globe* and *Vanity Fair.*"

"Are we supposed to eat the flowers?" Mickey squinted at the plate of risotto one little girl had carefully placed in front of him.

"Oh yes," Callie said, appearing at their table. She was still wearing the rosary Rafferty had returned to her, and she had on a long lavender sundress. Her hair was loose and adorned with flowers, like that of a hippie princess. "Lately we've been feasting on the bounty of Marta's new kitchen garden: pansies with our pancakes, squash blossoms with arugula in our salads, and basil flowers in our pasta."

"Hello, Callie," Ann said.

Callie nodded. She knew Ann had helped Marta with the flowers and had done her best not to run into her. Paul had taken no notice of Ann's presence on the property, which would have made her happy if she hadn't been so worried about him. He couldn't let go of his anger, and it was changing him.

Ann had made no move to speak with Paul earlier, but now she was looking in his direction. She asked quietly, "Is he okay?"

"He's just fine," Callie lied, turning to Rafferty.

Rafferty thought Callie looked precisely like her late mother. She'd dyed her hair back to its natural color. All she needed were bare feet and some patchouli oil.

Seeing Rafferty's eyes move to her feet, Callie looked down, too.

The gaping hole in the lawn was now completely covered by a metal plate, the sod expertly patchworked over it, to be reopened after the wedding so the grounds crew could finish the repair job. It was so perfectly woven that she could barely see the damage the root removal had caused in the otherwise perfect lawn.

"I hear you're responsible for all this pageantry," Rafferty said to Ann.

"Only partly," Ann said. "They hired a professional music director. And the girls chose their own flowers."

Callie had watched from her window this morning as the little girls had picked flowers to garnish each plate. They'd flitted through the maze of midsummer blossoms, stopping briefly to pluck things and place them in the baskets they carried. From the perspective of the boathouse, the children had looked like butterflies or the tiny fairies Rose had described in her stories about Ireland. Not the ones trapped in trees, but the beautiful ones who lived in the fairy mounds, performing magic for deserving passersby. The sight had calmed Callie's nerves and seemed to have had the same effect on Paul, smoothing over the most recent argument they'd had, one that had lasted most of the previous evening. They'd made peace before they went to bed, but they hadn't touched each other. Callie had tossed and turned, and finally decided to just get up.

She'd grabbed Rose's *Book of Trees* from the shelf where it sat next to Rose's ashes and taken it to the reading nook at the top of the lighthouse stairs. Before she'd opened it, she had stood for a moment looking out toward Baker's Island and the blackness beyond.

Rose had been heavily on her mind since the grounds crew had uncovered the roots of the tree. Callie had entertained the idea that she might scatter Rose's ashes under the stump. But after the vision of blood she'd had, she knew the area was not fit for Rose's final resting place. So many things she'd experienced recently were hidden, things that lay beneath: the reef at Norman's Woe, submerged and treacherous; the frescoes concealed for centuries under layers of smoky soot; the root hole, now covered with sod. There were caves beneath the palazzi of the Sassi, and there were caves under Pride's Heart. Indeed, there seemed to be things just below the surface of life itself, revealing themselves only at odd moments or when accidentally or intentionally disturbed.

She'd wanted to figure out a better place for Rose and had been hoping the journal would give her some ideas. So she'd sunk into the nook's overstuffed chair and turned on the light, extinguishing the panoramic seascape and creating multiple reflections of herself in the angled glass walls of the lighthouse. Taking a deep breath, she'd opened Rose's *Book of Trees*, fearing she would find a paranoia-laden manifesto, the scribbled prose of a disturbed mind. Rose had been penning in it so furiously in her last few weeks. Instead, Callie had discovered a work of art. Laced in a continuous pattern were sketches of trees, their branches extending from one page to the next, sometimes bared by winter, sometimes fully leafed. Veined oak leaves sprouted at the tips of random twigs. And then . . . what she'd thought of as a sampling of many trees resolved itself, and Callie had realized with a start what she was looking at. It was a single tree spreading across the pages. A Tree of Life, like the fresco in Italy. Its upper branches reached toward the sky, and its matching roots grew far into the ground, extending as deep as they were high. *As above, so below.*

The only words in the book had been names. The roots held the names of both the accused and the executed of July 1692: Rebecca Nurse, Sarah Wildes, Elizabeth Howe, Sarah Good, and Susannah

Martin, the five petals of the rosary she was wearing. She looked at the corresponding branches and saw names she didn't recognize, names sitting on branches that led higher and higher up the tree. At the very top were the names of Olivia, Cheryl, and Susan, each on a branch that had been broken. Near the highest branches, Callie found Rose's name, and just above it, on a branch that extended from Olivia's severed one, was her own. It was an unfinished work: There were many gaps, places Rose had not yet filled in, but the meaning was clear. This was a family tree.

Callie had stayed in that chair all night, in a trance, paging through hundreds of names, until the rising sun pulled her out of her reverie.

Now Zee's question pulled Callie back to the reception. "Have you ever seen anything so adorable?" she asked, indicating the flower girls as they continued presenting a plate to each diner.

"They are—"

"Excuse me," Ann interrupted. Without another word she dashed across the lawn and snatched a long-stemmed purple flower off a plate. "Where did you get this?" she asked the little girl who had served the dish. "These are fairy's bells. See this bell-like blossom? They're not good to eat, sweetie. They can make you very sick."

The girl started to cry. People turned to look.

Marta rushed over. "What are you doing, Ann?" She didn't hide her concern.

"Go back to your table," Ann said, waving her away. "I'll take care of this.

"Can you show me exactly where you found them?" Ann asked the child, as she scanned the other tables. She found two more fairy's bells and quickly snatched them off plates. The girl nodded and said she could.

"What was all that about?" Towner asked, when Ann rejoined their table.

"Nothing," Ann said. "Crisis averted."

Callie was looking at Ann. "Crisis?"

"Foxglove. Fairy's bells. Those purple flowers grow wild in this region. They are beautiful but very poisonous."

"Where were they, exactly?" Callie asked.

"In a patch just beyond the new kitchen garden, a section that must have been hidden by that tree stump they removed," Ann said.

Mickey looked at his plate as if it might bite him.

"Go ahead and eat, everyone, it's fine," Ann said, reassuringly.

Callie made her way back to the main table.

Marta picked up her fork and began to eat, and the guests followed suit, reassured that whatever crisis had gotten Marta's attention was now resolved.

The little girls, finished with serving, took seats at the long table by the orangerie and ate lunch together.

After the dessert course was served, the waiters filled the guests' glasses with the thousand-dollar port for the wedding toast. A large carafe of an even more valuable port had been poured earlier for the wedding party. Callie knew it was from the barrel that Paul had served her from that night in the speakeasy. Finn and Paul had both consumed quite a bit already. After the waiter refilled their glasses, Finn stood and raised his. He spoke directly to Marta: "To my wife, Marta. It's you. It has always been you." Finn downed his entire glass of port in one go.

What followed was a prolonged and numbing silence. Finally, Helen Barnes raised her glass and, following her lead, the rest of the shocked guests joined in the toast.

Feeling Marta's eyes on her, Callie took a sip.

Marta smiled but didn't drink.

Paul hadn't taken his eyes off his father. Though he'd already consumed quite a bit of the port, he didn't join the toast.

"Everyone, please join Mr. and Mrs. Whiting for dancing in the ballroom," Darren announced.

Marta stood and took Finn's arm, and the two left the main table and walked directly toward the house and then through the French doors just off the ballroom. Paul stood unsteadily and followed; he did not take Callie's arm, and she trailed a few steps behind the others. The crowd remained seated, staring after them until an usher appeared and gently escorted the guests to the house.

"Where are you going?" Callie asked Paul. While the rest of the guests had turned left into the ballroom, Paul had veered right, into the library.

The elevator was there, its iron grate open and waiting.

"The wine cellar's unlocked for a change. I'm going to get more port." He held the elevator door for her, almost losing his balance. "Alcohol's the only way I'll get through this ridiculous charade."

"Let's go back," Callie said to him. "To Matera. Right now. Let's drive to Logan, and we'll get a plane out tonight. We could be at the monastery by morning."

"No way," Paul said. He gestured for her to get in the elevator. She shook her head, and he shrugged; the door hit him as it closed.

She stood at the partners desk listening to the elevator's groans and creaks. She had a bad feeling; her gut was telling her to get away and not to look back. She glanced out the window, and, for a moment, she believed she could see the hole they had covered on the lawn. It was throbbing.

Sadly, she realized that Paul would never leave this place. He would choose his birthright over his own happiness. It was the family curse, the curse of both the Hathornes and the Whitings, and it went back generations. He wasn't free of it, and he never would be. It was more important to him than the happily ever after that he'd promised her. Marta was right. He would betray her.

She walked out of the library and went to the boathouse. Climbing to the top of the lighthouse, she looked out at Norman's Woe in the bright summer sunlight and sensed the presence of something far darker than she'd once imagined.

Clutching Rose's book to her breast and taking Rose's ashes, Callie descended the stairs.

Through the forest that separated the boathouse from Pride's Heart, Callie could hear music as the orchestra started up in the ballroom. She loaded her car quickly. Her fingers had swollen from the day's heat, and she had to run her hand under cold water and slick her finger with soap to remove the emerald ring Paul had given her. When it finally loosened, it flew across the room and rolled under the couch.

She crawled on hands and knees to retrieve it and carefully placed it on the table where he would see it.

She took the back roads, past the barn and the outbuildings, past the beach, turning left as she came to Route 127. She crossed the bridge, careful not to look in her rearview mirror. She didn't have the strength to make it back to Amherst, so she drove to the Hawthorne Hotel and booked herself a room. She got all the way to the sixth floor before she broke down and sobbed.

Rafferty stood in the doorway of the ballroom talking to Ann and Towner while they waited for Mickey, who had gone in search of a bathroom. Helen Barnes approached them and stood for a long moment looking at the threesome. "Well, isn't this a day of firsts?" she said. "Men and their mistresses! Have you ladies taken inspiration from Emily and Marta? How very European of you all!"

Rafferty stared, dumbstruck, at Helen and then at Towner. Mickey rejoined the group as Helen walked away.

"What's going on?" he said, when he saw the looks on their faces.

"Come on," Ann said to Mickey. "You promised me a waltz."

CHAPTER FORTY-ONE

July 18, 2015
<small>SALEM</small>

In the realm between life and death, time,
as we know it, does not exist.
—ROSE'S *Book of Trees*

TOWNER AND RAFFERTY DIDN'T SPEAK DURING THE DRIVE
back to Salem. They climbed the stairs to the coach house in silence,
the distance between them growing.

"I'm going to bed," she finally said. "Are you coming?"

"We have to talk," he said.

"We'll talk after. Come to bed."

"We need to talk now," he said, following her upstairs to the bedroom. He knew what would come after, had always known what would
happen when he confessed. He knew too well what "after" looked like.
It looked like the void, the place he feared most. *After* meant when she
left and he was without her. He'd been there once before, and it had
almost killed him. He wasn't certain he would survive it again.

"About what Helen said . . . Ann and I . . ." he started.

She held up her hand. "Never happened." She was removing her
dress as he spoke, kicking off her shoes and putting on her robe.

It was just what Ann had said when he'd tried to talk to her about
what had happened between them that night. Had the two women
talked about this? Feelings of betrayal and shame settled on him,
creating an odd blend.

"It did, though," he said. "I was there."

"Stop," she said, putting a finger to his lips.

When she took it away, he spoke again.

"I went to Ann."

"I know."

"I thought you had left me."

"I had."

He sat on the edge of their bed, tears of frustration and grief streaking his face. "I *went* to *Ann*," he said again, waiting for the full impact of it to hit her.

"I know," she said again. "And Ann brought you back to me."

He remembered her then, sitting on his porch in the early morning. "How?"

"I don't know." She held his face, wiping his tears with the sleeve of her robe. "But she did."

For the first time he noticed that Towner was wearing a black kimono, the same kimono he'd noticed Ann wearing that night. In fact, everything about Towner was the same as it had been that evening: the curve of her neck, the way the black kimono hung off her shoulders. "It was you."

She nodded, holding his stare.

"How?" he whispered.

"Time isn't linear."

She opened the robe and stepped toward him, exactly the same way she had done that night.

CHAPTER FORTY-TWO

July 18, 2015

*The banshee manifests as either a beautiful young maiden
capable of luring her victim toward death or an aging
crone, two aspects of the triple goddess. No human is
able to glimpse the third and most prevalent aspect,
the mother, yet she has been there all along.*

—ROSE'S *Book of Trees*

"I'M SO SORRY," PAUL SAID. "I DON'T KNOW WHAT'S WRONG with me. We can go back to Matera. I want to go. I need you. Just come back." His voice sounded strange, as if he were talking from a tunnel.

"Where are you?" Callie asked. She regretted answering her cell.

"The boathouse." He coughed once, then again. "I came looking for you, and I found the ring on the table." He sounded as if he were crying: ragged sobs that broke into a deep, gagging choke.

"Are you all right?"

"No," he said. "My heart—it's beating strangely. And there's a weird green halo around the moon."

She looked out her hotel room window, toward the west, where the sliver of waxing moon was just setting. There was no halo.

She could hear the sound of him retching.

"I'm sick," he said. "Oh, damn."

"What?"

"There's blood in it. A lot of blood."

She drove as fast as she could, pulling into the back driveway, the one nearest the boathouse. "Paul?" She rushed from living room to bedroom to kitchen to bath before climbing the stairs to the lighthouse.

He wasn't there, but a patch of bloody vomit was on the floor next to the phone. A scribbled note from him was on the table: *Meet me in the spa. Finn sick, too. Marta needs help getting him upstairs. Doctor meeting us there.*

She grabbed the note and sprinted through the woods to the main house, the huge pine trees spiking, pointing their shadows skyward, conjuring memories of fairy-tale forests and doomed children. The front door was locked, so she entered through the pantry. She called their names. No answer. There weren't any staff members around; there was no sign of Marta or Finn. They must still be down in the spa. Callie felt fear rising as she ran through the library to the elevator. She pushed the button, and as the lift crawled and clanked upward, she wondered what could be happening. Food poisoning from the risotto? Something worse?

She stepped in, her panic growing as the elevator descended slowly to the spa. The door opened to a dimly lit but empty room. They'd already gone. She had started to get back into the elevator when she spotted a dark figure on the floor, in the back corner near the sea well.

"Paul!" she shouted, rushing to his side.

There was no response. The only sound came from the oak sea well as the water lapped its walls, surging with the high tide.

Paul was passed out, facedown in his own bloody vomit. "Paul," she said again, shaking him to wake him up. She felt for his pulse; it was pounding wildly and skipping beats.

She tried her cell. No reception. She rushed to the house phone, picked up the receiver, and heard a busy signal. She hung up and tried again. When did you ever hear a busy signal? Someone must have left an extension off the hook somewhere. Damn.

She turned Paul onto his side, so that he would not choke if he vomited again, then tried the phone one more time . . . still busy.

She got into the elevator, pulling the heavy glass door shut behind her. Just as she pushed the up button, the lights went out, leaving the room in total darkness. The elevator didn't move.

She felt her way back to him in the blackness.

Rafferty was sleeping, the sheets tangled around him, when the phone rang. "What time is it?" he said as he picked up. The clock read 3:00 A.M. Then, hearing the voice on the other end, he dragged himself to a sitting position. "What's wrong?" He listened carefully. "You tried the boathouse, and Pride's Heart, and both their cell phones? Okay." He hung up.

"What's happened?" Towner asked.

"That was Mickey and Ann," Rafferty said, pulling on his pants and shoes. "I have to go to Pride's Heart right now."

"Ann had a vision?" Towner asked, and Rafferty nodded.

"What did she see?"

Rafferty hesitated before he spoke. "She says she saw the badb," he said.

Towner stared at him. "The what?"

"The banshee."

"She saw the banshee?"

"She heard it wailing. And there's something else," he said, starting for the door. It was something Mickey had said, but there wasn't time to elaborate. After the night they'd just spent together, leaving Towner alone was the last thing Rafferty wanted to do. But if he was right . . .

"Oh, God," Towner cried. "Hurry. I hear it, too. Callie's in trouble."

"Hail Mary, full of grace . . ."

The tide had pulled away, taking the water from the sea well. The lapping against the oak well had gone silent, and Callie's world had become the essence of nothingness. In the hours she'd been sitting with him, Paul had not come to, not even briefly.

She could no longer hear the sound of his breathing.

She comforted herself that he still had a pulse, though it was now so slow and weak she could barely feel it.

She'd yelled for help so many times that her throat was raw. She had even vomited herself, probably from fear. She'd tried the house phone again and again, hoping that someone had discovered the line off the hook, but she only got the busy signal. Finally, she prayed. She said every prayer she'd ever been taught, and then she began fingering the rosary and reciting her Hail Marys until she realized she'd been clutching the oak rose so hard her palm had started to bleed. She had likely created a new scar, a smaller rose inside the larger one.

Now, as if in answer to her prayers, she saw the elevator come to life and begin to rise. She could hear whoever it was as he or she climbed in and started to descend.

"Oh, thank God," she said, jumping dizzily to her feet as the door opened and the lights snapped on. "Where the hell were you? Did you bring the doctor?" Why was Marta's head haloed green? It was an odd vision. "We need to get him to the hospital right away. Help me move him."

"I don't think so," Marta said. In one hand she held a carafe of the magenta port and a long-stemmed glass, and, in the other, a knife. She looked at the bloody vomit. "Interesting. I wasn't expecting blood. The first phase of foxglove poisoning is marked by nausea and an irregular heartbeat. Then the muscles go slack. The final phase slows the heart, ultimately stopping it. I do regret that the little girls are going to be blamed for choosing the wrong flowers." She shoved the glass into Callie's hands. "You didn't drink the port at dinner, and you didn't toast our future as enthusiastically as etiquette requires. So now mind your manners and drink up."

CHAPTER FORTY-THREE

July 19, 2015
PRIDE'S CROSSING

Transgressors, may more quickly here, than else
where become a prey to the Vengeance of Him,
Who ha's Eyes like a Flame of Fire, *and,* who walks
in the midst of the Golden Candlesticks.
—COTTON MATHER, *The Wonders of the Invisible World*

RAFFERTY BANGED ON THE FRONT DOOR OF THE BOAT-
house. Inside, every light was blazing, but no one answered. He
crossed to the other entrance, slipping on what he thought was seagull
guano and then realized was vomit. Alarmed, he looked in the windows but didn't see anyone. He opened the door and walked in.

"Callie? Paul?"

He saw her ring on the farmer's table. On the floor next to it,
he discovered more vomit, bloody this time. He searched the rooms
quickly, making the climb to the lighthouse; then, finding nothing, he
rushed back down and outside, cutting through the woods to Pride's
Heart.

He tried the front door. Locked. The house was completely dark.
He rang the bell and pounded hard on the door. He hurried around
to the side of the house, trying each entrance as he moved. All locked.
The French doors of the ballroom were locked, too, but easier to break.
He hip-checked one of them, popping its latch.

The room was pristine. It was hard to believe a huge reception had been hosted in here only hours earlier. He rushed from ballroom to hall, flipping on lights as he went.

"Marta?" he called, announcing his presence. "Finn?"

There was no answer. No sound at all except the wind off the ocean.

He tried the kitchen first, then the library. Both were empty. He ran to the parlor, then the orangerie, calling their names before taking the stairs two at a time. "Finn?" he called, louder this time.

Nothing. Had they gone away for a few nights, like traditional honeymooners? He opened the bedroom door. Empty.

Rafferty moved down the hallway, knocking on doors, then opening them, calling fruitlessly to each of the Whitings as he moved. He made his way to the third floor, to the servants' wing, and knocked on the long row of white doors.

There was no one there. All of the servants had been dismissed.

The only place he hadn't looked was the wine cellar. He went back to the empty library, turning on more lights. The bar, normally hidden behind the bookcase, was turned at a right angle into the room, and he could see light below. Either they'd neglected to lock things up after the party, or someone was down there.

He walked behind the bar to the elevator and pushed the call button. Nothing. He could see down the shaft to the elevator at the bottom. He pressed the call button again and, once again, nothing happened.

There was a house phone in the speakeasy. He'd seen Finn use it on Thanksgiving, calling the kitchen for more glasses. There was probably one in the spa as well.

He walked to the partners desk and found the house phone off the hook. He replaced it on the cradle, then picked it up and pressed the button marked SPA. It rang, but no one answered. He stepped forward, and his foot stubbed something soft.

Finn's face was blue, and there was a trail of bloody vomit on the rug next to him leading to the couch. He must have tried to crawl toward the phone before collapsing on the floor. Rafferty knelt, trying to rouse him, but Finn's body resisted. Already rigor mortis had begun to set in.

Rafferty used his cell to dial 911. Then he unlocked the front door and left it open for the Beverly police. Back outside, the air was cold and moist as he moved toward the cliff. If someone was really in the wine cellar, he had to find a way down there. Rafferty had no light save the flashlight app on his phone, but the stars were bright, and the sky was clear enough to see the approximate location of the opening that Mickey had pointed out on the rocky, narrow beach below. The tide was dead low and just beginning to turn. He was going to have to climb down.

The cliffs were steep, falling at least fifty feet into the ocean below. He stood on the granite ledge, looking down at the crumbling staircase that was behind a padlocked iron gate. The last fifteen feet of stairs were completely missing. If he got down there, he might not be able to get back up. Still, he knew what he had to do. This was the only other entrance to the cellar.

Adrenaline pumping, he climbed up and swung himself over the iron gate, stepping off the edge of the cliff and lowering himself onto the crumbling staircase carved into the badly eroding ledge.

The uneven steps sloped steeply as he moved down toward the ocean. With each step, the stairway dropped bits of rocky granite that bounced off the beach below.

It was a longer drop from the last step to the beach than it had appeared from above. Rafferty lowered himself off the final step, holding on for a long moment before he let himself fall. He landed hard on hands and knees, scraping skin. Slowly, he stood, then looked up at the sheer cliff and the house above.

He might have just made a really stupid mistake.

"Drink," Marta demanded.

Callie stared at her in disbelief. "Why are you doing this?"

Marta smiled. "Do you really have to ask?"

Callie hadn't sipped much of the foxglove-laced port at the reception the way Finn and Paul had, but she had joined the toast, drinking just enough, she now realized, to have slowly begun to feel its poisonous effects, first with the vomiting, then the green-haloed vision of Marta she'd seen earlier, and now the muscle weakness Marta had just described. Unwilling and unable to grip properly, she dropped the glass, shattering it into a thousand little shards.

Marta tsked, flashing the blade in front of her; its silver appeared to strobe. Marta's dark hair seemed to strobe, too, turning colors as she moved. Where had Callie seen that before? Callie's knees buckled, and she slid down into the pile of glass, drawing blood.

"Be polite, for God's sake." Marta held the carafe of purple port up to Callie's lips. "Protocol demands it. Look, I'll even give you the toast. To marital bliss," she said. "Too little and far too late."

Callie turned her head.

"So contrary," Marta said. "So ready to refuse the libations. You've turned into your mother."

Callie stared at her.

I have another name.

The scent of licorice.

She's five years old, for God's sake!

The stone floor. The blood dripping down the walls and pooling at Callie's feet.

"It was *you*."

I have another name. Can you guess it?

"It *was* you," Callie repeated. "At the party with all of us."

"It was me in a few places," Marta said. "Though you might not have known me, I knew you."

The woman in red held out the chalice for Callie to sniff.

"The Wicked Queen."

"Never wicked. Humiliated, betrayed, unloved, but never wicked."

Callie felt sick.

"I was Rose's friend. From the center. I was never one of them," Marta said. "But they convinced Rose that what I was doing was worse than anything they were doing. I tried to warn her, but they turned her against me."

My Love . . .

Cheryl, Susan, and Olivia giggling.

Callie standing in front of the room, hands in the elocutionist's pose, reading the love letter aloud while the others hooted with laughter.

The Goddesses vowing revenge for getting them in trouble, for telling Rose what they were doing in her house.

Callie's own mother suggesting their revenge and the ultimate betrayal: "Let's take him."

It wasn't Leah who was the fifth petal of the rose. It was Marta.

"You were supposed to be at the blessing that night."

"Rose forbid it. She took your mother's side against me."

"She was kicking us out of her house! Because of what you told her."

"I told them not to go that night."

"To the blessing?" Callie wasn't sure what Marta was telling her.

"To him."

Callie remembered the man on the bed. The blood.

"What they were doing was wrong. Especially with a child around. Your mother convinced Rose that I was part of it, procuring men for them: the Goddesses' madam. But you were right. I was supposed to be at the blessing. And so I came."

The rift between the Goddesses and Marta had become a crevasse far deeper than the one at Proctor's Ledge. It may have been Rose who had recited Sarah Good's name that night, but Marta, Sarah Good's true descendant, could just as easily have spoken the name herself, because she'd been there all along, Callie realized in horror. The curse that Rose heard that night hadn't come from the banshee, it had come from Marta just before she pulled the blade across Susan's throat. When Rose told the police that she had seen the Goddess turn, she hadn't been referring to the one who'd been trapped in the oak, she'd been talking about Marta.

God will give you blood to drink . . . Callie heard the words she'd long ago erased from her memory.

"I have another name," Marta said again.

Callie stared at her. "You killed my mother . . . and the others."

"They deserved to die."

"And Paul . . ."

"Paul is not worthy of you. He's a Whiting. He would have betrayed you, the same way Finn betrayed me. It's what they do, the Whitings, generation after generation.

"I tried to warn you. You shouldn't have come back, Callie. You should have taken my advice and run for your life."

Callie stared at her. "You loved him. I know you did."

"Once," she said. "A long, long time ago, when I was a stupid girl who thought love conquered all. You were there, you know my name."

Callie felt the floor fall away. She was going to be sick.

"Say it."

"Morrigan."

Callie could see the blood dripping down the walls now, the same blood she had seen that night, first at the castle and later in the woods. She vomited violently, and Marta, with a look of revulsion, took a tiny step backward.

Summoning her strength, Callie got to her feet and rushed toward the elevator. Marta grabbed her, sliding the silver blade across her throat as Callie threw her voice against the wall, and it bounced back hard, throwing Marta off balance. Instead of skin, the blade caught the oak rosary, slicing it and scattering its beads on the stone floor. She slashed again wildly, and Callie felt the skin on her arm slice open, felt the blood running down her fingers as she fell back, slamming into the sea well. She grabbed at Marta as hard as she could, and they both tumbled backward into the frigid tidal waters fifteen feet below.

Rafferty walked the beach, peering at the granite cliff, searching for the opening that had to be there. When the beach ended, he found himself in water, first at knee level, then up to his hips. Incoming waves made it difficult to maneuver, and finally impossible, so he climbed, reaching a jutting plateau five feet above the water. The ledge was only a few inches wide, and he placed his feet sideways, holding on, white knuckled, as he inched along, looking for the way in.

He didn't see it until he had almost passed it. A few feet higher on the cliff, where the rock formed a natural indentation, was an opening of about fifteen inches. It looked like erosion, or a storm gash where the rock had tumbled to the sea below. He almost rejected it until the light from his phone revealed a stairway. There were no decent foot-holds to hoist himself with, and the first one he tried crumbled under his weight, sending rock falling into the black churn of turning tide.

He repositioned and pulled himself upward until he reached the split. Crawling inside, he saw a tiny opening, barely child-size. Bur-rowing, making himself as small as possible, and pushing his hand out in front of him in the darkness, he felt his way forward. A centi-pede skittered across his arm, sending a shiver down his spine.

He counted his steps as he moved, ten in all before he reached a framed opening and found himself in what could only be described as an upright coffin: wooden, musty, and damp. He could go no farther. He'd reached a dead end.

CHAPTER FORTY-FOUR

July 19, 2015
Pride's Crossing

*There is not one culture, nor is there one individual
who does not harbor a prejudice against those
they consider "other."*

—Rose's *Book of Trees*

CALLIE WAS DEEP INSIDE THE FRIGID BLACKNESS, KELP
lining the sides of the ancient oak, its hollow trunk slimy with marine
vegetation. Severed limbs stretched from the hollowed trunk of the
sea well as the tide receded to dead low. The sides were too slick to
climb, and so she floated, losing blood, certain she could feel it flowing out of her, as if the frigid seawater was pulling it. She could feel
the nightmare creatures Paul had described to her, their bony fingers
grabbing at her, touching her from one side and then another. She
thrashed, spinning around to face them, but each time they vanished
before she could see them.

What had Paul told her about hypothermia? Struggling made the
blood rush to the extremities, causing death much more quickly. She
should wait for the tide to lift her, the way Paul had done, but that
wasn't possible. She had to keep moving to get away from the bony
fingers that reached for her.

She was almost relieved when she felt Marta's human hands until
they found her neck, tightening, and dragging them both under.

Callie fought her way to the surface, struggling for breath, only to be pulled under once again, as a vision overtook her.

They were standing at the edge of the void, nothing but emptiness stretching before them. She couldn't breathe or move. She was trapped with Marta in the abyss, the emptiness that was eternal. *No,* she thought. *Not like this.*

Callie ducked her chin to her chest and grabbed Marta's tightening fingers with both hands, forcing them both deeper underwater, sliding one hand to Marta's elbow and loosening her grip, then using Marta's wrist and arm as a lever to turn her, until the two women came face-to-face. Callie looked into the empty eyes that stared back at her and saw for the first time what Rose had seen that night on Proctor's Ledge: not Marta, not the banshee, but the turning itself.

Callie didn't close her eyes against it, but made herself look.

It began slowly, a falling feeling as in a dream. She felt the water recede, leaving behind the scent of oranges. Then the music began, single notes. Was that the plucking of a harp? As quickly as she recognized the sound, the plucking stopped and was replaced by other notes, both distant and dissonant, tones she had never before been able to hear.

What had just moments before been Marta's bony fingers were now a braided witch hazel switch.

Every lash Marta had ever received, Callie now felt. The whipping became a rhythm, and as the switch struck, the emptiness deepened, the dissonant sounds became louder, first in disjointed disharmony, then crystallizing into words.

"What have you done?"

Strike.

"Nothing, Mama."

"Don't lie to me!"

Strike.

"I love him."

"They have taken everything from us. They can't have you, too!"

Strike.

"He loves me."

"He will betray you! The Whitings always do!"

Strike.

"He wants to marry me."

"You stupid, stupid girl."

Strike. Strike. Strike.

Callie felt the pulse of blood rushing to the reddening welts on Marta's bare thighs.

"He will betray you again and again! The same way his father betrayed yours, and his father before him!"

Strike.

And, for the first time, Callie understood the real meaning of Rose's phrase. Marta had courted the strike. By standing alone with a Whiting and against her family, she had incurred the rage of generations.

Strike.

The music of the lash was rhythmic. Callie felt her body convulse with each strike.

Now Callie saw Marta as a young woman arguing with Rose.

"Why did you tell me that?" Rose demanded. "You accuse them of unspeakable things."

"You need to know what they are doing in your house. For the sake of the child."

"You mean what *you* are doing!"

Marta stared at her.

"They told me. It was you who called yourself Goddess. You who first brought men to them."

"No, I swear! I never . . ." Marta insisted.

"Get out of my sight," Rose said.

Strike.

Marta holding Leah's hand, guiding her through a series of dark enclosures, then a long dark tunnel to the spa. "Are you sure Finn said to meet him here?" Marta turned. Leah saw the flash of a blade.

A slash; blood everywhere. Marta pushed Leah's lifeless body into the sea well.

Strike.

Glint of a blade. Three final slashes. The crevasse and the bloody, still-costumed bodies below.

Strike.

Marta looked around to make sure no one saw her entering the Left Hand Path. She unwrapped a cloth and handed Susan's white hair and a patch of skin to the old witch.

The witch looked at the hair, then the skin. She looked at Marta. "What have you done?"

"Nothing," Marta said, but the witch knew better.

The witch took a step backward, away from the trophies.

"I've given you what you demanded and more," Marta said. "Now give him to me."

"I cannot."

"Yes, you can."

"You must leave this place. Or be discovered." The witch stared at Marta, seeing all that she'd done. "The older one sees what you've become."

"I've become only what he's forced me to become," Marta said. "Now give him to me as you promised. Or I will confess that you helped me. Because you wanted these." She pointed to the trophies.

"I cannot," the old witch said.

"What?"

"He will marry the one who is with his child."

"I've taken care of her. He will not marry her."

"No," the old witch said, looking shocked as she scried and envisioned carnage. "She lives."

"Impossible." Marta shook her head.

"You have killed the wrong rivals."

Strike.

The music of the lash became another kind of music then, the sound of waves beating on the ledge below. Marta stood on the cliffs at Hammond Castle looking out at the searchlights, watching as they pulled her father's lifeless body out of the water. The Whitings were there as well, not with Marta and her mother, but standing on the opposite side of the cliff: young Finn standing with his mother and father, his arm around a young and pregnant Emily, a large wedding ring on her finger.

Finn's eyes met Marta's across the divide. Then he looked away.

As she watched her husband's lifeless body being dragged from the water, Marta's mother began to keen, an otherworldly sound that echoed across the cliffs and down to the water's edge. She pointed a finger at the Whitings and, in a voice not her own, intoned: "God will give you blood to drink!"

Callie gasped, choking on seawater that tasted like human blood, the curse of Sarah Good echoing in her ears. The music was unbearably loud now, not music anymore but pure noise. Callie tried to summon the calming notes of the solfeggio scale that she had heard in Matera, but the music was bound, just as Dagda's harp had once been.

Callie was floating in a viscous pool of warm seawater and human blood somewhere between life and death. She could feel her mother and the other Goddesses, who she now knew had ended up in the sea well with Leah, but when she reached for them, Callie grasped only bones. Then, from her mother, she heard one tone, lower and under the noise: "Ut." Just the first note of the ancient scale, but it was there.

The sound started softly, mournful at first, as if it contained every drop of sorrow that had ever existed in the world. She opened her mouth to join the tone, letting it echo through her, building the vibration. Time shifted and stretched. And in these eternal moments, as she came face-to-face with Marta, she saw the others who had died in the wake of this great sin that had been kept alive through the generations. Time stretched to encompass them all, then vanished completely, leaving them trapped in the abyss: accused and accusers together. Floating in a liquid that was more blood than seawater now, the blood of the living and the blood of their ancestors. The harp began to play.

And Callie could see that the abyss, the nothingness that she had been faced with, was not nothing but everything: every possibility that had ever existed in the world and every choice made. She felt Marta's pain as if it were her own. And in that moment Rose's last words came back to her: *Sometimes the only healing is death.*

The sorrow Marta felt, the anger that had consumed her, now turned to something else, something Callie had heard only once before. It was far louder this time, its sound pitching higher and wilder as it circled, swirled, and shrieked, pulling them both inside its vortex of fury.

CHAPTER FORTY-FIVE

*It was the lightning strike that finally freed the trapped and
much changed goddess. In a stunning act of self-sacrifice
from which recovery was not possible, the oak gave
up its own life to save the banshee.*
—ROSE'S *Book of Trees*

MOVING HIS HANDS ALONG THE WOOD, THROUGH COB-
webs, Rafferty searched for an opening. He knocked on the sides of the
coffin, hearing a hollow thump at the far corner. Running his hands
upward in the darkness, he located a latch, and, as he unhooked it,
the bottom of the coffin swung open into another, slightly larger one.

He moved into the second coffin and realized it was a closet. Beyond it was another, and, past that, yet another. The closets were
empty, just wide enough to stand in, and linked one to another,
bottom to corner, forming a chain of tiny upright rooms. Stepping
sideways through the openings, he moved forward. Each room was
slightly larger than the last until he found himself on the backside of
a real closet, something heavy blocking its opening.

He threw his full weight against it, forcing the door to yield, and
found himself standing amid a pile of papers and books that had
spilled from the bookcase propped against the outside of the door
he'd just forced. He recognized where he was from the strong smell of

port that had permeated the walls over the last century. He was inside the speakeasy.

He unlocked the door to the hallway, and, as it opened, the sound rushed at him like a hurricane siren, driving Rafferty to his knees. It felt as if all the rage he had ever experienced was contained in the sound, every affront, every inhumanity. He pressed his hands over his ears as the shriek shattered all the wine bottles in the racks. Then it stopped, taking with it all possible sound and sucking the world into a silence so pervasive that Rafferty was momentarily uncertain he had survived the banshee's rage.

Towner, Ann, and Mickey arrived at Pride's Heart together. Glancing into the library, they saw the coroner bagging Finn's body.

"What the hell happened here tonight?" one of the Beverly officers said to the EMT as the paramedics took Paul and Callie away on stretchers.

Intuiting both the origin and the cure for their illness, Ann climbed into the ambulance and accompanied them to the hospital. Mickey followed in Ann's car.

Towner waited for Rafferty.

Beverly wasn't his jurisdiction, but he was on the scene, and, given all the possible connections to Salem, the local cops wanted him in the loop. So Rafferty joined the Beverly police when they looked through Marta's office in the speakeasy. They found several books on poisons, including one that had been written by Ann Chase, indexing common plants and herbs, detailing their beneficial medicinal purposes as well as their dangers. They also found a small volume of Longfellow's poems with a romantic inscription from Finn on the occasion of Marta's twenty-fifth birthday, *To Morrigan from Dag*. This was significant to no one but Rafferty; he paged through the book of poetry until he found "The Wreck of the *Hesperus*" and the reference to Norman's Woe.

He joined Towner in the front hall of Pride's Heart.

"Oh God," she said, burying her head in Rafferty's chest, hugging him tightly. "Oh my God."

The call came in from Ann just as they were crossing the Beverly Bridge. Rafferty switched to speaker so Towner could hear.

"Callie will be fine. She's being treated at Salem," Ann said.

"What about Paul?" Towner asked.

"Paul was airlifted to Mass General. His heart is severely damaged."

CHAPTER FORTY-SIX

September 27, 2015
PRIDE'S CROSSING

> *Turns out it wasn't the crazy homeless woman,*
> *it was the rich bitch all along.*
> *No big surprise there.*
>
> —LIKESTOSAIL

THE BONES STARTED TO SURFACE AFTER MARTA'S DEATH. The root hole was uncovered so the grounds crew could complete their job, and when the tide went out the bones clung to the dark earth. A skeletal hand appeared, and the Beverly Police were called. They, in turn, called Rafferty.

The discovery caused a sensation. The Goddesses had been found. And so had the partial skeleton of Leah Kormos, her bones miraculously preserved, the result, according to forensic speculation, of high levels of calcium carbonate in the seawater. The cliffs around Pride's Heart evidently contained large deposits of limestone that had leached into the sea well as the cliffs eroded every year.

Rafferty speculated that Finn and Marta had relocated the bodies from the graves to the sea well sometime between Thanksgiving and Christmas. The dinner conversation about DNA and how easily it could be transmitted must have scared Finn, who had been intimate with at least one if not more of the victims the night of the murders. Callie subsequently had a vision that Marta had talked Finn into having the bodies moved to avoid being implicated in the murders he didn't commit. In all likelihood, Finn never suspected Marta was the murderer. He had likely paid off Patch Willis, the caretaker of Greenlawn Cemetery. Willis had recently retired from his position and left town, leaving no forwarding address.

Leah's remains had been in the sea well for much longer.

It was Callie's vision in the sea well that filled in the details of Marta's terrible history, but it had been Ann and Mickey's call the night of the reception that had made Rafferty realize she was the Goddess murderer. On Ann's vision alone he would have gone to Pride's Heart, just to assure himself that everyone was all right. But it was what Mickey said that had chilled him to his core. After the celebration, Mickey had been working on his belated wedding present for Finn and Marta, a merging of their family trees. When he traced Marta's back, he discovered her connection to Sarah Good.

Still, many questions remained unanswered. "The truth is we'll never know it all," Rafferty told Callie.

"For me, it's enough to know that Marta killed the Goddesses," Callie said. "And to know that my mother and the others are truly laid to rest. And I'm happy to see that not only was Rose vindicated but she was right all along."

"How so?"

"She was right about the oak. She was right that remains were hidden on the Whitings' property, though they belonged to the Goddesses, not to the original accused."

Callie told Rafferty about Rose's vision of the hanging tree, cut and floating down the North River to the Whitings' property. She didn't mention her own visions, ones that had become clearer since that night in the well: the Whitings' oak, the one Rose claimed talked to her, had spread its roots so wide it had become entangled with the far older oak body. And as the tidal water rose and fell in one it was mirrored by the other, creating a waterway that had moved back and forth for generations.

All this was only speculation, something she'd never share for fear of being perceived as every bit as crazy as Rose. But, in Callie's mind,

Rose was right. The trees had communicated their centuries-old message. They had done their job.

They gathered around the oak tree that Eva Whitney had willed to Rose. Archbishop McCauley was performing a blessing to consecrate the ground. It was just as Rose would have wanted, Rafferty thought.

September 27, 2015. Ann had told Rafferty that tonight marked the end of the tetrad lunar eclipses. It was a supermoon as well as the blood moon, and people around here were expecting weird energy and odd behavior; both the ER and the police force had put on extra staff. But, according to Ann, tonight marked the end of the weird energy that had begun last year with the first of the eclipses. He hoped she was right. Still, Halloween was right around the corner, and weird energy was a given. He'd have to reserve judgment until he saw what October brought this year.

Callie looked different to him; she had aged in the last few months. Maybe not aged, exactly. More likely he could see that something had shifted. While Paul was recuperating in the hospital, she'd taken charge, arranging Finn's and Marta's burials, dealing with Paul's doctors, and meeting with the Whiting Foundation to make sure their work continued.

Towner had confided in him that Callie and Paul were planning their wedding for next summer, after Paul had fully recovered. Rafferty said a prayer that this would indeed happen, and that they would have happiness in their life together. They both deserved it.

As if in answer, the oak moved in the sea breeze, and through its leaves he heard the words:

Sometimes the only healing is death.

It wasn't Rose's voice he heard. Nor had he heard the statement before. It was a sound that seemed to come from the rustling leaves and the ocean breeze. Still, it made him shiver. Or was it simply the wind that had chilled him? Rafferty told himself he was being ridiculous. Rose was the only person who heard trees speak.

He forced himself to concentrate on the words of the archbishop until he saw Callie look upward, as if she, too, were listening to the tree. Then she nodded, stepped forward, and began lowering the urn containing Rose's ashes into the hole he had dug himself earlier this morning.

One by one, they all stepped forward, each grabbing a handful of earth and filling in the hole, as, together, they recited the Lord's Prayer.

There was no gathering after the ceremony. Callie needed to get to the hospital to see Paul, and the archbishop had to get back to Boston.

Rafferty tried to shake off the words the tree had whispered. As everyone said their hasty good-byes, he got a call from the Beverly Police. Marta's autopsy report had come back.

"The cause of death?" he asked, by rote. Everyone speculated that she had drowned; the autopsy was only a formality.

The voice on the line spoke two words Rafferty had prayed he wouldn't hear but feared he might: "Cerebral hemorrhage."

EPILOGUE

October 31, 2016
PRIDE'S HEART

The task of the banshee is twofold: to sing souls across
the divide between the living and the dead, and
to ease the hearts of those they leave behind.

—ROSE'S *Book of Trees*

CALLIE SAT AT THE PARTNERS DESK IN THE LIBRARY WHILE her husband napped on the huge leather couch. Paul was still recuperating. Every day she treated him with the singing bowls—not in the spa but in the orangerie. Once it had been Emily's favorite room, now it was hers. They never talked anymore about returning to Matera. The lure of Pride's Heart was far too strong. Since they'd moved in, she'd discovered many places in the house she adored, but she hadn't set foot in the cellars again. She doubted she ever would.

She felt the changes in herself, the heightened connection to everything around her: the oak, newly planted where Rose's oak had once stood, and the owl who had taken up residence in its young branches. She could hear their whispers to each other carried on the breeze from the harbor. She felt the turning of tides in the pulsing of her own blood.

And she could see death on people she met now; she knew how and when they would die, and how gently their passings would go. Unlike Rose, she didn't tell the truth she knew they had no capacity to understand. Today, as she was talking with Rafferty, she'd seen how he would meet his final end. He would live a long and happy life and die in his nineties, his grown daughter, grandchildren, and Towner at his bedside.

She wondered about Rose's goddess, real or imagined; about the diminishment and the turning. Just as she knew it was possible for healthy cells to vibrate an unhealthy cell back into balance, she now wondered if it would be possible to return the goddess, who had turned killer, to one who was both powerful and compassionate—and if it was possible to hold her in stillness long enough to try.

In the meantime, she had set up practice in Salem, and returned to working with the elderly and the ailing. She'd begun to treat the dying as well, spending part of each day in music therapy with hospice patients, comforting their pain and easing their passage.

Today, she sat at the computer, finishing a thank-you e-mail to the mayor of Salem and another to the group of scholars who had confirmed, once and for all, that, as Rose had always insisted, it was Proctor's Ledge and not Gallows Hill that was the real hanging site of 1692. The same group had planned the plaque to commemorate that spot. Downtown, there was already a larger, serene memorial where the tourists could linger, but honoring this true place was long overdue.

The first thing Callie had done when she'd taken over the Whiting Foundation was to offer funds to help make the memorial happen. She hoped it would lift the curse that seemed to plague that neighborhood and lessen the collective guilt that Salem still suffered. Whether the tourists ever visited it or not, the city needed this for itself and for all the descendants of those who had been lost.

Callie finished her last e-mail, hit send, then checked in on Paul, who was sleeping soundly.

She made herself a cup of tea and sat looking out at the water. Then she opened Rose's *Book of Trees*. Gazing into the space between the branches, she finally saw what Rose had been depicting since the night of the murders. She took out her pen, turned to an empty page, and began to translate into prose the mysterious puzzle she was just beginning to understand.

I am a cipher . . .

ACKNOWLEDGMENTS

FIRST, I HAVE TO THANK MY HUSBAND, GARY WARD, FOR his continued support and "keeping me alive" during this writing process, which was by far the most challenging story I've "discovered" so far. Thank you for everything you did to keep me writing for the last five years.

In the same spirit, a huge thank-you to Dorian Karchmar at WME, who always knew exactly what to do, from story suggestions to dealing with legal issues, to finding this novel the best home it could possibly have at Crown. Dorian, you are amazing! It must be said. Thank you for making all this happen.

Thanks also to Jamie Carr and Laura Bonner at WME for all they've done to help. To Becka Oliver, who was there at the beginning. And also I owe a huge debt of gratitude to Allison McCabe, whose story sensibilities greatly enhanced my own and whose ongoing editorial advice kept me on track, helping me zero in on the real story I wanted to tell that was so deeply embedded within the maze of Salem's history. Thanks for that, and for so much more. And yes, Allison, there really is a Bunghole Liquors in Salem. You have the T-shirt to prove it.

My greatest thanks to Hilary Rubin Teeman, my editor at Crown, whom I now refer to as "the best editor in the world." Her vast knowledge, her accessibility, and her attention to detail are what make her a star, and I will be forever grateful for her amazing and persistent work on this manuscript, which she came to know at least as well as

I did, maybe even better. To any writers who lament the disappearance of old-time editors who once partnered with writers to craft the best narratives possible, I'm here to tell you that they're still out there. Thank you so very much, Hilary.

Thank you also to Rose Fox, at Crown, who read and reread and drew parallels I hadn't seen in my story, and whose knowledge of history was a huge help in the editing process. Thanks to you and to all those at Crown who are helping to bring this book to life: Molly Stern, Maya Mavjee, David Drake, Annsley Rosner, Rachel Meier, Rebecca Welbourn, Rachel Rokicki, Shannon McCain, Kayleigh George, Kevin Callahan, Joyce Wong, Linnea Knollmueller, Elizabeth Rendfleisch, Tal Goretsky, Andrea Lau, and Sally Franklin, as well as Susan Brown and Meredith Hamilton.

To all my readers around the world, without whom none of this would be possible. To those who have already read this manuscript, sometimes more than once, and offered invaluable comments. My husband, of course. Sarah Ditkoff. Susan Marchand, my devoted friend, who read and reread too many times to count and always offered words of encouragement. Therese Walsh, with whom I share a muse. Emily Bradford Nuell, who has read multiple drafts of all three novels. David and Cheryl Monahan. Mark Barry, whose legal expertise helped me fact-check Rafferty's work. Manda Spittle, for her psychological expertise and many voluntary readings. Whitney Barry. Lela Clawson-Miller. Joanne Bailey. Jeannine Zwoboda. Christiana Bailey and Pamela LaFrance, for their knowledge of music therapy and sound healing. The Warren Street Writers: Jacqueline Franklin and Ginni Spencer. Katherine Howe, for her writerly friendship, and also for her *Penguin Book of Witches*, a must-read for anyone doing this kind of research. Alexandra Seros, a wonderful friend and writer, who always helps me with beginnings. And to Eve Bridburg and all my friends at Grub Street for their ongoing advice and support.

And lastly, to the city of Salem, Massachusetts, my home, without which there would be no story. Generational guilt aside, this is a wonderful place to live, and it's the people who make it so great. The fact is, the present-day story I've written would probably be less likely to happen here than elsewhere in the world, just because we remember our dark history and embrace our "otherness" as a result. A special thank-you to the members of the Gallows Hill Project who have finally proven, once and for all, the real location of the 1692 hangings. To Kate Fox and the folks at Destination Salem and to Mayor Kim Driscoll. To the Salem Athenaeum, the House of the Seven Gables, and PEM. To Teri Kalgren and the other modern-day Salem witches who so patiently answered my never-ending questions. And to Pride's Crossing, where my grandmother once lived, a favorite place full of great memories.

There have been some changes for the sake of my story, but not too many: a bit of the interior of the Salem Public Library, a few buildings on streets that don't exist. *The Salem Journal,* which is fictional, is not to be confused with the *Salem News,* our very good local paper. Pride's Heart is a compilation of favorite places in and around Pride's Crossing. The names of certain characters come directly from my family. Helen Barnes was named after one of my great-grandmothers, as was Emily Sprague, representing a side of my family that came to Salem from England in 1628 aboard the *Arabella.* The Irish Catholic side of my family, who all came over much later, is represented elsewhere in many characters and in name by Mickey Doherty. All other names are fictional. And I have to say, I have nothing but respect for the police forces of both Salem and Beverly. Other than changes made to further the story, I've tried to keep things as real as possible when it comes to Salem and vicinity, though, please remember, this is all seen through my writer's lens. Perspective *is everything.*

ABOUT THE AUTHOR

© Scott Booth Photography

BRUNONIA BARRY is the *New York Times* and international bestselling author of *The Lace Reader* and *The Map of True Places*. Her work has been translated into more than thirty languages. She is the first American author to win the International Women's Fiction Festival's Baccante Award and a past recipient of Ragdale Artists' Colony's Strnad Invitational Fellowship, as well as the winner of New England Book Festival's award for Best Fiction. Her writing has appeared in the *London Times* and the *Washington Post*. She lives in Salem with her husband, Gary Ward, and their dog, Angel.

THE FIFTH PETAL

EXTRA LIBRIS

ESSAYS,
READER'S GUIDES,
AND MORE

Book Club Questions:
The Fifth Petal

1. Contemporary Salem is a safe haven for neo-witches, greatly enhancing the city's tourist trade, but there are many who want to "ditch the witch." Could a modern-day witch hunt happen in Salem again, and, if so, what might it look like? Are witch hunts happening in other parts of the world?

2. "You know who you are, you have always been other," Rose says in her *Book of Trees*. In what way is each character in the book "other"? Rose later claims every culture, and every individual, harbors a prejudice against those they consider "other." Do you agree?

3. Callie longs for home and family, and particularly for a mother figure, having lost her own mother at a young age. How does Callie fulfill that dream, and at what cost?

4. Is the banshee a goddess or a monster? Its power seems to reside in a woman's raised voice. How does that power manifest in the hands of the different characters?

5. At one point in the story, Rose tells Callie not to "court the strike." What does she mean, and why is this important to the story?

6. Social media is both a resource and a curse in the novel. The wealth of available information helps Rafferty with his case, but the opinions of anonymous posters also condemn Rose, mirroring Salem's accusers of 1692. Discuss the positive and negative impacts of social media.

7. Brunonia Barry, who lives in Salem, is often surprised by the generational guilt the city still suffers for the 1692 witch hangings. In what ways does this manifest in the story?

8. Sound and vibration feature in *The Fifth Petal,* with a capacity to both hurt and heal. How does the banshee's killer sound relate to vibration and music therapy? How does the music of the spheres that Callie hears during meditation relate to the ancient music heard in Matera?

9. Religion played a huge role in 1692 Salem, as did misogyny and fear of the unknown. Discuss Rose's quote: "Tell me what you want, and I'll

tell you who you think you are. Tell me what you fear, and I'll tell you who you really are."

10. Trees symbolize both the interconnectedness of all life and the roots of humanity in this story. How does the sacred oak help Rose, and what is the significance of the Tree of Life? What does it mean to Callie in her translation of Rose's *Book of Trees*?

Brunonia Barry's Bewitching Books: The Author of *The Lace Reader* and *The Fifth Petal* Shares Reads that Inspire Her

By Brunonia Barry

ORIGINALLY PUBLISHED (IN PART) ON READ IT FORWARD

With the publication of *The Fifth Petal*, I'm taking a moment to reflect on some of the books that have inspired me. This collection is eclectic: including historical accounts of the Salem Witch Trials along with fictional depictions and even some fanciful storytelling featuring modern-day witches who reflect the role strong women have always played in this continuing narrative. Like myself, many of the writers listed here were inspired by ancestral ties to Salem's executions. With blame and persecution of those we consider "other" as alive as ever in the world, Salem's cautionary tale remains relevant if only to keep history from repeating.

FICTION

A Discovery of Witches by **Deborah Harkness**
Fanciful as well as historical, Harkness creates a veracity within this trilogy that's difficult to achieve

in fiction. Like many modern witches, Diana Bishop tries to deny her powers, only to find them taking over her life. Intelligently romantic witch fiction with one of the most compelling vampires ever created. Deborah Harkness, herself a historian, has created a world of alchemy, magic, and mystery so compelling that you'll want to linger.

Practical Magic by Alice Hoffman

A classic, this book initially piqued my interested in all things magical. Sisters Gillian and Sally Owens are blamed for everything that goes wrong in their Massachusetts town. With aunts who are practicing witches—ostracized publicly, yet sought out when love spells are called for—this is a classic woman's tale. Humor, mystery, and great family dynamics make this one of my favorite stories.

The Heretic's Daughter by Kathleen Kent

The beautifully written story of Martha Carrier, hanged for witchcraft during Salem's hysteria is told by her ten-year-old daughter, Sarah. A heart-wrenching story that depicts the bleak life faced by the Puritan settlers and the land dispute that turns family members against each other, ultimately resulting in the accusations of witchcraft that send Martha to her death.

WITCHCRAFT HISTORY

A Storm of Witchcraft by Emerson W. Baker

This is one of the best accounts of the Salem Witch

Trials out there. While there has been much speculation about the cause of the hysteria, Baker cites a
number of factors responsible, all of which add up
to a perfect storm of cause and effect. As an added
bonus, Baker was part of The Gallows Hill Project, a
group of historians and scientists who recently veri-
fied the real location of Salem's executions.

The Salem Witch Trials by Marilynne K. Roach
Well thought-out and impeccably researched, this
day-by-day account of the 1692 witch trials mixes
meticulous details with illuminating psychological
insights, placing the reader in the courtroom with
the accused. Another must-read for anyone interested
in the subject. Roach was also a member of the Gallows Hill Project team, which recently identified the
hanging site at Proctor's Ledge.

The Witches by Stacy Schiff
Ambitious and well-researched, Stacy Schiff's account of the Salem witch trials tackles the scale and
scope of Salem's dark history, offering a detailed and
empathetic account and providing psychological insights that draw parallels to present-day struggles.
This is a big book, with multiple and diverse pro-
tagonists, and includes Schiff's theories about what
caused the hysteria.

**The Penguin Book of Witches
by Katherine Howe, editor**
This is one of the better source books for anyone interested in the historical accounts of the witch trials

of both New England and Europe. Howe's insights and writing style make this wealth of material accessible for all readers, not just those involved in research.

TREE COMMUNICATION

Trees of Inspiration: Sacred Trees and Bushes of Ireland by Christine Zucchelli

"From ancient times people appreciated the other worldly value of trees, singling out individual trees for special veneration." This is a beautiful book with photos of some of Ireland's most sacred trees, along with locations and the lore associated with each. From chieftain trees and royal oaks, spots where sacred Celtic ceremonies were performed, to judgment trees where lawsuits were settled, to fairy trees and bushes with their magic spells, these trees have very special significance for the Irish, and Zucchelli succeeds in bringing it to the reader.

The Hidden Life of Trees: What They Feel, How They Communicate—Discoveries from a Secret World by Peter Wohlleben

The author spent more than twenty years researching tree communication and came to the conclusion that trees exist in families similar to those of humans; parents living with children and supporting them as they grow. They have even been known to share nutrients with trees from other families when they are sick or struggling. I found this book a great metaphor for how we wish human families would consistently behave.

Suzanne Simard's research and her Ted talk:
https://www.ted.com/talks/suzanne_simard_
how_trees_talk_to_each_other
An inspirational speech detailing the fungal threads, root systems, and infinite biological pathways in the forest floor that comprise the web of communication between trees of different species and show how trees are "super-communicators." I recommend starting with Simard's TED talk. You'll never look at trees the same way.

MYTHOLOGY

Celtic Myth and Legend **by T. W. Rolleston**
A great general introduction to polytheistic Celtic Mythology with stunning illustrations. Broken into time periods, this is far easier to understand than other books written on the subject and a great read for anyone interested in the evolution of mythology and how the past influences the present.

The Banshee **by Patricia Lysaght**
Details the Celtic "death messenger" legends and various accounts of banshees, spirits who not only predict the deaths of family members but ease the hearts of those left behind. A well-known figure in Irish folk tradition, the banshee and her lore were passed down through oral tradition, evolving through the

centuries with changes in attitude and social mores. Lysaght traces the legend back to the eighth century and shows how the belief in banshees is still very much alive in Irish families today.

SOUND HEALING

Vibrational Medicine by Dr. Richard Gerber
An extensive explanation of human energetic medicine and changing attitudes about health and disease. Gerber details historical perspectives of science and healing and the evolution of the holistic approach, explaining that "doctors are beginning to understand that we possess unique energy systems that help to maintain health." Includes explanations of many new age methods including music therapy and sound healing.

RECIPES

Cocktail Recipe: Death in the Evening

This is the absinthe punch that was served at the fundraiser for Ann's Witches' Educational Council. It's a slight variation of a cocktail that Ernest Hemingway called "Death in the Afternoon" (named after his book). Hemingway advised caution, to sip slowly. Our characters in *The Fifth Petal* would have been well-advised to pay attention.

Death in the Evening

Add to punchbowl: 4 ounces iced champagne and 1 $\frac{1}{2}$ ounces absinthe for each drink. Mix until absinthe reaches a milky greenish opalescence. Serve in punch glasses and sip very slowly. Hemingway recommended 3–5 drinks apiece; we recommend one.

Lobster à la Newburg

The recipe Emily's family has always used for Lobster Newburg goes back through the generations, and was originally from Fannie Farmer's *Boston Cooking-School Book* written in 1896.

Here is the recipe as written in the cookbook:

2 pounds lobster
Slight grating nutmeg
$^{1}/_{4}$ cup butter
1 tablespoon Sherry
$^{1}/_{2}$ teaspoon salt
1 tablespoon brandy
Few grains cayenne
$^{1}/_{3}$ cup thin cream
2 egg yolks

Remove lobster meat from shell and cut in slices. Melt butter, add lobster, and cook three minutes. Add seasonings and wine, cook one minute, then add cream and yolks of eggs slightly beaten. Stir until thickened. Serve with toast or puff paste points.